THE ELEMENTAL CHRONICLES
BOOK TWO

Reaper

THE ELEMENTAL CHRONICLES
BOOK TWO

ROSS KINGSTON

First published in 2018 by Ross Kingston

Copyright © 2018 Ross Kingston

All rights reserved. No part of this publication may be reproduced, stored in a retrieval system or transmitted, in any form or by any means, electronic, mechanical, photocopying, recording or otherwise, without the prior written permission of the publishers and copyright holders.

A record of this book is held at the National Library of Australia.

ISBN 978-0-6481126-1-7

Reader reviewer: Kaitlyn Smith
Editor and proofreader: Claire Bradshaw
Designer: Lorena Susak
Cover illustrations: Livia Prima
Map artist: Marc Loths

This book has been typeset in Palatino

Printed and bound in Australia by SOS Printing Group

10 9 8 7 6 5 4 3 2 1

Keep up with The Elemental Chronicles on www.tecseries.com

*'Someone just went
and pissed off the Princess.'*

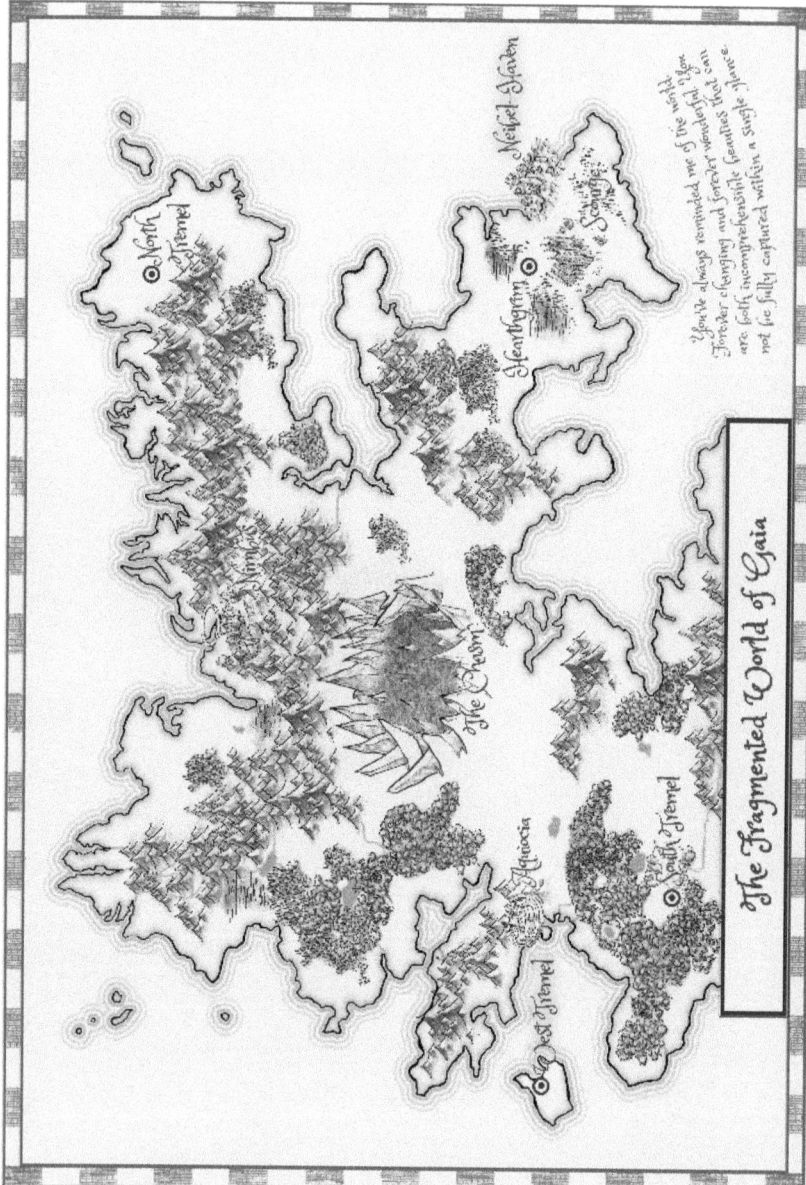

PROLOGUE

A BLOODY BEGINNING

The isolated village echoed with the sound of children playing in the green pastures as the adults went about their daily chores. The couple of hundred residents earned their living through the crops the fields yielded at different times each year, but there had been diminishing resources each harvest for the past six months.

In exchange for a portion of what they harvested, the Kingdom of Aquiocia offered the village its protection and assistance during times of need. It wasn't the only village to have such an arrangement and it was one many were thankful for. Oddly, once the crops had stopped producing food, the Aquiocian patrols had stopped making their rounds through the village.

The farmers had no idea whether the coincidence was a blessing or a curse. On one hand, their crops were becoming barren and desolate, but on the other, there were no knights persecuting them for it. In truth, it hadn't been their own doing. It was a side effect of the erratic weather that had been going on around their village. The closer you were to Aquiocia, the more you felt the chill of winter coming. Normally it would have been the perfect time to harvest and store their bounty away in the mills. Instead, winter had come earlier that year –

months earlier. There had been no sign of snow, but the frigid air had frost-bitten a lot of the potential produce. As a result, the kingdom's portion of the food was forfeited overnight.

The village had enough for itself, and the residents were sure the King would understand. After all, he had plenty of other issues to attend to, like the scandal surrounding his choice of wife. A commoner whose background was unknown to the public, or at least to those outside Aquiocia's walls. Rumours travelled fast, but not quite that fast.

None of this mattered to the boy of thirteen who was leaving a small house, the sound of his parents' yelling following him out the door. He had mid-length, jet-black hair that fell straight down across the upper part of his face, partially concealing the indifference emanating from his amber eyes.

He walked stiffly and yet with an effortless haste down the dirt path towards the road used by travellers. He never knew where he was going when he left the house. He knew he was expected to play with the other kids, but the only reason he did so was to stop people thinking there was something deeply wrong with him. Other children his age would hunt or spar after their chores. Some had even found early love within the tiny village and had started romances with the potential to go the distance.

But not he.

"He needs to go outside to fit in!" rang his father's voice from the house he had vacated.

"Fit in? They all know he's different! You can tell by the way people stare!" his mother retorted.

The conversation might have hurt or offended another child. The reality, however, was that this child felt nothing about their opinions or concerns. He never had. His entire life had been spent trying to recognise social cues and react accordingly. After a while, he had forgotten why he was putting up an act for others and promptly dropped it. Since then, his peers had taken to openly staring and even bullying the boy.

The bullying had always taken place from afar, as the culprits had always found the absent expression and amber gaze of their victim unsettling. Name-calling and rock-throwing were often the extent they could safely muster.

"Jex!" called the sweet voice of a thirteen-year-old girl.

The dark-haired boy turned slowly, as was expected of him. He found the source of the voice, recognising the girl with brown eyes and golden curls cut short as Clareen, the pretty daughter of one of the farmers his father worked alongside.

Clareen was one of very few people who ever addressed him with the respect of a human being. She was taller than average, standing only a couple of inches shorter than him. She wore a simple white dress that gently hugged her slowly developing physique. Jex assumed most boys would grow to find her attractive, but again, his inability to feel prevented him from forming his own opinion. The pretty smile and developing body that the boys were often heard praising between bouts of drool and grunts did nothing to affect Jex.

"Clareen," he acknowledged with a nod before turning away and continuing his stride.

"Jex!" Clareen called again, racing to catch up and walk beside him. "Where are you going?"

"I'm... not sure," Jex replied slowly, realising that he had been walking without purpose yet again.

"Come with me!" Clareen smiled, grabbing his hand and

leading him away.

Jex didn't know where she was taking him. He was barely aware of the dozen people watching him being taken away. After a moment, he decided to bask in the relief of not having to find something to pass the time.

It wasn't long before they arrived at their new destination. She had brought him to the edge of town and away from the houses. Even the people who had been watching them depart were just dots in the distance.

How did we cover so much ground so quickly? he wondered. *I must have faded out again.*

Jex had no idea why Clareen had led him out of the village and her smiling face gave no indication until her eyes darted down to the ground. Looking down, Jex noticed a small shrub covered in prickly thorns. At its centre was a single rose of brilliant azure, its petals lined with silver that glittered in the midday sun.

"An Aquiocian Rose?"

"Yes!" Clareen exclaimed excitedly. "Can you believe that one would be growing this far away from the kingdom?"

It is a flower. I'm sure it can grow any number of places, Jex thought, but said nothing.

After a moment, Clareen moved closer to her companion. "Do you know about them?"

"Of course. People say they bloom in blue at times of peace but change to red when there is strife nearby," Jex answered without emotion. "They bloom when love is prevalent."

"Exactly," Clareen grinned, taking another step closer. "Is it not romantic? Oh, what a dream it'd be to have someone present one to me."

A dream? Jex thought. *Something so small would bring her joy?*

Leaning down, Jex steadily reached into the twisted mess of thorns and yanked at the plant's stem. As he pulled the rose free, a thorn pierced his hand. Without a sound of discomfort, he retrieved the rose from its guarded home.

Clareen looked about ready to swoon as the dark-haired boy handed over the floral gift. It had been such a simple task, and quite obviously what the girl had wanted despite Jex's indifference.

The girl took the rose gently and seemed to be waiting for something.

What does she want now? Jex wondered, before recognising the look.

It was the same look he had seen a lot of the girls give the boys in the village before they would kiss. Is that what she wanted – a kiss?

Could I be wrong? Jex thought. *I suppose she has always been kind to me without needing to be, but why would she want this?*

Just as he was about to make the move, Clareen gasped in alarm. Following her gaze downwards, he saw the rose in her hand no longer held any hint of its former cerulean beauty and instead was a violent crimson lined with black.

"What is this?" Clareen demanded.

"I have no idea," Jex said bluntly.

For a moment they both stared at the flower's transformation. Just as Jex was about to say that his bleeding hand must have caused the change in colour, a crash came from the town, so loud they heard it clearly from their place on its edge.

"What was that?" Clareen asked in worry, sprinting off to investigate before Jex could answer.

Picking up the rose Clareen had dropped in her haste, Jex wandered back towards the town as well. He could hear a commotion as he got closer, but had no idea what it was coming from.

He found himself at the gate in front of his house. Uncertain whether to ask his parents or not, Jex was saved the trouble of making a decision when he was suddenly shoved from behind. He fell to the ground roughly, one hand finding the hard earth and the other ripped across the rose's thorns. Ignoring the physical pain like he'd always been able to, he looked up to see people running in all directions.

He felt the back of his shirt being pulled upwards and his light body followed until he was standing upright, an inch away from his father's angry face.

"What did you do, kid?"

"Nothing," Jex replied quietly, stoking his father's rage.

"A fine story that is! I'm sure that –"

Jex was almost shocked when his father's voice cut off and his eyes rolled to the back of his head as his body hit the ground.

He barely comprehended that his father was dead and that his blood was streaked up Jex's own clothing. It took a moment for him to realise that if his father had fallen, someone must have delivered the blow. Looking down, he realised there was a throwing axe embedded in his father's side.

"What did you do?" his mother shrieked.

"Why do people keep asking me that?" Jex asked.

His mother had no chance to respond before her head left her shoulders.

Jex watched on with mild curiosity as her body collapsed to

its knees and fell, spraying her son with blood in its descent.

Through the red haze, Jex saw his parents' assailant.

Before him stood a knight encased in dark, violet armour with translucent colours racing across its surface. The figure stood an impressive head-and-a-half taller than Jex and held an enormous sword with a single hand. The knight stared at the teenager soaked in his own parents' blood for a long moment before starting to walk away.

"You killed my parents," Jex stated, in the same tone that someone might have said the sky was blue.

"Anyone who dies is simply returned to where they once emerged from. Some return sooner than others," the knight replied without turning around. "Clean yourself and continue your menial life."

"Clean myself?" Jex looked down and finally noticed the dirt, grime and blood that coated the majority of his clothing.

Despite appearing soiled by filth, he had never felt cleaner. He had been dirty before, but the blood didn't worry him at all. As he fondled the scarlet rose, he realised the fact that it was his parents' blood covering him meant very little.

What is wrong with me?

"Farewell," the knight said softly.

"You're not going to kill me?"

"Why would I do that?" The knight's soft voice could barely be heard over the din of people screaming and fleeing the village.

"You've killed a large amount of people as it is, and I only speak of the ones within this village," Jex noted, referring to his home as if it was a foreign place to him. "Given that you're obviously the knight of legend, it stands that you've killed thousands."

"You do not tremble like the others leeching from this world's bosom. You do not fear death, nor do you fear me," the knight stated matter-of-factly.

If Jex had cared to listen for it, he might have even heard the mild surprise in the knight's magically altered voice.

"Why would I fear death? It's an inevitability. I've been able to sense its presence for as long as I can remember. As for you, Lucian, what should I fear from a man who has the ability to go after what he desires?"

"Profound. For a leech, anyway," Lucian noted as he looked back at the kid. He was thin, almost sickly so. But he had a certain aloof strength about him. Along with something undeniably sadistic waiting to awaken within his scorching amber eyes.

"Take me with you. You imprison souls, right? Take mine. I give it willingly," Jex offered.

"Why would you offer such a thing? Are you so tired of your life?"

"Either take me with you, or I will find you again," Jex said.

"Is that supposed to be a threat?"

"Take it as you will. The truth of the matter is that you are the only one who is doing anything that actually matters. Consider me curious."

Lucian seemed to gaze intently into the boy's very soul, sizing up his physical form along with his innermost thoughts. For the most part, the teenager in front of him felt like a blank slate. His soul seemed to be separated from the rest of the world in a big way, almost as if there was nothing holding him there as he floated through his life.

Then he found it. A vicious malice lying dormant within the

boy's soul, almost as if the indifference towards the outside world served as a facade to hide its existence. Regardless of what was holding it at bay, when the facade was broken, the malevolence within the young boy would surface with unrivalled force and brutality.

"No. You are unsuitable. I should purge you from this world as it is, but your life may just prove interesting yet. That is dependent on you being alive long enough to embrace it, of course," Lucian answered.

Jex was about to protest when he noticed the knight's armour flickering in and out of existence. After a few seconds, Lucian started to become steadily more transparent.

"You are leaving," Jex noted.

"Yes. My time here is expended for now. I squandered too much of it speaking with you."

"Jex!" Clareen's voice cried from behind as she raced up beside him. She looked terrified of the knight, yet felt safe next to Jex.

"What am I supposed to do?" Jex demanded of the knight, ignoring Clareen.

"A person's birth is not the start of their life. When they awaken and find their purpose within the world, that's when their life truly begins," Lucian said quietly, ignoring the question. "Most are simply leeches, draining the world of its strength. But you... You might have a chance at being something more. You too will know of the end coming for humankind, perhaps more intimately than most."

"How will I know when my life has begun?" Jex asked with the mildest hint of desperation.

Lucian responded by effortlessly lifting the enormous sword

in his hand and running it through Clareen. Her slender frame shuddered as blood sprayed from the massive cavity it created through her middle. She didn't make a sound as her life left her and Jex grabbed her, unsure what to do. Clareen's eyes were already emptied of all vitality as he gazed into them. Jex willed himself to feel something. Sadness, anger, wrath – even feeling joy would be a victory at that moment. Instead, he turned to face the knight as if he might offer some insight into what Jex should feel.

"The truly great are awoken through unconventional means. Awakening via blood is perhaps one such instance," Lucian said cryptically as he faded from view, leaving Jex feeling as lifeless as the corpse that was soaking his skin more and more with each second he held it.

Blood is the answer? Jex wondered, dropping Clareen's body carelessly. *I need more information. I will find him again.*

CHAPTER 1

AN OBJECTIVE MANIFESTATION

Where is everyone? Alicea wondered as she traced the walls of her castle's grand hall for the first time in months. Was it the first time? It didn't feel as though it was a new experience. It felt as though it was a repeat of events that had happened frequently in recent months.

But that was impossible; they had only just broken through the ranks of her own soldiers to reclaim the fair city she once called home. It was clearly just a case of her nerves playing havoc.

This reassurance didn't placate the rampant memories playing in her mind. Normally she had a firm grasp on her memories; they were never allowed to run free due to the potency of emotion they could invoke for someone with perfect recollection. But they were free to play here.

The events of the past months rushed her. They began with her creating a painting in her chambers before she was suddenly staring at a stone floor racing past as dirty leather boots carried her away. She was gazing at a brilliant fist-sized sapphire in the moonlight and when her eyes rose from the stone, they met those of a robed man behind a desk cloaked in shadows.

Orders were given, plans were made, and she found herself

under a waterfall, talking to the one within the stone. The voices melded together, forming the instructive tone of her teacher. She saw her kidnapper sprinting around a field of small streams, evading the strange bird she commanded. The bird collided with the man and the spray of mist formed a wall of liquid. Beyond the barricade was a legion of cerulean steel, and her friend was at her side. The wall fell in a clash of light that flooded her eyes and once it cleared, she was eye-level with the monster who had led her troops against her. The same monster who was still in control.

The memories faded to a blackness that wanted to last. Within the darkness were cruel, amber lights, small and ominous...

The Princess forced her mind to focus, but despite her efforts, it remained clouded. What was her task again? Oh, yes – to get to the highest balcony, from which her parents once addressed the people. From there she could put an end to the fighting.

Which way was it to the balcony again?

"What is wrong with me?" Slurred words she could barely recognise as her own fell from her mouth. "How did I even get here?"

She allowed herself to consider the question in a haze as she stumbled around the great hall in confusion. She felt drunk – not that she had ever let herself drink to the extent of knowing what true intoxication felt like.

Perhaps she had been drugged; the thought crossed her mind before disappearing entirely. She had not consumed anything to allow that theory any merit.

Alicea approached the staircases at the back of the hall

before falling into the side of a large ornamental fountain. Leaning against it for support, the Princess glanced upwards at her goal. Her vision failed her, doubling everything, and a cruel voice cut through the fog.

"Are we lost, Princess?"

"You! I know that voice!" Alicea exclaimed as she focused on the image of a dark figure.

Within the silhouette, sinister amber eyes pierced the darkness. Jex.

Everything around her began to blur uncontrollably as the man who had slaughtered countless innocent people stepped forth.

"Jex, what have you done?"

"You seem to be having difficulty standing, Princess," Jex mocked. "Allow me to aid you."

"No!" Alicea screamed as she lashed out at the water of the fountain with her mind. Calling it forth into a shield that stood shakily between her and her enemy, the Princess grimaced with pain. *How is this such an ordeal for me?*

"You have fought valiantly, but it was all for nothing." Jex smiled with malice. "You have already lost to me in both this world and the next! You are not ready!"

Jex reached behind him to the peculiar contraption on his back and yanked at it as Alicea felt the dizziness intensify. Her world reformed around her into colourful swirls of shapelessness before they faded to black, leaving her in absolute darkness.

The next thing she felt was her lungs burning for air as her body jerked upright.

"You will not take control of me like this!" she screamed

into the darkness before realising where she was.

She heard the sound of feet against dirt as a flame appeared in the room. On the other side of the light she could see her friend pushing aside a great animal pelt, his concerned face screwed up into a grimace. Alicea realised where she was and stifled tears at what had happened again for the umpteenth time.

"The same dream again?" The man's voice was thick with sleepiness.

"Go back to bed, Mr. Thief. I am used to it now," the Princess muttered.

"Well, I am still not used to you screaming in the middle of the night and waking up the entire village," the man replied in annoyance.

"It's not as if I am enjoying it myself!" Alicea snapped with fatigue. She hadn't slept well in weeks.

Receiving a sigh of exasperation as a response, the Princess bowed her head. It wasn't his fault. It wasn't his fault that at almost twenty-one years of age, nightmares of monsters were keeping her from sleeping. She lamented the thought of her age and where she was. By Aquiocian tradition, she was almost considered a full adult, and with that, her right to call herself Queen was secured without question. Instead, she was hiding in a small village, completely out of touch with her former kingdom.

"I assume that dawn is not too far away?" Alicea asked, suddenly feeling a surge of energy from the bitter thoughts.

"A couple of hours, maybe," the man replied as he turned away while Alicea changed out of the frock she wore to bed.

"Good. Then let us get a start on today's training."

"It would be best that you try to get a few more hours' sleep, Alicea," he responded wearily. He saw her sudden energy for what it was: an attempt to deny the exhaustion. An attempt to forget everything that had happened for just a little longer.

He couldn't blame her. He'd been there while she trained under a veteran mage's tutelage, learning to wield the untrustworthy force within her. He had watched her struggle to control the power only to be overwhelmed and fall. With her friend's aid, she had been able to awaken.

Only to turn the damned power on her own people... Rufus scowled at the thought before his expression softened. It was harder to stay angry at her now. His complaints seemed trivial when he thought of what had happened to Alicea.

"Have you forgotten what today is, Mr. Thief?" the Princess asked rhetorically. Nobody in the entire village was unaware of what the impending day held.

"Today is the day we march," Rufus answered, resigned.

"Today is the day we march," Alicea repeated as she straightened her tabard. "So, we must start training early. Let's go."

CHAPTER 2

THE MOTIVATION OF HATRED

The pair walked the same path to the training field that they had traversed every day for weeks. They always turned off just before reaching the original training grounds and headed to another smaller field; the original site was under investigation for a reason they were not privy to. The Chief had issued a village-wide order that the original training field be restricted. It had been a strange order to the Princess and thief, but they had decided the village's issues were their own, and had probed no further. They had their own issues, anyway.

The pair pushed through the brush and came to the small clearing where they had been sparring every day since the attack on the village led by Aquiocia's new commandant. The attack had been unprovoked and ruthless, but they had survived with minimal casualties thanks to the combined strategic efforts of Tremel's advisor and Setz, leader of the guild hidden away below Aquiocia's surface.

"Garnet is not here yet," Rufus muttered.

"So? We can spar without her," Alicea replied absent-mindedly, combing her hair with her fingers.

"I only bring it up because she usually dulls my weapons with her magic."

"Well, all the more reason for me not to get struck by you," the Princess shrugged as Rufus stared at her in the moonlight. "What is it, Mr. Thief?"

"Nothing."

"Tell me."

"It's just been quite a while since I've seen you wear that outfit."

Alicea took a moment to look down at her cerulean tabard with the emblem of her kingdom – the Aquiocian Rose – stitched to its front. Her legs were covered by black leggings and white boots that reached just below her knee. Alicea had taken to crafting clothing from the leftover pelts and materials the villagers had donated to her. She couldn't bring herself to hunt the animals herself, but she hated to see anything that once lived go to waste. She shrugged as she tied back the long, ebony hair that reached below her lower back, even when restrained. As her hair was removed from her face, the dying moon revealed discerning, lazuline eyes that shimmered in its light.

Her normally cheeky smile was missing; instead, her face displayed a persistent concern. It felt like the young Princess hadn't smiled in a long time, a slight frown taking its place in the past weeks as she worried for her kingdom and the coming battle. On top of her troubles, her nights had been plagued by recurring nightmares that offered her little rest and even less comfort about the current situation.

"This outfit is the one I wore when we first set out together. It was a time of adventure and conflict. It is only right that I wear it today."

Rufus sighed before replying. "I was just making an observation."

"And what exactly was the meaning of that observation?"

"It meant that it's nice to see you wearing it," Rufus said, immediately regretting his words.

"I'm glad that a symbol of my distress brings you such joy," Alicea snapped sarcastically.

"Weapons or hand-to-hand?" Rufus asked, changing the subject before another argument broke out. They had been arguing constantly since the battle.

"Hand-to-hand first. I need to learn to channel my energy into more than just my element. I also must learn to fight without magic," Alicea explained as Rufus tossed his daggers to the ground.

As the two combatants took their stances, Alicea noticed her companion's thoughtful expression.

"What is it?"

"I want you to fight with all you've got," Rufus announced as he tugged at one of the belts bound around his leg.

"I always spar at my full potential, even though I never win," the Princess replied bitterly.

"No, that's not what I want. I want you to fight, not to spar. I know you dislike fighting, but you must be ready for it."

"How do you propose I fight with my all against *you*?" she snapped with irritation. Her patience was at an all-time low.

"Picture me as Jex."

"What –" Alicea trailed off in confusion. "But you aren't Jex!"

"That's not the point. You hate him, don't you?"

"Of course I do!" Alicea snarled a little too viciously. There was something under her hatred.

"Then show me how much. He has killed countless

innocents. In fact, he boasts about it any chance he gets!" Rufus goaded and smirked when he saw it working.

Alicea's fists were tightening.

"Do not test me, Mr. Thief!"

"That's precisely what I want to do!" Rufus sniggered. "But if you don't have what it takes to fight the man who attacked this innocent village, then –"

Rufus had no time to finish his taunt as Alicea lunged at him, swinging her fist directly at his face. Blocking it easily, he pushed her back roughly. He had sparred with the Princess enough to know that she wasn't as delicate anymore and she could take a lot of what he threw at her. She didn't have his strength, but she was crafty. It had taken him a while to realise that he needed to change his style of sparring regularly to avoid the risk of her memorising his moves. Even a few quick exchanges were enough for the Princess to work out what he'd do next if he didn't shake it up.

Alicea responded by advancing again. Ducking under his guard, she landed two swift blows to his chest before jumping back.

Rufus laughed. "Is that it?"

The Princess' eyes had a pale glow about them as she stepped in, brushed aside Rufus' right arm with her left and shoved her open palm upwards to his jaw. Rufus followed the momentum and dodged the strike. Wrapping his arm around her petite waist, he flicked his leg behind hers and effortlessly pushed her to the ground. For a split second, he caught sight of the azure glow from her eyes, combatting the dying moon's rays. It was a warning sign. Over the past couple of months, he had seen the faint glow more and more often; usually during training.

Rufus received a swift kick to the guts from the enraged Princess lying on the ground. As he stumbled back involuntarily, Alicea flipped to her feet and rushed him. The pair locked arms and engaged in a struggle of raw strength. Rufus had the edge and he knew it as he pushed her back and yelled in her face.

"What's wrong, Princess?" he snarled. "What do you hope to do against the Reaper if you can't even hold your own against me?"

"Hold your tongue, Mr. Thief!" Alicea screamed back. She'd reached the point of genuine fury.

"I don't know what I was expecting!" Rufus laughed as he forced her back further and further. "You want to lead an army but can't even take down the peasant in front of you!"

"I can do this! I will help everybody!" the Princess grunted as she attempted to harness her rage.

"Then show me! Show me you aren't the sheltered brat I kidnapped a few months ago! Show me your strength!"

"I – am – not –" Alicea spat as the energy rallied within her. "A BRAT!"

Alicea twisted out of Rufus' arms and the last thing he saw was the Princess' eyes exploding with colour before she spun around in a pivot, her long ponytail whipping him across the face. Both of her open palms found the thief's torso and he felt an immense amount of energy discharge through his body as it was lifted from the ground and thrown across the forest floor.

Rufus was gasping for air as he struggled to his feet before giving up, allowing himself to fall into a sitting position on the ground. His laughter made it all the more difficult to catch his breath as the pressure subsided.

Alicea joined him. Her anger didn't subside completely, but a moment of forced happiness was preferable to rage. Her laughter gave Rufus a joy that he hadn't felt in a long while.

"That's cheating!" Rufus exclaimed between gasps.

"Hardly!" Alicea scoffed. "You had it coming!"

"I can't deny that!" Rufus conceded as he let his body fall back upon the ground. Looking up at the velvet sky and the first creeping rays of sunlight, his laughter reignited.

"What's so funny, Mr. Thief?"

"It's the outfit again!"

"What about it?"

"I was just thinking about how much you have grown in strength since the last time you wore it," Rufus admitted.

"I suppose that is true," Alicea nodded. "Though I worry that it won't be enough."

"You need to stop worrying so much," Rufus said, suddenly serious.

"How can I not worry? My people are in very real danger."

"That's true enough, but you have conquered every challenge put in front of you so far – so what makes you think this won't be the same?"

Alicea paused. He was right, in a small way; she had overcome a lot. Even in the limbo that had been the past couple of months, she had learnt a great deal, bolstering her abilities in combat and otherwise. She had even learnt how to replicate her friend's ability to take magical energy unto herself to increase her physical limits.

"I'm just scared, Mr. Thief. I'm scared that I will fail and that I won't be able to help my people."

"It's alright to be scared. Bravery is measured by your…"

"…by your ability to stand up for what matters to you, even when you're terrified," Alicea finished.

"You remember, then?"

"How could I not?" Alicea smirked. "It's the only profound thing I've ever heard you say!"

"Brat," Rufus snorted.

"Scoundrel," Alicea sniffed.

"Children," a third voiced added, and the pair looked up to see Garnet smiling as she walked into the grotto.

"Garnet!" Alicea greeted the older woman happily.

"Good morning, Princess. A fine display of combat, the pair of you," Garnet commended. "But it is time to prepare. Please return to the village."

Garnet disappeared into the flora of the forest as Alicea and Rufus climbed to their feet. Rufus noticed that the Princess was frowning yet again and placed his hand on her shoulder. The touch seemed to shock her, but he nodded reassuringly.

"You're going to do fine. Everyone is here for you."

Alicea smiled widely, brushed his hand away and raced off into the forest, leaving Rufus alone. From amongst the trees he heard her call, "Come on, Mr. Thief! Let's see if I can run faster than you as well!"

Rufus grabbed his blades from the ground and sprinted after the Princess.

Let's see about that.

CHAPTER 3

HEIR OF NIMBUS

"Welcome back, Kat!" came the voice of the innkeeper at the dingy pub in Hearthgrim.

Katarina smiled widely in acknowledgement and approached the bar.

"How goes business, Keeper?" she enquired, using the nickname he had earned by keeping the secrets of every patron he had ever had. Nobody knew his true name; he was always introduced simply as "Keeper", by both himself and others.

"Fine, fine, same as always," Keeper replied cheerfully, brushing down his white apron. "Back to see the strays you picked up on your way to Neibel-Haven, are you?"

"Something like that."

"They ain't here anymore, I'm afraid. They said to let you know that they were headed to Scourge's destruction site." Keeper pursed his lips ever so slightly. "But there is another who has requested to see you. I know your skin crawls at his very presence, but I think it wise you speak to him."

"My skin crawls? Oh, you can't mean –"

"As beautiful as always, I see, Kat!" came a slow drawl from behind her.

"What are you doing here, Arshen?" Kat snapped without turning away from Keeper.

"I thought I might stop in at one of your favourite haunts while I passed through." A hand fell on Katarina's shoulder. Katarina grabbed it and attempted to spin out of the grip, which resulted in the man pulling her close and binding her arms. The man named Arshen rested his face on Katarina's shoulder and whispered softly in her ear.

"Now, now, Kat. Now is no time to dance." His voice made her cringe.

"Let go of me or I'll take you through the roof of this establishment and into the sky before dropping you," Katarina threatened, before smiling at Keeper. "I'll pay for damages, of course."

"I only ask that you take any fighting outside." Keeper seemed amused. "Which is exactly what you'd be doing."

"Your call, pervert!" Katarina snapped as Arshen released her.

She turned and looked at the tall man dressed in the attire of a prince. He was remarkably handsome, yet it had no effect on her. She had known him for too long to find any part of him attractive. Those cunning green eyes and that hair with a sienna glow made it easy enough to see why the striking man could captivate almost any woman. The feebler-minded the woman, the easier she fell victim to his firm jawline and masculine physique. This had definitely played a part in forming his belief that any woman could be wooed, and that it was just a matter of time and effort. Katarina, however, only saw the puffed-out chest of an egotistical deviant.

Arshen had a royal guard on each side of him. They were dressed in green and gold, the colours of the kingdom to the north, Nimbus. Both appeared disdainful of Arshen's behaviour, but carefully arranged their expressions so the disrespect wasn't seen by the Prince himself.

"That's no way to treat someone who came to help you get back to your home," Arshen said with false indignation.

"I have no intention of returning to Nimbus yet, nor is it my 'home'. How did you get free of your duties this time, Prince?" Katarina asked, laying heavy mockery on his title.

"Well, I could tell you an epic tale of my escape, but for the life of me I can't seem to find a way to make me walking out the front gate seem exciting. Except that it was me doing it, of course."

"You just walked out?" Katarina asked, not sure if she was surprised or not. Realistically, the Prince of Nimbus tended to do what he liked on a whim, others be damned.

"Not exactly. I have my reasons, along with a goal."

"A new experience for you, I'm sure. Is it a goal that *doesn't* involve cheap wine and cheaper women? While I doubt it, I'd like to believe you're growing up."

"Is that jealousy I hear?" Arshen asked with a smirk.

"No, what you hear is the relief I feel every time you pester any woman who isn't me," Katarina quipped, with a meaningful glance towards Keeper. It was clear she wished to resume her journey towards Scourge.

"Oh, you are growing colder and colder every time I see you. Be careful – you may end up being as closed off as Amelia. Where is she, by the way?" Arshen asked, looking around them for any sign of Katarina's sister.

"Busy avoiding you, I'd wager. I'm not so lucky," Katarina replied, opting to withhold the fact of her sister's passing.

"It doesn't matter, I suppose," Arshen shrugged. "But you were right about one thing: my travels *do* involve a woman."

"You can pretend I'm surprised, if it makes you feel better."

"It does, and you should be interested. It affects a lot of people, after all." Arshen attempted to sound aloof, as if what he was saying was of little consequence. It was difficult sometimes. Katarina rarely took him seriously and never left herself vulnerable near him.

"I highly doubt that. What happens is between you and whatever unfortunate woman you have your eyes on," Katarina replied, her cold edge still strong. "Now, I have to find someone. Please leave me be and don't feel obligated to rush back from wherever you're going."

"Quite right, I must be off." Arshen smiled and leant closer. "I shouldn't keep a Princess waiting, like you do to a certain Prince."

With that, Arshen and his party were gone.

Katarina turned back to Keeper and sighed.

"He's calling them 'princesses' now?" she asked. "I'm yet to meet a whore worthy of that title."

Keeper looked concerned – a rare expression that generally meant something was about to go wrong.

"Katarina." He used her full name, another sign that he was worried. "I think he was referring to an actual princess."

"Meaning?"

"I have only heard rumours and I will look into it more, but I hear that the kingdom of Aquiocia has been undergoing changes," Keeper said uncertainly.

"Arshen is hardly one to get involved in politics, especially not another kingdom's," Katarina replied dismissively.

"Just the same, I'll look into it and gather what information I can. I will present it when you return from Scourge – I assume that's where you're going?"

"It is. With any luck, I can convince the Vassal there to come with me back to Nimbus."

"Be on your guard, Katarina. With the rumours and the fact that Arshen is actually moving away from his hole of alcohol and cheap thrills…" Keeper trailed off with a grimace.

"Indeed, it doesn't bode well. I'd like to think it idle coincidence, but…"

"But you know that very little involved with Arshen is coincidence," Keeper finished.

"Precisely."

CHAPTER 4

A ROGUE'S CONCERN

Alicea slowed to a jog as she entered the village and looked around at the villagers racing here and there in the morning sun. At first it looked like a state of panic, but she soon noticed that each person was carrying tools, equipment, armour or something else of use to the front gate. She weaved through the people towards Garnet and Kurok, the Chief of the small village. The pair were engaged in deep conversation, which came to an abrupt halt as the Princess approached.

Alicea glanced past them to see Rufus sitting with two identical young women, one with a long ponytail and the other with her hair falling messily. Although the Princess recognised the twins as Lori and Tori, whose presence in the village indicated that Setz's troops were here, she couldn't help but focus on the fact that Rufus had beaten her back to the village by a large margin.

"Do not be discouraged by losing a race to someone who runs for a living," Garnet smiled, seeming to read her mind.

With a nod, Alicea changed the topic. "What's the situation, then?"

"It is simple enough," Kurok grunted, his face riddled with fatigue. He had been sleeping almost as poorly as the Princess and his age wasn't helping. "We wait for the last of the men and women from the other Tremel settlements to be ready. They are stationed out in the fields where the last battle took place."

"Stationed? When did they arrive?"

"Last night. We did not wake you, as we know how much difficulty you've had sleeping recently," Garnet said kindly.

"I am going to speak to them now, if you would care to join me?" Kurok offered, noticing the Princess' anticipation.

As Chief and Princess strode through the crowd, Alicea tore her eyes away from the excited waving of the twins who had spotted her.

There will be time enough to talk later, hopefully.

Rufus took a large draught from his cupped hands as he stared vacantly at the now rippling water of the trough. The stream that circled the village had been deemed insufficient in supplying water to both the villagers and their visitors. The population gathered at South Tremel had exploded overnight and the stream had been left to the newcomers, with troughs of water littered around the village for its residents.

He'd heard them arrive; he was surprised the Princess hadn't. (Then again, she'd been so fraught with worry lately – it wasn't surprising that during the periods she was able to get to sleep, she slumbered deeply, if restlessly.) If it wasn't for Kurok mentioning that they had called in reinforcements, Rufus would have sounded the alarm for an attack on the village. There was no way to see thousands of shadows suddenly emerging from the forest and be at ease. The Chief had given the order that no one was to greet them in the night should they hear their arrival, and that everyone was to stay within their dwellings and rest.

The truth was that, on average, Rufus had gotten about as much sleep as the Princess herself. Whenever he would doze off in the hammock he'd erected outside her hut, his head would be filled with the sounds of her screams, whether she was battling her new night terrors or not. He supposed they were his terrors as well now, in some small way. He couldn't rest knowing that she could awaken at any moment screaming.

As a result, he was even less interested in meeting the new people at the doorstep of his temporary home. He needed a break. Instead, he settled for submerging his entire head in the crisp water of the trough. It was cold and fresh; his skin reacted by paling to the sudden coolness that enveloped it. Rufus held his breath for thirty seconds, pulled his head free, breathed, and repeated the process. After three more dives, he came up for air, shook his head violently and turned to a low voice addressing him.

"My sources tell me that the corrupted Council often refers to you as 'the Princess' watchdog'. Shaking your head like that makes me powerless to argue with them."

"What do you want this time, Setz?" Rufus snarled as he wiped the cool liquid from his face.

"You look exhausted," Setz observed, clearly noting the thief's sunken eyes and the black bags surrounding them.

"And you look ravishing!" Rufus replied sarcastically. Looking around the pair, he quickly noticed that nobody was in their immediate vicinity. Somehow, Setz had managed to speak to him alone in broad daylight. As an army rallied to march around them. The Guildmaster was beyond cunning.

Setz didn't reply at first, instead pacing slowly back and forth in front of Rufus. With his dark, billowing cloak, it looked more like he glided rather than walked. Rufus couldn't be sure, but he could almost see a hint of concern on his employer's scarred face.

"She's still ali—"

"I'm not here for Her Highness. I'd know if anything had happened to her." Setz sniffed, pausing for a moment. "I'm here for you."

"You travelled from Aquiocia to check up on me?" Rufus scoffed as he started to undo the belts holding his weapons. He'd been meaning to check on them that morning but hadn't had the chance.

"No. I came because everything in Aquiocia is currently on standby. My men and women are ready and in hiding. They await the Princess' return; they await her command. I am here to lend my assistance in any way I can. However, it appears that Kurok, Garnet and even the other Chieftains have everything under control. They are competent."

"Cut the shit, Setz. You're here to spy on them," Rufus snarled as his weapons hit the ground and he removed his coat to reveal the dirty tunic underneath.

Setz shrugged. "Call it what you will. Everything is in order, so I've come to ask how you're handling everything. In general, that is."

Rufus paused. Genuine concern from Setz was more off-putting than his ability to be everywhere and know everything. "Why do you want to know?"

"Why wouldn't I?"

"Fine." Rufus let himself fall to the ground and started rummaging through his coat, taking stock of what he had and didn't have. For a long moment, there was only the sound of him pulling everything from lock picks and whetstones to small blades and wire from the inside pockets of the garment.

Rufus finally caved.

"A few short months ago I was doing a job for you. Nabbing a stone, simple enough. Now this stone turns out to be some form of superpower that only the Princess can wield. We go in search of others and find a woman who nearly kills us with *her* stone by turning into a magical beast –"

"Yes, Lyrium's transformation was something else," Setz remarked nonchalantly.

"THIS WAS SUPPOSED TO BE A BODYGUARD JOB WHERE I WATCHED THE BRAT'S BACK WHILE SHE WENT LOOKING FOR PRETTY ROCKS!"

"Yes. I can see you're enjoying yourself," Setz said.

"Are we just turning a blind eye to the fact that we are about to attempt to storm Aquiocia itself?" Rufus muttered as he started stuffing items back into his coat.

Setz didn't reply. He didn't have to. He knew that Rufus' issue wasn't the job, or the siege itself.

"Look, I just…" Rufus trailed off as frustration got the better of him. "Setz, tell me what you think will happen here."

Setz glanced off into the distance for a second and took a deep breath.

"I believe that despite our best efforts to quash the chances of it transpiring, the Aquiocian Princess and the Reaper will cross weapons. People will die on that day, most of them innocent. The real question is – when the cerulean roses turn crimson, will the Princess find it within herself to fight with her all, or will she join her parents in the afterlife?"

Rufus' face cycled through a range of expressions before deciding on scepticism. "Planning on becoming a poet once this is all over, then?"

"What's the real issue here, Rufus?" Setz asked without humour.

"You seem convinced that she and Jex will go head-to-head. How can you say that without intervening more?"

"Because I appear to have more faith in the Princess than even you do," the Guildmaster replied with a glance around himself. He was clearly staying clear of people for a reason. "I've spent enough time here. I –"

"How is she supposed to win when she can't even wield a bladed weapon?" Rufus asked, his gaze focused on his blades. He couldn't look the Guildmaster in the eye. Not while he was vulnerable with concern for Alicea. "From where I'm standing, she doesn't stand a chance."

"If I've learnt anything over the years, it's that every single person has the capacity to kill. You might think of the Princess as a pacifist, but have you ever tried touching her hair?" Setz replied.

As Rufus looked up to snarl at the man for making a joke, he found himself alone. He was surrounded by men and women undergoing errands and preparations. He could make out snippets of conversation about the newcomers and deducted that introductions were to begin shortly. He knew it was time to get himself – and his gear – together. Throwing the coat over his shoulder and hastily tying the blades back in place, he went off in search of familiar faces.

CHAPTER 5

THE FALSE KING

The morning sun's rays saturated the royal chambers with their warmth as Arissam scowled at his reflection in the gaudy, full-length mirror before him. Its gold trimming and red jewels clashed violently with the room's theme of silver and azure, but he wanted to stand out from the traditional Aquiocian royalty in any way he could. As a result, he'd slowly begun to replace various items in his chambers with furnishings designed to contrast with anything "Aquiocian".

The results of his insecurity had made many a visitor's eyebrows rise as the royal chambers steadily transformed from a place of elegance and beauty to a storage room of ostentatious items. While the library in the east of the great chambers remained untouched, the massive four-poster bed was the only piece of furniture that remained in its original place. Arissam couldn't quite explain it, but there was something truly exhilarating about sleeping in the bed of the kingdom's late rulers.

His face had grown worn over the past few months since Jex's return from Tremel. He had been furious that Jex had not only failed to seize the Princess or the stone, but had returned without a single man he'd left with.

That man's insolence has cost us far too much time! Arissam thought for the thousandth time, prompting the same bad mood he'd had been battling for months to resurface.

He knew that he was partly to blame himself. As soon as they'd had enough infected with the curse, he'd given them the order to march. He'd wanted the loose end that was Alicea to be snuffed out immediately and the stone returned to Aquiocia. Now, they had two Vassals to contend with and from the reports, the people of the village had not fled as he'd assumed they would.

"NONE OF THIS MAKES ANY SENSE!" Arissam roared, picking up a gaudy bronze chair from beside the mirror and slamming it into the shimmering surface.

The priceless glass shattered into thousands of pieces, showering the ground with its glittering remains. The servant behind him didn't flinch or say a word. He was the thirty-second attendant of the new King since his takeover and was currently holding onto an impressive streak of eleven days without being beheaded for incompetence. He'd learnt from the thirty-one attendants prior to him that the best way to stay alive was to simply let the King feel whatever he needed to feel without comment. In fact, not responding was often the only way to avoid strife.

Unless he made eye contact, like he was doing now.

"Your Majesty, is there something I can assist you with?" the young man asked, standing up straight like a soldier ready for battle.

"Yes," Arissam sneered. "You can tell me how a powerful man like *Jex the Reaper* could possibly fail to bring a bitch like Alicea to heel!"

The attendant didn't reply; the King had forgone eye contact.

"Perhaps you could go on to tell me how he could not only fail to do that, but fail to get any information on the second Vassal, either!" Arissam's voice was rising again. "And finally, tell me how he managed to get the entire legion of cursed men destroyed in the process!"

The attendant had almost fallen into a daydream designed to block out the King's rant when he noticed the King was looking him in the eye again.

"Well, if I might be so bold, I daresay that it would have ended very differently if you were leading the charge. I believe it was your absence that let Jex run amok." The attendant spoke with honeyed words. It was a simple tactic: cater to his King's ego and simultaneously speak ill of someone he fears. It worked every time.

This day was no different.

"You're right there, son!" Arissam declared as he walked towards the library's archway.

That was close. If I had lost my focus, I'd have lost my head.

"You know, I always come to this abomination; yet I never enter!" Arissam announced with a wave of his hand towards the entrance. "It's like something always gets in the way of me investigating – not that I have any use for a damned library."

"Of course you don't!" the attendant agreed, meeting the King's eyes again. "What information could a library possibly offer you that you don't already know?"

"Precisely, my boy!" Arissam grinned with self-satisfaction, turning back to the library's entrance. "Although, it is MY property and I really should –"

"Your Majesty!" A panicked voice interrupted the King as a young girl burst into the chambers. She wasn't dressed well

– sporting clothes that barely passed for rags – and Arissam knew her for what she was immediately.

She was one of the test subjects he had personally selected for the curse. He'd deliberately chosen a few dozen children to be afflicted so the contagion could be passed on quickly should they need more people bending to their will. Children were useless in combat, so there was little chance of losing them in battle if they were never sent. Yet they made for good messengers; they were not only eager to please their superiors, but the idea of a bloody curse consuming their bodies was enough to terrify them into submission.

The end goal was to have complete and utter obedience throughout the kingdom. Although he now had enough soldiers under the effects of the curse to quash any insubordination, there had been a perilous couple of months where Arissam had operated on fear alone. Nobody knew what the contagion was, exactly; even Arissam wasn't certain what Jex was doing, but it had worked a treat. The more they infected, the easier it was to spread, and the first place he had delegated the accursed were the outer gates. He didn't want any substance to the rumours going on outside of Aquiocia, and the ill kept those who were uninfected trapped within the city walls until it was their turn.

That's right. I'm in charge now. Arissam grinned at the thought before finally focusing on what the child before him was saying.

"– and she's coming!" the girl finished in borderline hysterics.

"What?" Arissam frowned as he stepped away from the library's entrance. "Who is coming?"

He knew the answer even before the girl opened her mouth, but it didn't stop him from violently slapping her across the face when she uttered the Princess' name.

"You do not speak her name! She is nothing to this kingdom!" Arissam snarled. "Or perhaps you'd like to go the same way as some of your little friends, hmm?"

The girl didn't reply. Instead she attempted to bury her face in the stone floor to stifle her whimpers of pain. She had seen enough of her friends brutally punished on the tyrant's whim; showing discomfort in front of him only ever made it worse for the victim.

"How many?" Arissam asked before leaning down and screaming into the girl's ear, "I ASKED YOU A QUESTION!"

"You should become a father someday," came a slow drawl from the doorway.

Arissam shook his head slowly to regain his composure. He knew Jex's voice all too well; he also knew the man was currently breaking their agreement.

"Jex, why are you –"

"Most of the village of Tremel, thousands of hunters from the other settlements, and I swear there is another faction working alongside them." Jex counted off his fingers from his place propped up in the arch's frame.

"Did anyone see you?"

"There's an army about to march on your new kingdom and you're concerned about people seeing me?" Jex laughed. "No, any who might have seen me were... persuaded to look the other way."

Anyone listening in might have thought bribes or violence were the way Jex got around the city, but Arissam knew better. Once the Reaper's influence had made its way into the blood of a victim, it was easy for him to manipulate the host. Realistically, despite his violent nature, Jex probably made it to the royal chambers without physically hurting a single person. The thought brought limited reassurance.

While Jex being seen wasn't the worst possible thing, it still made Arissam's life a little more complicated. He had taken charge of an entire kingdom in the past few months and while the sight of Jex reinforced the fear of Aquiocia's people, it also made people ask questions. Questions about where he'd come from and where he had been, especially from the countless people who were old enough to remember the late King announcing the execution of a man corrupted by foul magic.

The riskiest part was when they were seen together, as Jex rarely acted submissive to the new King. Arissam had taken the throne with the Reaper at his side – that was the story. Yet anyone looking closely could see their dynamic was not simply King and underling. More questions…

"You seem to know something of the coming force." Arissam brushed down his silk tunic as if dealing with the girl in a heap on the floor had sullied his attire.

"I do indeed!" Jex exclaimed with an enthusiasm that was out of place. "I also know that we can meet them head-on."

"You said you believe they have help – another faction?" The King gestured towards the balcony at the west of the chambers. Jex followed as the King's attendant helped the young girl to her feet. Seemingly forgotten, the servants remained in the chambers as their superiors took to the balcony.

"I did," Jex replied, his face alive with excitement as he leant against the archway – out of the sight of anyone looking up at the royal chambers from below. "Damned if I can work out who, though. My bet would be –"

"They are from underground."

Jex didn't reply. He had theories, none of them conclusive. There had been rumours of an underground society floating around since he'd emerged from his prison, but every time he attempted to question someone, they simply looked equal parts scared and confused. He was also reluctant to make himself too obvious to those uninvolved in the current campaign, as incompetence tended to infuriate him and cause unnecessary scenes. While the idea of drama was enticing through the bouts of boredom, outright panic within the city would distract him from his current course. The course that led him to the Princess.

"They are from underground," Arissam repeated, this time in a growl.

"What's it matter where they are from?"

"It doesn't, so long as we remain within the city's walls."

Jex finally moved to Arissam's side, grabbing his shoulder and smirking as Arissam flinched. The King was still uneasy around the Reaper.

"Would you like to tell me what would happen, should we leave the city's influence?"

Arissam didn't. He loathed the idea of revealing any more weaknesses than necessary, even to his most powerful resource. But he knew that now Alicea was marching towards him, it was best for his champion to know exactly what limitations they were faced with. After a measured breath, Arissam spoke.

"If I leave the walls of this city, I will be struck down before

I can take a single breath."

Jex looked intrigued, his sinister eyes running over the coward playing the King. For a few moments he found himself entertained simply by trying to work out exactly what the King was afraid of.

"What's outside of these walls, *Your Majesty?*"

"Assassins," Arissam answered simply, before raising his hand and clicking his fingers. His attendant scurried to the bedside table and opened a drawer, rummaging for something inside.

"Any King who doesn't have assassins after his head is a pathetic King indeed," Jex observed as the attendant returned with a scroll.

"Open that," Arissam ordered.

Jex did so without breaking eye contact with the King. It was only when the scroll was completely unfurled that Jex finally looked down to see a blood-red rose impaled by a dagger emblazoned upon the surface of the parchment. The emblem glowed faintly with a purple luminescence and Jex knew immediately that he was holding some sort of enchantment.

"I'm going to need a little more information."

"Forbidding enchantment. Tricky stuff," Arissam sniffed as he waved his hand dismissively towards his attendant.

Once they were alone on the balcony once more, the King continued.

"It doesn't work on just anything. The subject has to have some degree of power to begin with. This emblem was taken from an assassin I managed to have captured and interrogated just before the King and Queen left for the Plains. Do you know what the assassin told me after a couple of weeks of torture?"

"What?"

"NOT A DAMNED THING!" Arissam snarled in frustration. "I knew Axeal knew something about the assassin's purpose, though I couldn't just ask him about it. I didn't want him to know I knew of their existence. So, I did the only thing I could think of. I requested a gifted mage to assist me in ensuring there would be no more lurking in the shadows. I had him take this man's arm, and dive into the secrets behind the tattoo. Again, we found nothing."

Jex was getting bored. The story felt like it was going nowhere, and its sole purpose was to reiterate that Arissam was a failure. Jex crossed his arms impatiently.

"The mage discovered that the markings did indeed have power, but their nature was hidden well. He weaved an enchantment upon it so that anyone bearing that emblem couldn't enter the kingdom. He couldn't make it absolute – even forfeiting his life to the spell wasn't enough to guarantee its success. Which is why the enchantment is dependent on this scroll. It's a conduit for the spell's power."

"If it was so difficult, then how do you know it even worked?"

"Because I'm standing here telling you about it."

"Why *are* you telling me this?" Jex asked suddenly, his eyes squinting against the rising sun. He still wasn't accustomed to so much exposure to sunlight.

"Because retreat isn't an option," Arissam answered quickly, walking back inside to conceal the scroll once again in the bedside table's drawer.

"So long as I'm in command of the troops, retreat was never on the cards." Jex grinned. "With your leave, I will prepare them. I'd say we have less than a week."

"Do it."

Arissam and Jex began to make their way out of the royal chambers.

"What of the peasants?" Jex muttered, glancing at the pair behind them.

"Oh, I hadn't thought of that." Arissam turned at the doorway, taking in the distraught-looking girl and the stoic expression of his thirty-second attendant.

Arissam smiled, and without breaking eye contact with the girl, he nodded towards his attendant.

"Kill him."

The girl looked horrified. It was a command she'd heard a few times, usually accompanied by a cursed knight striking someone down.

"I – I can't…"

"You can." The cruel King turned to Jex with a smile. "And you will."

The King left the chambers, and Jex looked over the servants with the slightest hint of a smirk.

"Do what he asks and the curse will release its hold," he said as his bandaged arm began to glow.

As the Reaper turned and left to ready the soldiers of Aquiocia, the young girl's heart exploded with the pain of searing venom coursing through her chest as the transformation began.

CHAPTER 6

THE COURAGE OF THE TORTURED

"I – I don't understand what – WHAT IS HAPPENING TO ME?" The girl's shrieks were met with the solemn expression of the King's attendant.

He knew he could leave the girl, who was now crying tears of blood, but he froze, the same way he had every time one of his friends had been consumed by the infection. He knew what would happen here. He would watch on as the girl was devoured from the inside out. The blood in her veins would boil and curdle from the venom borne of the Reaper's magic. She would die slowly, consumed by a curse she didn't deserve. And he would watch in terror.

What the young man *didn't* expect was that the girl might turn her blood-obscured gaze to him. At first he hesitated at the sight of the victim bleeding from the pores of her face, but quickly gained his bearings when he remembered she was a foot and a half shorter than him and sickly thin. She was decaying right in front of him, encased in her own blood.

"It was... They were..." The girl spluttered, thick strands of crimson falling from her mouth as she tried to gather her thoughts. "UNDERGROUND!"

He couldn't understand what the girl was trying to put together. His blurred mind thought over the words and he glanced towards the King's bedside table.

Underground? The assassins?

The attendant wasn't allowed another thought before the blood-doused girl leapt at him. Taking him by surprise, her tainted, searing blood burnt through his fine clothing and began to scorch his skin. As his flesh gave way to the assault, the tainted blood began to seep into his own.

The girl felt a vicious strength amidst the haze of pain. She was barely eight, and yet she'd seen more than most people in her time. She also knew that she'd be dead within half an hour. That was the longest she'd ever seen one of her friends last under the effects of the curse. As her tiny hand found the attendant's oesophagus, she closed her thin fingers and crushed his windpipe with her new strength.

They made me into a monster... I... Her thoughts broke away. She focused on destroying the scroll. Then she stopped. *He'd... He'd know...*

The girl sprinted towards the exit of the royal chambers.

Underground... Underground... UNDERGROUND!

The girl sped down the spiral staircase leading to the second-floor balconies. She barely noticed her surroundings; she knew the palace well and had precious little time to take in its splendour one last time.

They had come for the orphanage first, demanding children and not explaining why. The knights had spoken only to give orders and otherwise remained silent as they rounded up the hungry and the abandoned. The children had been dragged away, terrified and despondent. Then the experiments had begun, and she was amongst the few who remained.

Now she had a mission. She had a mission for herself and

for her friends. She would be with them soon. But first, she was going to strike back at the one who had tormented them.

She no longer felt the fear that came with being infected. She'd already endured being separated from her parents and living at the orphanage. She'd already survived being selected to become a test subject and she'd already lived in terror as she served her cruel superiors. Now she felt free, despite the fact that her body was falling apart with each step.

As she burst into the audience hall, she barely saw the handful of people watching her as she stumbled across the grand chamber, making her way to the eastern branches. Nobody stopped her – nobody dared. There wasn't a single clean-blooded person in existence who'd want to risk infection while apprehending an already doomed victim. It made the girl's job easier.

Her blood-soaked feet hit the eastern corridors and she made her way towards a doorway leading to a courtyard housing half a dozen destroyed statues. The statues formerly depicted the images of the late royals and were now missing large pieces of their original forms – a result of Arissam's tantrums.

She realised the curse was approaching its climax when her pores erupted with small torrents of gushing blood. She reached the doorway and felt her blood eating away at the door handle at her fingertips. Slamming against the door as she turned the handle, the girl fell to her knees upon the lush grass. From there she crawled. Inch by inch, she dragged her liquidising body towards her target – a manhole in the centre of the pavement.

She made it. Barely. Her brain was starting to burn inside her skull.

The gurgling sound of blood in her throat, she groaned as she pushed the lid aside. Without a second of hesitation, she threw herself down the dark manhole. She barely felt the impact of falling fifteen feet straight down. She realised that most of her muscle mass was now the equivalent of acidic crimson jelly. What remained of her body squelched and slid across the surface of the sewer floor as she attempted to call out to people she wasn't sure actually existed.

"Helppphh!"

The girl couldn't be sure whether the orange glow of a torch was her imagination or not. The person holding it was clad in a black robe with the occasional crimson blur etched into its fabric. What she assumed was long silver hair fell across the figure's featureless face. The girl had no idea if what she was saying was intelligible, but still she tried to speak.

"Besshshide shable!" She gurgled and coughed. "Shroll, enshaaandment blokett asshhashins! Deshroy shroll Kingsh besshide –"

"Rest," the figure said quietly.

The girl listened, allowing her burned eyes to close and death to lay its claim. The man watched over the bubbling mess of blood and body matter before speaking in the same quiet voice.

"Recruit some unmarked civilians for clean-up in the eastern courtyard."

"Yes, Master," a voice behind him confirmed.

"What does this mean, Setz?" another voice asked from the darkness.

The Guildmaster didn't reply for a long moment, his eyes still examining the cooling remains as they steadily burnt through the stone beneath them.

"It means that the courage of a tortured child can be quite the game-changer."

CHAPTER 7

A SQUIRE'S MISSION

"Get your head down, damn it!" a man's voice hissed from behind Jex. The order wasn't directed at him; they very rarely were after he received the initial brief from higher up the chain of command. Arrive at the village, wait until nightfall, observe the bandits troubling the hamlet and intervene if needed. Simple.

The people within the dwellings at the base of the hill didn't know about the company of ten knights hiding on the hilltop. The knights had deliberately kept their presence a secret to avoid anyone in the hamlet giving away their plans. So far it was going well, save for Wenalt's inability to lie still.

"It's not easy to lie flat in full-plate armour!" Wenalt whined as he attempted to get comfortable.

"Gods help me, you're more of a Princess than the newborn back in Aquiocia!" growled their Captain.

Captain Reicel was an older man who had seen his fair share of battles. He had more grey hairs and wrinkles from stress upon his forty-year-old face than he'd have liked. He had voluntarily given up on rising any higher than Squad Captain at the age of thirty, instead staying at his current rank and working with knights who showed promise throughout their training. Despite his lack of ambition, squires all throughout

Aquiocia and even other cities often dreamt of being taken under Reicel's wing. A recommendation from him was an immense step towards the higher ranks of full knighthood.

Jex hadn't expected to be chosen. He hadn't even applied to train under Reicel, or really thought about it. Reicel had approached him, saying that Warmaster Maxim had seen him in the field and requested that he accompany the rest of the party.

Given that he'd only joined the military in order to become more competent in combat and survival, Jex had seen little reason to say no. Though he had learnt early on to keep his motives for joining to himself. When he'd arrived in Aquiocia, exhausted and starving, he had found out the hard way that telling the people offering him food and shelter of his goal to find Lucian often led to them screaming that he leave their house. It had been a steep learning curve – people hated honesty.

All those people I met upon arriving in Aquiocia... They still just linger and do nothing with their lives. I've been in the city for the better part of four years and yet I see the same problems repeating over and over. All the while, people bellow for change. They all want to change the world, but they won't lift a finger to do so, much less put their head on the chopping block.

His cynical thoughts did nothing to distract him from his task. He saw the shadows within the trees even before his Captain did.

"Target spotted. Possible courses of action include taking the initiative and striking first, luring them into a trap in the hamlet by using the residents as bait, waiting for them to cross the –"

"Damn it, kid, I get the point!" Reicel muttered in response to Jex's monotone. It wasn't a secret: Jex unnerved the Captain.

Jex didn't apologise – he never did. Those who knew him wondered if he'd ever even considered the concept of an apology. One thing they did know was that he didn't actively avoid apologising so much as he didn't seem to realise when he'd done something wrong.

The party of ten turned their gaze back to the movement in the trees with curiosity. They were definitely bandits; the knights could make out the rough clothing worn by each of the poorly concealed ruffians. Their numbers were the real mystery.

Though the forestry surrounding the small village wasn't what anyone would call dense, it was enough to conceal their ranks. The Captain and his men may have had the vantage point and element of surprise, but the bandits were scattered and possibly plentiful. Couple that with the fact that they had cover from arrows and it became a situation Reicel didn't think highly of.

"Twenty-two," Jex announced in that same monotone.

"What?" Reicel asked in surprise.

"There are twenty-two bandits," Jex replied simply.

The Captain twitched. While he wanted to discredit the kid, he found himself believing him instead.

Jex himself didn't understand exactly how he knew how many there were – just that he could feel them. It was like the dull thud of a hefty drum was thumping in his ears, and the sound was coming from each of the bandits hiding in the forest. He knew it wasn't natural, but he felt a similar rhythm every time he sparred or trained with his peers. It happened whenever those around him were excited in some way or another.

Over time, the ability had been honed to focus only on that which he found interesting. He hadn't trained himself. Whatever the phenomenon was, it had adapted to its surroundings and his own needs. As a result, even though the men beside him were shifting with anticipation, Jex didn't hear the sound of drums from them. He couldn't hear anything coming from the village, either, meaning they had no idea that the bandits were here.

Villages all around this area have been attacked by a group of bandits and yet they don't even have lookouts? This is another case of people wanting something done but not doing a thing to help themselves, Jex thought as he tightened the tie holding back his shoulder-length, pitch-black hair.

He'd grown it out upon getting to Aquiocia in the hope of changing his appearance so that those he'd unnerved didn't recognise him in passing. But his fiery amber eyes did nothing to help people forget the unnatural-looking child, and things didn't change as he grew into adolescence.

Thankfully, most of the people in the castle barracks had seen the Council Chairman known as Setz. The Chairman had similarly coloured eyes, so the grief Jex endured had lessened greatly. It also helped that he spent any time he wasn't training hiding away in the barracks. He'd sit for hours looking at and taking in absolutely nothing, simply waiting to be called upon by his superiors.

"We could lure them into a trap. Get them to chase one of us and break cover. I'm wearing very little armour, so I'd probably be the fastest," Jex noted.

"Are you suggesting I use one of my men as bait?" Reicel asked in surprise. "How do you even know it'd work?"

"The reports said the bandits always take hostages so the rest of the village doesn't fight back. I don't make for an imposing figure, so they'd probably try to take me."

The Captain didn't reply, and the rest of the knights fell into complete silence, even their breathing slowing as they waited for their commanding officer to reply. Everyone was thinking the exact same thing: it was a damned fine idea. Not only was it likely to yield results, it removed Jex from their immediate company. While most of the knights had learnt to deal with having him around, very few genuinely liked it. Wenalt was one of the few exceptions.

"You aren't going out there alone; I'm going with you!" he declared. Jex's eyes ran over the young man offering to run with him. While his incessant whining was a chore, Wenalt was a doer. Jex respected that and nodded slightly.

"Bastard kids get crazier each year," Reicel muttered, reflecting on the many times he, too, had been reckless on the field.

Gazing over the land below, he acknowledged that the ground levelled out nicely from the hill where they hid. Realistically, the bandits wouldn't hurt those they wanted to use as hostages, and if they immediately ran back towards the hill, the knights would be able to pick off at least some of their numbers. It was risky, but it was also brilliant in its simplicity.

"Strip the armour, Wenalt," Reicel ordered suddenly.

"Sir?"

"Well, you aren't going to stroll towards the village dressed as a knight, are you?"

"Oh, right!" The squire nodded, backing away from the crest and allowing two of the others to help him out of his heavy plate. Thankfully, he was wearing frayed shorts and a tattered tunic beneath. Save for their equipment, squires had very little of value. Wenalt had inherited his armour from his family upon being accepted as a squire. He was considered lucky amongst his peers.

Jex was already dressed in black trousers, shoes and tunic, all slightly sun-bleached. He had adopted black as his predominant colour long ago when he had realised that it suited almost any occasion. If people weren't asking about his attire, that was one less thing he had to explain about himself.

He appeased his commanding officers by wearing a simple leather vest beneath his tunic. None of the other squires had any idea why Jex would choose minimal armour when they had access to a variety of hand-me-down resources. Sure, the stuff supplied usually stank and had some questionable stains, but it blocked a weapon well enough. Jex had only selected a light vest after multiple bouts of questioning from Reicel.

"Ready," Wenalt announced. Reicel nodded.

"Now, everyone, ready your bows and remain hidden. Wenalt and Jex, I want you to approach the city at a comfortable pace. You need to seem relaxed and at ease, understood?"

The squires nodded.

"As soon as you catch sight of the bandits moving towards you, run back to us. Unfortunately, taking your swords is not an option, so be careful."

The squires abandoned their weapons and started down the hill towards the village. Neither seemed particularly uneasy about the plan, but they showed their feelings in different ways. Jex was focused, his face expressionless as always, save for his intense eyes. Wenalt, however, was doing enough talking for them both. It was clear that he relished the chance to get up and move around after staking out the village for the past thirty hours.

"Ya know, I hear that once you graduate to knighthood, you get a pouch of gold AND you get to meet the King and Queen!"

"Mm." Jex nodded absentmindedly.

"Imagine that, an entire pouch of gold!" Wenalt crowed. "Do you think we will get to meet the Princess as well? Wouldn't that be a treat!"

"If you continue to talk about the palace so loudly, you will blow our cover," Jex warned. His companion lowered his voice.

"That's a fair point. Sorry, Jex."

Jex shook his head slightly to dismiss the conversation and noticed movement in the brush across the field. Doing his best to look surprised as a burly man burst forth, Jex stood his ground with Wenalt.

"Oh no, bandits!" Wenalt yelled with a fear that was surprisingly convincing as he turned and ran back the way they'd come.

Jex was about to join him when the thumping of the drums became louder with each beat. After several rhythmic thuds, the sound caused his head to ache. He noticed that about a dozen bandits were now sprinting towards him. To them, Jex looked like he was frozen in fear. The lone squire could do nothing to prevent the men from getting closer as they rapidly covered the ground between them.

The bandits... They fell for it, but what is wrong with me?

Jex doubled over with his hands clasped against his temples.

It felt like an enormous rush of blood was pulsing through his head. He grabbed at his wrist in an attempt to feel for his pulse, only to find his heart throbbing steadily with a calmness that was completely out of place. But he was hot. With each flood of blood that pushed through his arteries came the sensation of being blasted with a torrent of scalding water.

"What's wrong with the kid?"

"Who cares?"

"Just grab him!"

The voices sounded like they were leagues away, but Jex knew their owners were close. Though he couldn't see them through a haze that had turned crimson, he knew exactly where each of the seven bandits were, and from which direction each was approaching.

Then his vision cleared.

"I feel..." Jex had no idea what he was trying to say as he eyed each of the men reaching for him.

It was too late to run, but his daze was broken when an arrow suddenly found one of the bandits' necks. Jex's body finally responded, his hand racing across the middle of one of the men who had reached him. Stepping to the side, the young squire found the bandit's short blade and liberated it from its scabbard before burying it into its owner's sternum.

"I feel..." Jex repeated emotionlessly.

The short, bloodied sword was lighter than the longswords they were instructed to use during sparring practice. It made it easy for Jex to autonomously engage in combat by weaving through the enemy ranks, slashing at their exposed limbs. He could hear everything: the bandits' surprised grunts, the whizz of arrows soaring through the air, the pounding of the heartbeats belonging to the rest of the bandits joining the fray.

"I feel..."

As the confrontation came to an end, Jex stood panting with twenty lifeless bodies encircling him. At least a dozen of the corpses had vicious lacerations across their bodies from where he had butchered them with their comrade's weapon. Jex wasn't aware of the blood staining his clothes and skin, much less the remaining two bandits fleeing the scene.

His mind barely even acknowledged the knight running down the hill towards him, all the while barking orders at the squires behind him to stay back. Reicel reached Jex and grabbed him forcefully by the shoulders, ripping the blade from his hand.

"What in the name of King Axeal was that?" the Captain demanded.

"I feel –" Jex repeated as Reicel slapped him across the face as hard as he could with his gauntlet.

"Enough games, Jex!" the Captain bellowed as his squire raised his head from the blow with a look of realisation. He finally understood the feeling.

"I... I don't know... I just... reacted," Jex muttered softly, speaking an untruth that neither man quite believed.

"Get back to the crest!" Reicel snarled. "Do not move until I return from the village!"

Jex nodded, turning away from the Captain and marching back up the crest. A smile made its way across his face.

Alive. I felt alive.

CHAPTER 8

AN INCOMPLETE RALLY

"Hail, cousin!" A loud greeting met Kurok and Alicea's ears as they exited the village's main gates.

The sight took Alicea aback. The plain between Tremel and the forest caused great wonder to the Princess, ever since a few months ago when she and the Vassal of Earth had combined their strength, changing the landscape from level ground and turf to dense marsh.

Over the weeks, the swampland had dried up and slowly formed cracked mud and unlevel patches of green flora. The damp landscape couldn't have hoped to last long in the warm climate that persisted even through the winter months, which had been expected to settle in for some time. Now, across the plain were countless tents made from animal skin.

Hundreds upon hundreds of people dressed in animal pelts were going from tent to tent, assisting their brethren. These people had managed to come here in the dead of night, set up and wait until the morning – all without her knowledge. It was... unnerving.

The greeting had come from a man in his fifties, garbed in a bear pelt that clung to his impressive physique. Even at his age, the man had muscles growing upon muscles. As he got closer, his height became apparent to the Princess as well. He looked just shy of seven feet tall.

The man wore a brown beard with flecks of grey scattered through it. His forehead sported a massive scar that looked like someone had tried to cut off the top of his bald scalp. His skin was brown like those of South Tremel, but it had a bronze sheen and a leathery texture from over-exposure to the sun's rays. As he approached, Alicea's nose twitched at his scent.

She recognised it, and her mind raced backwards to when she was five: her parents had taken her to the coast that lay to the west of Aquiocia for the first time, and the same smell of brine and sand clung to the behemoth of a man before her. It was obvious that he hailed from the island settlement of West Tremel.

While Alicea had been aware of people living outside her own continent, she had been surprised that one of Tremel's settlements was out there. Arok had mentioned that when the Fortress of the Forest had fallen, a lot of Tremel's people wanted to get away from the site and the memories attached to it. For many, the shame of their home being decimated was too much to bear.

She had never realised just how prideful they were as a people until that moment.

"Hail, cousin, yourself!" Kurok finally replied with a grin before turning to Alicea. "This is Dairok of the West. Dairok, this is Princess Alicea."

Alicea resisted the urge to take a step back out of caution. The hulking man practically drowned out the presence of the morning sun, bathing her diminutive form in shadows.

"How are you, little Princess?" Dairok laughed as he bent down to look Alicea in the eye.

The gesture was not appreciated.

"I can hear your booming voice from your head's place in the clouds just fine, thank you. Do not patronise me."

"Ha! The little Princess has a big mouth!" the man bellowed as he patted her on the head. His hand could quite possibly have crushed her skull if he had a mind to do so.

"While I appreciate any and all assistance to my cause," Alicea said, using both hands to swat away Dairok's before turning to the Chief, "tell me that we have some brains to accompany the brawn?"

"That is where I flourish, one would think." A soft but firm female voice entered the conversation and a young woman approached.

The woman appeared to be around Alicea's age of twenty, with long, sandy-blonde hair that caught the sun's light and shimmered in response. Behind each ear was a large feather clipped into her hair. Her almond-coloured eyes continually darted from one direction to the next, as if paranoid that an enemy would strike at any moment. She did not have the strong physique of the other hunters; instead, her small frame was clad in a cloak of feathers, revealing nothing. As the woman stepped closer, Alicea felt a shift in the energy around her. The change was the newcomer, and she was not to be crossed.

"Who is this?" Alicea asked.

"Silrok," Kurok answered. "Daughter of Salrok. I assume that her presence means her mother was not strong enough to make the trip."

"Your assumption is correct," Silrok explained, a slight frown on her face. "Normally I would watch over the village while my mother charged off to battle. However, it appears that the roles have reversed in this campaign. Instead, it will be me who fights at the side of the Aquiocian Princess."

"You're a mage," Alicea observed.

"I am a shaman," Silrok corrected coldly. "Mages are tearing this world apart. Shamans fight alongside the world."

"I have been informed that I am a mage," Alicea replied curtly, her head tilting slightly.

"Indeed, you are. You're the very worst kind. Wielding the stones as a tool and ripping the life force from the world itself at an accelerated rate."

"I'm not sure what you are talking about, but it sounds like you think you could do a better job."

"The Vassals are chosen on magical aptitude. This has become evident over centuries of records, of which I have read many. They are not chosen on anything except magical strength. How else can you explain one of the stones choosing a Princess who lost her own kingdom to corruption?"

"And what exactly do you mean by that?" Alicea asked in a tone more threatening than she intended. Anger was building within her.

"I mean to say that neither you, nor Lyrium, nor any of the other Vassals selected by the stones are or were worthy of their strength."

"Well, I suppose I should consider myself fortunate that it's not for you to select the Vassals then, shouldn't I?" Alicea forced the words through clenched teeth. She didn't want to lose her composure in front of so many people.

Silrok shrugged. "You may consider yourself whatever you desire. It is the world's wellbeing that I find interesting. Not an immature Princess playing at politics."

"You are an infuriating woman," Alicea muttered.

"Then it is fortunate that I am only here for the time it takes to correct your situation," Silrok goaded.

"That is probably enough, I think," Kurok finally intervened as Dairok looked on in confusion. It was clear that cattiness was not something he was familiar with.

"Is there not a third leader we must meet with?" Alicea asked, attempting to drop and ignore her conversation with Silrok.

"Aye, but the clan members from the East will not be joining us, I'm afraid. We, uh… had difficulty finding them."

The Princess looked at Kurok, then the two others, and nodded thoughtfully. There was clearly something the gathered Chiefs weren't sharing, but despite being royalty, Alicea felt the information wasn't owed to her. She eyed the pair that had led their people to her. They seemed competent enough despite a shaky first meeting.

"I thank you both for coming to my aid. It was not mandatory, and yet you both travelled for a battle that was not yours to fight. You have my deepest gratitude."

"Forget about it, little Princess! Nothing like a good brawl against evil!" Dairok laughed as Silrok averted her eyes.

"That woman – what is her problem?" the Princess muttered under her breath as she watched Dairok and Silrok walk back towards their camp.

"Silrok of the northern settlement. She is a defiant woman," explained Kurok. "She has a strong dislike of mages and believes the world is crumbling beneath our very feet as we fight for the stones. Her hatred of the stones is second only to her hatred of the mages of Neibel-Haven."

"A reservation like that may prove detrimental," Alicea observed.

Kurok smiled, taking her by surprise. "Silrok may have a lot of pent-up hatred towards mages, but she is loyal to Tremel before anything else. She is an ally well worth having. Besides, better her here than her mother. Now, *that* is a woman with a grudge…"

"I will take your word for it," Alicea conceded.

"We march in one hour. I suggest you speak to whoever you need to or do whatever you have to do before we leave," Kurok advised with a weary nod towards the village.

Alicea found she wanted to see Lori and Tori after all, and nodded in appreciation before jogging back the way they had come.

It'll be nice to speak to some people who will be happy to see me.

CHAPTER 9

THE PARTY ASSEMBLES

"Princess!" the twins exclaimed together before practically diving at Alicea for a hug.

"It's been…" Lori started.

"…way too long!" Tori finished.

"Argh! Enough!" Rufus grumbled in annoyance.

The twins and Rufus sat by a small table fashioned out of a tree stump, having taken it upon themselves to oversee the preparations of the village. Rufus was lazing in a deer pelt he had strung from the overhanging roof as a hammock, and the twins had adopted a long log as their seat.

Alicea took her place next to the twins.

"How are you?" she asked kindly.

"We've been missing you and Ruffie a lot," Lori admitted as the Princess smiled warmly.

"As if!" Tori scoffed. "We haven't had time to miss anyone!"

"Setz has been keeping us very busy," Lori nodded, allowing her fatigue to flicker briefly across her face.

"Really? What has he been keeping you busy with?" Rufus asked, rolling over with sudden interest in the conversation.

"Can't tell ya!" Tori laughed.

"By offering information on your mission to those uninvolved, you only invite failure." Lori recited words that

Rufus recognised as Setz's.

With an irritated grunt, Rufus rolled back over in his makeshift bedding away from the girls, at which they all giggled – Alicea included.

Before Alicea could ask anything further about the twins, a loud crash sounded beside her as a log as big as the one they were seated on fell to the ground. The Princess nearly leapt out of her skin from nerves, but the twins exploded with laughter.

They had seen it coming.

Looking up, the Princess saw a short yet well-built man with messy hair grinning widely. The man had the pelt of a black bear draped over his shoulders, dragging in the dirt behind him. Beside him was a woman a couple of inches taller, with chocolate waves of hair bouncing around her shoulders and a deer pelt serving as her cloak. Two long, brown, rabbit-like ears protruded from her curls, standing up as if at attention.

They were two Tremel warriors ready for battle, but to Alicea, they were friends.

"Lyrium, it's so good to see you! You too, Arok!" Alicea exclaimed as her pounding heart recovered.

"Princess," Arok nodded quickly before striding over and playfully punching Rufus in the arm. "Do you ever stop sleeping?"

"Aye, I occasionally take a break from sleeping to eat," Rufus joked back, swatting his friend away.

"It is good to see you again, Prin— Alicea." Lyrium corrected herself at the last second as she took her seat. After so long on the road, it was easy to focus on the titles the pair had left behind.

Arok and Lyrium had been gone from the village for the past few weeks, representing Kurok in their bid to gain the assistance of the other tribes. Before the separation, Lyrium and Alicea had forged a close friendship that made the distance between a hunter and a Princess null and void.

"Same to you. I have missed you greatly," Alicea admitted. It was true that she had made a lot of friends, but not many of them were women she felt she could confide in.

"Then you clearly haven't been training hard enough!" Lyrium laughed, scratching at her long brown ears. "Gah, these things itch more than the rest of my body combined."

"I suppose we will have to wait and see if the training has made any difference," Alicea chuckled.

"Today is the big day!" Lyrium declared suddenly, abandoning the assault on her irritated ears. "It is almost time to march, and here we all are!"

"Not all of us," Arok observed, taking a seat next to his beloved. "Any of you heard from Stefan?"

"Stefan? The man you two went into the ruins with?" Alicea asked.

"The same," Arok said with a grimace. "He is nowhere to be found."

"He didn't partake in the battle, did he?" Rufus wondered. He'd been thoroughly distracted during the conflict.

"Nay, he was too injured and was forced to rest. My father said he hasn't been seen since before we left to meet with Dairok about this issue," Arok revealed. "But he can't work out when he went missing. Father said to keep it quiet, but I expected him here by the time we got back…"

"He didn't tell anyone where he was going?" Lyrium asked.

Alicea thought it strange that her friend seemed to know nothing about what Arok was saying.

"Nay," Arok repeated. "I don't understand. I know he wasn't part of this village, but he had been here so long that I expected him to be around forever."

"It could be that he doesn't want to get wrapped up in all of this," Alicea noted. "If he is not from here, then maybe he returned to his homeland?"

"He would have told me!" Arok insisted. "I don't even know where he is from! Whenever I asked, he just said that his home is wherever he is at the time."

"Makes sense enough to me," Rufus muttered. The group turned to him. "What? Makes sense that he'd like to roam free without any obligations."

"Is that what you would like, Mr. Thief?" Alicea snapped as the twins giggled at the brewing argument. "To be obligation-free so that you may run off and do whatever you please?"

"I know a trap when I see one," Rufus mumbled, not meeting her eyes.

"I'm sure he will show up," Lyrium comforted Arok as Alicea glared in Rufus' direction.

Before Arok could reply, the sound of a loud horn echoed through the village and everyone leapt to their feet. Rufus practically fell from his hammock, then addressed the party.

"Well, that's irritating. I assume that means what I think it means?"

"Aye." Arok nodded grimly. "It's time to march."

CHAPTER 10

THE ARMY MARCHES

The combined force of Tremel's gathered warriors was an unusual sight to behold. Partly because they had not come together like this in two centuries, but also because Alicea never thought she would see the primitive-looking men and women lined up in a formation designed to march on a castle.

A few of the warriors had taken the form of crows and other birds. They had taken to the skies in all directions, to warn the bulk of the force – standing a few thousand strong – of threats from any direction.

In Alicea's brief examination of the army, she realised that the Tremel she had made a second home within was well and truly the smallest of the tribes present. She had been told this before and had even studied it. But to see a portion of the other settlements dwarf the entirety of South Tremel was fascinating.

Just how magnificent was the Tremel of old…?

The plain's cracked and dried earth seemed to bring unease to some of the warriors. The Princess had heard some of the army's shamans discussing the impact magic had had on the ground beneath them. Alicea had ruled it out as simply rearranging the elements of Earth and Water to create a landscape more favourable to their struggle.

The shamans, however, seemed to be of the opinion that lasting damage may have been caused. Though the exact details were lost on the Princess, she was in no mood to approach them about the matter.

"Alicea," Rufus greeted softly as he walked up behind the Princess.

"Mr. Thief. What can I do for you?"

"I wanted to know if you required me by your side for the first leg of the march."

"Do you have somewhere better to be?" Alicea asked. Before she got a response, she saw the twins standing at a safe distance behind the thief, both seemingly waiting for something. "You wish to march with Lori and Tori?"

"Personally, I don't care. But the twins asked to –"

"Go."

"You aren't upset?"

"Of course not!" Alicea exclaimed, genuinely surprised by the question. "They are your family. Now, run along."

Rufus was still stunned as he slowly retreated, occasionally looking over his shoulder to see Alicea shooing him away. She watched her friend join up with the people he considered his family and found herself longing for her own – especially in what was to follow. Having a family member on her side would have made her feel more confident in herself, if only a little.

"Correct your posture. A Princess should stand tall for the people who are about to fight for her," Garnet quipped as she appeared beside Alicea.

"A true Princess should not have to attempt a siege on her own castle," Alicea replied bleakly as she straightened her back. It was difficult to refuse Garnet's advice.

"A Princess does not feel sorry for herself. A Princess soaked in self-pity would make a truly subpar Queen," Garnet lectured, catching her eye. "Are you ready?"

"Yes," Alicea replied without hesitation, despite her anxiety. "Let us begin."

"Warriors of Tremel!" Garnet's voice boomed through the plains as she fed it magical energy. "Whether you hail from the South, West or North, we thank you for coming to our aid! We stand to gain a great deal. In the name of Princess Alicea of Aquiocia, we will hunt and destroy the evil that now plagues her kingdom and furthermore – this land!"

Three figures joined Garnet's side: the leaders of each of Tremel's gathered settlements. Their voices joined Garnet's and Alicea could feel the energy surging throughout the army that had gathered for her. The men and women were drawing excitement and adrenaline from their leaders' words.

"We came here for a battle that our men haven't seen in hundreds of years!" Dairok roared. "Let's crush these weak-minded dogs!"

"The Princess has called to us – we must answer!" Silrok cried. Alicea's lips pursed. She knew there was a message hidden in Silrok's words.

"We have proven that we can defend against a great threat time and time again! Now it is time for us to show that we can bite back!" Kurok cheered. "For Tremel, for this land and for the rightful Queen – we march!"

"FOR THE RIGHTFUL QUEEN!" Alicea's ears were not ready for the thousands of people crying out in response. She could still feel them ringing as the force began moving forward.

Her eyebrows rose as the warriors started jogging for the forest. Those tasked with scouting ahead had changed form into birds or deer to increase their pace. Others like Dairok, however, lumbered along the ground in their mountainous bodies, keeping up with the main force. Even Silrok was running alongside her own little retinue of warriors, her owl-feather cloak lifting just enough to reveal thin yet muscular legs carrying her at a rapid pace.

In the Princess' confusion, she spotted Rufus and the twins running happily amongst the massive legion of pelt-wearing soldiers. Alicea was forced to smile as they turned it into a game, the twins trying to catch Rufus.

She was relieved to see that the majority of the force began to slow to a steady march once they hit the forest's edge.

"Do you plan on standing around all day staring, or are you going to join them?"

Alicea jumped at Garnet's voice. She had forgotten the Chief's advisor was even there. "They don't seem particularly organised!" she remarked.

"That's the idea. No enemy will know exactly how many there are as they march. But you best believe there is a formation in there that every warrior is following," Garnet replied.

"Is Mr. Thief a part of that formation?" Alicea asked, nodding slowly as she began deciphering the patterns the warriors were following.

"No. He and Setz's forces are best left to their own devices."

"Speaking of Setz's forces, I've only seen Lori and Tori. Are they the only ones he sent?"

"I would have thought you'd know that just because you

can't see Setz's men, doesn't mean they are not there," Garnet quipped. "Now I suggest you hurry up or you will get left further behind!"

With that, Garnet's body started to mutate in a fashion Alicea was now familiar with. After a few moments, a deer stood before her. The beast picked up a small satchel in its mouth before taking off after the soldiers, leaving the Princess alone.

You had best hurry, Princess. Garnet's voice echoed through her mind as she looked back at the running water coursing along the outside of the village.

Alicea smiled.

I think it wise that you focus on your own pace, Garnet.

Garnet was about to respond when she noticed an odd shadow above her. Looking up, she saw a peculiar transparent bird the size of a small hut, flapping its wings steadily to keep afloat as human legs dangled on either side of its neck.

The Princess had created her own mode of transportation.

CHAPTER 11

A SQUIRE'S PROMOTION

She's here again – I can feel it. There, hiding at the door.

Jex pushed the stray black hairs behind his ears and glanced towards the doorway leading out of the knights' mess hall. He had come in to eat an hour after everyone else had left, as usual. Like always, the young apprentice chef had been there to toss him the leftovers without conversation before vanishing from the hall. Jex liked that. What he didn't like was the feeling that someone was watching him.

Sure enough, the door the apprentice had closed was now slightly ajar, and peering from behind it were the eyes of the Princess, glittering under a fringe of dark curls. She wore a dress of sky-blue material that was likely worth more than his monthly pay, along with a look of poorly masked fear.

Why? Why is she here? The damned child is only now approaching her third birthday and she is already too curious for her own good. Can I not eat in peace? I disturb no one and only emerge from the barracks when summoned. Why is she everywhere I am? Watching. Just watching. Waiting. She's waiting for it.

What is "it"? Whatever it is, she knows it's there. Those ice-cold eyes see all. She's nervous like everyone else, but there's a difference within her fear. Others think I'm disturbed. But she knows they're wrong. She knows that I'm far worse…

What am I even thinking…?

"Your Highness," Jex said with forced politeness as he rose and bowed deeply. He had practised the procedure endlessly during his squire years, which were rapidly coming to an end. That afternoon was his graduation – he had almost made it.

The child who was the Princess of Aquiocia squeaked and vanished from view. Jex was familiar with the practice, and by the time he had taken his seat and resumed his meal, Alicea's face was at the door again.

Jex took a measured breath. He wasn't angry or irritated; in fact, he couldn't remember a time he'd felt either of those emotions. They were a foreign concept to the young man of seventeen. But he was perplexed, perhaps even unnerved. He knew he wasn't going to get any answers from the child, despite her being able to speak as well as any eight-year-old.

Alicea had been able to hold a fluent and relatively complex conversation with child or adult alike since she was two years of age. She could read and even scrawl the written word. She was nothing short of brilliant, the pride of both the royalty and citizens of Aquiocia. But despite her comprehension of her surroundings and the fact that she was a Princess, her voice was silenced whenever Jex was nearby. It was a development that wouldn't have mattered if she would only stop following him around.

"Can I help you, Princess?" Jex asked in the same polite voice.

After a moment of silent staring from both parties, Jex changed his tactic.

"Don't you usually have an entourage?" he asked. "How did you escape the watch of the knights?"

"I memorised their patrol routes."

Jex nearly choked on his food as Alicea spoke softly. "Y-you what?" he spluttered.

"The northern watchtowers change hands at midday and the next patrol doesn't come past for another eight to eleven minutes. The knights aren't due back for another three hours and forty-three minutes, and the additional patrols do not commence for another four hours and twenty-two minutes and four hours and fifty-six minutes respectively. My entourage believes that I am napping."

Jex almost felt surprise. He had heard that the Princess was intelligent beyond her years, but this was ridiculous. How could she possibly have worked all of that out so swiftly when the knights themselves had their rosters memorised and burned?

"Might I ask what brings you here, Your Highness?" Jex enquired, forcing himself to speak civilly.

"You frighten a lot of people."

"Do I frighten you?"

"Yes," she replied quietly, looking down.

"Then why are you here alone, if I scare you so much?" Jex asked, slightly puzzled. It was odd for him to feel genuine interest in someone's life.

"There are two knights posted at the end of the hall, the watchtowers' changeover is complete, and a patrol will be along in less than one minute. Additionally, if you hurt me, it won't be overlooked like the missions you've been assigned to."

"You're clever."

"I am," the child-Princess agreed. "Well, I must be off."

Before Jex could respond, two knights appeared beside the

Princess to gently scold her for running off. With a wary nod of affirmation to Jex, the knights took the young girl away.

❖

The sun had barely risen, and yet in the great courtyard, there were hundreds of men and women lined up in the same formation in which they had been trained. Each wore a shining suit of brand-new, sky-blue armour emblazoned with the image of the Aquiocian Rose. Sky-blue was the colour of recent graduates to knighthood. Steadily, as one achieved merit, the colour of their armour would be replaced with deeper hues. The greatest officers actually had the freedom to wear whatever they liked. It was a freedom Jex longed for. Most generals would wear heavily and intricately adorned full plate to show off their prestige; Jex would prefer to run headlong into battle wearing only a comfortable pair of trousers.

The morning was warm, but there were no complaints, as the people gathered there had accomplished what they set out to do. They had made it. In a few moments they would be addressed by the King and elevated into fully fledged knights.

Jex shifted uncomfortably in his armour. He'd only worn what he called a steel shell a few times before, and only when absolutely required. Squires didn't have money, and often had to settle for secondhand leather armour or nothing as part of their training. Most found it unpleasant; Jex found it preferable to the steel plates. He hated the lack of freedom.

His squirming was interrupted by the massive doors leading into the audience hall suddenly opening. Through the doors came the Warmaster Maxim, a young, handsome man with crimson hair ablaze in the morning sun. The gathered squires all saluted and Jex followed suit half-heartedly. He had heard the stories of the great man before them as often as anyone else. But admiration still eluded him.

Following Maxim was Captain Reicel. He had gone ahead that morning to put forward his final recommendations. Jex knew that given the incident involving the bandits, he was lucky to even be graduating. Oddly enough, it seemed that Reicel hadn't told anyone about it, and while the rumour mill was abuzz in the barracks for weeks after the fact, no punishment had come about.

Before Jex had a chance to think about how lucky he had been, the man they had all been waiting for emerged. King Axeal stepped forward in all his magnificence, wearing an immensely thick ceremonial robe adorned with diamonds and sapphires stitched into its precious fabric. In his right hand was a sheathed blade encrusted with more precious stones. He strode forth with confidence and pride. A wide grin was stretched across his face, highlighting his neatly trimmed beard and strong jawline as the sun made his form explode with shimmering brilliance.

The man was quite statuesque at an impressive six foot five, with a fair amount of muscle filling out a robe that, on anyone else, would be oversized. Beside him stood a beautiful middle-aged woman with short, dark hair that reflected the morning sun's rays in the same way he'd seen the Princess' own curls do so. Queen Adele was a full foot shorter than the King, with a slender body. Her deep blue eyes shone with a mischievous wit and Jex couldn't help but wonder about her.

He had always thought about Adele with the closest thing to reverence he could muster. The woman had been a wanderer, homeless by choice as she travelled and practised her magic. It was said that she would travel to places of famine with food before utilising her magical gifts to purify the contaminated water. She would help those suffering to regain their strength before moving on. No one really knew her intimately until she was spotted by King Axeal. The pair had told the masses that they had fallen for each other mid-combat. They claimed that with each spell and each collision, they became that much more certain they were meant to be.

What rubbish. A ridiculous notion. Though it does not change the fact that this woman was both powerful and arrogant enough to take on a King in battle. Axeal isn't just any King, either; he is hailed as one of the greatest. I can only wonder how much is to be expected of their offspring.

As Jex's mind floated to the Princess, he caught sight of the young girl in her mother's arms, supported by Adele's hip as she walked. To Jex's distaste, Alicea was already staring directly at him, despite the hundreds of knights around them.

How did she see me so quickly?

The King and Queen seemed unaware of their daughter's fixation on Jex as they beamed at the gathered squires. The impressive party stopped at a small podium crafted solely from sapphire and silver, where King Axeal placed his ostentatious blade and looked out at soldiers who had been training in his name for the past several years. His face beamed with a pride that was absolute, and the men and women standing before their King felt it.

Except for one.

"Oh, what an impressive group we have gathered here today!" Axeal's voice boomed. It was always louder than anyone expected. "You…"

Axeal seemed to have difficulty finding the words – and it wasn't an act. The King of Aquiocia had always been known to become emotional during speeches. It was a sign of just how much he loved Aquiocia and its people, although sometimes it made it difficult for Jex to believe that he was actually an exceptional warrior and mage.

"You've made it!" Axeal declared simply. "You have made it through the rigorous training and study to become knights of Aquiocia. Plenty tried, and more than half gave up the path of the soldier. Do not condemn those people in your own hearts; do not think yourself superior, as everybody undergoes the same struggle to find their place in this life. Someday they will find theirs, as you have found yours."

The King was making it up as he went, and everybody knew it. With a subtle clearing of her throat, the Queen attempted to speed her husband along.

"From here you will walk the path of guardians. You will protect the people of this fair city, helping them in many ways. You will travel, and you will experience many –"

"Father, they didn't train for so long just to listen to you speak for the sole purpose of hearing your own voice!" a voice chimed in from the Queen's direction – Alicea scolding her father.

The entire crowd of squires desperately tried to stifle their laughter. Axeal looked as if he'd been slapped as he glanced towards his daughter in disbelief. Any other ruler would have felt ashamed or embarrassed to be reprimanded by a child in front of his knights, but not Axeal. Instead, the courtyard was filled with hearty laughter bellowing from the King's chest. His mirth only intensified as he encouraged the knights to laugh at his expense.

"Apparently I have said enough, my soldiers!" Axeal chortled with tears in his eyes. "Well, let us not invite the wrath of the child – let us begin the ceremonial proceedings!"

What followed was the most casual imitation of a knighting ceremony that Jex could have imagined. Line by line the knights stepped forward, taking the blade from their King before kneeling and offering it back. It was purely symbolic, an unspoken vow to say that despite title and rank, they would both serve the sword as it would serve them in return.

The procedure was professional, but the King laughed and made jokes with each of the newly knighted squires so they would walk away chuckling and smiling.

The men never broke formation as the King ran the ceremony and the sun crept ever higher until afternoon became dusk. Adele had put Alicea down. Dissatisfied by being placed out of sight of Jex, Alicea had immediately walked over to Maxim and ordered him to lift her up. Now she was comfortably perched on the Warmaster's shoulders, resuming her observation.

She is relentless, yet I can't discredit the idea that she is somehow important. But I can't feel it. I don't feel anything for her apart from unease. What is it about her that makes me so unsettled?

Jex barely realised it was his line's turn to kneel and receive the King's blessing. Despite his lowered head, he couldn't help but gaze out of his peripherals at the Princess. Sure enough, she was staring straight back, right up until Axeal reached him.

"Ah, yes – Jex, isn't it?" Axeal asked with a wide grin as the Queen looked up with mild interest.

Jex had to take a second to find his voice.

"That's right, Your Majesty."

"Relax, my friend!" Axeal laughed as he followed Jex's gaze. "Ah, she's a sweet child, eh?"

Jex didn't know how to answer.

"Why don't you say hello to Jex, sweetheart?" Axeal suggested to his daughter, who glared back at her father and Jex in equal measure. "Strange – normally it is a superhuman effort to keep her quiet and stop her from bossing everyone around."

"Well, I'm sure that is something she will grow out of, Your Majesty."

"Oh ho!" Axeal exclaimed as he clasped Jex's slender arm with his own meaty paw. "Assumptions like that are a sure way to get a knight in trouble, my friend!"

Axeal broke into heavy guffaws as he performed the knighting procedure with Jex and moved on to the next squire. Jex refused to look at the Princess again, though her gaze continued to bore through him.

After what felt like an eternity, his line was dismissed and allowed free time to celebrate. Jex moved so fast he almost missed out on the pouch of gold that was handed to him by an attendant surrounded by seasoned knights at the gate. Muttering his thanks, Jex made his way outside the courtyard and started his long trek around the outside of the castle walls to the rear entrance, where the barracks were.

The sooner he could be alone with his thoughts, the better.

CHAPTER 12

THE FORGOTTEN KNIGHT'S MESSENGER

"Servant!" Arissam bellowed as he blustered around a corridor.

He'd received a message, and he tore the parchment out of his pocket to read it for the fifth time.

The hunters of Tremel have come together and are marching.

The message wasn't signed, nor was the handwriting recognisable. He had found it upon the throne, sitting there with the audacity to ruin the King's mood. The letter hadn't mentioned it, but the Princess would be marching with the residents of Tremel. Arissam knew that Tremel's people had been scattered, so for them to gather and march had to be a calculated move. It left him precious little time to act.

"I said SERVANT, DAMN IT!" he shrieked.

Part of him didn't *want* to act. Part of him, the mildly deluded part, believed it could be a prank, a joke. He wanted to entertain the part that suggested an inconsequential person had planted the scroll, but he couldn't. He knew Alicea, and her parents before her, well enough to know that this was exactly the kind of plan Aquiocian royalty was famous for.

So what? Arissam simmered down slightly. *What's she going to do? She won't announce her presence for fear of the curse activating. From the reports, she can't stand death. I'll just throw her people at her until...*

His sobering thoughts trailed off when he caught sight of a simply dressed young man of about seventeen. He was obviously still going through the awkward stages of teenage years, but he stood with the confidence of a man with purpose.

"Finally!" Arissam snapped. "Find me something to take the edge off! You have two –"

"I have all the time in the world," the teenager said lightly, barely concealing the sadness in his words. "Truly a terrible sensation, knowing you have an eternity to…"

The pair stared at each other, the King bewildered, the teenager distracted.

"Are you defying me?" Arissam's rage resurfaced. "You are my servant! My subject, my pawn!"

"I am all of those things, though not yours." The teenager bowed his head. "I planted that message, as he willed it. The Princess marching is no issue. Retrieve the stone."

"Who sent you?" Arissam snapped. "I will have him brought before me for this affront!"

"He will appear when he wills it, when he is ready." The young man shook his head with a remorse that looked out of place. "He will take what he wants and discard the rest. Retrieve the stone."

Arissam stood still for a moment before storming towards the young man, his hand raised. An inch before colliding with the insolent teen's face, it was caught at the wrist. The boy had next to no muscle on his frame, his arms appearing pale and weak. Yet he effortlessly stopped the assault.

"He has many servants, many of whom are far less mundane than myself. There is a reason the world has begun to forget. There is a reason for everything." The teenager spoke forcefully but his eyes remained pleading, as if seeking salvation from the tyrant King. "When he returns, make sure you are on the right side of a collapsing world. Retrieve the stone."

Arissam attempted to resist the casual way the teenager pushed his arm aside, as if there wasn't a full-grown man on the other end trying to lash out. But the strange visitor turned and began to walk back towards the audience hall, silent and deep in thought.

Retrieve the stone.

CHAPTER 13

SILROK'S APPRAISAL

The combined forces of Tremel had come to a stop within the Aquiocian forestry shortly after Garnet's enhanced voice had echoed through the ranks. Their war horns sounded swiftly in response to show they had received the order.

Looking down at the tiny figures below her, scampering through the trees to get into a position that only they knew, Alicea spotted a small, vacant clearing and mentally issued the order for her great mount to land. As she touched down, the swan gracefully fluttered across the soft turf towards a small spring and broke down to its base form, becoming one with the current.

The Princess heard a derisive sniff behind her. "Impressive, for a mage."

Spinning on the spot, she saw Silrok waving to her private guards, who nodded and hung back from the confines of the clearing. Silrok's cloak of feathers dropped from her body, revealing smaller pelts that preserved her modesty. She marched towards the Princess.

"So, it's a confrontation you want, then?" Alicea smirked in spite of her rising unease.

"Do not tell me you have sunk to the primitive level of the violent brutes you keep company with," Silrok snarled.

She reached behind Alicea's head to the tie keeping her hair secured, yanking it so forcefully that both women's eyes were locked together.

"What are –"

"Close your mouth!" Silrok demanded. Alicea fell quiet, but not as a result of the order. Silrok's eyes had turned pitch-black and the Princess couldn't turn away from the endless void within their sockets. Alicea felt nothing at first, then a sharp irritation inside her mind. It was as if someone was rattling around in her head as they searched for something.

Then it was gone.

Alicea returned to the real world and Silrok's eyes returned to their rich almond colour as she pulled her cloak back on. She looked confused, suddenly regarding the Princess warily, as if she hadn't initiated the interaction.

"Did you read my mind?"

"Do not be ridiculous," Silrok scoffed, though the sound was insincere, as if masking something. "I am not capable of reading someone's thoughts. I am only capable of catching a glimpse of them as a person. Even then I am unable to get a completely accurate portrayal. Sometimes I get an idea of their aptitude for combat; other times I get a sign of their religious beliefs. It is not a perfect technique – not yet, anyway."

"Then what did you get from me?" the Princess asked through clenched teeth. She had been taken by surprise and was starting to see the affront for what it was.

"Not a great deal, between your natural defences and your friend blocking out a lot. I did manage to catch sight of what hounds you day and night, what shadows you whether you're asleep or awake."

"You saw my parents," Alicea muttered, somewhat relieved it was something almost everyone knew.

"No." Silrok shook her head and Alicea looked up in surprise. "I saw death."

"That's what happened to my parents!" Alicea insisted.

"It's what is happening to your people."

"I –"

"Would you close your mouth and listen, just once?" Silrok snarled impatiently. She portrayed disdain, but an undertone of desperation had crept into her voice.

Alicea bit her tongue, wanting to strike Silrok. The audacity of the shaman was more than the Princess could accept. How could this person be so different from Lyrium and yet still be from the same tribe?

But that wasn't quite true, and she knew that deep down. While the ancestors of Tremel may in fact have been as one in the past, it was no longer the case. She did not know the finer details of the split that had turned Tremel from one tribe to four, but it was no excuse for Silrok's behaviour.

"You're a more complex person than I gave you credit for, Your Highness," Silrok conceded after a moment, with the mildest hint of respect. "You feel the pain of others perhaps even more than you feel your own."

"What would you know?"

"Only what my mother has deduced through the information supplied to her," Silrok conceded solemnly before adding, "I apologise. I had to know."

"Had to know what?" Alicea snapped. Her patience had waned.

"Whatever the technique was willing to offer me. I…" Silrok

regarded Alicea cautiously. "I didn't delve into your mind. I mean, I *couldn't*. Neither you nor the thing in the stone would allow it."

"Your point, Silrok?" Alicea snapped again, but the woman nodded. She had just confirmed that there was something within the stone protecting her. Alicea didn't care.

"What I saw, the glimpse I caught from afar, it's... It's terrifying in there. How do you –"

Silrok cut off at a sound behind her and Alicea felt a wave of relief as Rufus stumbled into the small grotto, nodding to the Princess before looking around anxiously. The conversation was taking a turn she didn't like, and his entrance was timely.

"Can I help you, Mr. Thief?"

"You can help by keeping quiet!" Rufus hissed at the Princess. Her eyes narrowed.

"Why is everyone telling me to be quiet?" she snapped. "I am a Princess and –"

"There he is!" Lori's voice broke through from the brush.

"Hiding behind his Princess again, the big coward!" Tori's voice replied from the other side of the clearing.

The twins burst from their respective hiding places and Rufus was gone almost instantly as they gave chase.

"I am not *his* Princess!" Alicea growled as she found herself alone. Amongst the commotion, Silrok had taken her leave.

CHAPTER 14

AN INSTRUCTOR'S CONCERN

"Alicea!" Rufus' voice broke the Princess' daydream.

Alicea had found a small pond with minimal hunters gathered around it. The pond had formed after recent heavy rain. It made its way down the various streams and rivers, only to be cut off from its source as the sun took its due day to day. Now, the small body of water shared a similar solitude as the Princess sitting cross-legged at its edge, watching the tiny swan dance across the water's surface. The peculiar bird's head constantly became one with the pond as it bobbed for the small fish residing within.

"Tell me something, Mr. Thief. How do you manage to sneak around when you insist on making such a commotion just by greeting me?" Alicea asked, clicking her fingers so that the swan came to her.

Rufus grinned as he sat down beside her. "I did pretty well sneaking around a castle once."

"I assume you speak of a different occasion to the one where you simultaneously failed to keep me unconscious *and* alerted the better part of the kingdom's residents to your existence?" Alicea asked as she reached out to pet the small bird.

"In my defence, I'm not convinced you being unconscious guarantees you shutting your mouth. They were always going to find out."

Rather than arguing further, Alicea raised a single eyebrow at her companion.

"From Princess to Commander, huh?" Rufus changed the subject, producing a small bundle from his pocket that caught Alicea's eye. As he unfolded the ball of leaves and spiced meat, he continued, "Not really a change most Princesses take on in their lives."

"It is not so strange; I am only fulfilling my role as an Aquiocian royal. It is our duty to fight," Alicea said softly, her eyes never leaving Rufus' food. Finally, he noticed.

"Really?" The thief sighed, handing over half of the meat. "I'm trying to speak to you and you want my food?"

"I also desire silence, but I will have to settle for the food," Alicea quipped as she nibbled at the spiced meat and eyed the remainder in Rufus' hand. For someone so high-maintenance, her love of basic food was bizarre.

"Oh, have it!" Rufus huffed, tossing what was left to her. "You know, you have very simple taste in food for a Princess. I thought you'd want fancier meals than this!"

"Sometimes simplicity is best, be it food or company." Alicea smiled cheekily as the blue of her eyes deepened.

The pair sat in silence for a moment before Alicea spoke again.

"Mr. Thief?"

"Hm?"

"Thank you for being with me through all of this."

Rufus shrugged. "It's what I'm paid to do."

"Yet it's not the reason you do it. So again, thank you."

A long moment passed between the two where nothing

needed to be said, before Rufus found the exact words to make his friend smile.

"I realised it a little while ago. There's nowhere I'd rather be."

"Thank you, Mr. Thief." Alicea smiled, her voice lowering as she leant over and wiped a smear of dirt from his face. "I suggest you start moving again."

"Why?" Rufus asked, irritated at Alicea mothering him.

"Because they've found you," she whispered.

Rufus was on his feet and sprinting towards the trees as two figures burst from the bushes behind Alicea. Shrieking about being betrayed by "Ruffie's Princess", the twins resumed their pursuit of the thief.

When silence filled the small grotto again, Alicea looked back down at the cygnet pecking at the water again with a frown.

"You are literally made of water – why is this pond's existence so difficult for you to accept?" Alicea asked before saying in a louder voice, "Hello, Garnet. I'm surprised you have time to spare just to come and speak with me."

You grow ever more perceptive, Alicea. Garnet's voice entered her mind as a crow descended from a neighbouring tree and underwent the transformation into its original human form. With a shrug, Garnet stepped into the pond and began to wash her body, much to the bird's disgust.

"To what do I owe this visit? I thought you'd be far too busy," Alicea asked.

"Everything is organised. Are you doubting my management capabilities?" Garnet asked with the mildest hint of humour.

"Don't be ridiculous. These people would be lost without you, myself included," the Princess said with outstretched arms. Her pet retreated from the rippling water and found its place in its owner's lap. Now, it was eyeing the woman who had the audacity to interrupt its investigation of the pond.

"I wanted to ask what your intentions are after we take back the castle, along with a few other questions. Consider them my own curiosity," Garnet revealed without turning around.

"I will seize the castle and return the kingdom to order."

"I know that, Alicea. The question is: *how* are you planning to accomplish this task?"

"I am contemplating various courses of action as we speak. There are quite a few things to consider, as I'm sure you are aware."

"Are you being deliberately vague?"

"Yes."

"Why?"

"Because I don't know yet!" Alicea snapped. "I've been trying to sit here in peace and think over the best way to approach the issue, and so far all I've accomplished is being interrupted by your random questions and having to babysit Mr. Thief!"

Garnet continued to wash herself as if the outburst didn't take place at all. Her silence paid off when her student flushed a slight shade of red.

"Garnet, I'm sorry."

"For what?" Garnet replied, her back still turned.

"For yelling at you?"

"Don't be," her mentor said dismissively as she finally turned to face Alicea. *"Gladirus: Movdul."*

Alicea's eyebrows rose slightly as the mud and rocks at the bottom of the pond slowly began to rise to the surface before breaking free of their waterbed. The soaked soil moved and began to mould into the form of a chair in the middle of the pond. Once the back and arms of the earthen seat had formed, Garnet took her place upon it like a naked Queen of the grotto.

"Has this changed from a conversation to an interrogation?"

"If that mentality helps you find answers to my questions, then carry on." Garnet smiled slightly as a thin layer of earth made its way across her skin and came to rest, as if she was wearing a skin-tight frock of soil. "Alicea, I'm worried that you might hesitate at the wrong moment."

"Oh?"

"I've seen your body and mind at work, especially since the battle at Tremel. You've become exceedingly competent in most facets. I can see your determination and your resolve. I know that you love your people and I know your heart seeks vengeance."

"You think that if I'm confronted by Jex directly, I will buckle and waver," Alicea said with a distasteful click of her tongue.

"A lot of people believe that," Garnet reasoned.

"A lot of people?" Alicea repeated, absentmindedly stroking the swan. "A *lot* of people?"

"Of course." Garnet shifted in her natural seat, now completely covered in soil from the neck down. "Did you assume they would all follow your orders without questioning why you were the one giving them?"

"Of course not!" the Princess scowled as her eyes flashed with annoyance. "I recall expecting no one's assistance back in Kurok's hut at the end of the last confrontation. I remember crying in front of Mr. Thief and Lyrium as I panicked about the people of your village dying because you sheltered me. I distinctly remember –"

"Good," Garnet interrupted quietly. "So then tell me what your plan is."

"We will strike the enemy, not the kingdom. We will secure the safety of the innocent, and then…" Alicea trailed off as the plan fell short.

"And then?" Garnet pressed quietly.

"And then we will corner those responsible and bring them to heel."

"What if they refuse?"

"Then they will regret the day they betrayed both the kingdom of Aquiocia and its people," Alicea said with a viciousness that was unusual for her. It was only a flash of ruthlessness, barely a moment, but it was there.

Garnet nodded, her lips pursed in thought as her wise gaze looked over her student.

"Stick to your beliefs, Alicea," Garnet said suddenly as she rose from her seat. Her body began to shed the soil as she mutated into the form of a crow and took to the sky. As Alicea watched Garnet's departure, she thought over the conversation and had an idea.

CHAPTER 15

A BRIEF RESPITE

"So, ya ready?" The booming voice of a man did nothing to surprise the Princess as she slowly made her way through the forestland.

She had decided to walk with the main force while they slowed their pace to a swift, seemingly disorganised march. Though most people who looked at her – and there were many – could sense her desire to be alone in her thoughts, the observation had not registered with Arok, who was now heartily greeting her.

"Good afternoon, Arok," Alicea replied simply, keeping her swift pace through the already well-trodden brush. A lot of the force had trampled over her makeshift path and made it relatively easy for her to navigate, even in her slightly impractical choice of heeled boots.

"Nay, say it nicely!" Arok laughed as Alicea's eyebrows rose. Her focus on the road ahead remained unwavering.

"I believe I greeted you in a sufficiently pleasant fashion. Now, how can I help you?"

"Well, you could start by smiling. It's to be a siege, not the death of Gaia, after all!"

Alicea's knuckles tightened around the staff of water she'd ordered her swan to transform into. She had been using it as a marching aid to keep her balance in the rougher spots, but she suddenly had the urge to smack her new company with it. The humidity of the forest wasn't helping her mood. The heat had come on in the span of an hour and Alicea had begun to notice the weather's peculiar behaviour.

"Arok, I do not share your ability to confront every problem with a delusional sense of –"

"Nay, say it nicely!"

"I will speak however I desire," Alicea hissed, still not breaking her forward gaze. A few people were glancing over at the exchange, but attempted to remain inconspicuous.

"Feel better?" Arok grinned, matching the Princess' stride and walking so close to her that they were almost shoulder-to-shoulder.

Had Alicea not been so irritable, she'd have been forced to admit that the way Arok could saunter through the forest with a massive war hammer in one hand while smelling like a well-utilised tavern was impressive.

"What – do – you – want – Arok?" Alicea asked through a clenched jaw.

"I want to know how my prinny friend is doing."

"Your prinny… I'm a Princess, not a prinny. I don't call you a *barby* or a *hunty*," she snapped, climbing over a massive log that had fallen to the ground.

"Aye, Rufus was right." Arok grunted as he hurdled over the log, using a single massive arm to propel him over.

"That'd be a first for him."

"Ya scared." Arok's tone was serious. The sudden change in demeanour made the Princess glance at him for the first time.

"Well, consider me reassured that Mr. Thief can finally pick up on the most obvious of emotional developments. What a massive stride in his own personal development!"

"Ya know, half the time when you speak, I have no clue what ya sayin' at all." Arok shrugged with a swig from the half-dozen wineskins slung over his shoulder. "But I want ya to know that it's all going ta be fine."

"Fine?" Alicea's sapphiric eyes flashed electric-blue for a split second as her head snapped to Arok. The brief eruption of colour in her gaze was enough to make the barbarian uneasy, but he grinned again.

"Aye, fine."

"Arok, right now I am attempting to deal with my own plethora of responsibilities. I do NOT have time for games." Alicea had stopped walking to gain his attention. In spite of her expression of controlled fury, Arok shrugged.

"Aye, well I'm dealing with my own shit as well. Top o' that list is my friend being upset. I know what Garnet said."

Alicea didn't reply for a second. She knew exactly what Arok spoke of, but it took a moment for her to realise how he might know.

Lyrium?

"Aye," Arok repeated for the third time with a nod. "Garnet told Lyrium. Lyrium told me."

There really are no secrets between those two, Alicea realised.

"I want you to know something." Arok smirked as the Princess scowled again. "I don't care if ya royalty or homeless – you are Alicea, and you are my friend. My friend with a silly name. Nothing else matters. Now, let's go show 'em why you don't take someone's castle without asking!"

Alicea didn't reply, and at first she couldn't. Arok's outlook was so simple and short-sighted. The situation before her – no, the situation before them all – wasn't so easily pushed aside. Nothing about the coming struggles suggested that it'd be easy to take back the kingdom. Yet somehow, in the tiniest of ways, she felt better.

Watching her friend lumber off into the thick forest towards the moving crowd, she noticed Lyrium waving to her as Arok joined his lover. The happy-go-lucky man turned around and grinned back at her before taking off with Lyrium to join the march.

The Princess didn't know how to feel. After a moment of conflicted emotions, she looked up at the sunlight attempting to break through the canopy of growth. Suddenly she knew what she needed, and she could feel it responding to her call. The forest's residents watched on as leaves and thin branches gave way to the massive bird crashing through the roof of the forest.

The massive swan collided with the earth with a sound like a boulder being dropped into the ocean. The bird flailed around for a second, barely avoiding striking Alicea in the flurry as it gained its bearings once more. With a final puffing of its aqueous feathers, it looked down at its smiling master.

Let us fly, little one, Alicea mentally cooed, refusing to acknowledge that it was anything but small.

The swan responded by letting fly a geyser of pristine water from its mouth into the air, before lowering itself closer to the ground so the Princess could climb aboard. Once seated at the base of its neck, Alicea tapped the massive swan on the wing and the pair left the ground. The swan's thin legs boasted surprising strength as they leapt into the air. Its beautiful clear wings caught the light of the sun as they effortlessly lifted the Princess into the air.

They left the confines of the forest, and Alicea allowed a small smile as the air met her face with force. Looking back down, she saw the force shrinking as she encouraged her mount to take her higher. She'd never flown for any reason other than practicality, and despite having grown in strength as a mage, she'd only commanded her pet to grow in size a handful of times. Just enough to assure her that she could do it at any time. She had learnt a great deal of tricks utilising her element, whether taught by Garnet or by herself, but she couldn't believe that she'd never actually flown just for the joy.

She felt the connections with countless people lessen and vanish. She recognised the last one as Garnet's: a hint of concern before begrudgingly letting go. Her tutor didn't like her being alone, but it wouldn't be for long.

Sitting just below the thin clouds of the otherwise empty sky, she noticed the greying clouds to the west. They were travelling towards Aquiocia, signalling a storm. Alicea didn't care at that moment; the conflict to come didn't exist yet. She tapped the swan on its back and it came to a halt, flapping steadily to keep its position in the air. The wind was picking up from the direction of the clouds, and she knew it wouldn't be long before the force below her and the storm both reached Aquiocia.

She wasn't sure what she was supposed to feel. She had been certain that getting away from everyone would clear her mind and at least tell her what she was feeling. Instead, there was a pit within her where everything had gathered. The remorse for those who had died and everyone rallying to her cause. The dread of confronting her family and kingdom alike, knowing that she might have to kill. Then there was Jex, right at the centre.

A man who shouldn't even exist. He had been executed; her father had seen to it personally and her mother had confirmed it. He had been a blight on Aquiocian history that had been expunged, yet here he was, refusing to be forgotten.

She loathed him, but the guilt she felt wasn't solely for the deaths of the innocents. A portion of her guilt resided with Jex himself.

I'm to blame for this... Alicea admitted to herself, a bittersweet acknowledgement to past mistakes that offered both relief and pain.

She spent what felt like hours staring at the ominous grey clouds in wonder. Her long ponytail billowed in the wind as her pet happily kept its master on high. In truth, only ten minutes passed before the Princess realised she was probably out of range for Garnet to contact her. She wasn't ready to come down, but she tapped the swan's back once more and the great bird began to descend steadily.

She didn't know why it had helped so much, but Arok's carefree approach had driven her to find a semblance of freedom, however fleeting. As she reached her regular altitude above the highest trees, the Princess laid back, her feet dangling on either side of her water-made mount, and tried to quash the dread.

Nothing in the immediate future is going to be pleasant. But I will deal with it as it comes.

❖

I suggest you make your way to the clearing a few leagues north-east of your current location, Princess. Garnet's message was short and to the point.

Alicea had been lost in her own thoughts, lying across the back of her pet as it steadily glided through the air to keep pace with the army below. The Princess had been wary of the potential cold while flying in the last of autumn's days, but had found nothing but a mild chill. It was inexplicable, how the heat had transformed into a chill so quickly, but it felt wonderful. Somehow, the cold of the high altitude and coming storm hadn't worried her at all, despite her lack of warm clothing.

She'd lost herself completely and utterly within her own head for hours, the only thought interrupting her being the occasional warning from Garnet, informing her that she'd flown too far in one direction or another. Otherwise she'd happily dived into memories of her training, the recently transpired events, and even certain people – Rufus, Lyrium, Arok, the twins. She hadn't seen much of any of them save for Rufus checking in now and then, only to be chased off by the twins in their never-ending quest to catch him. They had been relentless for days on end, and Alicea had worried they would exhaust themselves before she had spotted Rufus tending to them one night around a fire built by the hunters.

The twins had worn themselves out and fallen asleep next to the warmth of the flames to escape the biting cold of the impending winter. Alicea had watched Rufus appear out of nowhere and drape a massive blanket of feathers over the twins, before disappearing with a smirk at the Princess and a finger to his lips. The next morning, Tori had awoken in a rage that her mark had been so close, yet she'd missed her opportunity to grab him. With a violent shove of her twin and an explanation that their newly acquired blanket was Rufus mocking them, the chase had resumed.

Alicea smiled, her thoughts returning to Garnet's message. She found the clearing in the distance, but rather than descending immediately, she ordered her mount to hold its position when she spotted something else of interest. The mountains that had been so far in the distance that morning were considerably closer now. She hadn't even noticed in her trance-like state of reminiscence.

As the Princess' eyes ran over the sight before her, she saw something that made her heart flutter. There, in the far-off distance, she could see the outposts of Aquiocia on the main roads used for travelling merchants and citizens alike. She hadn't realised what they were at first. There were no signs of life on the roads and it appeared that they hadn't been used in weeks, perhaps even months. Gazing at the distant structures and landmarks, the Princess couldn't help but entertain a sensation of undeniable dread at the sight. It wasn't just what lay ahead that gave her a foreboding feeling; there was something wrong with the kingdom, and she knew it wasn't her imagination.

What in the world is going on here? Alicea wondered as she looked in the direction of the castle in the distance. She couldn't make out the heart of the kingdom from where she was. Her heart ached for a moment when she realised that if she couldn't see it, they probably couldn't see her. The thought made her impatient, but also brought relief.

If I might be so bold, Garnet's voice sounded in her mind once more, *I suggest you come to the clearing and get off that bird before someone spots you and tries to shoot you down.*

Oh, alright, I'm coming! Alicea grumbled as the bird turned downwards sharply and commenced its dive towards the clearing.

CHAPTER 16

AN UNLIKELY ASSEMBLY

"What are we looking at?" Kurok asked as Alicea landed in the clearing.

The Princess leapt from her mount and walked towards the fallen tree that Garnet, Arok, Lyrium, Rufus, Kurok and the other Chiefs had gathered around. It was swiftly approaching dusk, but the dying sun hit the clearing with enough light to make fire unnecessary.

As she approached the makeshift war table, Lori and Tori appeared from the brush and raced towards the giant water swan, beginning their own examination of the peculiar bird.

"Welcome, Princess," spoke a voice Alicea had not heard in quite some time, as a man garbed from head to toe in a black cloak appeared from the shadow of the great tree.

"Setz!" Alicea exclaimed happily. "When did you get here?"

"I have been nearby for quite some time," Setz revealed. Alicea's eyebrows rose.

"How long?"

"Long enough. Fret not. You have been doing well in all regards," Setz said, allowing a small smile before his gaze turned to Rufus. "As have you."

"I'm not here to impress you, Setz," Rufus sniffed.

"Yet here you are at my request," Setz replied before turning to the rest of them. "To answer your question, Kurok. We are at a crossroads and a decision needs to be made."

"What kind of decision?" Alicea asked.

Garnet sighed. "A decision regarding the assault on the kingdom. Logically thinking, using the Underbelly as a base and striking from the many passages and manholes around the city has its merits. Setz has kept the existence of the Underbelly a secret, even with the change of power above. They have suspicions of an organisation working from the shadows but no solid evidence, so it is certainly viable."

"How many will die this way?" Alicea asked. Rufus grunted. "What is it, Mr. Thief?"

"It's you and your constant search for a peaceful resolution!" Rufus snapped.

"Is there a problem with that?"

"The problem is that sometimes there just isn't one. This isn't the same as the attack back at Tremel. We are on the offensive this time."

"Do you think I am an idiot, Mr. Thief?" Alicea asked suddenly, causing Garnet to sigh again and the rest of the leaders to look at the thief for his response.

Rufus shrugged. "I think you're a brat."

"But not an idiot, then?" Alicea replied, ignoring the insult. "Very good, because I happen to be well aware of the fact we are on the offensive!"

"Rufus is right, Princess," Setz interrupted before the thief retaliated. "Defending, in a lot of ways, makes it easier to control losses. Attacking may see a lot more casualties, as our opponent has no interest in a peaceful resolution. In fact, my sources say that the Council currently in command considers the people of Tremel savages who should be eradicated."

"Why would they think that?" Alicea cried.

"Because Tremel got in their way," Rufus muttered.

"Who cares? We will crush them all the same!" Dairok declared. Everyone shook their heads in exasperation.

"We most certainly will not, you oversized oaf!" Alicea snapped.

"Do not speak to your only allies in that tone or you will find yourself alone or dead, Princess," Silrok interjected coldly.

"Threaten her again and you will find yourself in a similar situation!" Rufus hissed.

"Enough!" Setz's voice echoed through the clearing. It was the first time in years that he had raised his voice.

The entire group fell silent and Alicea noticed that a few warriors were looking over in interest. Lori and Tori, however, were still completely captivated by the large bird.

"Glare at each other all you like," Setz said evenly, looking at each person in turn. "But remember that we are a team."

"We haven't forgotten," Arok piped up, pumping his chest enthusiastically.

"At the very least, Arok and I will do as the Princess bids," Lyrium added as Alicea beamed at her friends.

"What would you have us do in regards to the assault upon the castle, Princess?" Garnet asked with a significant look. Her expression suggested that their previous conversation was firmly in her mind. Alicea took a moment to consider both the question and the fact that Garnet had referred to her title before answering. It was a clear indication of the faith the tutor had in her. She couldn't falter here.

"Many of you can take the forms of various animals, from

birds who can fly high to deer who are swift-footed," the Princess said thoughtfully. "But the greatest trait you share is that you are hunters."

"Are you planning on telling us what we already know for the whole night?" Silrok asked sarcastically.

"No," Alicea said quietly. "Ideally, we would apprehend the kingdom's leader and demand a surrender."

Setz nodded slightly as Kurok crossed his arms with a raised eyebrow. There was a shift amongst the leaders who had joined the ranks just before the march.

"Tell me what you'd do." Alicea turned to Silrok, who looked around herself as if she couldn't possibly be the one the Princess addressed. But she answered, "Avoiding bloodshed can send just as great a message as slaughter, if delivered correctly. If there was a way to take prisoners safely, it would serve our desire to avoid unnecessary casualties."

"We don't have a camp or cells to keep these prisoners in," Dairok interjected, though not aggressively.

"For the immediate situation, we can live off the resources we brought with us along with those of the land, but even we have our limitations," Garnet added.

"My people can aid with supplies, but every time a unit of mine mobilises, it's a chance for the enemy to catch wind of the organisation," Setz conceded gravely.

"In other words, if you want prisoners, you need to do it quickly and sustainably, and there are walls between us and them," Kurok said, his eyebrow still raised.

Alicea glanced at Setz, and the Guildmaster knew what the look meant. She was counting on him apprehending some prisoners. Discreetly, he returned her glance with a slight shake of the head that said "impossible".

While there was no clear reason why a master of the shadows and his army of assassins couldn't abduct a few prisoners, Alicea knew better than to question it in front of the others. Instead another idea came to her, perhaps riskier but quicker and more effective.

"Aquiocian legions are a thousand strong." Alicea smiled at Silrok as the beginnings of a plan came together. "With Garnet's help, could the shamans create deep holes that could hold a legion?"

"With a little time, we could hold multiple legions," Silrok said shortly, glancing towards Dairok. "You would need guards."

"You'll have them," Dairok said grimly with a nod.

"If the enemy gains any idea of our numbers then we may need to accommodate more than one legion, but it's unlikely they will send more than one out, if they even send that. We will need to goad them out." Alicea turned to Setz. "How easily could you get false information to the Council?"

"So easily that the fact you have to ask borderlines on being an insult."

"Very good," she nodded, turning to Silrok and Garnet in turn. "Then I wish for your quickest men on land, the people able to take flight and your strongest mages, all in respective formation so that I may address each one. Setz, I require your men to be ready as well."

"They always are, Princess," Setz replied with an edge of amusement. "They always are."

Alicea met Garnet's critical eye as her mentor began to speak.

"You intend to lure out these knights and claim them as prisoners. I assume there's another side to this we are missing?"

"There is. It involves a party being inside the walls. Mr. Thief, you along with Lori and Tori will be needed, so stay close to me," Alicea ordered.

"What of us?" Lyrium asked, gesturing to herself and Arok.

"You command the stone of Earth, so I need you to remain back with the mages. Aid them in their coming endeavour along with Garnet and Silrok. Arok, protect your lover."

"Ha! I like nice and simple!" Arok crowed.

"I assume my men and I sit and wait, then," Dairok grumbled, clearly feeling more than a little left out.

"You, along with your men, will be serving as guards to the traps, along with the muscle to convince those hesitant to fall into them. You are my added assurance."

Dairok eyed the Princess critically for a moment before grinning, obviously pleased with his role.

"You have not told me what you plan to do," Rufus asked Alicea with narrowed eyes. Clearly Garnet wasn't the only one suspicious of the Princess' evasive approach to being questioned on her motives.

"I will be within the walls of the castle, but you will be in the city," Alicea revealed.

"Why will I be there?"

"You will know when it's time. Now, if there are no further questions, we should all prepare."

There were some uneasy gazes directed at each other, but the war party steadily dispersed. Garnet lingered long enough to give Alicea a long, expressionless look, before nodding slightly and leaving. Alicea could hear the twins talking to the massive swan as if expecting it to strike up a conversation with them.

"That was…" Alicea trailed off as she looked for the word to describe how she felt, commanding people to prepare for battle. Although she wasn't at peace doing so, she didn't feel as horrible as she had last time.

"You're planning something stupid, aren't you?" Rufus asked.

"I'm planning for what I believe needs to be done," Alicea replied coldly.

Rufus stared at the distracted Princess for a moment. Before he could help himself, he found his hand raising and gently pushing back a long wave of the Princess' hair she'd deliberately left out of her ponytail. At first, she looked up at her companion with genuine confusion, but then her eyes flashed and her expression turned so withering that Rufus couldn't remove his hand quickly enough.

"Never – touch – my – hair!" Alicea growled.

"Noted." Rufus put his hands up in mock fear as her eyes paled.

Her fury evaporated when she glanced back at the twins jumping in front of the bird. She turned to Rufus with a cheeky smile.

"Do it!" he smirked.

With a snap of the Princess' fingers, the large bird exploded into a torrent of water as the twins screamed in surprise.

"That should keep them on their toes," Alicea laughed.

CHAPTER 17

BLADE AND FLAME

The young man groaned from his place in the debris. Pushing the messy brown hair off his face with his spare hand, he used his sword arm to climb to his feet.

Looking at the scorched face of his sparring partner, he raised his sword in front of his body and focused on the blade. The metal glowed angrily, a sign of its wielder's irritation, before erupting with flames that bathed its length. With a flick of the hilt, fire coursed along the ground in a thin line towards the opponent.

The swordsman's contestant had fallen victim to the Fires of Forever – an ancient magic said to have been created by the dragon, Scourge. It was said that those burnt by the mystical flames would be forever sealed within the place in time that the injury was incurred. A legend that had proven credible to the swordsman since he arrived in the city dedicated to the dragon.

His opponent sidestepped the flames and brought his own burning blade across his body, letting fly a wave of flame. The young swordsman laughed, and met the wave of fire with an open palm. The blaze reacted by dispersing, leaving only a thin haze of smoke.

The burnt man nodded in approval and barely had time to

deflect a blow from the swordsman as he leapt through the smoke. The pair exchanged blow after heated blow as their blades' fiery energies met and separated, only to reunite and clash again.

The surprise attack had worked. The young swordsman could feel his opponent losing his edge. With a quick feint to the right, the swordsman slid his foot behind his opponent as their blades met for the last time. The scorched man lost his balance and crashed to the ground. As he struggled to get back to his feet he found an inferno-engulfed blade in his face, and at the other end of it, a breathless young man with honest green eyes that were filled with pride.

"That's probably –"

"Concede!" the young man yelled with enthusiasm.

"You need –"

"I said concede!" the man yelled again as if his life depended on it.

"I concede! Now get your blade out of my face!" The scorched man laughed laboriously as the prideful youth stepped back.

The man with the charred skin climbed to his feet as his youthful opponent released the energy required to keep his blade alight. Sheathing his weapon, he stretched and groaned loudly while looking around.

The pair had left quite a bit of destruction in their wake. At the beginning of the day there had been the shells of houses, which had now been levelled by the training exercises they had just undergone. It didn't matter. The young swordsman had trained with the other man for long enough to know that come tomorrow, the houses would all be back to how they were. The curse of the Fires of Forever never failed to deliver.

"You did well today, Chase," the man offered as he, too, extinguished the flames of his blade.

"Ha! First time I've ever beaten you!" Chase panted. "You weren't holding back, were you?"

"Most certainly not." The man's tortured face twisted into a smile. "This victory was your own. I misjudged how much your affinity with Fire has grown. To dismiss my own spell like that was the move of a scholar. I applaud you."

"To be honest, I didn't know if it would work – it would have made for an awkward recovery period if it didn't," Chase admitted.

"I would never throw anything at you that you couldn't handle," the tutor quipped. Perhaps he had been holding back after all. "How is your hand?"

Chase knew which hand he spoke of. He pulled the glove free to examine the damage. Blackened and charred, the lines in his previously healthy hand pulsed an angry crimson like embers beneath charcoal. It hadn't changed over the past few weeks. It neither worsened nor healed – not that he had expected it to. A wound inflicted by the stone's flames was an injury to last a lifetime.

Perhaps longer still.

"No change, Namier," Chase said with a shrug.

Namier seemed to lose interest in the conversation at the sound of the name given to him. It was merely a play on the people of the city's true identity – "The Nameless" – but they were known as a whole. For someone to have a name solely for himself seemed odd, and brought with it a sense of unease.

Before Chase could ask if his instructor was alright, he was interrupted by the approach of a woman in a practical, full-length dress. Beneath her flaming red hair were green eyes flecked with orange and guarded by half-rimmed spectacles. The woman moved timidly and yet with a more-than-capable grace.

"Hello, Temp!" Chase called. He was met with a small smile.

"Chase," Temperance replied warmly. "It is almost time to attempt the extraction."

The young man's face fell. He knew that the extraction of the stone within her had been coming for some time. He just hadn't expected it to arrive so soon.

Namier looked up with an expression of curiosity that was painful to behold. He seemed as though he wanted to say something, but instead simply nodded.

"If these people can remove the stone, then I am less likely to lose control. You know this, Chase," Temperance said quietly. She hated to stoke his concern.

"You barely survived the procedure of taking on the stone. There is too much risk!"

"Is this really about whether or not the stone is fused with me?"

"What else would it be about?" Chase asked guardedly.

Temperance approached her friend and gently ran her fingers over his scorched hand. A logical woman, she had deduced early on that Chase was very much still a boy in many ways. Boys didn't like being vulnerable.

"I was supposed to cover that," Chase said hurriedly as he pulled his glove over the burnt hand, wincing at the leather rubbing over his blackened flesh.

"Don't," Temperance ordered, removing the glove.

"I don't want to look at this."

"You need to," Temperance insisted.

"Why?" Chase muttered. He took a moment to look at his swordplay instructor, then shook his head. "I cannot forgive myself yet. I may not ever be able to do so."

"A noble sentiment, to be sure," Namier interrupted for the first time. "Guilt can be a powerful motivator. But know that guilt will only nurture a hollow strength; a fragile weapon that will shatter when you need it most. It isn't until you find the courage to forgive yourself for the sins in your life that you will obtain the clarity you need to be the best man you are capable of being."

Chase was exhausted. His head started to throb as he tried to understand his instructor's words. Rather than dwell on it further, he opted to lose himself in Temperance's encouraging smile.

"If you insist on going through with this, then I will stand by you." Chase forced a smile back.

"Thank you, Chase. Now let's get you cleaned up before we go to the cathedral."

❖

Chase hit the hot springs like a pig would hit fresh mud – by charging and hurling himself at them. Located within a large cavity in the southern reaches of Scourge's ruined perimeter, the hot springs were originally an underground haven hidden from the sun above. The stinging water made his flesh steam, and his skin was soon giving off the same white wisps as the springs themselves.

He couldn't feel the heat – at least, not like someone

unaligned with Fire might have. Although the temperature of the debris-filled water might have been enough to peel back the skin of another, it ran off Chase in refreshing waves.

His first experience with the sultry spring had been unpleasant. The thick steam had made it hard to breathe and being in the water had felt like standing in flames. But he had endured it, and the springs had inflicted no lasting damage.

Chase had come to the conclusion that Namier had known what the spring would do to him when he'd shown Chase the hidden location. Chase had gone there each day after his training, but not once did he mention his experiences to his instructor. After bathing for the first time – a thoroughly unpleasant and almost intolerable experience – he had almost told Namier what had transpired. But the moment he opened his mouth to mention it, he had sealed it again. Somehow, it seemed more important to keep some of his trials to himself. Now, he relished the thought of being able to return each day.

Chase looked down through the atmospheric steam at the sooty water running down his body. He often wondered about the redundancy of bathing within the ruined city. The soot and filth in the water didn't make him any dirtier – not for any longer than the day, anyway – but neither did the dirt from outside the spring. He knew that everything ultimately returned to the way it was at the beginning of the day, and that probably included all the dirt and dust he attracted. But it did beg the question – what was the point of bathing?

"I trust you haven't drowned, Chase?"

Temperance's voice made its way through the dense air and he realised he'd come to a standstill while pondering Scourge's mysterious curse. "As alive as ever, Temp!" he crowed towards the lip of the destroyed roof.

He could barely see Temperance's obscured silhouette through the haze, sitting atop a rock with a large tome-shaped object in her hand. Though no one could know for certain where Temperance was looking, Chase was positive her eyes hadn't left whatever text she was reading. On top of the other unpleasant aspects the first time he'd bathed in the spring, there had been an air of embarrassment, as Temperance had sat at the upper rim and read then, too – and every day since.

Chase hadn't had the greatest options for bathing in the tower, and those he had were shared. A fear of being naked around others seemed foolish then, but meeting Temperance had sparked a desire to be clothed.

"How goes the reading?" Chase called as his splashing resumed. He could almost feel Temperance's eyes narrowing at the question.

"About as enthralling an experience as the last time you asked," she responded as Chase scolded himself internally. He asked the same question every day.

It was frustrating: each day seemed to reinforce a standing between himself and Temperance that he wasn't entirely sure he was happy with. It had become clear over the time they spent together that Temperance wasn't one for small talk – or talking much in general. When she opted to speak, it often held a weight that was reinforced by knowledge and well-constructed thoughts. Chase liked that – no, he *adored* that. But he found himself longing for an everyday conversation with his unlikely companion.

He wanted to be able to ask how her day had been without her smouldering, intelligent eyes clouding over with confusion at the question. He wanted to know more about her, but had no idea how to probe the topic. It seemed she knew everything worth knowing about him, and the more she took in from her quiet observations, the more Chase felt as though she saw him as a foolish child.

I am foolish, but I am no child! he thought, his unharmed hand lashing at the simmering water in irritation.

By all accounts, Temperance had recovered with both haste and poise from the traumatic experience of being fused with the legendary stone of Fire – not that Chase could know for certain. It appeared that she had a naturally pragmatic and logical nature about her, and did not trouble herself with unnecessary thoughts or activities, like dwelling on the past or bathing in Scourge.

Not that I've thought of her bathing, Chase thought, knowing it was a lie.

He'd also come to the realisation that Temperance was possibly quite a bit older than him. While he had assumed a couple of years separated them, he could feel the gap in maturity between them more with each passing day. Allowing himself to sink deeper into the water, Chase's curiosity got the better of him.

"Say, Temperance," he started, trying to sound more mature than he felt. "Might you enlighten me as to how old you are?"

Chase could hear her shift slightly, as if getting comfortable, but her silhouette still didn't divulge whether she was looking at him or not. Either way, he could feel that her attention had shifted to him.

"Are you succumbing to a fit?" Temperance asked, seeming genuinely concerned.

"I... No – what?" Chase stuttered.

"Is the heat getting to you? I worry that I might have overestimated your tolerance for it."

"I feel fine!" Chase cried. It was mostly true – most of his body felt nothing short of refreshed. His stomach, however, felt ready to empty itself through his oesophagus.

Temperance paused for a moment before adding, "Your choice of words regarding my age was unusual for you."

"I was trying to sound more mature," Chase admitted, quietly desperate for the moment to be over.

"Oh, I see," Temperance replied. He heard her flick through the pages of her tome. "I only ask because you sounded like an idiot. I am twenty-eight years old."

Chase grinned. He was embarrassed, but he'd succeeded in getting Temperance to talk about herself.

"That's a great age, Temp!"

"Chase, please dress yourself and leave the hot springs. I honestly fret that you're unwell."

CHAPTER 18

THE POWER OF A NAME

Chase scruffed his head roughly with a surprisingly clean rag. He knew that in time the water would return to its usual place of its own accord, but it didn't stop the habit of drying himself. What he *had* become accustomed to was the ability to toss the rag away and know that it would eventually return to where it had originated, clean and ready for use once more.

As he finished drying his hair, his eyes fell on one of the Nameless. Chase stopped dead to prevent himself from walking straight into the scorched man, who was eyeing Temperance with a mix of curiosity and reverence. The cursed villager had become so fixated on her that he'd stopped in the centre of the path.

"Uh, greetings?" Chase opened uncertainly, waving an unsure hand in front of the newcomer's face as Temperance took a hesitant step away from his intense gaze. "You're making her uncomfortable. Can we help you?"

The Nameless snapped to attention, ember eyes turning to Chase before he fell to the ground and grovelled.

"Please accept my apologies!" the man cried.

"Apologies… What?" Chase muttered.

"I was instructed to request that the Vassal of Fire please come with me before going to the cathedral! The one you named bid me do so!"

The one we named? Namier? Chase's mind whirled. It must have been the influence of spending so much time with Temperance; he was starting to overthink things.

"Namier is considered different now, is he?" Temperance piped up, her hesitance gone. "The first time I spoke to one of the Nameless, he was chosen at random, wasn't he?"

Alright, maybe I'm not the over-thinker.

"That's right, My Flame!" the man said from the ground.

"My Flame" – so that name is sticking, is it? Chase thought bitterly. He didn't know why, but every time the name was uttered, he felt a strong urge to hit whoever spoke it. Irrational, sure. But it was how he felt, and the fact that Temperance had seemingly taken it in her stride didn't help. She hadn't brought it up, though, and he didn't know how to.

"It appears we have inadvertently given Namier a promotion." Temperance turned to Chase, breaking his gloom.

"What do you want to do about it?" Chase asked, rallying his senses.

"We can strip him of the position immediately, if you so desire!" the Nameless declared, so suddenly that Chase couldn't grasp whether he was eager to demote Namier or to please Temperance.

"Don't be ridiculous. The fault lies with me," Temperance announced firmly. "I have acted without thinking and the action shall remain in place. If there is one thing the people of this village have learnt, it's to live with the consequences of their actions. I will be more perceptive in the future."

Chase could still see the uncertainty on his companion's face and acted before the Nameless could rise and see it for himself.

"I think *Your Flame* would appreciate it if you would lead us to where Namier instructed."

"Of course!" The Nameless stood, looking at Temperance and Chase in turn. "But I have to warn you that once we arrive there, only My Flame may enter with me."

"But –"

"Chase." Temperance's soft voice stopped his objection. Their eyes met, and after a brief moment, Chase nodded slowly.

"Very well. But I'm following for as long as I'm allowed."

"Good for you, Chase." Temperance smiled slightly at the small victory her companion had taken for himself as they followed their escort's lead.

CHAPTER 19

THE TYRANT OF AQUIOCIA

"Interesting." The balding former Chairman smiled. "But you have no confirmation?"

"We cannot get close, my King," a shaking messenger said with his fifth bow.

The man who stood before the messenger wore a cerulean cape that was far too large for his slender, untrained body. The cape had belonged to the late King Axeal and had been donned by the Chairman shortly after his political takeover of the throne. It looked ridiculous on the man's poor form, but not simply because it had been designed for a much more statuesque figure. It exuded a certain majesty, and the people who laid eyes on it had come to respect it as part of their great King. Now, it was an unfortunate reminder of how Aquiocia was swiftly plummeting in every regard that had once made it great.

The treasury was depleting at an astronomical rate, seemingly used on nothing at all. Whatever the gold was spent on wasn't to improve the kingdom itself. The Council had shown very little interest in bringing the Princess home after their first attempt, claiming that they were currently in negotiations with the terrible barbarians in the south to get her returned safely to the kingdom. Some believed various conspiracies relating the missing gold and Princess, including some involving the Council having to pay large sums to keep her alive. Other rumours suggested that Alicea had taken the gold herself. Regardless of the whispers exchanged in the marketplace, every civilian had felt the drop in their quality of life – be it the price of food going up, or the curfew the knights had instated under the orders of their new King.

Now, as soon as the day turned to dusk, the people of the fair kingdom would rush to pack up their stalls and shops to make it back to their homes before the sun concluded its descent. Some of the smaller traders didn't even bother unpacking their wares of a morning; any customers they might have had knew that haggling was no longer an option. Some merchants took advantage of the situation and vastly raised their prices, knowing that people would pay it to avoid being caught outside their homes after dark.

Some travelling merchants refused to even visit Aquiocia out of fear, for business or otherwise. They refused to live the way put before them and recoiled at the idea of serving the self-appointed King. They left and were never seen again.

"Ahem." The former Chairman cleared his throat loudly.

"A-Apologies, Your Majesty, K-King Arissam!" the messenger stuttered. Failing to refer to the new King with ample awe was often a death sentence.

"That is much better. It is good to see the people are learning after all." Arissam smiled as he stroked his patchy beard. The former King had often let his stubble grow. On Axeal it had an air of masculinity. On the current King it looked like a teenager's first bout of facial hair. "Now, perhaps you can explain to me why our scouts have continually failed to get closer to the savages marching towards us?"

"They simply disappear, Your Majesty!"

Arissam's eyebrow rose.

"K-King Arissam!"

"They disappear, you say?" Arissam asked sceptically as he looked up at the soldiers on the balconies above. "That's very interesting. Why do they disappear?"

"We have no idea. The higher officers have reported that they've tried sending both single covert spies and groups of trained rangers. In every instance, they have not returned. There…" The man stopped himself suddenly.

Too late.

"What?" Arissam asked in mock curiosity as the messenger hesitated. "Please, share your theories with us, young man!"

"There was one who returned… H-he reported that a man vanished in a blast of smoke. The officer swears that in the scout's place stood the… Princess of A-Aquiocia." The messenger looked as though he might lose consciousness as he shook like a man standing in a frigid lake. His next words echoed throughout the hall as hope climbed into his voice. "People are saying t-that… that Princess Alicea is coming back!"

"But surely that's impossible, isn't it? I've told the entire city about her capture and the efforts we are implementing to retrieve her unharmed." Arissam smiled. "What was the officer's name? Is he a credible source?"

"Lieutenant Lerung has never been anything but honest and reliable, King Arissam!" the messenger confirmed. The knights on the balcony shifted restlessly.

"Well then, isn't that unfortunate?" Arissam said as he

slowly rose from the throne.

"I-I don't understand, Ki—" The man had no time to finish his sentence before a dozen crossbow bolts found his soft flesh, piercing his vital organs before following through to the stone floor.

Arissam's good humour was gone. He raked his nails through his thin beard in irritation. After a moment, his head snapped up to the knights above, whose eyes had turned the colour of burning, bloodshot amber.

"Find this Lieutenant and bring him to me immediately. Send a message to his men by killing half of them!" he snarled.

"Which half?" The men spoke in unison.

Arissam paused for a moment before his smile returned and he responded pleasantly, "Let them decide amongst themselves."

CHAPTER 20

THE LOYAL LIEUTENANT

Lerung was surprised, to say the very least, as he was dragged into the late King and Queen's chambers to see the self-appointed leader of the city standing at the window. Despite being practically thrown into the room by knights who said nothing, the Lieutenant got to his feet and bowed deeply. He would always show his loyalty and love for the crown, if not the man currently wearing it. He was just one of many longing for the days when Axeal and Adele were upon the thrones, and it showed in his appearance.

After weeks of constantly searching the plains and neighbouring towns for any word or sign of the Princess under the order of the new King, his blond hair had started to thin, and his skin had become pasty and frail from hiding in the shadows during stakeout operations. His brown eyes had hardened, losing the kind aura they'd once given off. He had jumped at the chance to join in the search a couple of months earlier, as he knew there would be no higher honour than to rescue the Princess who had been taken captive.

But he had quickly realised that something was wrong.

Firstly, he'd found out through the rumours of his men that the Council had known where she was the whole time. Secondly, he'd been ordered to sweep the neighbouring towns in search of her. These two revelations alone had cemented the belief that they were hiding information, yet he couldn't refuse the orders.

What would I have done? Gone rogue? he thought as Arissam turned around.

"Lieutenant Lerung, I assume?" the King asked pleasantly.

"Yes, Your Majesty?"

"King Arissam is the preferred title," he corrected as he ran a hand over his freshly shaved face. He'd abandoned the attempt to grow a beard and had it removed. Just in time, too; it had been barely an hour since giving the order to retrieve the man in front of him.

"It is an honour, King Arissam." Lerung bowed deeply.

"I'm sure it is. Rumour has it that you have spotted the Princess?"

"Yes, King Arissam. There is a possibility it was her." Lerung felt himself starting to sweat under his pale blue breastplate. He'd known it would get back to the King, but he still had little idea how he'd handle the impending conversation. "The details are in my report. I can get it for –"

"This report?" Arissam interrupted, producing a scroll from within his cape. "Yes, I've taken the time to read it quite thoroughly. It says an exceptionally well-trained ranger disappeared in a cloud of smoke and when the smoke had cleared, the Princess was spotted. Care to explain further?"

"I wrote that I *believed* it to be her. There is every chance it might not have been."

"That is true. Thank you for the correction." The King smiled as he paced the room. After a moment he appeared beside Lerung and whispered in his ear so softly that even the knights in each corner of the chamber couldn't make out his words. "But that's the lie, isn't it? You know it was her."

"There is no way to know for cer—"

"Do – not – lie – to me," Arissam spat, not removing his lips from their place an inch from Lerung's ear. "We both know you saw her. There aren't a lot of women who look like that particular royal bitch, don't you agree?"

Lerung felt a pang of anger but suppressed it by remaining silent.

"I asked you a question, you pathetic excuse for a knight!" Arissam bellowed, now standing in front of him. "Did you see the bitch, or not?"

"Whoever you speak of, I did not see," Lerung answered with a forced calm as his stomach turned. He detested the idea of lying to the crown, but it wasn't the crown he was lying to. "There was no bitch there, King Arissam."

"If you do not stop playing games I will have you beheaded right here for treason," the King threatened.

"Do what you will," Lerung replied, surprised to find that he suddenly found the idea of death revitalising. After being conflicted for so long about his purpose in finding the Princess for the Council and false King, death seemed like an easy way of escape. If he died protecting the Princess in this small way, it could almost be considered an honourable way to die.

Is it honourable to search for a way to make longing for death seem less despicable? he thought. *Probably not. But given the situation, I doubt I will be offered a better alternative. Princess Alicea, please come back and see to this tyrant. I have no right to ask anything of the crown, but your people need you.*

Lerung's thoughts and Arissam's interrogation were cut

short as two knights with burning eyes entered the chamber and stared at the King, awaiting acknowledgement.

"What is it?" Arissam snarled.

"They refused to choose which half of them would die today. They are being held in the main barracks," the corrupted knights said in unison.

"What? How dare they disobey me!" Arissam bellowed, before he suddenly smiled and scratched at his freshly shaved chin. He glanced at Lerung. "Actually, this is for the best. Come with me, Lieutenant. I have something to show you."

❖

Lerung had no idea why he was being escorted towards the knights' barracks. He had even less idea why there didn't appear to be a single soldier in the training grounds as the King led the way across the courtyard and to the barracks' doors. With a wave of his hand, the two knights following Lerung grabbed him roughly and forced him back. He didn't utter a word. He was ready to endure whatever was going to happen next.

Arissam gave an unsettling smile and knocked on the heavy timber doors. Surprisingly enough, he then walked away, putting distance between himself and the building.

After a few moments, the heavy doors opened.

The sight of an older knight poking his head out from inside was almost comical as he looked at Lerung first with confusion, before nodding upon seeing Arissam. Disappearing back inside, the training field fell to absolute silence. Lerung was about to ask a question when the doors opened again.

Practically falling from the building were men and women dressed in their undergarments. The first thing he noticed was that for each person who lacked clothing, there were two encased in cerulean steel. Next, he started to recognise the distressed faces, and after a moment he realised exactly how many people were there.

There are one hundred people without clothing here, Lerung thought miserably as he was pushed further back by the knights to make room. He knew how many, because he knew who they were. *Which means there are two hundred armed knights.*

The almost-naked men and woman must have been told what was expected of them; despite being clearly terrified, they lined up in four equal rows of twenty-five, as if prepared to march. The knights, on the other hand, had formed a perfect circle around everyone present – save for the King, who stood sneering from outside the steel wall. Lerung could only look on at his soldiers, his eyes reflecting the most sincere of apologies, as two knights forcefully relieved him of his armour. He had no idea what they had done, but he knew that he was somehow at fault. It was clear, even now in his faded trousers and worn tunic, that he was the superior officer of the stripped men and women. The nakedness almost seemed symbolic. After all, he knew they hadn't been serving the same crown they once swore allegiance to for quite some time now.

"These people were given a task," Arissam began, as though he was preparing to tell a great tale of old. "They were told to elect an amount equal to half of their total number to die. A simple request, if I might say so. But they could not accomplish even that. Can you imagine, Lieutenant? Aquiocian soldiers are amongst the best in the land; their loyalty is unmatched.

Yet here they stand in defiance of the crown."

"Why?" Lerung croaked. Arissam mockingly cupped his ear. "I ASKED YOU WHY!"

"Because Aquiocia needs order." Arissam shrugged, making his way into the circle and approaching a ginger-haired woman on the end of the first row. "Who is this woman?"

"Her name… is Regalinete," Lerung replied after a moment of hesitation. He wasn't going to insult the naked woman by feigning ignorance of who she was. "She's a superb archer and scout. Two children, both boys. Her husband has passed."

"Fascinating. You seem to know your underlings well." Arissam smiled as the woman cringed at his touch. "Will she be the first of the required fifty, then? Hm? Will you save or kill her?"

The entire field was silent as Lerung struggled to comprehend what was happening.

"My soldiers are my people. They are family. I can't –" Lerung's words caught in his throat as Arissam produced a knife and buried it hilt-deep in Regalinete's sternum. He heard the simultaneous preparation and aiming of two hundred crossbows, but the display was pointless. He wasn't going to give the King the satisfaction of reacting. Though his expression was stoic, his stomach had dropped to his feet.

"Well then, that's one." Arissam grinned, wiping the blade on the twitching woman's cloth. "Only forty-nine to go."

"Why do my people have to die?" Lerung struggled to keep his voice level.

"Because you have spread falsehoods of the Princess returning. She is held captive in –"

"Lies!" a woman's voice cried from the ranks of naked

soldiers. "Do not give this monster the satisfaction, Lieutenant Lerung! We die here serving the rightful Queen!"

"Silence!" Arissam bellowed as Lerung smirked in realisation.

"I get it now." His smile grew. "Oh, how I finally understand."

Everyone watched on as the Lieutenant's face flooded with realisation. The reason for the King's fervent actions and questioning finally dawned on him. The King put on a façade of calm control when addressing the masses, or in the company of anyone with power. But he was a cowardly lunatic who simply knew what face to wear.

Lerung let go of the fear for the people he thought of as family, dropping it like an unwanted package and kicking it to the side. He knew there was no way to make it out of this situation alive. He'd seen the kind of man Arissam was all too many times. It didn't matter how many people they commanded, or how big the land they ruled – they were sustained by the fear of others. He'd always found it ironic, as so many of the tyrants he'd met were in fact cowards.

Some soldiers met their ends on the field of battle, others in less dramatic ways. Lerung was going to meet his by calling out the false King.

"Tell me something, *Your Majesty*," he drawled, his exhausted face struggling into a look of smug satisfaction at the hesitation on the King's own. "Just how terrified are you of the rightful Queen?"

The question hung in the air, like the uncomfortable chill of a winter's morning. Nobody wanted to move; nobody dared as the King began to shake visibly with rage. Arissam's head snapped back and forth between Lerung and the knights surrounding them, as if genuinely surprised that the man who insulted him was still standing.

"I asked you a question," Lerung continued, taking a step towards the furious King. "Is it her rightful claim to the throne that bothers you, or something else?"

"Kill him!" Arissam roared. "I fear no one, least of all that useless bitch! Kill him!"

"Do it!" Lerung called. The soldiers around them hesitated as the Lieutenant slowly pivoted, arms outstretched to emphasise that he was unarmed. "Take my life! The kingdom I was once proud to be part of is gone! Take my life!"

The stripped soldiers let out a cheer. They knew the situation as well as their leader.

"Take us all!"

"Do not feel guilty! We are not infected as we know you are," Lerung bellowed at the knights, Arissam frowning in confusion. "We know you have no choice but to obey this coward!"

Lerung knew the crossbowmen surrounding him were grimacing under their helms as they lifted their crossbows and pointed them towards him and his companions.

"You know more than you let on," Arissam noted.

"That's always the case," said Lerung. "But my information is incomplete. For example, I don't know what they're infected with, or how they got that way. But I know this." The Lieutenant allowed himself to chortle in amusement. "The Princess is coming back, and she won't forget this."

The false King nodded slowly, as if weighing the words. With a thoughtful shrug, his face broke steadily into a wide grin as he approached the Lieutenant. Lerung gasped as the sharp sting of a short blade pierced his stomach and the false King's hot breath invaded his ear once more.

"I know she'll return. In fact, I'm counting on it."

The sound of dozens of crossbows unloading their deadly projectiles filled the air shortly after the King turned and left the Lieutenant to fall, blade still buried in his stomach. There were no screams and barely a stray grunt of pain from the brave ranks of naked men and women. No final words were needed between the soldiers and their Lieutenant; they would have sullied this moment of bitter honour.

We have lived as a family. We have trained and persevered as a family. Lerung smiled with lips painted crimson. *It's only right we fall as one.*

CHAPTER 21

SETZ'S BRIEF

Alicea's brow furrowed in annoyance. She was mostly irritated with herself and her inability to put her thoughts of the coming battle to the side. They were only a day's hard march from the forest's edge and Aquiocia's doorstep. The anticipation would not let her be as she forced herself to recline against the thick tree she had adopted away from the bulk of the army.

She hadn't been allowed to wander too far away this time and the idea of flying had been outright forbidden, despite the steadily setting sun. The argument that nobody would see her at night fell upon Garnet's deaf ears and despite their difference in titles, Alicea had buckled.

While she had stormed away from her mentor, her feet had remained grounded. Something about the head shaman made her feel like a child who'd just learnt to speak. She felt like she could argue all she liked, but ultimately, she'd be doing what the elder dictated. The Princess hadn't felt that way since her own mother had last given her an order, which only added sorrow to her frustration.

She had rebelled in her own feeble way by going to the very edge of the camp and turning her back to everyone. She'd even ordered her familiar away to exercise her hollow authority. Now, she sat under a tree in silence as the sun rose in the distance, its light barely filtering through the thick canopy.

The army would rest that day, or that was the plan. They would travel the last leg of the journey under the cover of night. It would allow them to arrive at dawn and immediately begin the operation Alicea had concocted. The revelation that she wanted the assault to take place during the day had been a surprising one to the other leaders, but they quickly agreed that it was a good idea – the enemy was far more likely to act as the Princess predicted they would in broad daylight.

Despite being around twelve hours away from their destination, some of the force had already set to work. While many of the hunters rested, there was also a large number who had pressed forward in a tireless march. They were mostly gifted shamans and a few of the more heavy-handed hunters. Quite a few scouting parties comprised of both hunters and assassins had been dispatched in search of enemy forces, but to Alicea's delight and Rufus' dismay, very few had been found.

The scouting parties had been ordered to subdue and only to kill if absolutely necessary, but the lack of enemy scouts meant that something was awry. While the lack of death pleased the Princess, Rufus had continually reminded her not to get complacent and that it didn't sit right with him. This had resulted in him being banished from her presence as well.

The Princess wasn't oblivious; she'd already spotted the thief some thirty yards away, sitting on a large boulder and eating while he kept track of her whereabouts. At first it had annoyed her. She had ordered him to disappear, not sit and gawk at her from afar. But her anger quickly dispersed when he allowed the twins to race up and finally catch him at long last. She had watched them laugh for a few seconds before the twins had fallen silent and joined the thief in his observation of her.

He deliberately lost the game to see that I didn't come to harm. Alicea allowed herself a small smile, its lifespan short.

She was about to swallow her pride and wave them over when her attention was drawn elsewhere.

"Good morning, Your Highness." The quiet voice had Alicea smiling grimly. She wasn't surprised that Setz had managed to approach without her noticing.

"Someday, I shall hear you coming," she quipped as she turned to the Guildmaster.

"I hope so, for that is the day I shall finally retire," Setz returned with a glitter in his eye. "The twins and I must take our leave shortly."

"Just you three?"

"I doubt you'd notice any others missing."

"True enough. That would result in far too many people retiring right when I need them."

Alicea finally turned to face Setz. Her eyes missed nothing as she looked over the man she'd known since birth. It was true that Setz had aged considerably since they'd first met; it had been two decades, most of which she could recall infallibly. His face held a fatigue invisible to most; Alicea loathed that part of her gift. Most people didn't watch those around them age day to day. Most only noticed it now and then, yet she missed nothing.

The drastic changes in a person's appearance she could handle, like the day Setz had returned to the kingdom covered in the vicious lacerations that still scarred him to this day. There was the initial shock and concern, then it was gone. It was the miniscule changes that vexed her; they were persistent. The ever so slight deepening of a laughter line on someone's face after a night of rejoicing, or the minute fading of colour in someone's eyes as they witnessed more of what life offered... Whether it had been a day or a year since seeing someone, the immaculate and cruel comparison of past and present forced itself upon Alicea, and she was reminded that death forever crawled towards them all.

Meeting new people didn't come with that despairing reminder. There was nothing for her to compare them to. It was the first and last time that she could appreciate someone's appearance without the morbid undertones she felt every time after.

"You look tired, Setz," Alicea noted, her own tone exhausted.

"I might say the same about you." Setz's eyes flickered over the Princess' form before he changed the topic. "Your plan for the assault on the castle is a sound one."

"Providing it works," Alicea interjected.

"Providing it works," Setz confirmed quietly. Too quietly.

"What aren't you telling me, Setz?"

The Guildmaster didn't bother questioning how she knew he was holding something close to his chest. He'd wanted her to ask.

"Your plan involves my men, and perhaps even me, storming the inner city – a superb idea that few would see coming in most situations."

His praise didn't sit well with Alicea. "Are you telling me it will not work as well as I assume in *this* particular situation?"

Setz didn't reply immediately, instead allowing himself

to take in the image of Rufus and the twins watching before speaking again.

"Your enemy knows I exist – or rather, he suspects it," Setz revealed grimly.

"I fail to see an issue with that. Plenty of people know of you; that doesn't mean that they ever actually see you coming."

"True, but Arissam has seized the throne with a tight grip."

Alicea was on her feet at the mention of the Chairman's name. She'd never liked Arissam, to the point that she'd barely even considered him family. He'd always kept his distance from her – which, as she grew up, she had come to appreciate more and more. It had been a simple task, leaving the affairs of the kingdom to the Council, knowing that her uncle was at the head of it. She'd known about his forced ascendance to the throne, but hadn't spoken to anyone about it.

Not even Rufus. How could she begin to explain that her uncle was the cause of Aquiocia's issues, or that he was the one she recalled within The Elemental Chronicles?

Alicea stood and paced, her hands balling into fists and unfurling several times. For a time, she appeared to be looking for something to hit. She paused, eyes closing for the span of a breath before reopening. Taking her place back at the base of the tree, she finally responded.

"So, my uncle remains at the heart of Aquiocia's issues." The statement was for herself more than anything. But her next question was enough to surprise even Setz. "Why haven't you killed him?"

Setz didn't reply immediately. The Princess knew the Guildmaster was choosing his words carefully. Assassination of a family member tended to be touchy subject for some.

"Because I am unable to."

"Why?" Alicea asked in puzzlement, searching for clues on Setz's face.

"I haven't been completely truthful with you, Princess. For that I apolo—"

"Either explain yourself or close your mouth, Setz," Alicea snapped. She was exhausted and furious – at him for holding something back from her, at herself for not realising it.

"Very well. I have not been able to step foot into Aquiocia for some time now," Setz said vaguely.

Alicea said nothing, waiting for him to continue.

"One of my men was caught within the kingdom and he never returned," Setz revealed solemnly. "As with anyone who goes missing, I send one of my elite, or I go myself. In this instance I elected to investigate myself. The second I attempted to enter the city, I was repelled by a foreboding energy. Try as I might, I could not dispel the enchantment after months of attempts." It was obvious the story had been weighing on him for some time. It was heartbreaking for Alicea to see the guilt in his expression.

"What about your other men? Could they not –"

"I utilised every single resource I had trying to dispel the enchantment. Fortitudes were tested and lives were lost, but to no avail." Setz's eyes flickered to Alicea. "It wasn't long before I realised I'd been outmanoeuvred."

"What made you come to that conclusion?"

"Your parents didn't make it."

Five words. The same five words that had been delivered to her by a messenger, driving her into a depressive spiral, threatened to do the same all over again.

"I'm aware of that, Setz," she replied coldly.

"Your parents didn't make it," Setz repeated. "Then I found myself barred from the kingdom. All of Aquiocia's most influential candidates were removed from the city, and we couldn't get to you."

"Mr. Thief managed to get to me. Rather haphazardly, but he managed it."

"Yes, a lot was pinned on Rufus' success. It took quite a while to mould Rufus into the amicable young man he is now." Setz smirked and held his arm out away from Alicea. The Princess watched on in silence as a scroll materialised in his hand. With a quick glance over the parchment, the Guildmaster nodded and the scroll disintegrated into ashes. "He could have been killed at any point in our efforts to secure the stone and yourself."

"If there's something in place forbidding your guild's entry…"

"Rufus is not marked by the guild's brand, nor are the twins," Setz cut in softly.

"The brand is what forbids your entry." Alicea didn't know much about enchantments, but this made sense. "I assume that if you could simply burn it off, you would have already done so and killed Arissam?"

"A thousand times over. However, removing the mark from one's body has some rather dire consequences. Unfortunately, while I'm more than willing to accept them, I have too much involvement in the coming events, and it would be unwise to remove me from the equation just yet."

"You sound like you've already calculated where you'll die!" Alicea joked, her smile fading as quickly as it had appeared when Setz grimaced slightly in response.

"My men will be there, Your Highness," he said in a forceful tone. "I must leave now with the twins, but you can mark my words: we will be there for you."

"I expected no different, but how –" Alicea's voice cut off abruptly when she looked up to see that Setz had vanished.

Spinning on the spot, she searched for the twins, only to see Rufus sitting on his own. Alicea's shoulders slumped and she took her place back against the tree, her knees drawn up to her chest.

Just how many steps is Setz ahead of me? How many strings is he pulling behind the scenes? What does he see in the future that no one else does?

CHAPTER 22

VANQUISHER OF KNOTS

The high sun did nothing to cover the shadows leaping over fallen trees and the odd mound of hay. They raced through the farmland on the outskirts of the walls leading to the city, doing their best to keep their heads down so that at the very least, their faces wouldn't be seen. There were very few guards, as Alicea had predicted. Nothing ever happened in the farmland, and even the residents appeared to have retreated to safety within the walls. It was hard to believe that the force approaching the city gates included their Princess. It was even harder to believe that the general population didn't know she was within the ranks.

If they knew I was here, there would have been an uproar... Alicea pondered for a moment. It was tempting to simply announce her arrival and let her people revolt. But she couldn't.

Garnet had floated the idea of projecting the Princess' voice across the land, like she had done at the skirmish of Tremel. Alicea had dismissed the idea, knowing very well that should the people in the kingdom hear her, they'd immediately rebel against anyone who stood in the way of their rightful Queen. The problem with that was that she had no idea how many civilians had been afflicted with the curse, and if she pulled such a gambit, thousands might immediately perish or be compelled to fight. Garnet had questioned her at length about the risk of Jex triggering the curse anyway, but Alicea had simply shaken her head, smiled and replied, "He'd never risk missing the chance to kill me."

The shadows came to a halt, crouching behind a large bale of hay and an abandoned wagon of still-fresh fruit. With a flick of his violet hood, Rufus' face peered around the wagon and took in the fields from a different angle. He could see everything from the gates leading to the city to the forest's edge, though the force of hunters remained invisible. Looking towards a lone house surrounded by upturned soil, he saw their target. It was the same house they had visited when they had departed Aquiocia for Tremel in the first place.

Although there was no one around, they knew that Setz's contact would be there awaiting their arrival. Lori, Tori and many of the others under Setz's employ had already gone ahead to ready themselves for the coming operation, leaving Rufus to escort the Princess alone. It was for the best, really; small groups attracted less attention, and as Alicea had pointed out, Jex would expect her to be heavily guarded.

"Ah, good..." Rufus nodded, satisfied with what he saw. "Soon the fields will be flooded with knights charging towards the – *are you brushing your flaming hair?*"

Alicea's hand stopped mid-stroke, eyes narrowed in irritation.

"Yes, I am, Mr. Thief. I would thank you not to hiss at me like an irate child."

"And I would thank *you* to realise that you're amidst what will soon be a warzone," Rufus retorted as he tried and failed to confiscate the brush.

"Impending disaster is absolutely no excuse to look like you've just climbed out of a pigsty. Have some pride, Mr. Thief," Alicea quipped.

"This is unbelievable."

"What is unbelievable is the fact you're under the impression that occasionally running your hand through your hair constitutes it being groomed and maintained," the Princess scolded as she inched closer. "Now, hold still, and maybe I can salvage this mess before you look completely homeless and unloved."

Rufus found himself speechless as the Princess started running her brush through his hair. He couldn't think of a single thing to say, sarcastic or otherwise. Alicea's comb found every knot, but not once did the exercise hurt as she expertly untangled his dusty hair. After a few minutes, the feeling of the comb running through his hair ceased and with a quick movement, Alicea reached around and placed the brush in one of Rufus' front pockets.

"There, all done. You may keep that, as I no longer want it." Alicea tilted her head. "Oh, look at you with your neat hair. I'd say you could almost pass as being employed, Mr. Thief."

He laughed.

He laughed so hard that he had difficulty stifling it. When he finally succeeded in banishing the chuckles, he bowed his head slightly.

"Princess Alicea A. Aquiocia, Vassal of Water, Rightful Heir to the Aquiocian Throne and above all, Vanquisher of Knots!"

"I feel the last title is the most prestigious and the one this world needs most," Alicea smiled. "Now, let's move while it's clear."

CHAPTER 23

IT BEGINS

"This plan is awful!" Dairok exclaimed as he attempted to hide his impressive form behind an equally large boulder.

It has its merits, Silrok replied through telepathy as she bounced across the surface of the boulder, taking in the surroundings.

Dairok stared in surprise at the small bird that Silrok had become, but said nothing. He looked around at the countless other men hiding in the brush: some in trees, others in the dirt, but all equally well-hidden. If it wasn't for the fact that Dairok was a trained hunter, he would never have seen the men and women concealed in the woodland, much less the traps they had crafted from vines and other natural materials.

Another giveaway to one trained in the art of hunting was the over-abundance of birds hiding in the trees. All were completely still, sitting in absolute silence.

"I thought you hated the Princess – and now you're defending her?" Dairok groaned.

I do not hate the woman, and I am not defending her. I am merely giving this plan due consideration and an appropriate amount of praise. After all, we are enabling its execution.

"Gah! What am I missing here?"

It is very simple: the enemy will charge the forest in search of the

Princess. They will fall to the traps of the hunters and mages. Our job is to apprehend as many as we can.

"What if that doesn't work?" Dairok demanded. "It won't go that smoothly!"

I believe the Princess knows it is impossible not to kill some of the soldiers. That is why brutes such as you are amongst our ranks. To ensure that, should the plan fail, we have the muscle required to crush the enemy.

"That doesn't sound like the Princess we were talking about. Sounds like she's scared of fighting, to me."

Of course she is, but she will do what needs to be done.

Dairok gave up on the conversation, seeing no way to come to an agreement with the other stubborn Chief. He turned his attention to a deer racing towards him through the brush. It came to a stop in front of him, kicking up dust in its haste. Noticing a blue ribbon around its neck, he nodded. It was a messenger.

The young voice of a man entered their minds. *Chief Dairok and Chief Silrok, I bring news. The gates have opened.*

"Aye! They are coming!" Dairok exclaimed.

Would you close that immense mouth of yours before you give away our position?

"Aye, sorry, Silrok. But still, great news!" Dairok said.

You may leave, Silrok dismissed the young man, and the deer sprinted off. *They won't be far off, given that the message was delivered on foot.*

"Well, whose fault is that?"

It had to be done. Birds in the sky at the time of war is a tell-tale sign of enemy activity. I thought you knew of these things?

Dairok was about to respond when he saw something shift

out of the corner of his eye. One of his men was moving his hand slightly. The Chief watched closely before nodding.

"They are here."

Stick to the plan.

CHAPTER 24

A PLAN AND A LINE

Alicea was momentarily mesmerised by the large, enchanted orbs that floated near the ceiling of the Underbelly, giving off brilliant light to the residents who were loyal to Setz, and casting those who meant harm into blindness. She'd seen them before, of course, but returning as a somewhat accomplished mage made her consider the theory behind the spell itself. How did the orbs see the motives of every person who walked into their light?

"Are you going to tell me my role in all of this yet?" Rufus asked impatiently, breaking Alicea's reverie.

"The Princess wants a distraction, would be my guess," Setz said, his tone knowing.

"The army of hunters drawing the Aquiocian forces out the front gate isn't enough of a distraction?" Rufus asked, voice dripping with sarcasm. He knew he'd soon be separated from Alicea, which meant she'd be that much more vulnerable should things go sour.

"I need them to be unaware of what is going on around them," Alicea explained patiently as they made their way through the streets of the underground settlement. "Once the Aquiocian force realises their people are being trapped, they will attempt to retreat towards the castle itself. That's common sense."

"So, you want them to come back to find me?" Rufus asked in surprise. "Look, Princess, I know we've had our issues, but –"

"The Princess has no intention of you being caught or killed," Setz said quietly.

"Of course not, Mr. Thief!" Alicea scolded. "You will take the twins into the city and set alight the festival stores."

"Set alight the – that will turn the entire city into a fireworks display!" Rufus protested.

"Yes, and I'm sure it will look beautiful," Alicea replied.

"Where did you even get an idea like that?" Setz asked.

"I saw something akin to it the night I was kidnapped. There was a large purple cloud. I suppose you could say that *you* gave me the idea, Setz," Alicea smiled.

Setz nodded. "I assumed as much. Rufus and the twins are to go alone so as not to draw attention, I assume?"

"I was hoping they might be assisted by your men," Alicea said. Setz's revelation about not being able to enter the city was worrisome, but he had promised to be there.

"Understood. I will organise some of my best."

"You say that as if there was a chance I'd ever be happy with this arrangement," Rufus muttered, glaring at Alicea.

"What is the problem, Mr. Thief?"

"Nothing." He turned away.

Alicea glanced from Rufus to the twins, who had been ignoring her since she had made the swan explode in their faces. Lori smiled slightly, while Tori simply stuck her nose in the air. Clearly, the latter was far more accomplished in the art of holding a grudge.

"The quickest way to strike the festival stores is from the eastern upper-class district. I will go now and await the command," Rufus said, veering off the dirty path away from the party.

"Lori, wait!" Alicea stopped the milder-mannered twin.

"Yes, Princess?"

"I say this knowing full well that you will anyway, but look after him. We…" Alicea paused a moment. "We all have our part to play. Tell him… I am sorry."

"Ruffie is very tough. He will be back to argue with you before you know it!" Lori said with a smile.

"The men will report to Rufus directly. You will make your move according to their report, which will be sent directly from me," Setz ordered. "Good luck, Lori. I have full faith in both you and your sister. Now go." The second twin raced off.

"It is time for the last pieces of this plan to fall into place," Alicea said, drawing a deep breath.

"I will be with you every step of the way," said Setz.

"No – you will be here, ready to strike alongside your people."

"Then I will organise a small band of my men to watch over you as well."

"You need all the men you can get!"

"An order to leave you defenceless is one that I cannot fulfil," Setz replied, ending the debate. Alicea knew that there were certain things Setz wouldn't stand for. It was the reason her father had trusted him above any other advisor who stepped into the Aquiocian halls. She could remember her father saying, on more than one occasion, "Setz is a man who'll draw the line at foolishness, and gods know I need that in an advisor."

Alicea made a point of keeping her eyes forward.

"As you wish."

CHAPTER 25

RESOLVE

Alicea and Setz walked together in silence. The Underbelly appeared deserted, its residents having already rallied or returned to their homes. There wasn't any need for the hidden city's lockdown, but once the shadows of the Guild had begun to shift, everyone had taken to their homes.

At that very moment, Alicea felt the safest she had been in months, perhaps even longer than that. Knowing what she did now, it wasn't a stretch to consider the possibility that she could have been assassinated at any moment from the time of her parents' passing. It made sense that Arissam hadn't made that move, though; there were few ways to make the Princess completely disappear without heavy backlash from the public. They would have revolted.

Or would they? she wondered. *Something has placated the people – they believe whatever the Council has told them. Whether it's faith or fear, they are allowing the Council full control.*

The sullen Princess and unreadable Guildmaster continued what felt like a meaningless trek towards the Guild's main hub – the massive pillar in the centre of the shadowy civilisation. Alicea noted a path she had seen before, as dirty and poorly maintained as the rest of them, but unmistakably the one she had traversed with Rufus the first time she'd arrived in the

Underbelly. Her memory traced the route they'd taken to get into the Underbelly all those months ago. She recalled each path that branched off as they'd walked through the city, and each stone corridor of the canals before that.

Comparing what little she knew of the underground layout to the manholes above, she figured there were at least three exits she could find without an issue. There was also the potential of a fourth, and it was of great interest.

Alicea kept her eyes forward so as not to draw attention to what was keeping her mind busy. She had put her end goal to the side, as if it was inconsequential, instead solely focused on finding a way out of her current situation. Her first assumption was that she was subconsciously trying to run away from the battle before her, but by taking that path, she would be doing quite the opposite.

And Setz wouldn't be able to follow, she thought, perplexed by the realisation that she wanted to leave him behind. She wanted to do… *whatever* it was alone.

She knew then what it was: she had been rattled. The doubts of the people around her had gotten to her, Garnet's words had burrowed into her own self-doubt, and now she felt she had something to prove. She knew that wasn't true, of course. There was no reason to abandon or forsake their current path; things were falling into line. To act rashly now would invite disaster.

And what about after this is all over – what then? Will the people have faith in me then? Or will they still consider me inadequate? Will I still consider myself so?

"Is something amiss, Your Highness?" Setz asked, making a point of staring directly ahead.

"No, everything is as well as could be expected. Why do you ask?"

"Because you're wearing the same calculating gaze you wore as a child before... Well, I'm sure you know firsthand," Setz finished.

"I... I just need to be alone with my thoughts a moment," Alicea admitted. She had appreciated the silence surrounding them, but it still wasn't quite the same as being truly alone. It was a morbid realisation, that the solitude she had endured so long had become so desirable.

"Take some time for yourself, but do not tarry. Your friends and comrades still need your leadership," Setz said lightly.

"Yes, just a short while..." Alicea murmured as she branched off the path they were on and began to follow a side street.

She could feel Setz's eyes on her as she wandered the new path, attempting to look casual as she veered off. She knew Setz was suspicious; she didn't know that he knew exactly what she was doing. The Princess had little tells that gave her away to those who had known her long enough. Things like her eyes changing intensity to reflect emotion, or a certain trance-like expression she wore as she steadily deciphered a challenge in her head.

One of her favourites as a child had always been navigating the castle without being seen, and while Setz couldn't hope to completely understand how the Princess' mind operated, he knew she had already formulated a plan. She had sifted through everything she knew about the underground canals, entrances and exits. While she lacked experience underground, she could call on any memory that revealed a manhole and work on constructing a rough layout of the underground. If she hadn't glanced at a map of it before, of course.

She will be running by now... Setz thought grimly. *She will be running as fast as she can in hopes of reaching where I can't go. She knows I can stop her if I wish...*

The Guildmaster stood in the centre of the street, watching the corner Alicea disappeared around as if expecting her to reappear at any second. He was conflicted, if only for the moment it took for him to realise he had received an order: a silent command from a woman too ashamed to utter it.

Good luck, Your Highness. The Guildmaster turned and returned to his headquarters.

CHAPTER 26

A SQUIRE'S WEAPON

"You've done a fine job, Jex," the crimson-haired Warmaster commended.

"Thank you, Sir," Jex replied automatically as Maxim turned back in his saddle to examine the company of knights guarding the carriage behind them.

"You've all done a superb job!" he called. The compliment was met with the resounding cry of fifty men and women.

The company of soldiers had been marching for the better part of a week towards Aquiocia. They had been charged with a top-secret task and Maxim had meticulously hand-picked each of them. There had been more than a small amount of grumbling when the cargo they had received was simply a large ornate box they were forbidden to open. Only Maxim and the Chairman of the Aquiocian Council had been allowed to briefly open the box and peer inside. Then, with a small nod to each other, the knights were on the move, back the way they came.

The grumbles had come from the men desiring action. A lot of them wanted battle and the glory associated with it. The Warmaster had smiled at the men gathered around him at night as they'd tell him tall tales of their alleged bravest moments. Maxim hadn't called them out once, instead seeming content to listen to their fabricated stories of heroism. It was the price he paid for refusing to march during the night. As he'd explained to the knights, they were more susceptible to an ambush while in motion, and at night, even more so. The revelation had only made everyone more curious about their mysterious cargo.

The Chairman had said very little during the journey, often occupying his mind by reading and writing on long scrolls of parchment. The Chairman received quite a few visitors for someone who was on the road. Men and women dressed in black would appear before Maxim and he'd simply nod and let them approach the carriage, where they'd receive instructions from the man named Setz before disappearing.

Even Jex had felt slightly curious about the proceedings. But both Warmaster and Chairman were uninterested in answering any questions, and curiosity aside, it wasn't a knight's job to speculate. They had been offered the mission and it came with a nice bonus upon completion. The entire situation had felt strange, but Jex wanted the extra coins. With the reward he'd be able to visit one of the blacksmiths in the upper class. He'd never felt comfortable wielding the issued longswords, so he hoped to have something crafted specifically for him.

He had no idea what weapon he'd select, but he'd heard high praise for one of the blacksmiths who claimed to be able to "craft the weapon the individual was meant to wield". What that meant exactly was beyond Jex's comprehension.

"Why'd you become a knight, Jex?" Maxim asked, smiling, his friendly green eyes looking over his subordinate. The Warmaster had asked Jex to ride next to him both to and from the meeting point. It had sparked some nasty whispers amongst the ranks, which had shortly been silenced by the Chairman looking out the window of the carriage with a glare that would make most men cringe.

"Why not?" Jex shrugged. "It's one of very few professions where you are able to make a difference."

"Oh?" Maxim nodded thoughtfully. "Make a difference in what way, exactly?"

"I don't know that part yet," Jex admitted quietly. "But I can't stand the idea of just existing. I have to make some form of mark."

"Why? Some people are quite content with what others might call a menial life. There are those with families, or small businesses. There are those who –"

"There are those who made it to the status of 'Warmaster' at the age of twenty-five and proceeded to obtain dozens of medals and awards for bravery and the like."

Jex glanced at his superior officer quickly to see if talking over him had sparked irritation.

It hadn't.

"A fair observation. Though I doubt there are many who could have obtained such prestige so young without help, connections and a tremendous amount of luck. Wouldn't you agree?" The Warmaster smiled.

"I don't believe in luck," Jex muttered. It was true; luck was a concept that clashed greatly with his ideals. The thought that someone could be shaped by something that might happen on the whim of some force of fortune was ridiculous.

"What do you believe in?"

Jex didn't answer. It wasn't a case of him not wanting to converse; he just didn't have an answer to give.

What do I believe in? he thought. *I'm not sure. It seems there isn't a great deal worth believing in. What do others believe in? Luck? Gods? Fate? Does it even matter?*

"Another thing I don't know yet," Jex finally replied, somewhat bitterly. He was swiftly becoming tired of the constant probing he received.

"Different people realise what is important to them and what they believe in at different points in their lives," Maxim said. "Different events and experiences can cause those realisations to come forth. Whether they be pleasant, like the birth of a child, or unpleasant, like a death in the family. Some even come to realise amidst combat." Maxim seemed to be on a tangent, but Jex noticed that when he had mentioned combat, his tone had changed. Looking up and following Maxim's gaze, he spotted what the Warmaster was referring to.

In the distance, over a small crest of land, half a dozen heads poked out from around the littered trees. It was an ambush, and Maxim had spotted it well before anyone else.

There's one of the many reasons he was titled Warmaster at such a young age.

"Jex, I believe it is your move," Maxim smiled.

"My what?"

"Your move," the Warmaster repeated. "Unless you wish to forfeit the opportunity to claim the flow of the coming battle, I suggest you seize the momentum of the conflict before it even begins. Direct the men. Direct me."

Jex was about to protest when he realised exactly what Maxim was doing. He was giving Jex exactly what he wanted. The power to *do* something and make a mark. He wasn't going to squander it.

"Very well then." Jex turned to the knights behind him. "Shields at the ready! Rally around the carriage – I want an impenetrable wall of steel and resolve defending the carriage and its cargo!"

At first the knights all froze at the command. Surprisingly, about half of them started moving to follow the order even before Maxim nodded in affirmation. The Warmaster turned to his temporary commander with a small smile and asked, "And my orders, Sir?"

"I don't recall giving a second set of instructions," Jex replied.

"Ha! Understood!" Maxim exclaimed with a nod. Pulling at the reins, his horse took off towards the carriage to join the ranks as another link in their defence.

No sooner had the knights taken their positions than they were forced to raise their shields in response to a storm of arrows launched from the other side of the low crest. Jex was surprised to see so many of the lethal projectiles, but knew the numbers meant nothing as they collided with the thick steel shields. Jex groaned in annoyance – he hated shields. Especially when they proved their worth by protecting him. It was like the stupid thing was taunting him every time arrowhead met steel.

The barrage of projectiles resulted in a few casualties. Though the knights' training had indeed borne fruit in the way they defended themselves, many of the horses within their ranks now had sharp arrows embedded in their flesh as they fell to the ground. The soldiers knew what to do. They rolled with their falling steeds, unhooking their legs as they landed roughly on the ground. Quickly rolling away from their dead beasts, they were upright and shielded once more.

"Next move, Commander!" the Warmaster's voice rang out from the crowd that was still mounted.

Jex didn't falter. "Mounted units, I want you to charge!"

"You *want* us to charge?" Maxim scoffed. "I hope you'll say please and thank you once this is all over!"

"Enough! You *will* charge!" Jex yelled with a shake of his head. "Kill them! Subdue them only if you're certain it is safe to do so! Your lives before theirs!"

The mounted men and woman were already in motion by the time Jex had finished giving the order.

"Now THAT was a command!" Maxim roared as his steed thundered past towards the enemy.

Jex was about to join the charge when he noticed the sudden emergence of their opposition. All at once, dozens of warriors were running out from their thin cover and charging headlong at the advancing horses. Parts of their bodies were fitted with pieces of armour, but for the most part they wore the thin material usually seen on peasants.

Jex realised what had happened. These were citizens of some village that had been contracted to assault and overwhelm the company of knights. It was a feat that was almost certainly accomplishable as the dozens turned to hundreds.

Desperation... Jex thought. Jex didn't necessarily care about where they had come from or if they were regular citizens. If you attacked a company of knights, they were going to defend themselves. He realised the idea of everyday people charging them and meeting their ends triggered the same apathy he'd felt when his own village was slaughtered by Lucian.

Shouldn't I feel something more... normal?

Jex pushed the thought aside and focused on the possible reasons for the attack instead.

Someone forced their hands... They must be crushed. There were too many, but Jex charged anyway, bellowing, "Hold your position! Crush any who come close without hesitation!"

His body tingled with a sensation he'd never experienced when the air was filled with the cries of "Aye, Sir!"

The feeling was gone as quickly as it had appeared, but Jex knew he'd felt it.

You suit being in command. A voice Jex couldn't place entered his mind.

What was that? he thought, but it was already gone.

Jex didn't have time to ponder it further; he had joined the fray. The slight gradient of the hill was filled with people charging towards the knights.

The two forces collided.

Jex immediately blocked out the sounds of screams and battle cries; they were of no use to him. It was a talent he'd taught himself, an invaluable tool, to be able to ignore unimportant sounds in a skirmish.

There was only one downside.

Jex grimaced as the rhythm of countless heartbeats entered his mind.

There were a lot more than he was accustomed to. Then again, he'd usually only block out the sound around him when he was lying in bed. At most, he'd pick up the slow rhythm of his sleeping comrades' hearts. Then it was almost soothing. Now it was chaos. The peasants were terrified. It was a fair response. Despite having superior numbers and the capacity to win, a lot of them were going to die.

"What will you do now?" Maxim called out amongst the perpetual drumming as he slashed at a man who came too close to his steed. Jex hadn't even realised he'd reached the combat zone, much less that he was next to the Warmaster. Maxim's ornate longsword shone in the midday sun, glittering with diamonds as its wielder ruthlessly cut down his opponents.

He doesn't hesitate, yet he feels no joy.

Jex held his position for a moment. One of the villagers called out as they pointed towards Maxim.

"Look at 'is sword, fellas! He's their leader, I bet!"

"Damn it!" Jex cursed, but not at the hundreds of men and women now sprinting at the Warmaster. He was cursing his incompetence.

I can't think! They will overwhelm us. Do I even care? Damn it. What – do – I – want?

"We rally!" Maxim's voice echoed around the plains. Enhancing his voice was a magical ability almost every officer had. It was forbidden to lesser knights, lest the voices around the battlefield become too convoluted.

"A wise suggestion." A soft voice came from the ground beside Jex's mount, travelling despite the chaos.

"Chairman!" Jex exclaimed, looking down at the clear face of the thirty-something-year-old man. He wore a dark cloak of burgundy and pinned to his chest was the crest of the Aquiocian Council, catching the light. His silver hair was tied back in a ponytail and while his eyes were the same rare amber hue as Jex's own, the Chairman's portrayed wisdom that defied his age.

"Sir, if I could suggest –"

"You will return to the carriage. Guard it with your life. Do not touch the artefact under any circumstances."

The Chairman was whispering, yet neither Jex nor Maxim had difficulty hearing him. Jex couldn't work out why.

"Sir, I —"

"Jex, go!" Maxim ordered. "Chairman Setz has authority beyond even my own and is second only to royalty. You will obey!"

"I will obey!" Jex cried as the chain of command was established. It was almost a relief knowing exactly where he belonged, even if it was on the other end of orders. With an about turn, he was charging back towards the carriage. The only luck they'd had was the fact that their opponents didn't have horses.

"Shields up!" the men around the carriage cried, and Jex realised he was in trouble. Taking his hands off the reins, he attempted to clip the shield to his back in hopes of protecting himself from the next volley of arrows. Then his horse faltered.

Jex was on the ground before he knew it. His left arm met solid dirt with a crunch that triggered excruciating pain through his body. He weathered it well, barely emitting a sound as he was hurled to the ground. Though he could endure the pain, the shock had already begun to cloud his mind. His vision was blurred as he finally came to a stop and found himself looking up at a clear sky filled with descending arrows.

Unfortunate... Jex thought without emotion. He was more annoyed with the way he was about to die than death itself.

It was a surreal moment, as his mind threatened to succumb to shock and his death fell from above. There was no avoiding it, and he knew it. Time seemed to slow as he reflected on his life. He'd heard of seeing one's life at the moment of death, but he'd never put much stock in it.

Rightly so, he thought as he realised that all he could think about was the Princess constantly staring at him. Wherever he went around the castle or barracks, there she'd been. He was genuinely surprised he hadn't caught sight of her on his current quest.

Jex realised the arrows must have found him, that he was dying. The delirium he was experiencing must be death claiming him, because he couldn't believe what was standing over him.

There must have been half a dozen exact copies of the Chairman gathered around him. They looked over him before they turned to the sky and vanished. In their place, a cloud of smoke spread out like a blanket before engulfing his entire body.

Suddenly, the sounds of battle he'd blocked out returned as the smoke caressing him vanished too. Jex found the energy to sit up quickly, looking around in confusion. He was sitting atop the carriage. Even the knights standing guard looked up at him in surprise.

"Wh-what happened?" Jex spluttered, his head snapping towards the sky. "The arrows!"

"The smoke!" a female knight called out.

"Your arm!" a man cried. "Is it alright?"

The question was rhetorical. Jex looked down at the limb that was bent at odd angles in three places. There was blood everywhere.

"It doesn't hurt." It wasn't surprising to find he wasn't feeling the pain.

"Get inside the carriage, damn it!" a grouchy knight ordered, and Jex had to admit that it was the smartest course of action. He was useless where he was.

With the aid of a few knights, Jex was lifted from the top of the carriage and helped to climb into its confines, where he slumped onto one of the luxuriously cushioned seats. He was never one for the finer things; he'd always felt them unnecessary. But his body felt the relief supplied by the comfort he found. Looking around, he noticed the carriage was illuminated by a strange orb of light no bigger than the pommel of his sword. It hovered in the air seemingly of its own accord, offering its light to the inhabitants.

Jex sat upright and sighed, allowing a moment of tentative peace, when he noticed the viewing window at the front of the carriage. It was designed so the person inside could pull aside the cover to see what was happening outside. The windows on the side of the carriage had a similar shutter over them. Jex bounded over to the one at the front and ripped it aside to reveal the battlefield.

What he saw had him blinking rapidly, as if his eyes were trying to wipe away something that didn't belong in the spectacle before him. Judging by the number of peasants that had stormed the fields, they should have overwhelmed the knights. There were hundreds of villagers as opposed to their platoon of fifty or so men.

I wonder how many of the fifty are left. The thought crossed Jex's mind but didn't linger. He was far more interested in the dozens of doppelgangers of Setz that were constantly appearing and disappearing from the field of battle.

The clones occasionally lashed out at the unfortunate peasants, but whatever incantation Setz was using was clearly for confusing the enemy rather than slaying them. Sadly, it seemed their enemies knew that, and only redoubled their efforts in trying to overrun the knights.

Setz's magic is unreal, Jex thought. *But it might not be enough here.*

You have your own strength to call upon. The voice from the battlefield entered Jex's mind. This time it was louder; this time he couldn't mistake it for his own imagination. It was a low, almost sinister-sounding voice that somehow remained impartial to the events unfolding before Jex. Before the conversation had even begun, Jex knew that whatever the voice was, it didn't care about what was happening.

A demon, is it?

An interesting assumption, but one that is largely dependent on the person's perspective.

What would you call yourself?

One half of an ever-clashing whole.

That isn't useful.

It wasn't designed to be, the voice replied, amused.

I assume you're the cargo. Jex turned away from the battlefield and looked at the large rectangular container sitting in the middle of the carriage floor. He couldn't say he was curious, exactly, as he didn't care for the cargo itself. But he did feel a drawing sensation towards the ornate chest – or rather, what was inside it.

I'd call you perceptive, but it was an obvious conclusion.

Yes, it was. I ask again because I'm unable to open the chest – what are you?

I am one half –

Enough of the games! Jex snapped, surprised by the genuine irritation he felt. It turned out even he had his limits. *At least tell me why you're speaking to me.*

The enemy has an army, the voice stated.

That they do, Jex acknowledged grimly as he turned back to the small window to see that the peasants had multiplied again. *Where are they all coming from?*

You could hear them all, their heartbeats. You know they will keep coming. The people charging the Warmaster and Chairman will continue to grow in number. These are the souls of those living in the various villages around this area. Alone they are weak; together they swarm.

"How do you even know this?" Jex muttered out loud.

I have a similar talent, though I hear the hum of their souls rather than the beat of their hearts.

Similar? There is someone like me?

Indeed.

Jex was finally curious despite himself. He preferred the indifference he had become accustomed to feeling. It was a struggle to return to the issue at hand rather than playing the voice's mind games.

"Unless you have a suggestion on how to deal with this situation, I do not wish to waste my time speaking with something I'm forbidden to interact with," Jex said. He didn't know why, but speaking aloud added an air of finality.

There was a long moment of silence before the voice dragged Jex's attention back.

I do.

CHAPTER 27

A SQUIRE'S TEMPTATION

"You want me to *what*?" Jex exclaimed, looking around quickly. Though it didn't seem the carriage had let the sound escape, he remained concerned that the knights outside would hear his conversation. He knew that whatever was speaking to him could read thoughts directed towards it, but he hated the idea of talking on its level. Whatever "it" was.

Wield me, the voice repeated.

Perplexed, Jex weighed his options as he stared out at the steadily tiring Chairman. Setz was at the centre of the fray; the peasants surrounded them, forming a semi-circle upon the hill. His doppelgangers had formed a wall of shadows to repel the enemies and their assaults. Though effective, every now and then one or two would push through and kill one of the copies, which would detonate into a cloud of smoke before reforming. Anytime one of the civilians made their way through, they'd be cut down by Maxim before they could get to the cloaked man he was guarding with his life.

The Warmaster was the only man left on their side, and he proved himself to be a veritable wall of cerulean steel. Though it was a herculean effort, Jex knew the villagers wouldn't stop until the two men in the centre were crushed, despite being able to turn and seize the cargo. They had their targets, and they weren't strategists.

I don't even know what you are. How am I to wield you?

Open the container and it will be made clear.

I am forbidden to do so.

Are you also forbidden to save your leaders? To save your comrades? I know you don't particularly care for their lives, but I never thought you were the kind of person who would sit and do nothing.

Jex knew he was being manipulated, but he took solace in the fact that it was exactly what he wanted to happen. Yet again he found himself in a situation where he had no idea what to do. To have a direction pointed out to him was nothing short of a gift.

Wielding you. Is it so simple? Jex asked as his hands found the clips securing the container and the feeling of desire grew. *I wield you, save my people and put you away?*

That is what you are about to attempt, is it not?

Part of him warned against what he did next, but he didn't care. Lifting the surprisingly heavy lid upwards revealed the inside of the container, which was lined with a violet cloth that glowed ever so faintly. Jex recognised it for what it was: an enchanted cloth designed to keep magical artefacts in check. The artefact that lay inside was a longsword with a blade the colour of obsidian. The silver hilt was encrusted with rubies right up to the guard that elegantly folded around its wielder's hand. The blade was three-and-a-half feet of pitch darkness that moved with the light being emitted from the orb floating around the carriage. The metal extended out from the hilt in a perfect display of symmetry, despite the fact that it appeared to be in constant motion.

The thing that surprised Jex most about the weapon wasn't the unique materials and craftsmanship that evidently went into its creation. What drew him in was the sight of a crimson ribbon coiling itself around the weapon, like a serpent making its way up the length of a tree branch. The colour of the strange material contrasted against the onyx-black blade as it constantly made its way to the tip of the weapon, only to disappear and start its journey from the pommel once more. It was a continuous and seemingly self-defeating purpose, but it was one that Jex found himself enthralled by.

The ribbon reaches its goal only to begin anew. What a redundant purpose. It is as if its only goal is to exist. It wants to exist forever, even if only in this state of limbo. This ribbon reminds me of so many people I have met. Demanding their right to linger in this world, and yet never doing anything with the gift of their existence. I loathe that.

I can still hear you, the voice interrupted with amusement. *Wield me and make your mark.*

Jex found himself smirking as his left arm stretched out for the artefact before him. He didn't even realise it was his broken arm that was reaching for the prize. The warnings of the Chairman and everyone else faded from his mind.

I will.

❖

Jex's crippled hand wrapped around the hilt of the blade and the response was instant. The pain in his arm vanished briefly, only to return in excruciating waves a moment later. The brutal sensation shot up his arm, lingering on each of its breaks and fractures as they melded back into their original state. Jex felt his lungs burning – he was screaming. For the first time in his life he couldn't suppress or ignore the pain he was in, and he was terrified.

I don't understand! his mind wailed as he slumped back in his chair, his eyes rolling to the roof of the carriage. *What is going on?*

In his panic, Jex saw that the crimson ribbon was no longer coursing across the blade. Instead it was now bound to his wrist, effectively tying him and the weapon together. The blade glowed with thin tendrils of darkness and even the red jewels were alive with energy. By grabbing the weapon, he'd brought it to life. Now, as he screamed from the agony spreading through his body, the blade was well and truly in control. It could kill him if it so chose, and it certainly seemed its intention.

Through the pain, he heard a familiar voice bellow a single word directly into his mind.

FOOL!

Chairman? A single clear thought rang out from amongst the anguish.

Jex had no time to think about the implications of Setz knowing of his disobedience as the pain consumed his thoughts.

Why are you doing this? he mentally screamed at the blade.

Consider it my toll in exchange for my power. I suggest you utilise it before your body and soul give out.

The words were cold, but they broke through. Jex knew what he had to do. Clarity filled his mind as he finally stifled the wails he was emitting. The pain was still there, and he could feel his body being burnt away from within, but he was going to make it count. As he slowly pushed the pain to the side of his mind, he felt the power surging within him. The more of the pain he ignored, the more he could tap into the power and understand its nature and strength. It was sinister – Jex knew that. But it was fair. It hadn't lied about what would happen; it simply hadn't mentioned the repercussions. Knowing that as the wielder, he wouldn't have cared anyway.

How can I care so little if I live or die and yet still want to make my mark on the world?

Jex banished the thoughts and called his new power to the surface with a flick of his restored wrist. The blade erupted with a burst of sinister light that blew the roof of the carriage skyward. The knights who had been listening to the screams saw a figure cloaked in shadows launch through the sky towards the fray, like a bird of prey shrouded in corruption. The knights taking cover from the sudden destruction of the carriage knew who it must have been, though no one on the battlefield who saw the dark entity soaring towards the sky could know what had happened.

Jex still felt the agony gnawing at his entire body, though it had dulled. He knew he could only suppress it for so long and that after his will to ignore it gave out, he'd be overwhelmed and crushed from the inside out. Glancing quickly at his wrist, he saw that the ribbon had expanded up his entire arm, scorching the flesh and skin around it to a mess of cauterised wounds and infected blood. As Jex defied gravity and approached the field of battle, he knew it was his left arm that would be first to rot away.

I hope it takes the rest of me with it.

Jex was surprised for a moment by the fact that he wasn't scared of flying at all. He had to be at least a hundred feet in the air, yet he had full faith that he would land unharmed. He couldn't work out if it was self-assurance or a side effect of the blade's power, but he felt mostly at ease. Even the ravenous pain waiting in the corner of his mind for its chance to devour him was of little concern; he was about to make a mark. His mark.

BOOM!

The earth rattled with the impact as Jex finally made his landing. Countless men and women from each side were lifted right into the air by the force of the man crouching in the centre of the blast zone, his sword impaling the turf beneath him. Pillars of negative light burst from the earth below, rupturing soil and soul as every human who wasn't a conduit of the dark energy perished immediately. It didn't stop the flow of mindless men and women who were now rushing Jex at the sight of the blade. Their courage might have surprised him if he could feel anything but loathing for them.

"Death awaits you," Jex muttered towards his enemies as the tendrils of darkness surrounding the blade began to encompass his entire body.

A fine attitude, the blade said approvingly.

Jex barely exerted himself as he lifted the blade into a backswing. The air before him was sliced through by the same light that had offered him temporary flight. The moment the light found each of the peasants, their skin succumbed and their flesh ruptured as they were cut in twain by the guillotine of the blade's raw power. The weapon's discharge flew into the distance before finally fading away.

The rest of the people watching on as hundreds of their allies were dismembered and mutilated by the evil light suddenly halted, reconsidering their charge. But it was too late.

"More," Jex ordered softly.

As you wish, the blade answered smugly as its wielder felt another burst of the nightmarish energy and the pain intensified.

"Insignificant dogs," Jex grunted as he grimaced at the now fleeing men and women. "Perish."

The blade lifted from his side, its tip pointing directly at the dense crowd that was tripping over itself in its attempt to run away. The blade knew what to do; another blast of dark light akin to the one that destroyed the carriage exploded from the peculiar metal. The blast met the fleeing people with the force of a ballista bolt, powerful enough to puncture a castle wall. The blast travelled further than Jex could see, not slowed by the pitiful resistance of those who were in his way. What he did see was hundreds upon hundreds of people meeting their ends as their bodies gave out and dissolved in the detonation of darkness.

Seems you have a gift for slaughter, perhaps even one for genocide. A pity that your body will not survive the hour; I could have used someone like you, the blade said, almost apologetically.

You need someone like me? Simple. Stop this process of destruction within my body and we can arrange something. I've long since wanted to find my calling, my reason for existing. Perhaps this is it.

I'm afraid that is impossible. Your body cannot withstand this onslaught, and if you must know, I am not deliberately doing this. Furthermore...

Jex realised the blade was hesitating. *Furthermore... What?*

You are – how to say – unsuitable.

Jex's amber eyes widened behind the aura of shadows before hardening again.

"Unsuitable? I've been told that before," he sneered. "Allow me to show you who is unsuitable."

Jex was grinning despite the rejection. It was the same dismissive response he'd received from Lucian. The difference here was that he wasn't a helpless child. Now he was powerful, and he felt unstoppable. While he knew it to be only temporary, he wanted to make the most of it.

Grasping at the energy with his mind, the tendrils of darkness began to recede inside him. The torn ground beneath him began to shake as he drew more and more of the blade's power unto himself. The pain was becoming unbearable. With each second the agony threatened to topple him, and he knew that he had reached a completely new level of strength from the energy within him. For those few moments, he oversaw his fate, and though it was a grim one, he relished the freedom and the choice.

"Have you regained control?" a man's voice cried out, filled with a mix of authority and trepidation. Jex looked up and noticed that Maxim was standing ten yards away from him, approaching cautiously with his arm outstretched as though trying to reach something. The man was covered in blood and grime, but aside from being riddled with fatigue, he seemed fine.

"Warmaster..." Jex muttered the title, but Maxim heard him without issue. They were the only people for hundreds of yards now; Jex could have whispered.

"That's right, my friend!" Maxim nodded. "It is I. You need

to drop that weapon or the curse will take your life. I am not returning to Aquiocia without you!"

Jex laughed. "I am a dead man already. You know more about this sword than I do; you should know that I will die here."

Maxim nodded grimly. "I know it to be a very real possibility. But I can't leave a soldier behind. It isn't how I run things, my friend."

"Stop – calling – me – a friend!" Jex's aura flashed and the earth's rumbling intensified. "I am a soldier, nothing more. And I'm going to make this count!"

"This lunacy is a side effect of the blade, Jex!" Maxim pleaded, barely staying upright on the shuddering land. "But if you release that energy, you will kill thousands of innocent people!"

"Innocent? Those pathetic mutts attacked us!"

"Jex, I refuse to believe you are a fool. We both know that something wasn't right about the way they attacked. I need you to rally yourself here, soldier. I need you to regain control!" Maxim's voice stuttered from the shaky foothold he was trying to establish.

"No. This..." Jex looked down at the blade with a cruel smile. The ground began to shake so violently that Maxim was knocked off his feet. "This is my mark."

Maxim's sense of hearing failed him as everything fell to silence. The very atmosphere around him felt like it was being dragged inward towards Jex before a stillness washed over the solitary pair. Everything felt like it was moving at a tenth of the speed it should, from the smile flickering across Jex's face to the stored energy emerging from his being, blazing forth in all directions like a dome of shadows and darkness. In the fleeting moments before the energy hit him, Maxim swore he could see the shadows of countless wolves in the haze of darkness tearing towards him. He couldn't react when a cloaked figure appeared before him. Maxim's body vanished, and the figure was engulfed by the sinister explosion.

The energy ripped up the land for leagues in all directions. Trees, hills, people – everything was immediately eradicated by its brutal influence. When it dispersed, all that remained was Jex, who was only standing because his body had seized up in absolute agony. It felt as though countless more explosions were detonating throughout his body. He couldn't move, breathe or do what he desired most – scream. The insufferable anguish coursing through him was seconds away from petrifying him in a state of perpetual torment. Through the trauma, Jex barely noticed the cloaked man appear directly before him. The man's face was bleeding from countless lacerations and most of his cloak was missing. What remained was unbound silver hair that had fallen free across his bloodied face and his critical amber eyes.

"Know this, Jex," Setz said softly. "If it wasn't for my loyalty to the crown, I would let this blade devour your soul entirely. I would watch it take shred after shred until absolute chaos reigned free in the last dregs of your mind and body. I would not offer you the mercy of a true death until you atoned for every person who died at your hand today, by having those same soul-starved wolves gnaw at the very essence that gave you life. Remember that when you awaken in your new and well-deserved lodgings. The King and Queen of Aquiocia are the *only* reason I am not abandoning you to be tortured for an eternity that would outlast the gods."

Setz's words were cold, but Jex understood their meaning well, despite his mind screaming over them. The Chairman's hand waved across his eyes; the pain dulled and Jex's body was finally released from its position, allowing him the relief of collapsing onto the upheaved soil. He barely registered the blade's ribbon releasing his wrist as he coughed up blood and finally lost consciousness.

CHAPTER 28

A LIFE FOR A CHANCE

"I assume you are ready?" Setz's cold voice filled Keenin's ears.

The assassin elite had returned to brief his master on the preparations and found him standing in the middle of an abandoned street. The order for the Underbelly's citizens to remain in their dwellings had been given, and he had been ensuring it was adhered to. It quickly became obvious to Keenin that Setz wasn't interested in hearing anything further than that the men were ready to strike.

He was far more concerned about the Princess he had allowed to leave his care.

"I am. But where is the Princess?" Keenin asked hesitantly.

"I don't recall questioning me as being part of your job," Setz replied, so softly that Keenin had to strain his ears to hear the words. The venom in them, however, was exceptionally clear.

"I apologise. What would you have me do?"

"Word has been received that the castle is empty save for the remaining Council members and a few stray knights. Granted, these are not men who are directly bound to me, but the bulk of the Aquiocian force is either coming back through the main gates or manning the walls. The civilians are either hiding inside their houses or have been moved to other enclosures." Setz finally glanced at his underling. "Rufus has done something foolish, enabling Alicea to do something worse."

"Would you have me intercept her?"

"I would have you lead the assembled men to the surface. Their job is to meld with the shadows. Strike down only those who seek to harm our people, succumb to the curse, or seem to be about to stumble on our plan," Setz ordered. "They will spread through the city, but your presence is not to be known. If you locate the Princess, you will apprehend her."

"By force?"

"Short of killing or maiming her, yes," Setz confirmed, still gazing down the empty paths. "The men will have to use force to some degree, as Her Highness has become a lot stronger over the passing months."

"You're speaking as though I will have a different job to the rest of the men," Keenin noted quietly.

Setz didn't reply. Was he hesitating?

"Sir, may I speak freely?"

This made the Guildmaster turn and look over his underling. Keenin had never requested to speak freely. After a moment of thought, Setz nodded slightly.

"This is the first time the men will emerge inside the walls of Aquiocia in over a year. What did you mean by saying I will lead them?"

Setz's scarred face didn't flinch at the question.

"Your target is in the royal chambers. Something hidden in the bedside table of the false King. I'm uncertain exactly what the target will be, but you will know it when you see it."

"I will retrieve –"

"You will destroy it immediately," Setz interrupted, his voice lowering.

"Very well. And Rufus?"

"If you manage to find him after you complete your task, you will likely find the Princess. They have spoken many times of dreams she has been having. But our information is incomplete, and it appears that she only shared the details of the dreams with Rufus," Setz explained. His next words had the tone of a man holding something back. "It was an oversight on my behalf, one I should have pursued further…"

Keenin waited a long moment for his master to continue.

Surely there's more to this…

"Meet with Rufus' party, defend them in their efforts to reach their target, and then immediately disengage to pursue your own target in the royal chambers. That will be your part in all of this."

"Understood. Is it now safe to enter Aquiocia?"

Those were the final words spoken between them. As Setz produced a long, thick hunting knife from his cloak, a bittersweet smile clawed its way onto Keenin's face. Taking the brutal weapon, he took a knee like a man swearing allegiance, before rising and walking away from his master.

For what it's worth, I'm sorry. Setz watched his subordinate disappear into the shadows. *My consolation is knowing that you are not.*

CHAPTER 29

KNOW THY ENEMY

There's one... Lyrium thought, crouching amongst a mess of brush and trees. *And another, and another!*

Lyrium continually spotted glints of metal in the distance within the forest's confines, but whenever she caught sight of one of the enemy soldiers, they disappeared. She was in one of the deeper sections of forest the Tremel force currently occupied, but for none of the soldiers to reach her was unnerving. With a glance at the dozen or so birds hiding in a tree behind her, she was taking a moment to stretch her cramped limbs when an Aquiocian soldier stepped out from behind a tree.

The soldier froze at the sight of her, as if expecting something bad to happen to him just by making eye contact. Lyrium could see a very real fear in the blue eyes behind the silver helm before they hardened, and the man took a step towards her.

No sooner had he made the move than a vine wrapped around his ankle and his body was lifted six feet into the air, smashing his head into a large rock on the way up. His helmet fell away, revealing a dazed knight with a large bruise growing up the side of his face.

Lyrium knew there were countless traps spread throughout the forest, though she was surprised to see one so close to her.

It explained why very few soldiers were even getting through, but was also proof she had lost focus. Looking around, she made out a few more traps hidden within her proximity. She'd completely left the real world, lost in her own thoughts, residing far away from what was going on around her.

She knew she shouldn't move too far, lest she fall into one of the traps designed to protect her. Being young, and having been thrown into the teachings of a shaman instead of hunting, her knowledge of traps was somewhat lacking compared to the man now crashing down next to her.

"Arok." Lyrium greeted her lover with a swift kiss on the cheek.

"That's me." Arok grinned, looking around. "There are traps set all around us, so we should be safe for the moment, unless the whole damned army comes directly for us!"

"Have you received any news on how the battle is going?"

"Aye. A few of the enemy have been taken out, but a lot more captured. Just the one legion at this point. They are clueless – guess they expected a straight-out battle."

"Well, that's good news. Alicea's plan is working!"

"Aye, for now," Arok agreed quietly.

Lyrium barely noticed his solemn look in her own soaring hope. Everyone, herself included, had hesitated at the Princess taking charge. She hated herself for doubting her friend, but the Princess had only picked up a weapon for the first time a few months ago, and now she was leading an assault on her own kingdom. It was true that her friend had been training in arts of combat and magic, but Lyrium wondered just how much she could have learnt in the time she had spent with the other Chiefs.

She exhaled slowly and focused on the positives, trying to quash her reservations. Despite her inexperience, Alicea had called every move their opponents had made well before they'd made it. A legion had indeed charged out the front gates upon hearing rumours and "sightings" of the Princess. She had successfully predicted that Arissam's blustering nature would order them to charge the forest and gain the upper hand while his enemy "rested" from the trip. As a result of his brash order, hundreds of men had already been captured and trapped within massive pits hollowed out by shamans and guarded by hunters and assassins. More pits were being prepared as the existing were filled.

Alicea's words echoed through her head. *The forest is your home, and the assassins reside in the shadows of its floral canopy. Why would I hamper our odds of success by making you leave?*

Lyrium grinned at the memory of Dairok's face when he'd first heard the plan, and then again when it was implemented. "Attacking by defending?" he had scoffed, only to roar the same words with outright enthusiasm when he saw that it was working. Alicea herself hadn't seen the barbarian's change in attitude, as she had left the battlefield quickly to pursue her own part of the plan.

Whatever that might be.

"What's wrong?" Lyrium asked Arok softly. He shifted uncomfortably.

"Garnet. I talked to her while I was laying the traps," Arok began, taking a deep breath. "She doesn't think the Princess' plan is going to last."

"Why not?"

"She thinks there are too many variables, or something."

Arok frowned. "She said they will likely retreat soon and regroup, or worse."

"What did she mean, worse?" Lyrium asked, already knowing the answer. "They will activate the curse again!"

Arok nodded grimly. "Aye."

The pair fell silent at the thought of the curse taking hold of their enemies again. Last time they had been lucky; they had thrown their weapons into the swampland created by the melding of Lyrium and Alicea's magic. But the enemy was well and truly armed this time. Alicea outright refused to address her people, knowing full well that should she attempt to appeal to them, Jex would activate the curse. He had done it before – why not again?

It was best to leave them thinking they had hope of finding her.

So long as I don't address them, they will storm the forest thinking I'm your captive. It is unlikely that Arissam will give any orders to the contrary, as he is an angry and brash man. The second I address either of them and make it known to the soldiers that I am acting of my own accord, they will activate the curse, and I can't estimate the number of casualties that will result in. We will allow their façade to remain in place. No, we will reinforce it for them. Then we will shatter it.

"Oh, there is one other bad thing you should know," Arok muttered, clearly not liking what he was about to tell her.

"What is it?"

"He's been seen on the field of battle. He ain't real aggressive yet, but he is there."

"Does Alicea know?"

"They have sent word."

"Then we must have faith."

"Aye. We must place our trust in Gaia." Arok's face steeled as he stared dead ahead.

CHAPTER 30

MISLED INFANTRY

Garnet's body grew and altered as she underwent her transformation from feathered to human form. Naked and exposed, she was handed a long garment, which she swung over her head and across her body before addressing the gaping hole in the ground before her, expanding across what was once a peaceful clearing.

The chasm was four men deep, its edge surrounded by a mix of burly hunters and mages from the various tribes of Tremel.

The hole was filled with hundreds of Aquiocian soldiers, some of whom had begun to return to a conscious state. Garnet had been making her rounds to the numerous makeshift prisons the people of Tremel had crafted under the order of the Princess. The old woman had to concede that so far, the Princess' plans had worked marvellously.

These soldiers had all been trapped by the mages' magic, the superior strength of the Tremel warriors, or the crafty traps littered throughout the forest by the hunters. All the victims were relocated to one of these holes, which were watched closely by Dairok and his men.

While it was a suitable task for the barbarians, their hospitality towards their prisoners was somewhat lacking. This often meant it fell to Garnet to speak, on behalf of both the prisoners' wardens and the Princess herself.

By the time Garnet reached the edge of the pit, some of the soldiers were already in uproar as they attempted to awaken their comrades and scale the dirt walls of their prisons. Some of them managed to make some headway up the walls, only to be pushed back down, all the while threatening and swearing at their captives.

"If you have enough energy to curse and carry on, then you have enough energy to close your mouths and listen!" Garnet's magically enhanced voice boomed across the dirt-crafted prison.

"What do you savages plan to do with us?" one of the knights screamed.

"Nothing at all," Garnet replied, causing the captives to fall silent. "Listening now, are we?"

"Tell us why we have been taken prisoner!" the same man demanded. Garnet took a closer look at him.

He was wearing a different helmet to the others. On each side of the helm there were steel wings, serving no purpose but decoration. *Or to show rank*, Garnet concluded. *He is probably a squad leader at the very least.*

"The answer to that is very simple: because the Princess wishes you no harm!" she finally responded.

"Bah!" the soldier scoffed. "You expect us to believe the savages who took our Princess hostage and wish to overthrow our kingdom care what she wants?"

It was the same story she had heard from every visit to the containments. Those in charge didn't need the curse to brainwash the soldiers anymore. The Council of Aquiocia had succeeded in convincing them that the people of Tremel were criminals, responsible for the disappearance of their Princess. Who could blame them for believing it?

"As I have told many of your fellow soldiers already, that is not the truth. In fact, we fight for the Princess at this very moment!" Garnet's words had no sooner left her mouth than the soldiers were in uproar. They had taken insult.

"Let us see her, then!" one voice rang through.

"Stop with the lies and release Her Highness, Princess Alicea!" a female voice called.

"Enough!" Garnet's voice boomed through the forest again and the soldiers fell silent, watching and waiting.

After a moment, Garnet elected to speak once more. This time, however, she was a lot quieter and far more forceful.

"I do not care what you believe," she began in an icy tone that made some of the knights squirm. "I do not lose any sleep over what ignorant lackeys think of me, or my people. But if your faith in Princess Alicea has faltered so much that you believe she would be our captive, then you are in for a surprise."

"We only want our Princess to return to us safely!" the first man replied, slightly humbled.

"Then I suggest you restore your faith in her!" Garnet snapped. "For she is no more our prisoner than I am your enemy. We care about this land, but our affections are miniscule compared to her love for her people and for all of us. So sit down and be quiet. I must go and tend to the woman you claim you are all here for!"

Garnet did not wait for a response before she shifted into the form of a crow, her robe dropping to the ground as she flew into the trees and out of view.

The soldiers looked to one another in unease, their eyes all turning to the man who had been their voice. With a sigh, he said, "At ease. We await word from our Princess!"

"Aye!" the soldiers chorused.

CHAPTER 31

SHAMANS OF TWO GENERATIONS

Silrok sniffed as a crow landed on the rock beside her. The acting Chief of the northern forces had taken a position on the north-eastern outskirts of the forest, effectively the hinterlands of Aquiocia's gaze. While by no means the edge of the kingdom's reach, she was content knowing that no one was likely to see her here, perched cross-legged on the high branch of a magnificent tree.

Her eyes resembled pools of ink as she watched over the Aquiocian plains, where the soldiers had marched forward and been captured. She had been surprised by the thousand men who'd emerged from the main gates, following an order issued by a man who had promptly disappeared into their ranks.

She had expected more troops. Instead, a single legion had formed and marched on the forests. She had also expected a far grander display of authority from the figurehead. Silrok had heard countless stories about the Aquiocian armies. They were brave and loyal to a fault, but their leaders were susceptible to ostentatious attire and grand boasting, regardless of the way Gaia's favour leant on the battlefield. Yet the man named Jex had become one with the soldiers so fluidly that even Silrok couldn't keep track of him.

Her first assumption had been that Jex intended to locate the Princess and surprise her, as he had done in the last battle. She had heard the story and critiqued it at length, despite knowing that Jex wasn't a run-of-the-mill adversary in a skirmish. Having never met him in combat, she could only form an opinion from the history she'd heard from others. Even someone as critical of stories as she was had to admit he sounded like someone who shouldn't be underestimated.

"Your Princess' plan has started out well enough. We will have our prisoners soon," Silrok said to the crow beside her as she watched the plains steadily clear. Their numbers dwindled as they made it to the forest's edge, and the authorities of Aquiocia seemed uninterested in sending more.

She has the Aquiocian eye for warfare, Garnet acknowledged.

"I pray Gaia does not let that eye lead her the same way it led her parents."

It is on that note that I've come to you, Garnet revealed. Silrok's eyebrow rose a fraction but her attention never left the battlefield. *Alicea and Rufus have gone underground.*

"Was that not in the original plan? One would think being hidden away with criminals would offer her great cover."

It would, except that I don't believe she is with Setz anymore.

That got the northern shaman's attention. With a blink, her eyes returned to their almond hue and focused directly on the bird sitting next to her. Despite her immediate dread, Silrok kept her voice low. Although she was hidden away in the thick foliage of the tree's branches and leaves, she didn't want the half dozen hunters below them to overhear a conversation between those of command.

"Then *where* is she?" Silrok hissed.

I am uncertain –

"Unacceptable!" Silrok exclaimed, quickly realising that her voice was too loud and reaching out with her mind instead. Gently, Garnet's own consciousness welcomed the northern Chief into a private and silent conversation.

The Princess is the only reason we are here. That insolent child cannot just go off on her own in times of war!

I understand your frustration, Silrok, Garnet conceded, allowing her to vent for a moment before adopting a firmer tone. *I believe I know where she went. I intend on finding her.*

You'd leave the ranks of your own people for her? Silrok snapped incredulously.

I'd leave the ranks of my own people in your hands to retrieve the entire reason we are here, yes, Garnet replied evenly.

She'd known Silrok would be the most difficult to convince; that was why she had approached her directly, rather than sending the quick mental message she'd relayed to Kurok and Dairok. Despite the recipients being unable to respond, she had sensed their immediate surprise and then their dismissal of the issue. Kurok knew Garnet would only ever do what was for the best, and from what she had gathered of Dairok, he didn't rightly care what she did.

Now, the furious acting Chief was glaring at Garnet with a loathing that faded steadily as she processed the information.

"Fine." Silrok had verbalised the word. It was obvious to them both that she did so to distance herself from the intimate nature of a private telepathic conversation. It wasn't surprising – such a means of communicating felt like being crammed into a chest together, with walls of both parties' thoughts pressing in on them.

Fine?

"Leave."

Silrok, I will tell you what I've told Alicea many times – I have precious little time for tantrums. Speak your mind.

The younger woman hesitated, shifting slightly on her perch.

"You knew her mother – the Queen. Adele," Silrok spat out, clearly not savouring Garnet's mothering tone.

I did. What of it?

"Does she know?" Silrok asked quietly, her eyes turning dark as she examined the plain again. The Aquiocian ranks were even thinner; she wondered if it was due to the brewing storm.

Does it matter? Is that really what you wanted to ask?

"I suppose not. What I'd really like to know is whether you'd have done all this had you not known the late Queen."

No, Garnet replied firmly. Silrok's eyes snapped to her just in time to see her feathered form ruffle in discomfort.

Had she hit a nerve?

I most certainly would not have done all of this under other circumstances, Garnet elaborated. *But Silrok, you need to understand that knowing Adele personally is but a fraction of the reason I'm here. I understand your prejudice towards mages and I understand that it's exacerbated by the fact that Alicea is a Vassal.*

Silrok opened her mouth to interject but closed it immediately.

But this goes so much further than Adele and Alicea. The Queen saw this coming for a long time. She might not have known the threat's identity, but she knew its nature. She put her faith in Alicea, for good reason – she is exceptionally gifted. But you need to trust her.

TRUST HER? Silrok blasted Garnet telepathically. *Trust the woman who just ran off on her own in the middle of a war centred around her living or dying? Have you completely lost your mind?*

Garnet spread her wings suddenly and took to the sky, leaving the fuming Chief behind.

Trust her, Silrok.

CHAPTER 32

THE LAST STOKER

Temperance's lips pursed at each new sight she passed.

They had left Chase at the blown-out archway that was once a grand doorway to a wealthy home, now left as dust and ash in its perpetual cursed existence. Chase had protested being left behind again, but a quick reassuring smile from Temperance silenced him as she descended a dark stairwell that presumedly led to a basement or cellar.

The stairs had been steep, taking the pair over five minutes of silent descent to finally reach the bottom. Now they walked a well-lit corridor lined with hundreds of torches held by the stone hands of humanoid statues. The statues weren't the main attractions of the tour, nor were they depicted as aiding those walking the halls so much as illuminating the images of dragons behind them. Every dozen or so steps revealed a new display of a man using the light of his torch to examine the exquisite murals and it tugged at Temperance's heart to continue walking.

After another few minutes, Temperance finally spoke.

"This passage..." she began slowly, the Nameless almost falling over himself in excitement at her voice.

"Yes, My Flame?"

"This passage is untouched by the curse," Temperance said

with finality, as though she was deciding on an answer in a test.

"YES!" the Nameless crowed so loudly that Temperance's stomach fluttered. The sudden noise echoed up and down the corridor.

"The flames didn't reach below the city, then," she continued with her theory, stifling her unease by looking at each of the images in turn as they walked past. "Which means there might have been survivors – people of Scourge who weren't cursed by the rage of the dragon."

"Indeed." A new voice shocked Temperance and her eyes snapped forward.

She hadn't realised they had been approaching the end of their stroll underground. Before her was an enormous cavern opening up to reveal a perfectly crafted dome beneath the surface. Her eyes widened in wonder at the faint crimson glow that hovered across the singular wall that encompassed them, offering light to everything within. As Temperance stepped inside, she was careful to note that the corridor's path did not expand in width upon reaching the chamber, instead staying the course to a circular plateau in its centre. Below the platform was a massive pool of crimson essence, reaching just below the lip of stone they were standing on.

Once she was certain she wasn't about to wander off the path, Temperance allowed herself a few moments to take in the mural surrounding her. She realised that the image started from the entrance and panned right, following the wall's surface around until it met with its origin. Her cursory analysis revealed that it was a timeline of Scourge's history, something of great interest to her – but it would have to wait.

The newcomer spoke once more.

"Good morning, My Flame," the voice offered.

Temperance immediately noticed the difference between this voice and that of the other Nameless. It held none of the rasp nor the labour the other man struggled with. Next, she saw that only the left side of the newcomer's face was scorched with the same painful burns that now existed on Chase's left hand. The man was clad in a shiny, almost royal-red robe that hung only from his unharmed right shoulder. Sewn amongst the robe's fabric on his right was a scabbard housing a short sword, though it appeared more ornamental than anything.

"There were those untouched by the flames of the dragon; they were not offered the same extension of their lives as the vast majority," the man continued with a chuckle. "Look at me, speaking as though this curse was a gift."

Temperance elected not to respond. She couldn't help but sense the man wished to speak more than he desired to listen.

"The statues you saw." He waved towards the corridor from which Temperance had emerged, smiling coyly. "I suppose someone as perceptive as you can hazard a guess as to where those untouched by the flames are now?"

Temperance knew. The thought had crossed her mind the second she'd laid eyes upon the statues in the corridor.

The man loosed a satisfied sigh before turning away from her and looking up at the centre of the cylindrical mural. Temperance followed his gaze to a particular point on Scourge's timeline. It wasn't hard to discern what he wished her to see as her gaze fell upon the image of a woman shrouded in flames, hovering above the panicked faces of the people below.

"Oh my…" Temperance uttered her first words as the image came to life and the enraged woman rained a storm of flame down on the fleeing victims.

With a flash before Temperance's eyes, the mural became all too real, revealing the brave mages of the past attempting to combat the tormented Vassal. Her vision swirled, and her perspective changed. Suddenly, she was watching the mages launch their fiery spells directly at her. Fear welled within her before it was crushed by a fury that was not her own. The mages' spells were absorbed and returned to their casters with far more ferocity.

She saw a woman carrying two young children, screaming and running from their house seconds before they detonated. It took Temperance a moment to realise the explosions were caused by her own hands, coated in incandescent fury. Those who didn't succumb to the flames within their homes were rewarded with the inferno that was their city. The flames leapt between their houses, bounding around the scorched streets. Each new spark erupted into furious plumes of the Vassal's rage. Those who made it to the city's edge were met with a wall of searing essence reaching to the sky.

The brave charged the wall and were immediately thrown back, a new set of inextinguishable flames engulfing them. The clever erected barriers around themselves, only to be crushed under the sheer might of the Vassal's magical energy before joining their kin writhing on the ground.

High above the labyrinthine inferno that was the city of Scourge, the Vassal of old and Temperance herself wailed in agony as one. Temperance could feel the rage within the Vassal as she endured the terrified screams of those being burnt alive around her. Temperance barely collected herself in time to avoid becoming enraged herself. It was only the knowledge that what she was seeing had to be a collection of memories that enabled her to keep herself in a state of strained calm.

It didn't stop her senses heightening in empathy for the past Vassal. She'd felt that same rage, that same overwhelming compulsion to destroy everything and everyone around her. She had heard those screams.

Not again. Temperance's resolve denied the possibility, and she found herself staring up at the mural again.

The Vassal glared at her through the image and Temperance felt her judgement. She was being looked over, like a prized beast reviewed by an appraiser. Then she was done, and the whole scene was enveloped in a white-orange blaze that scoured it from existence and returned the mural to its original, motionless state.

It took Temperance several moments to look away from the mural and back to her host, who was already observing her reaction. Part of her hesitance to tear her eyes away was curiosity. How could she not be interested in the secrets it clearly housed? The other part was anxiety – what she saw had deeply shaken her. It had been terrifying to be engulfed by the power of the stone now housed within her; it was worse still to witness the destruction firsthand, however briefly.

"Scary, yes?" the man chortled, as Temperance's eyebrows rose behind her spectacles.

"Scary?" Temperance found her voice. "Yes, I suppose on some far-off plane the word 'scary' might begin to cover the nature of what I just saw – what they experienced..."

"What *we* experienced," the man corrected, taking a step off the platform and onto the crimson wisps of light. A shroud of luminous essence gathered beneath his feet, allowing him to walk upon it towards the beginning of the mural.

"You were there," Temperance said. "Though you appear to have suffered fewer burns."

"Correct, though I suffered enough to be awarded this persistent atrocity that some in this city still call a life."

The man continued to wander across the pool of essence as his words echoed throughout the chamber. Somehow, despite the things he was uttering, Temperance didn't feel that he was bitter. Annoyed, perhaps, and almost certainly perplexed. But not bitter.

"Who are you?"

"I'm one of the Nameless."

"Who *were* you?"

The man shot Temperance a smile.

"I had you brought here to speak about your plans to extract the stone within you."

The man had sidestepped the question, but after several weeks of being in Scourge and receiving little to no information on the stone itself, Temperance allowed it.

"You must be concerned," he said suddenly, his voice solemn. "I've heard from many that you've been asking about the stone at every chance. I know the decision to extract it wasn't a simple one; and while the Nameless are not one to question Our Flame's word, might I ask *why* you'd wish to remove it? I assure you the process is quite dangerous, even should it work."

"I would think that the people of Scourge would know better

than most," Temperance countered. "The Nameless have seen the chaos firsthand on two different occasions."

The man smiled again and Temperance had to stop herself from scowling.

"Indeed, they have!" His full voice echoed throughout the grand cavern as he gestured towards the expansive mural.

"Why would I want to keep it?" Temperance asked coolly. Information was being withheld and the scholar within her loathed it.

The man turned back with the same pleased expression and Temperance could feel herself growing nervous. She hated not having the answers; it was part of what made her so great at anything remotely related to history – she didn't quit until she knew the secrets and people were asking *her* the questions.

"There's a difference between then and now. There are some similarities between the Conjuration of Scourge and the Vassal's Awakening; I'm sure you can hazard a guess as to what one of them might be."

"They were both out of human control."

Temperance's answer wasn't greeted with a reaction from the man; instead, a large portion of the mural directly across from her began to react. At first, she thought that maybe it would show her another scene from the past, and she didn't know if she was ready. But the section depicting the enraged Vassal steadily faded until another corridor revealed itself. Temperance wasn't even surprised – she'd have been more shocked to learn that the cavern *didn't* hold more secrets.

"Let's walk," the man grinned, but then he hesitated.

Temperance held her position until she heard the faint sound of scuffling feet behind her.

"Chase," she muttered, shaking her head.

Temperance couldn't help but grimace when she heard her companion mutter a curse from behind her. The scuffling had stopped, and without turning around, she knew that Chase was attempting to take in the cavern's glory for the first time.

"Chase, I was under the impression that you'd wait for me?" Temperance said softly, despite being somewhat pleased he'd come. The man who was to escort her deeper underground had already begun to unnerve her.

"Yeah, sorry about that, Temp..." Chase responded sheepishly. He hadn't prepared an excuse.

"It appears your friend was concerned – and rightly so, as a lot more time has passed for him than it has for you," their host said, smiling yet again.

"I've only been here awhile," Temperance said.

"Walk with me," the man repeated before glancing at Chase. "You may accompany Our Flame, but you may not speak."

Chase nodded eagerly, happy to match Temperance's pace and keep his mouth shut.

"Your friend had been waiting a few hours for your return," the man revealed as they walked towards the new corridor. "Scourge is literally burnt unto time itself, as you're well aware. Anything bathed in the flames of the Dragon God remains forever scorched, cursed to stay in place within the passage of time. Of course, this is not without effect on the world around us. A large city afflicted by the Fires of Forever houses enough residual magical energy to affect the passage of time in its immediate vicinity, sometimes quite erratically."

Temperance nodded. It was an answer – an answer that made sense despite her knowing little about the magic itself.

"Your friend is not bound by time, at least not as thoroughly as myself, this city or the Nameless," the man continued as Temperance shot a look at Chase. "His hand... It will remain forever burnt, but the rest of him remains unbound by the Fires of Forever. For now. I know not whether it is simply that only a small part of him is afflicted, but I can feel the flame of his being fighting against the curse."

This new revelation gave Temperance pause, and Chase looked as though he had countless questions himself, all of which he was forbidden to ask.

"Do not lose yourself so deeply in your own thoughts that you fail to take in that which is around you," the man said suddenly, drawing their attention to the ornamentation of the corridor walls. Like the first one, statues that were once people lined each side, holding torches up to new images. The artwork moved slightly in the light of the torches, so slightly that Temperance wondered if she was imagining it. A quick glance at Chase's expression told her that he saw it as well, but wasn't going to comment.

Most of the images depicted rather mundane scenes, from a woman feeding a child at her breast, to a man tending a field of wheat. The corridor wasn't straight like the last and although it was subtle, Temperance could feel the winding of the path she was on. Occasionally the trio would come to a fork or crossroad in their tour, but there was never a question of which path to take as their guide led them further into the catacombs.

"These images are much more... tame?" Temperance spoke the last word hesitantly when she realised the reason behind the mundane depictions of Scourge's previous citizens. Each display showed a civilian going about their everyday lives, and offering light to the scene was...

"The statues..." Temperance stopped walking to examine one of the light-holders. In the darkness of the catacombs, the somewhat blackened stone hid some of the definition, but after circling around to look at the subject face-to-face, Temperance uncovered another fascinating clue about the people of Scourge. "The people in the images and the statues illuminating them match..."

"Within each of us is a flame. A flame that we hold dear, a flame that persists even after death."

Pieces fell into place.

"The flames of each of these statues – they are residual energy from the host."

"Correct." The man smiled, glancing between the statue and Temperance. "Through a ritual crafted by the first of our people, those who meet with death are forever memorialised in blackened stone, and their life force feeds the flame illuminating a mural of their lives. No citizen of Scourge is ever truly forgotten."

Temperance nodded. It was a strange practice, but no stranger than any other she'd encountered, which made it easy for her to decide on her next question.

"Who *were* you?"

The man answered with a tsk. "Come, let's walk."

Temperance's expression flickered in annoyance, but she was enjoying herself. In some ways she'd have preferred to explore on her own, but having a guide, however elusive, was a boon. Now that she'd discovered the connection between the statues and the images they overlooked, she couldn't help but check each one in passing, despite knowing they'd all be the same as the image before them.

She saw priests performing various rituals she didn't understand, including one undergoing the "Blackening" that resulted in the statues lining the catacombs. She saw what appeared to be Scourge's answer to warriors – scores of robed men and women with flaming swords, once known as the "Flame-Touched". She walked on in a trance until she reached a blank slab embedded in the wall, barely visible from the flames behind them. It had no one to illuminate its face and no image to show.

"We've reached the end," Temperance deduced.

"Of the dead, yes. There are countless fixtures such as this awaiting their occupants, but those who remain are not permitted to perish," the man explained. "However, if we proceed a little further, there is still something I'd like to show you."

"I worry about those waiting for me at the cathedral," Temperance admitted, though it didn't stop her feet from eagerly following the man at his new, swifter pace.

"I assure you this will not take long. I also assure you they will wait. The Nameless are quite adept at doing so."

The darkness of the corridor was banished by Chase's silent lighting of his blade. Temperance smiled at her companion as he remained a step in front of her, holding the flaming sword ahead so she could see where she was walking.

Their guide smirked at the gesture. He was obviously accustomed to the darkness of the catacombs and the look he shot Chase seemed somewhat unfriendly. Perhaps not outright loathing, but there was a certain amount of resentment within the fleeting expression. Neither Chase nor Temperance noticed as they continued down the lengthy and considerably less crowded corridor.

The lack of figures to investigate allowed Temperance's mind to piece together other parts of her observations. A few theories rolled around in her mind, but the first one she voiced was: "You're the crypt keeper, then."

"Correct, in a sense." Temperance could hear the humour in the man's voice. "I am what's known as the 'Stoker'. I tend to the Catacombs of Embers."

"I assume there is more to the job than simply patrolling the corridors?"

"Correct again. Everyone who undergoes the Blackening is also connected to a Stoker. Once, it was the norm for a dozen or so departed to be connected to a single Stoker."

"I haven't seen anyone else..." Temperance noted uneasily.

"The job of a Stoker is to observe the flames of the departed, and, in the rare case that they falter, offer a portion of their own essence as kindling to the blaze. Of course, with the curse playing its part..."

"You never die."

"Indeed. Even if the flames of these people ever began to fade, they'd rekindle the next day, as decreed by the curse itself. There are only a few that begin the cycle with a weakened flame. Sometimes I refuel them; other times I don't bother. It doesn't change, one way or the other." There was a bitterness in the man's voice now. Temperance's questioning had revealed what ate at him.

It wasn't difficult for her to work out that the person leading her was the only Stoker left and that there had once been others; perhaps they were even his friends.

"How many have we walked past?" Temperance asked aloud, biting her lip. She was too curious for tact.

"None. They have their own chamber. It was – *is* – a place of honour."

Temperance nodded.

A place he may never be allowed to rest. A place denied to him despite his continual contribution. How very cruel.

"Do you want to die?" she asked suddenly.

Her question remained unanswered as firelight encompassed her from all sides. She had been so engrossed in the conversation with the Stoker that she hadn't noticed where her feet now trod. There were dozens – no, hundreds – of the Blackened gathered within a grand chamber. Some figures were sitting or crouching while others stood upon the enormous, chamber-spanning plateaus. The platforms were lowest on either side of the trio, rising every few strides back from the first, like a staircase designed for giants. The Blackened upon them exhibited various degrees of stationary excitement and intrigue, each with their torch ablaze.

Temperance raised her hand slightly as Chase instinctively clutched his blade. Her anxiety didn't subside as she stepped forward to examine what the Blackened were transfixed on. In the centre of what looked like a colosseum arena was another person: a woman the colour of charcoal, garbed in similar robes to their guide, who was now smiling again.

Chase almost protested as Temperance rushed forward to examine the woman, but he managed to catch himself. The Stoker followed slowly, appearing beside the enthralled Vassal as she began her observation.

She knew who the Blackened woman was. Anyone who made it this far could hardly fail to put the pieces together.

"The Vassal of Fire..." Temperance muttered in reverence.

The previous Vassal was an inch or two shorter than Temperance and a great deal thinner, though that was probably accentuated by her lack of clothing.

I should be ashamed. My first thought upon finding a previous Vassal is that she's skinny?

Temperance scolded herself for her superficial observation as she took in the sunken, tormented eyes and the look of terror on the woman's face. Her hands were held out to her sides, palms to the ceiling, encased in flames far brighter than any of the others in the room. Temperance could feel the heat, but it wasn't unpleasant. The fury the previous Vassal must have felt during the chaos was gone, leaving only her fear to fuel the life-flame within her hands.

The stone no longer lent the deceased woman that unreal power. While the essence that came from the statue suggested she was once a superb mage, to Temperance it seemed almost... pathetic.

The rest of the Blackened woman was unremarkable, but Temperance struggled not to think so low of the former Vassal. Despite genuine effort, she could not bring herself to look at the woman before her favourably; the most she could muster was condescending pity.

What is wrong with me? I never think like this!

"I admit I expected something more... flashy," their guide said suddenly, jolting Temperance out of her reverie.

"Flashy? It's a statue – a corpse... No, I –"

"It is what it is, My Flame," he said with an understanding

nod. "But I'm afraid I was referring to a flashy response from you."

"Me?"

"Yes. You bear the stone within yourself; I expected some form of reaction, should two Vassals meet. I suppose I was wrong?"

"What did you base this theory upon?"

"Emotions, My Flame."

"Emotions," Temperance repeated flatly.

"Yes." The man gestured back the way they came, and the party began their trip back to the centre confines. "Surely in your studies you've noticed a direct link between the emotions of a mage and the potency of their magical energy?"

I've noticed, yes. I've even lived it. I've endured the burden of another's fury, Temperance thought bitterly, but she merely nodded.

"Did you want the being within the stone to react?" Chase asked suddenly, breaking his promise. The Stoker, however, didn't seem angry.

"My, what a loaded question," he grinned. "No, I can't say that I *desired* another... fiery confrontation."

"Then what *did* you desire?" Temperance pressed.

"Honestly, I am unsure. These catacombs... They lack excitement."

Neither Temperance nor Chase could tell if he was lying.

They soon realised they were back in the first chamber. Temperance glanced around in confusion, but said nothing.

"I assume you'll be going forth with the extraction?" the man asked politely, as if they'd just met all over again.

"You've given me no reason to alter my plans."

"No, I suppose I haven't." He smiled. It almost seemed... genuine.

Temperance's unease was growing again. Chase gently pushed her towards the opposite corridor. "Time to go, Temp, the others are waiting," he muttered.

The Stoker didn't break his gaze, nor his smile, as he watched Chase usher the current Vassal of Fire from the grand chamber.

What a shame. She can bear the burden of the stone, yet she seeks to be rid of it.

CHAPTER 33

OLD RIVALRIES, NEW ALLIANCES

Rufus had spent the past twenty minutes sitting on the ground, back against the stone wall of the canal, watching the manhole above him. Small rays of sunlight were shining through the gaps in the lid. They were orange, signalling the day's end. He rubbed his eyes, showing extra attention to the scarred one. Soon it would be dark, though the thought barely even occurred to the thief. They'd been there a while, long enough for the torches on the wall to steadily become brighter as the light above began to fade.

His two companions were directly across from him, separated by a small three-foot-wide stream of dark water. Lori was squatting down with her head against the wall, eyes closed. Tori, on the other hand, had her arms crossed and was tapping her foot impatiently, a practice that was quickly working Rufus' last nerve.

"Do you have to?" he snapped, and Tori stopped for a moment.

Watching Rufus glare at her, she raised her foot slowly before slamming it to the ground once more. Rufus leapt to his feet. "That's it! You pair go back to Setz!"

"No! We are here to help you, Ruffie!" Tori smiled, pleased that she'd got a rise out of him. It hadn't been difficult; anyone could tell he was on edge.

"All you've done is irritate me," he grumbled.

"I'm just excited! This is our first job together!" Tori exclaimed. Rufus had no response. He knew how much it meant to the twins that they finally had the chance to accompany him.

"There is no one I'd rather have with me," he said after a moment, making Tori beam and Lori open her eyes.

"Really?" Tori asked.

"There isn't a certain Princess you would prefer to be here?" Lori followed up coyly.

"Bah! She would just get in the way!" Rufus scoffed, finding himself in slightly better spirits. "We need speed and stealth! Two things she is not particularly good at."

"Then why were you so concerned about leaving her before in the Underbelly?" Lori pressed.

"That's...." Rufus began before trailing off. "That's about something else."

"What is it?" Lori questioned, getting to her feet and looking curiously over the murky canal.

"It's about the dreams, huh?" Tori interjected sharply.

"How do you –" Rufus stopped himself. "Actually, I'm not even surprised. You two really need to find a new way to pass your time that doesn't involve spying on the brat."

"You should stop calling her that," Lori suggested softly.

"Yeah! Besides, the Princess is amazing!" Tori exclaimed. "With her walls of water, and her staff and her giant pet swan!"

"That's not a pet!" Rufus said in exasperation. He knew he'd already lost before his mouth even formed the words.

"What would you call it, then?" came the twins' predictable follow up. It was painfully obvious the pair had been watching and, perhaps even worse, listening to the Princess a little too much.

Rufus was about to reply when he sensed something close by. With a quick glance he saw that the sun's rays had given way to night. The only light they had left was that of the steadily dying torches.

"I know you're there. I assume it is time to move?"

"That it is," answered a voice Rufus knew.

From the shadows a darkly clothed man appeared. As expected, Rufus could not see his face clearly under the black cloak with red trim that only Setz's elite force wore. But he still knew the man. He might not have guessed his identity while he lingered in the shadows, but the voice was unmistakable.

"The one who always gives me grief when I need to see Setz – wonderful!" was Rufus' snide greeting. "I was looking for a way to make this whole situation more undesirable."

"For the purpose of getting along, call me Keenin," the man offered with an air of indifference and a glance at the twins. "Our differences will be put aside during this mission. Both I and the men I command will see you safely to your target – you have my word. Or perhaps more importantly, Setz has my word under the Dark Oath."

Keenin turned towards Rufus at the mention of the Oath.

"You made that kind of oath over something like this?"

"Despite our problems, outcast," Keenin spat, "the people below here believe in the Princess and what she has accomplished so far. Many men would make the exact same oath to be a part of her return to the throne."

"What's the Dark Oath?" Lori asked curiously.

"Something you are never to take," Rufus snarled before turning back to the featureless man. Giving up on the idea of seeing Keenin's face, Rufus' eyes settled on his torso. Despite being concealed, it was hard to ignore the fact that Keenin's left arm was tucked away under his cloak.

"You're wounded," Rufus noted, both curious and amused. He couldn't deny that the idea of Keenin in pain pleased him somewhat.

"I am capable," Keenin replied shortly.

"Have you seen combat already?" Tori asked with a hint of enthusiasm. She was always keen for action.

"No," Keenin answered, a little too quickly. It would have simplified things had he lied. "I have another task to attend to after this one. Timing is key and incompetence has no place here. Allow me whatever moments we have here as a respite before what is coming."

Rufus' disdain for the man remained firmly intact, but he let the questioning go. He somehow knew Keenin was telling the truth: that whatever came after escorting them wasn't going to be pleasant for him. He had a job, and so did they. Thankfully, the twins followed Rufus' lead and held their questions in check.

"Do what you want," Rufus grunted.

"Thank you." Keenin nodded, pressing his back up against the stone wall and closing his eyes. "We leave as soon as the bell tolls."

CHAPTER 34

SHADOWS AMONGST SHADOWS

The gaps in the lid of the manhole had been dark for what seemed like an eternity before the bell finally rang. The long, drawn-out sound signalling curfew rang throughout the chamber as the small band nodded to one another. Rufus and the twins climbed the ladder as quickly as possible while Keenin seemed to vanish from existence.

As the trio pushed open the lid and stood in the streets of Aquiocia, a small grunt escaped Rufus' lips.

"What in blazes happened here?" he muttered as he looked around.

Every house appeared to have aged dramatically in the months that had passed. The stalls that merchants once stood at looked as if they hadn't seen use in decades. Cobwebs and dust replaced the goods on display, and even the precious, once high-quality timber they were crafted from seemed to have crumbled away, losing its quality impossibly quickly.

Many of the houses' windows appeared to be permanently nailed shut, as if to keep out looters and the like. It wasn't just the houses – every single building seemed to be boarded up like fortresses crafted from decaying resources.

But most unnerving of all was the absence of children playing in the alleyways between houses. Even with the light drizzle settling in from the coming storm, there would usually be a few excited by the sky's impending light show, defying the curfew and continuing to play until the night watch would come and chase them home. Rufus knew this because it was the perfect time to make a hit; the guards would be short-staffed as they hurried to get the kids home.

"Things have changed here, Ruffie," Lori muttered softly.

"That they have." Keenin's cold voice came from behind the trio, though he could not be seen. "I suggest you start moving. There is a reason children no longer play after dark – or at all, for that matter."

Rufus rolled his eyes at the ominous message and looked down to see Lori with a terrified look on her face as her sister bounced from foot to foot in excitement.

"Nothing is going to happen to you." Rufus smiled at both of them before continuing. "Your job is to follow me and assist, but even more important is that you look after each other. You run together, understand?"

Lori nodded with a small smile and Tori seemed ready to burst with anticipation.

"All right then!" Rufus grinned. "Let's see if you pair can keep up!"

With that, he turned and sprinted down the road. His footsteps were swift but silent from years upon years of practice. To his pleasant surprise, he found that he actually had to look over his shoulder to see if the twins were following. They were, almost as quickly, and just as quietly.

"You two have turned out just fine," Rufus muttered proudly to himself.

Racing through the unnaturally aged and damaged streets of

the upper class, the trio did not stray from the path leading to their target. The area seemed deserted; save for the occasional candlelight in some of the windows, Aquiocia seemed robbed of life entirely.

This was precisely why Rufus was surprised when three soldiers barrelled out from behind one of the stalls in an attempt to intercept them.

Before any of them had time to react, the shadows cast by the moon's rays seemed to shift and the guards dropped to the ground.

"Keep running!" Rufus yelled back to the twins.

"What was that?" one of them cried out.

"That was our protection!" Rufus called back. "Now belt up and keep running!"

He was met with no response from the twins, but glanced back to see them still behind him. His heart started to race when he saw countless more silhouettes giving chase behind them.

"We are being followed, Ruffie!" Lori cried.

"Let's take 'em down!" Tori called eagerly.

"Do not slow down, and for the sake of every fictional god – belt up!" Rufus yelled back.

With another glance behind him, Rufus could see the silhouettes falling one by one. Keenin was keeping his word and his men were performing admirably. *Perhaps he isn't such a bastard after all.*

The thief finally spotted their mark, a massive wooden warehouse around three times as high as the houses around it, spanning the length of an entire block. The building was considered a hazard by many of the citizens due to the fireworks stored within, and there were very few dwellings within arrow-shot of the great barn. There were only a few stalls that brave merchants tended, but even those were pest-ridden, their wood decrepit.

This place would be locked tight against thieves, Rufus thought quickly before noticing a window above the large double doors, about twelve feet up the wall. *Alright, girls, I hope you're ready.*

Rufus reached the doors, found them locked and turned to see the quickly approaching twins. With a quick glance towards the window, they understood what they were to do.

Lori pulled her short bow from her shoulder and nocked an arrow as Tori drew her twin blades. In perfect harmony, the pair launched their weapons towards the window. The projectiles collided with the thin glass and it shattered instantly.

The twins had no time to feel pride in their teamwork as they charged towards Rufus, who bent with both arms outstretched. The twins' feet each found one of Rufus' hands and they were lifted effortlessly into the air.

Their light bodies vaulted elegantly through the night sky until they slammed into the wall, their hands grasping at the windowsill as they scrambled inside. Both were fortunate enough to be wearing light armour and gloves of tanned leather, rendering the glass fragments harmless.

Rufus took a second to observe what remained of the numbers chasing them before he heard the sound of metal hitting stone and the large doors opened behind him. As the thief stepped inside, Lori pushed the doors closed and Tori lifted a heavy beam of iron to sit across them, resealing the entrance. The sounds of surprised gasps and metal falling to the ground outside signalled the end of the soldiers' pursuit – and their lives.

"Keenin has taken them down," Rufus whispered to the twins as he reached out and grabbed the back of Tori's clothing. "Stay here a moment."

The twins looked at Rufus in confusion before taking in the warehouse's interior for the first time. The first things they noticed were the countless solid timber boxes stacked upon each other on either side of the companions. The walls of containers continued for yards upon yards, forming a makeshift corridor that started from the door and led in towards the heart of the building.

The lighting was horrendous. Save for the small amount of moonlight shining through the now bare window frame above them, there was no way to discern if their path was obstructed or not. There was barely enough light for the trio to see the path at all as it stretched off into the darkness.

Rufus saw what appeared to be a faint light in the distance, though he couldn't be sure he hadn't imagined it. But Lori whispered, "There is light on the other side."

"I was thinking…" Tori started slowly with a meaningful look at her sister that was almost lost in the darkness. "If this was barred from the inside, then how did the person who barred it get out?"

Rufus nodded as Lori's mouth shifted uncomfortably. He had already thought of this and was surprised that Lori hadn't; she was usually the more rational thinker of the two.

"What is the plan, then?" Lori asked quietly.

"The way these containers are stacked makes it a bad idea to climb them," Rufus muttered. "They nearly reach the ceiling anyway, and we can't risk falling, or them dropping and making too much noise."

"So, we are forced to follow the path?" Lori asked. "In the dark?"

"We have to. Lighting a flame around the fireworks here could mean us getting caught in the explosion. There are wards within the walls to contain an explosion, but they won't help us."

"How do you know that, Ruffie?"

"This… isn't the first time I've tried to commit arson in Aquiocia," the thief responded hesitantly as he pulled a thin wire from inside his clothing.

"A slow-burning fuse." Lori nodded, a gleam in her eye. "Find the other exit; attach the fuse to a viable explosive that will have a chain reaction after we have made our escape."

Rufus stole a glance at Lori, surprised at the interest she was showing.

"Couldn't we just light it up here?" Tori asked impatiently.

"It might work," Rufus conceded. "But we'd have to run the same way we came, and I can't guarantee there aren't more men waiting for us. Keenin will be long gone by now. At least if we find another exit, they won't be able to predict where we will come from."

"Chances are that the larger fireworks are towards the centre of the warehouse, anyway," Lori added encouragingly.

"Then let's go!" Tori insisted.

"Stay close," Rufus muttered as the three became shadows melding into the lightless confines of the warehouse. Before long they could see nothing, either in front of them or behind;

their eyes refused to adjust to the absence of light.

Feeling their way through by brushing their fingertips across the walls of stacked boxes, the trio inched towards the light in the distance. As they drew steadily closer to the unknown source, Rufus noticed that the light moved occasionally, and that it cast the same illuminating glow as the orbs of the Underbelly. He wondered if the twins had noticed the same thing.

What does this mean? Rufus thought before it dawned on him.

Spinning on the spot and spreading his arms outwards, he brought the twins to a stop.

"What the –"

"Shush, it's me," Rufus whispered. "Have you both noticed the light?"

"What about it?" Tori grumbled, pushing Rufus' arm away.

"It's the same as the ones in the Underbelly," Lori replied. "You're concerned about a mage being stationed here?"

"Aye," Rufus muttered, his eyes darting around pointlessly in the blackness.

"What's the problem?" Tori asked. "The mage probably isn't even here. Setz leaves the Underbelly all the time but the lights never fade."

"Setz is a brilliant mage," Rufus replied before snarling softly, "Don't you ever tell him I said that!"

"So, we take down the mage. I still don't see a problem, Ruffie," Tori pressed.

"The problem is that this light offers no sight to those who mean the caster ill intent. The caster will see us, but we won't see them," Rufus explained.

"Really? How do you know all this?" Lori wondered.

"Between Setz and the brat, the knowledge was forced on me."

Lori made a show of clearing her throat softly.

"Oh, fine – the *Princess* forced the knowledge down my throat. Better?"

"Much better," Lori responded, amused.

"Don't think I haven't noticed that she is winning you two over to her side –"

"Can we please get going?" Tori whined.

With what seemed like his hundredth sigh, Rufus gave in and the trio continued their slow progress.

Rufus found himself becoming impatient at the slow pace and painful silence. When he was by himself, he relished it; silence meant safety. But with the twins following, he felt more apprehension than he had ever experienced on a job before.

"Why hasn't the light gone out?" Tori muttered to her sister.

"I assume because we have not seen the caster yet, so we cannot mean them harm?" Lori wondered.

Their exchange was interrupted by Rufus stopping them again after finding his fingers grasping air. With stiff movements, he crossed the path and confirmed that their current corridor branched into two additional directions.

"There are two paths," Tori murmured.

"Of course there are – why wouldn't there be?" Rufus rolled his eyes in the darkness to no one's benefit.

"Is there a problem, Ruffie?"

"Trying to decide which way we should go."

"We could split up?"

Before Rufus could dismiss the idea, he heard voices. He quickly shushed the twins, his ears straining against the silence. They weren't alone after all.

The enchanted light was on the move, this time with some purpose. He watched the light change direction regularly as it danced across the ceiling. The people were making their way through the maze that was the warehouse.

Rufus' heart began to pound in his chest as he weighed up their options. Running back the way they came wasn't possible; the mission would fail, and they couldn't even see the window anymore – they would be sitting ducks in the corridor. Was it getting darker?

He couldn't set off the fuse now, either. The explosion would kill them, and besides, he wouldn't get through the thick timber of the containers without alerting the patrollers.

Rufus quickly pulled the twins towards him so their backs were against the stacks of boxes. Once they were out of view, he quickly voiced his concerns.

"So when they get to us, we'll go blind?"

"Not blind, exactly – you'll just receive no light from their magic, but they will. I think."

The three stood in silence amongst the darkness for a few moments as the voices got closer and closer, their light spreading up the corridor.

"Do it, Tori," Lori whispered.

"Do what?" asked Tori.

"The thing you do with your eyes closed."

"What are you two talking about?" Rufus hissed.

"But you said it was unnatural!" said Tori.

"It is, but we have no choice," Lori pressed.

"If you two have a plan, I'd like to hear it," Rufus remarked, anxiously watching the light moving across the ceiling.

"No time for that, Ruffie!" Tori said. "I need you both to be quiet and stand back a bit."

Tori exhaled and drew the air back in slowly. Her next breath was considerably quieter, and the following was completely silent. She could hear her own heartbeat and banished the sound through sheer power of will. After a moment, her world was as silent as her vision was saturated in shadows.

If you wish to master this talent, you need to focus. I am not suggesting you apply your undivided attention to the task; I am commanding you to banish everything else to the void. Then, and only then, do you strike.

Setz's training took hold and Tori focused on the voices of the people approaching. There were three of them. They were only a short distance away now and the light was bathing the corridor.

It was time.

As soon as she managed to remove their voices from her ears and mind, Tori stepped out from behind the corner with her eyes tightly closed.

Rufus and Lori waited with trepidation, but forced themselves not to move. The guards yelled in Tori's direction and a split second later, the light vanished as the caster became aware of their presence. The ill will was established, and the magic took hold.

Through all of this, Tori perceived nothing. It was only when the knights were upon her that she heard what she was looking for. A heartbeat.

She struck, and from the knight's point of view, he had just been stabbed by a thin blade wielded by a girl with her eyes shut tight. Tori's slender blade pierced his chain-link armour and found his heart. All she heard was the sound of a struggling heart losing the will to fight.

It wasn't the cry of surprise from the other lightly armoured knight accompanying the mage that alerted Tori to his whereabouts; it was his precious heart, which had started pumping at an accelerated rate due to his newfound fear.

The blind assassin's blade led the charge as Tori impaled the second knight before he even drew his sword. She heard the satisfying sound of his essential organ spluttering and spewing blood everywhere.

The mage stood a short distance away, and only after his second bodyguard collapsed in a bleeding, writhing mess did he find the courage to raise his arms in surrender.

It was too late. The focused assassin couldn't see the gesture, nor hear any words the mage might have offered her.

Tori heard her mark – the rapid beat of a drum. She flicked the blade almost casually through the darkness and punctured the mage's vital organ. It was over before he hit the ground.

Tori was shaking as she strained to hear any sign she had failed, but the night had returned to silence. As the last beat of the mage's shuddering heart ceased, the illumination from the orb that hung just above its enchanter returned its light to the victor.

Rufus looked down at the three corpses in surprise, his eyes adjusting to the light now floating above Tori for reasons unknown.

"How was that, Ruffie?" Tori smiled shakily.

"After this is over, I will be asking Setz what the hell he has been teaching you pair..."

"So damned unnatural..." Lori muttered.

CHAPTER 35

TARGET OBTAINED

The trio broke into a steady yet silent jog, the only sound light rain upon the high roof. The light from the orb not only made it possible to see their surroundings, but followed Tori relentlessly. As Lori had pointed out, her sister seemed to be its new master, and if they were to come across another enemy, they would have the advantage. They had never heard of magic changing hands at the death of its conjurer, but none of them knew enough to counter it.

What worried Rufus was the presence of the mage in the first place. Aquiocia had very few mages with any real talent at their disposal; to see one conjure a spell that Setz himself utilised made him uneasy.

Maybe the new King has been outsourcing? Rufus thought. *Setz should know about this...*

After racing through the corridor for a few minutes, they found another fork in the path. Rufus noticed a doorway faintly illuminated by moonlight filtering in from a window above. The door itself was slightly open.

Then he realised.

"Those guards were not actually stationed here – they were a patrol that we had the bad fortune of encountering."

"That makes sense, Ruffie," Lori nodded. "They were just

patrolling through to the other entrance and coming back this way after."

"I'd say the bad fortune was theirs, not ours," Tori laughed.

"Don't get too ahead of yourself. We all know that could have gone badly," Lori warned.

"You're just jealous!" Tori accused.

"Belt up, the pair of you," Rufus ordered in a weary tone that made the twins forget their argument.

"What's wrong, Ruffie?" they asked in unison.

"Mages," he said coarsely before clearing his throat and continuing. "There are mages patrolling the city."

"Been that way for a couple of months," Tori confirmed.

"Setz believes the King thinks having mages will protect him against the Princess," Lori explained, pronouncing Arissam's title with disgust.

"What? He thinks the mages will just deal with her? They are –"

"Not Aquiocian," Tori said quietly.

Rufus paused a moment. "What does that matter? The knights outnumber them and if they saw –"

"The knights are not guaranteed to be themselves any longer," Lori stated, imitating her sister's low volume.

Suspicion filled Rufus.

"He's had you watching the palace," he said, attempting to keep his anger in check. They were on a mission. The fact that Setz had been risking the twins' lives so carelessly would have to wait.

He was waiting for a response from either of his companions when he spotted something of interest. He stalked across the corridor towards one of the containers to find one of the lower right corners splintered and punctured. Inside the cavity, he could just make out the colourful dyed parchment used to decorate the explosives that lit up the night sky.

"Well, that's a lucky find," Lori noted with a hint of excitement.

"Why are you enjoying this so much?" Rufus wondered aloud.

"No reason! We have just found our target, is all!" Lori insisted.

"I'm not sure I believe you anymore," Rufus said, his tone resigned. "Let's tie the fuse and get out of here."

"Tori, go and gently push holes in all the containers you can!" Lori ordered.

"Huh? Why?" Tori questioned, looking at Rufus.

Rufus glanced at the twins and nodded. Tori shrugged and began making her way down the corridor, gently carving small holes in the boxes with her sharp blade. She was careful not to wander so far that the light couldn't aid her companions.

"You seem to know what you're doing," Rufus observed, absentmindedly rubbing his eye.

Lori smiled. "All ladies have their secrets, Ruffie."

"Alright, if you keep saying stuff like that I will forbid you from seeing the Princess at all!" Rufus grumbled. "You're sounding more like her every damned day."

"That's not as much of an insult as you think it is, Ruffie," Lori giggled before adding, "You're bringing her up a lot. Is there something you'd like to share?"

"I am not having this conversation with you, Lori."

"If you tell me what is on your mind, then I will think about telling you what she said back in the Underbelly after you left," Lori said.

"I am not interested in what the brat – Princess – has said about me," Rufus insisted as he focused on the fuse. "I just want to get this over with!"

There was a long pause before Lori whispered, "She... She said she's sorry, Ruffie."

Rufus stared at Lori for a moment, watching the shadows from the distant light lingering on her face. He scratched at his scar, paused, and swore under his breath.

Lori smiled. "You plan on running to her after this is done."

"Running to who?" Tori asked, appearing beside them. "Ah, whatever. We all know who Ruffie would run to. I stabbed about thirty, will that be enough?"

"That's great, sis."

"Aye. Let's make for the door," Rufus suggested as he unravelled the fuse. "Watch my back."

The twins led the way towards the open door as Rufus unravelled more and more of the fuse. Leaving plenty of slack and ensuring it wouldn't catch any of the boxes on the way, he was relieved to see the fuse was just long enough to reach the door. He didn't want any complications.

From the outside of the great warehouse, Rufus saw that this side of it had fared no better than the other. But that was not his primary concern.

"Where'd I put my flint box?" he wondered, before being nudged out of the way by Lori.

In her hands were two small rocks that she scraped together, a spark flashing between them. It burnt just long enough for the fuse to light and start its slow advance towards the end of the corridor.

"Well, girls," Rufus began with a deep breath as the trio stepped further and further back. "Target found and met and all that other stuff you two like to harp on about to Setz."

"We can make sure it blows up, Ruffie," Tori said with a smirk.

"We will report back to Setz and get to safety. Now go!" Lori insisted.

Hesitating for only a second, Rufus nodded.

"Thank you both," he said, quickly embracing them and disappearing into the night.

As his feet carried him through the dark streets towards the heart of the Upper District, a single thought repeated itself over and over.

Don't do anything stupid. Damn it, woman. Don't do anything stupid.

CHAPTER 36

OUT WITH A BANG

The still air of a night held hostage by strife met Keenin's bare face for the first time in hours. Pulling the hood of his gear back roughly with his unbound arm, he relished the sensation of water falling from the sky. For a man who was soon to meet an excruciating end, the simple pleasure of a cold drizzle was a welcome indulgence.

The assassin turned and smirked at the two shadows approaching silently behind him. He stroked his well-maintained shadow of facial hair and looked over the dark figures with his equally shady eyes.

"Count?" he rasped, slightly short of breath.

"Twelve."

"Fourteen."

"Bah! Pathetic effort, you pair. Twenty-two for me!" Keenin scoffed, though his accomplices knew it was a hollow boast at best. Their squad leader had never been the bloodthirsty kind. A perverted gambler, sure. But he never relished death; it was simply his job.

No, they knew their boss was scared, but not of their impending death. They had voluntarily given up the Guild brand, and they knew what that meant. As soon as their respective limbs had been severed, their life force had begun to evaporate. They could stem the bleeding, but the actual flow of energy that kept their bodies intact and able couldn't be resisted or ignored. Such was the way of Setz's magic. You removed the mark and your body was siphoned of life.

Surrounding the trio was the occasional bush littered with roses. It wasn't surprising to see fewer flowers these days due to the new government's negligence. What did they care about a few crimson-tinged roses? The Captain knew he shouldn't care about them either, but their colour only added to the true source of his fear.

Keenin was scared he wouldn't accomplish the task before his body gave out.

"Enough gawking," he snarled to his subordinates. "The ropes!"

As the pair reached into their travel packs, pulling free lengths of thick rope reinforced with wire, Keenin turned around and looked up at the forty-foot wall he had been resting against. Had he a second arm, the climb would have been a simple task. The reality was driven home as he heard a metal contraption deploy and latch onto stone. His men were already scaling the wall, legs clinging tightly to the durable tether as their right arms feverishly lifted them higher and higher.

Keenin wasn't about to be shown up by his subordinates. He leapt at the rope on his right, grabbing it with his remaining hand, and went to work trying to catch his men. What would have taken twenty seconds with two hands took well over a minute without. By the time he felt his men grab the shoulders of his gear and pull him onto the top of the wall, Keenin was cursing under his breath. It wasn't the pain that had him swearing; it was the waste of time.

Under normal circumstances, the other men might have left their leader behind. But not that night. That night the mission didn't come first, because they knew none of them were returning home after its completion. That, and because there was a reason that Keenin didn't have his own spare rope.

The squad leader wheezed as he rolled over tentatively and produced a small hand-crossbow from his travel bag, its luminous ore handle fashioned into a spike. The glowing metal swirled with shadows. Its wielder took his shot. The bolt soared through the sky with the same shifting shadows upon its tip disappearing into the night. There was a soft shriek, like a sword being sheathed, and the silence returned. He'd hit his mark: the royal balcony across the courtyard.

There was no way he was going to miss. Not after Setz came to him directly and requested he begin training to fire with his non-dominant hand. He hadn't asked a single question – he didn't need to. His trust in his master was absolute. So much so that when the one who'd offered him a home requested he die, he had already stretched out his left arm on a table, ready to serve.

It was simply the way of the Guilty Blade.

Slamming the spiked handle of the hand-crossbow into the stone surface of the wall, the energy contained within fused weapon and wall together as one. They had their way across. The handicapped trio didn't hesitate in rushing to the suspended tether, semi-somersaulting into the air and clasping the lifeline between crossed legs. Despite being upside down, despite their exhaustion, the struggle continued.

Keenin's face was drenched in more sweat than rain from

the continuous exertion. He couldn't help but replay the same thought over and over.

I will see this done. It was the right choice...

He wasn't what anyone would consider "gifted" in the magical arts. He could infuse certain items with his energy, allowing tools to operate beyond their original functions, but he was no spell-slinger like the stories led him to believe about the Princess. Despite this, he knew a Forbidding Enchantment when he encountered one.

He could feel the energy in the air nibbling at his skin. It wanted to banish him from its home. It wanted to crush the intruder it had been charged with keeping from its master. But it couldn't. Because the condition that gave the enchantment purpose had been removed. The magic knew that Keenin and his men were once threats, but it had no reason to believe they were now.

"You feel that, boys?" Keenin grunted laboriously.

"Aye," the pair breathed back.

"The damned enchantment can't do shit!" Their leader chuckled under his ragged breath as he looked down at the dark courtyard.

Shadows shifted in the moonlight overhead and the assassin couldn't help but feel a measure of peace making its way through his dying body. He had expected a more painful process. He was exhausted, yet it wasn't unpleasant dragging himself across the tether suspended in the open air. He felt no anticipation, no anxiety about his impending doom. He was where he was supposed to be – hanging upside down from a rope with two other men, just a short distance away from the royal balcony.

What...? Keenin's eyes flicked towards a fountain in the corner of the courtyard. From his perch, the spray of water looked like a high-pressured stream coming from a chandelier of ornately carved stone. *Shit!*

Keenin's order to move quicker was redundant as one of his men fell from the tether to his death. His second subordinate made it, struggling over the pale blue banister as a crossbow bolt whizzed past and clipped Keenin's lifeline. He was a sitting duck, but his comrade wasn't about to leave him. Keenin saw a flash of bright, crackling light coming from where he had noticed the soldiers.

"Risky," he noted as his comrade pulled him to safety.

"That wasn't me!" the man wheezed.

Keenin chanced a glance back at the fountain just in time to see a silhouette amongst the crackling flashes receive a barrage of crossbow bolts.

"Boss, there's no time."

"You're right," Keenin gasped. He was down to his last moments as he hobbled into the royal chambers and made his way to the bedside table. "Light!"

"Aye," the man whispered, reaching into his pocket and selecting two objects to strike together. The chamber filled with the same crackling light as the courtyard.

Keenin finally reached the table with all the exhaustion of an old man. It didn't hurt, but his body certainly wasn't living up to its age of almost thirty. Even as he paused a moment, he received no relief. He flung open the drawer, its contents spilling across the chamber floor.

"Boss, you –"

"Quiet, I can do this!" Keenin hissed with a cough. His

breathing was becoming more ragged by the moment.

His underling didn't respond, and it took a moment for Keenin to realise that the *clack* echoing around the chamber was the sound of a reloading crossbow. His body instinctively dropped and rolled, a bolt soaring over his tumbling frame and embedding itself into a large pillow. Through his dizzying thoughts, Keenin realised that he hadn't even checked to see if the false King was in his bed.

Sloppy.

"Hold!" a quiet yet authoritative voice rang out.

Keenin didn't know whether the command was for him as he came to a stop on the floor. His hand was under his limp body; he was finally at his limit. His eyes rested on the corpse of his accomplice before finally gazing up at the entrance to see King Arissam and two crossbow-wielding knights. Their weapons were held upwards, pointing towards the roof in Aquiocian style. They were on standby; the order had been for them.

"An assassination attempt? For me?" Arissam asked mockingly. "You flatter me!"

Keenin didn't reply further than a groan of effort. He couldn't move his hand properly.

"Your boss probably could have sent better candidates for the job. Did he have no one better suited for murder than two incompetent gimps?" Arissam laughed openly, glancing at the knights to make sure they were following in mirth. He had completely misread the situation, and Keenin knew it.

"Heh. 'Fraid you're about to find he chose just the right men for the job." Keenin chuckled hoarsely as feeling in his arm returned and his hand found what it was looking for.

The two new crossbow bolts buried in his chest barely slowed him as he produced another dark-swirling crystal fashioned into the shape of a crude dirk.

"I was always good with crystal work," Keenin murmured in a peculiar state of serenity, looking at his company with a bleeding smile. "Setz was a ruthless leader, but he allowed me one small concession."

Both King and guard looked on in surprise until Arissam noticed that the makeshift dagger wasn't the only thing in the dying man's hand. He also had a piece of parchment. A piece that appeared to be lined with a faint glow. Arissam finally realised the true target of the invasion and fled as the intruder plunged the crystal into his own chest.

Branching out from the new wound was the blistering colour of tempered iron lining his veins. Despite the sensation of magma making its home within his arteries, Keenin only smiled at the knights frantically trying to reload their weapons.

"He always said I could go out with a bang."

CHAPTER 37

A SQUIRE'S ATONEMENT

The image of a blue-stoned roof that glowed faintly filled Jex's blurred vision as his eyes struggled to open.

I'm... awake? I'm alive?

His mind was sluggish and slow to recall what had happened during the commoners' riot. Steadily, the details came back to him, leading right up until he reached out to grasp the artefact they had been charged with retrieving and protecting.

The blade!

As Jex attempted to rise, the pain he'd felt throughout the time he was bound to the blade returned, shooting from his left arm through the rest of his body. He screamed. Then he screamed again. He wailed in an agony so prominent that he couldn't even hear the voices yelling for him to quieten down. For a moment that felt like a lifetime, he was alone once more with the anguish he'd been dealt by the blade's touch. Then it was gone.

"That's better," Jex heard a man call from his right. "Keep quiet, you scum!"

Where am I?

Slowly and tentatively, Jex turned his head downwards. The pain throbbed slightly but allowed the small movement, and he saw that his left arm was bandaged in gauze that was stained black, as if it had been soaked in infected blood. Disgusted, he stifled a moan out of fear of bringing on another wave of pain. Deciding that he'd deal with it when he was fully awake, Jex tried to observe his surrounds. It took him a few moments to turn his head slowly, so as not to antagonise his condition, and take in that he was locked in a cell. All that was between the stone walls was the bed he was unable to leave, a chamber pot and a small table and chair bolted to the floor. The exit was barred by a door with thick, glowing metal beams criss-crossing over each other. Anyone could see in and out, but not even the smallest child could get through without touching the clearly enchanted metal. Even if he was well and able-bodied, he wouldn't be going anywhere unaided.

Jex lay there for hours – or at least, it *felt* like hours. He had no frame of reference in the cell, which offered only the pale, azure glow of the stones as light. He wasn't completely unhappy with the time he was given to lie upon the thin mattress. He could feel his body trying to rally against the pain and heal, but it was obviously going to be a slow process. All he could do was lie there and reflect on what had happened.

The blade... It made me crazy, Jex thought. *As soon as I heard it beckoning to me, I knew I had to have it. I had to be the one who wielded it. Why did it hurt me, though?*

He couldn't work it out. The blade had said that it wasn't causing him pain deliberately, but could its word even be trusted? No. To trust the word of a being that had caused the massacre of potentially thousands was nothing but a fantasy, and a stupid one at that.

Stupid? The same kind of stupidity that's required for someone like you to believe you didn't relish every second of those people dying? The kind of delusional idiocy that would make a murderer think they were not responsible for slaughtering thousands of people. That kind of stupid?

Jex's mind and conscience were teaming up against him and he knew it. He also knew that the voice in his head was right. He enjoyed both the power and the slaughter of those leading a menial life. To crush those in his way was liberating. There was no question what he was supposed to be doing or who he should be answering to. He had simply unleashed himself on the insignificant, and it had felt wonderful.

They weren't doing anything with their lives anyway, so what's the problem? They couldn't even take the sword from me. What a joke. That was their entire purpose for being there!

Jex's bitter reverie was interrupted by the clanging of metal on metal. Someone was tampering with the door leading into the cell. He was relieved to find his body didn't punish him too harshly as his head turned instinctually towards the sound.

His moment of curiosity was shattered when he saw who had arrived to speak with him.

"Setz," Jex croaked in a pathetic attempt to greet the man gliding into the cell.

"Jex," he replied shortly, placing down a bowl of food, a jug of water and, easily the most eye-catching, an ornate knife, whose blade shone with the same faint light of the walls.

There were many times in the following minutes that Jex tried to break the silence, only to find his throat too hoarse and his lungs too exhausted to speak. Setz watched him silently, a blank expression on his scabbed-over face. Jex realised that if Setz's mutilated face was already healing over, he'd been in his prison for a few days already. Setz's previously clear and perhaps even distinguished face had endured its flesh being shredded by intense magic – the same magic Jex had wielded ever so briefly.

What now? Jex wondered. He wasn't surprised that he felt very little remorse.

"Jex," Setz repeated, finally. "I'm here to inform you of what happened on our return to Aquiocia. I understand that you must be in quite a lot of pain, and you must understand that I simply do not care. Blink once for yes, twice for no. Do you understand why I am here?"

Jex blinked once, slowly. Even that small motion felt like a colossal physical feat.

"Excellent. Then I will begin," the Chairman said quietly as he produced a scroll from his cloak, letting it unroll until it almost reached the stone floor. "The company was confronted by an ambush and Warmaster Maxim initially placed you in charge. Upon realising that the situation was too much for you, he and I took over the role of commanding our troops and repelling the enemies. Would you agree?"

Jex blinked once and Setz checked off something from the parchment with a dark feathered quill.

They aren't going to lie? Surely this will put the Warmaster under scrutiny for putting me in command, so why not lie?

"Your eyes tell me you're surprised. While I can hazard a guess at why, it is irrelevant," Setz said softly, looking down at his scroll once more. "Upon attempting to retreat, you were assaulted, and I transported you back to the position we were holding. Is that accurate?"

Jex blinked and the Chairman scratched at the parchment.

"Upon arriving back at the carriage, you proceeded to open

the cargo and wield the artefact within to extinguish the lives of two thousand and fifty-six civilians of neighbouring villages. You also murdered forty-two Aquiocian soldiers and attempted to take the life of Warmaster Maxim, before finally grievously harming the man reciting this to you. Is this the truth?"

That's why they aren't lying, Jex realised. *Because when he puts it like that, I look like a murderous psychopath.*

Setz sighed at the sight of the prisoner blinking twice. He'd known it wasn't going to be so simple, but the fact remained that the man before him was unstable. He could see it, even if the Warmaster and the King himself refused to believe it. Setz began to speak slowly as he rolled up the scroll in his hands.

"Despite the very real fact that the rest of the people there that day believe it to have been the cursed blade's doing, I know that you at least had some part in the deaths that took place," Setz explained, his amber eyes boring into Jex as if he'd like nothing more than to finish the job then and there.

Jex twitched involuntarily as he tried to remain motionless. Frustration was building up inside him, and he had no idea why. He also couldn't fathom why the frustration was so rapidly turning to blatant anger and loathing. It made him uncomfortable, and lying still became an arduous task as his body begged him to move in a bid for restless relief. Instead, all he could manage was a hoarse whisper that would have been unintelligible to anyone else.

"The blade... made me..."

"The sword made you do it?" Setz sniffed. "Of course it did. This is the same blade you were expressly forbidden to touch, Jex. Do not try to pin the blame on the artefact."

Setz grabbed the knife, turned on the spot and was walking towards the exit when Jex muttered something that caused him to stop briefly.

"It felt like... like it was part of something... It was so angry that it brought my own... to the surface. But... there is more to it – ARGH!" Jex's wheezing turned to a wail of anguish when a cough escaped his throat, triggering a violent pulse of pain through his body.

By the time he'd recovered, the cell door was locked and Setz was nowhere to be seen.

CHAPTER 38

A SQUIRE'S VISITOR

The knight sheltering the Princess jumped and yelped in shock as the prisoner threw himself at the bars of his cell. He was feeling better, and while the action caused him a dull sensation of pain, four days resting in a cell had helped him to recover.

"What? Scared of a man locked in a cage?" Jex taunted loudly as he ran at the bars again. "You're a damned knight, but all I see is a coward trembling inside an iron casket!"

"You see what you want to see! Of course he is scared, and that is nothing to be ashamed of!"

Jex looked down towards the faltering voice and saw the Princess glaring up at him through tear-filled eyes. Her shaking legs barely held her tiny frame upright as she attempted to stare down the enraged prisoner. For reasons best known to the Princess, she had seen fit to visit Jex that day. Jex had not shared the same enthusiasm.

"Don't you preach to me, you child. Princess or not, I am beyond –"

"You're angry! It's normal – get over it!" Alicea screamed as she pushed her ebony curls away from her ashen eyes.

Jex appeared to seize up momentarily, as if weighing up the significance of what he was hearing. *Was* he angry? He'd never felt true fury before, save for when he was bound to the dark blade. All he knew was that there was a desire welling up in his chest – that part he understood all too well. He understood that he wanted nothing more than to rip out the pompous brat's throat, but he also wanted her to suffer first. For that, he needed to calm down. He needed to get out of the cell; he needed to be normal.

I need them to think I'm simply a normal man who touched the wrong blade. Then when I get the chance, I can murder the little bitch, Jex thought, before catching himself. *Where are these thoughts coming from?*

"That's better!" Alicea beamed as Jex looked up again.

The pair stared at each other intently, as if trying to discern what the other was all about.

"I – I'm sorry. It's just the blade..."

"Yes?" Alicea tilted her head slightly.

"It made me lose control and I... I hurt all those people," Jex muttered, looking at his hands. He hoped against hope that he was putting on a convincing display of regret, because it was the furthest thing from what he was feeling. But he wasn't unaffected like he had been with previous deaths; this time he felt something. Joy, release – a euphoria. He had revelled in the feeling of freedom and excitement.

Alicea nodded, though neither prisoner nor knight could tell if she believed what she was hearing. "Are you sad?"

"Sad? Why would I feel sad?"

"Sadness is sometimes a component in feeling remorse," Alicea stated, as if reciting something she had read. "Do you feel remorse? Regret?"

Jex didn't respond. He wasn't sure how to. Thankfully, his

silence was answer enough for the Princess to move on to the next question.

"A lot of people lost those they cared for. Do you have anyone you care about?" Alicea asked casually. "Perhaps your mother or father? Other family?"

"Dead," Jex muttered.

"I'm sorry. Do you miss them?" Alicea asked kindly.

More silence filled the cell before Jex finally spoke.

"No."

"Why not?"

"They were a waste of life. I've accomplished more since their death than they both did in their lifetimes."

"I see," Alicea muttered, with a disappointment that seemed out of place. "And what of the people you killed? Were they a waste of life?"

Silence.

"I'm certain they wouldn't like me saying this to you – though they'd probably be more concerned with the fact that I'm here at all – but Father and Maxim actually believe you."

"Th-they do?" Jex deliberately stuttered, glancing at the knight. He seemed to have rallied a semblance of courage, aiming a stoic glare at the prisoner.

"Indeed. Although Setz claims otherwise," Alicea said bluntly. "He claims that you're a liability crafted from a dormant malice and that you should be executed."

"What do you think?" Jex asked, barely stifling his irritation at the fact he was trying to appear innocent for the sake of a child.

Alicea looked down solemnly. "I think they are all wrong in one way or another. Yet I also feel they are right in some respects. My opinion is that whatever happens, you need to be gone from Aquiocia as soon as possible." Her head snapped up towards the exit and she began speaking more quickly. "Whether you meant to harm those people or not, it happened. I could never allow that to become a regular occurrence. Luckily for you, it is not my decision to make."

The Princess flicked her hair and mouthed a quick countdown. As she reached zero, three knights suddenly rounded the corner and appeared in front of the doorway. Yelling at Jex to stand back, they ushered the Princess away from the "dangerous prisoner". Jex barely heard the demands for space as he stepped back from the cell's bars; he was already lost in his own thoughts of what was to come.

Was he scared? No. Angry? Furious. But above all, he was determined.

He was determined to find a way out of the cell and continue his life until his chance revealed itself. His chance to make an even bigger mark than he'd made on his last task for the kingdom of Aquiocia. He didn't need the sword for what was to come. It had shown him enough.

The next mark I make will dwarf the last.

CHAPTER 39

A MISTAKE OF THE WISE

The crackling of the fireplace would have been enough to soothe most men, but Setz wasn't one of them. Though it did offer warmth and a brief illusion of peace, he wasn't in search of it. Eyes closed, he sat at his table, as still as an upright corpse.

Listening. Sensing. Waiting.

Discipline wouldn't let him panic, but his resolve wouldn't let him forget that the Princess had slipped away from under his nose. No – he had let her do so. He knew where she was headed; he also knew he couldn't follow.

Not yet.

His amber eyes flickered open to see the door to his office opened by a hesitant man in a dark cloak.

"I apologise, Master –"

"Leave," Setz whispered. The man vanished, leaving the door open for a woman to bustle in. With a murmur from her, Setz's wooden table offered her a seat by bending and twisting its form into an offshoot with a flat surface.

"Setz."

"Garnet." Setz shifted slightly in acknowledgement. "What can I do for you?"

"Your men have not taken to the city," the shaman noted. "Meaning something is preventing you from doing so. I haven't worked with you before, I've met you only a handful of times over the years, but can I assume that you have taken measures to rectify this?"

"I have," Setz said flatly.

"Good. Because the Princess going off on her own is the worst news we could have hoped to hear. We lose her and everything we are doing is pointless. Without someone to put on the throne, Aquiocia as we know it will fall."

Setz blinked.

"How perceptive of you to realise she was gone," the Guildmaster noted, mostly for his own benefit. He hadn't considered the notion that Garnet might notice so quickly. He'd assumed he'd have enough time to find her, but instead all he was able to do was wait.

"How gracious of you to acknowledge my perception," Garnet offered in mock politeness as she crossed her legs and clicked her tongue. "I've spent enough time with the Princess to sense her energy signature. I know when she's moved too far away from me or when something is interfering with my ability to sense her. The moment she dropped off the map, I came to you. I had *hoped* it was because she came underground."

Setz didn't reply. Instead he weighed up the implications of Garnet's abilities. Like any accomplished mage, the Guildmaster had immediately recognised her as a gifted mage commanding the Earth, along with small traces of talent elsewhere. What he hadn't picked up on was her clear aptitude on the sensory side of magical abilities.

This meant that on top of her prowess in commanding the Earth and her talent for sensing and identifying those within a large radius, she was also quite capable of concealing it all, allowing those around her to know only what she desired.

"Choose your next words carefully, Setz. I only plan to ask this once," Garnet began slowly, her dark eyes boring into his own. "What is stopping you from retrieving Alicea?"

Setz wasn't threatened. He was impressed.

"There is an enchantment in place, forbidding those with the brand of the Guilty Blade from entering Aquiocia," Setz revealed, almost nonchalantly.

Garnet took a stilted breath, as if trying to control exasperation.

"I find myself disappointed in you," she admitted.

"No more so than I am in myself," Setz countered softly.

"What do you plan on doing?"

"I'm waiting."

"For?"

Setz fell silent again, his eyes moving from Garnet's flame-lit face to the hearth itself. The Guildmaster's expression was one of serenity mixed with realisation.

"That," he replied, suddenly on his feet and making his way towards the door at an unnatural pace.

"Setz, where are you –"

"You wanted to know what I planned to do?" Setz asked, pausing just long enough for Garnet to nod warily. "Then I suggest you keep up. Come. It's time to take the fight to them."

CHAPTER 40

LOVERS AND FIGHTERS

Advance, but only to the edge of the forest! Garnet's previous message echoed around Lyrium's mind. *Capture as many soldiers as you can but do not leave the safety of the forest. The less that return to the castle, the less resistance we have to contend with. They will not allow us another chance at luring them into the forest.*

It felt like a long time since Lyrium had received the same message as the rest of the force, but she continued, moving swiftly along the forest floor and leaping over the traps she spotted with her lover ambling along beside her.

"Be careful of the vines here," Arok muttered as Lyrium narrowly dodged a hanging trap designed to restrain a soldier.

"You didn't hold back on the number of traps you set up," she commented. Arok grinned. He was good at his craft and the admiration of the woman he loved never went unappreciated.

The pair continued to charge through the forest, but the advance was uneventful. There was no sign of either Aquiocian soldiers or Tremel hunters. All they could see was thick trees and thicker brush. To her right, Lyrium caught sight of one the breaks in the flora that had been used as a place to keep the captured guards. Oddly enough, there was no sign of anyone guarding the pit.

Coming to a stop, Lyrium turned to Arok, who huffed up

behind her. Thankful for the quick rest, Arok sat on the forest floor and looked up at his partner. Sweat dripped down his face and Lyrium realised he had been working harder than anyone – laying traps, reporting to Garnet and all the while carrying the massive war hammer his father had passed on to him.

"Take a moment, love." Lyrium smiled as she looked around.

"What's the problem?" Arok grunted as he leant back onto the overgrown roots of a large tree.

"It's not a problem, exactly. It's just… Was any order given to move our prisoners from the pits?"

"Nay, they were to be kept separate to minimise losses if one of the locations was found and raided," Arok said, shaking his head and reaching for his wineskin.

"How many pits in total?" Lyrium pressed.

"Five, I think, maybe more now," Arok answered, confusion creeping into his voice.

"Did every hole have men stationed around it?"

"Aye, of course they did. Lyrium, what is wrong?" Arok asked, rising to his feet.

"Arok, where are we?" she asked suddenly.

"What kind of question is that?"

"One that I need answered. You know this area better than I," Lyrium hissed.

Arok took a moment to take in his surroundings, his eyes resting on various trees before shifting to the sky, finally ending his search with a nod as he saw the plain north-east of where they were standing.

"We are near hole number three, the closest one to the edge

of the forest that leads to Aquiocia. In fact, if you walked around three hundred paces that way," Arok pointed in the direction opposite to the plain that had caught Lyrium's attention, "you would find a path regularly used by travellers to get to Aquiocia."

"We must be very close to the forest's edge, then!" Lyrium exclaimed, putting pieces together that Arok couldn't follow.

"Lyrium, it's your turn to answer my questions now. What is wrong?" he asked quietly.

Lyrium pointed towards the plain. "There is nobody guarding that hole."

"How do you figure that?" Arok asked in surprise as he craned his neck to see what Lyrium could.

"I don't know it because of my eyes, Arok. I know because I can *feel* it." Lyrium sighed. She had hesitated in telling her lover about her developing talents. "Ever since connecting with my stone and training with Alicea and Garnet the past few months, I can sense the presence of people, especially those aligned with the Earth like I am."

"That would be a nice trick. So, you can't feel anybody over there?"

"I can't feel anyone aligned with Earth, but I can feel something... But I can't see anything, and it would be stupid for us to charge in there."

"How has no one else noticed this happening?"

Lyrium stopped to think. It was a good question. Could it be that whatever had happened was hidden from the rest of the forces? How could this have escaped Kurok's attention, or Silrok's? It was especially difficult to think that Garnet hadn't noticed.

"I don't know, but whatever it is, I know something is wrong. I just can't see what it is," Lyrium conceded.

"Could it have something to do with you being a Vassal?"

"Maybe. Unfortunately, I don't know enough about that either. But you may have just given me an idea..." Lyrium trailed off as she produced the fist-sized stone from her pocket. It emanated a faint sepia aura, with a surface of moving earth.

"You're going to charge in with the stone's power?" Arok asked in disbelief. "I like the plan, but if ya lose control, then I won't be able to stop ya."

"I will only tap into it enough for it to heighten my senses so I may see what's going on there."

Arok didn't understand, and that was fine. Lyrium barely understood it herself as she pushed the focus of her mind outwards slowly, before focusing on the stone.

You need my strength. The stone's deep voice was indifferent; Lyrium had become familiar with its almost apathetic nature. They had come to an agreement weeks ago that it was best to keep communication to a minimum – a nice way of expressing that Lyrium still held a lot of resentment towards the being within the stone, a feeling that was mutual.

I only wish for a little, enough to enhance my senses enough to see what is happening in the distance.

There was no reply, only the feeling of a light trickle of energy coming from the stone and entering Lyrium's reserves. Placing the stone away in her pelts, she focused her sights on the field ahead. The effect was almost instant. Lyrium's vision became tunnelled and yet much was revealed that was previously hidden from view. Now she was aware of the tiny insects going about their business as if a skirmish hadn't just broken out around them. Birds on high flew past the battlefield, completely at ease with their lot in life.

But none of this was the least bit interesting as the young shaman's enhanced sight homed in on the plain in the distance. As if sensing what she wanted, her eyes zoomed in on the hole that was so far away. She couldn't see what remained in the pit, but she could see clearly that there was no longer anyone guarding its wide expanse.

Lyrium was about to release the energy being fed to her when something caught her attention. A small group of people appeared to be fleeing the scene in the distance. As the last one escaped her view, she caught sight of the Aquiocian emblem on the soldier's sleeve.

"There are four – maybe six – Aquiocian soldiers fleeing from the location, and yet no sign of our men," Lyrium revealed.

"How is that possible?" Arok wondered. "Were they killed by half a dozen soldiers?"

"Pft, doubt it. It is far more likely that someone played a trick on our men," Lyrium replied, stretching out her limbs.

"What are you doing?" Arok's eyebrows rose; he made no effort to conceal his approval of her toned physique.

"I'm going to ask the bastards personally," Lyrium smiled, raising her fist to get her meaning across. "Care to join me?"

"This is a reckless and foolish plan," Arok muttered before taking a draught from his wineskin and grinning. "Let's get going!"

CHAPTER 41

MISDIRECTION

If the soldiers fleeing back towards the castle were surprised by the hunters emerging from the brush and tackling two of their men, they didn't show it. The unfortunate pair that had taken the fierce impact sprawled to the ground, where they lay motionless.

"Oh, come on – I didn't even hit you that hard!" Arok threw his head back and let the laughter flow from his lungs. Setting traps for hours on end had become monotonous, and he relished the outright assault on the enemy.

The three who remained on their feet didn't move. The hunters hesitated – why were the knights not drawing their swords?

There were a few odd things about the middle knight's appearance. The first was that he did not appear armed; the second was that his armour had clearly been made for a shorter man. The chest plate did not sit correctly, and the greaves did not cover the full length of his shins. The only reason the armour was wearable was that the man was thin enough to slide into it.

The last thing setting this soldier apart from the others was the fact that he had straight, pitch-black hair that fell from underneath his helmet and down his shoulders. The aura the man gave off made him seem familiar, but it felt like a less potent version of something Lyrium had experienced before. Like a familiar drink made by someone who went light on the spirits, the person's aura felt diluted.

Before she had time to comment on the strange appearance of the knight, he removed his helmet to reveal the amber eyes of the murderer the Princess had feared since childhood.

"This is a bad turn of events," Arok noted, smile wavering ever so slightly.

"Jex," Lyrium muttered, the fear starting to gnaw at her.

"In a sense, yes," the man responded in a strangely gurgled voice. "Two savages out on their own when the rest of them are working so hard?"

"What is wrong with your voice?" Arok asked. It was a fair question – Jex sounded like he'd swallowed a branding iron.

"Nothing. It is like this when I am in this form." The gargling did nothing to hide the cruel undertone.

Before Lyrium and Arok could respond to this strange answer, the two men on the ground started convulsing erratically. Lyrium didn't have time to move before every gap in the soldiers' armour began to secrete thick red liquid, while a sickening squelching sound filled the air. The sound rose steadily in volume before the bodies in the armour exploded, spraying blood through the steel caskets.

"It seems that these accursed bodies are out of time," Jex said thoughtfully as the two beside him started to undergo the same process.

"What is this abomination?" Lyrium demanded.

"This is just a little talent I have; one that you're very fortunate to see. The only others lucky enough to view this happening were the fools guarding that hole. Well done, though," Jex commended. "The Princess' ability to shirk her duty to fight is truly magnificent."

It was Arok's turn to demand answers. "What did you do?"

"It is merely an extension on the curse that plagues the men and women of Aquiocia. Eventually, after they have been under its influence long enough, they rot and decay. Generally, it takes years for it to adapt this far, but for some the taint spreads much more swiftly." Jex attempted a laugh that sounded more like he was choking on his own tongue. "Whenever I take full control, the body begins to deteriorate at an exponential rate. Some people just can't handle real power."

"You're not the real Jex," Lyrium muttered, to herself more than anything.

"I'm not, and this body's destruction will not remove the curse. I've been through… Oh, so many by now…" Jex's imitation gloated, though it appeared thoughtful through the pain plaguing its degradation.

"Why don't ya come out now and I will spar with ya myself!" Arok threatened.

"I might just do that." The imitation wheezed in agony as the two knights on his flanks collapsed. "But I have something to take care of… Go look in the pit. Witness the futility of your struggle."

The man's head began to sweat blood profusely, and the pair barely had time to leap behind the large trees before his head exploded in a geyser of blood. The red liquid scorched everything it touched, leaving severe burns on the plants it showered.

Glancing around the tree he had used for shelter, Arok quickly confirmed the death of the final soldier before turning to Lyrium.

"The... The pit," she said, absently wandering towards the hole that served as a prison.

She didn't bother looking for the hunters who had guarded the pit; she practically tripped over their corpses. Something within her forced her to stare ahead, to ignore her fallen kin strewn across the forest floor. She pushed forward. She knew what was likely waiting for her in the pit, but she had to confirm.

She had to.

At first, Lyrium couldn't react. A part of her acknowledged her lover behind her, cursing and muttering a hurried prayer to Gaia. The rest of her took in the gruesome spectacle below. The bottom of the hole simmered with thick, crimson liquid that scorched the various pieces of cerulean armour embedded in what had become steaming sludge.

Lyrium exhaled slowly when she saw the singed pelts of her kin mixed in with the rest of the gravesite. She felt her body react, stomach roiling and throat tightening, eyes blurring slightly as her muscles trembled. Her face remained impassive, as if desperate to hide what she was feeling from her audience of one. She acknowledged the bodies of the hunters atop the pit. While their deaths appeared to have been brought about through combat, the tainted blood was streaked here and there, burning whatever it touched – be it plant or skin.

The body we saw him in... It wasn't the first. Can he jump from body to body...?

"I can only guess that whatever you're thinking isn't good

news for us," Arok said, a weak attempt at a joke. He was periodically guzzling from the skins tied over his shoulder. The taste of wine masked the taste of bile his stomach threatened to bring up.

"He was never here..." Lyrium muttered. "He... never left the city..."

"So?"

"Alicea needs to know. We need to get word to her and –" Lyrium caught her lover's evasive eye. "What is it?"

Arok hesitated.

"What do you know, Arok?" Lyrium asked, confused. The idea of him keeping something from her was a foreign concept.

"I checked in on Dairok at another hole on the way here and he mentioned something about Garnet trying to find her. She ran off," Arok revealed, not meeting Lyrium's eye.

"What?" Lyrium hissed. "She's gone? Why did she –"

"All questions I dunno the answer to."

Lyrium slammed her fist into the nearest tree. The death toll for both sides had jumped in minutes. Now, their leader was gone, and Garnet was preoccupied with finding her. Things were falling apart.

Jex will keep jumping into the bodies and killing them all, along with any of our own nearby... He's known everything that's been going on and... A look of horror crossed Lyrium's face.

"He knows," she muttered, looking to Arok in desperation. "He's been watching all along. He planted these men!"

"What? I dunno what ya on about!"

"Arok, who knows she's missing?"

"The Princess?" Arok frowned. "Uh, Dairok, Garnet, few messengers maybe..."

"He knows she is in the city."

Realisation dawned on Arok.

"The bastard was in the pits!"

Lyrium's head was whirling. They had no idea how to locate their friend and there was every possibility their enemy was expecting her. They had known the curse killing the knights was a possibility, but they couldn't have predicted Jex transmitting part of himself through the cursed.

There was no way we could have known... Lyrium reasoned. *But... did she account for this?*

"Lyrium?" Arok waved his hand in front of her face. "You alright?"

"We didn't see Jex at Tremel until he had Alicea where he wanted her. How did he do that?" Lyrium asked, knowing the answer.

Arok frowned.

"He's waiting..." Lyrium whispered before falling silent. She had never felt so useless. Everything appeared to be going their enemy's way and her friend was marching into his waiting arms. She couldn't help – she couldn't even decide on a course of action.

Lyrium was spiralling, and she knew it. She tried desperately to cling onto something that would bring back her will to fight, but the confusion was too much. She could hear the rumblings of her lover saying something, but her mind refused to make sense of the words. What could he possibly say to help?

"LYRIUM!"

She looked up at Arok's face, which was twisted into a look of anger.

"We going or not?"

"Going where?" Lyrium asked absently.

I repeat, another legion approaches. They are rallying at the city gates. Silrok's voice echoed through Lyrium's mind for the first time. She caught a small sensation of satisfaction from the telepathic link, as though the messenger had achieved something she had been striving for.

"More...?" Lyrium muttered, gathering her bearings.

"We ain't capturing these ones!" Arok announced, tilting his head over his shoulder to his mounted war hammer.

Lyrium's muscles tensed. She knew what the enemy was doing. She knew what purpose the marching soldiers served now. It wasn't going to happen again.

That bastard just made his first mistake, she thought viciously. *He just gave me something to hit.*

CHAPTER 42

STRIKE BACK

Lyrium raced through the forest, her partner calling for her to slow down. She did, barely. She didn't know the forest as well as Arok, which allowed him to keep pace somewhat. She slowed to a brisk walk when she saw the forest's edge, her senses pricking at the anxiety of the hunters stationed on the front lines.

She pushed past a few younger hunters, their protests falling on deaf ears. Arok hurriedly offered reassuring smiles and small words of apology as Lyrium took her place at the front of the force, standing just outside the forest's edge.

It wasn't the first time she had been so close to Aquiocia, but it might as well have been as she gazed across the rough roads leading to the forest, along with those headed east and west. Deserted, of course. But for how long?

It didn't matter; she could see the massive gates in the distance, and with a touch of aid from the stone, the legion gathered before it. Lyrium didn't see soldiers – she saw shells of human beings. She saw tools utilised by a cruel lunatic. Their lives meant nothing to him and she forced herself to look at them the same way. It was easier than dwelling on the fact that she was about to strike out at her friend's people. She would deal with the guilt later.

Should I get the chance...

The force shifted and began marching forward. Lyrium turned to a group of hunters behind her.

"Messenger, your fastest!" she barked, and an anxious teenager clothed in the feathers of countless birds raised his hand. "Get this message to Silrok of the Northern Settlement. Jex can jump from body to body amongst the cursed. The soldiers in the pits are spies and dangerous. Pit three is compromised. Action required. Lyrium."

The teenager's face had visibly whitened in silent horror, but he nodded before bursting into light and taking to the skies as a bird of prey.

Lyrium breathed a sigh of relief, which allowed the anger in her to rise. She knew the message had to be sent before taking action. Before...

"What are you doing, Lyrium...?" Arok's concerned voice came from her left as her senses hit a new level. She was watching the marching legion as if she was a dozen strides away. She could hear the metal on the road as if she was marching alongside them. She caught traces of their trepidation as her unwavering focus settled upon them.

Lyrium didn't respond; she waited. She simmered and festered within her rage for what felt like an eternity. Then...

Message received, understood.

Lyrium's being exploded with light. Cries of surprise rang out from the hunters as a brilliant sepia glow burst forth, surrounding her body and drowning out the daylight. The gathered force backed away from the ethereal beast that had encompassed Lyrium's form.

The beast rose to its hind legs, displaying its impressive

torso of ripped and torn muscle. Its sheer size devoured the Vassal within, but it remained transparent, so that all could see the look of fury upon her face. Lyrium opened and balled her fists, the beast mimicking the action with paws big enough to crush a deer's chest. The power ran through her; it was her own. For now.

Her rage melded with the beast's, its face twisted into a canine snarl adorned with cunning eyes. Its fur was on end, its long tail lashing back and forth in anticipation. Lyrium's furious, determined gaze never left the approaching legion. Once the savage form was established, she growled with a sound more beast than human.

"He won't reach the forest. He dies today."

She didn't wait for a response. Her body was on all fours and in motion. She cleared the field effortlessly, leaving the medley of cheers and distraught wails behind her as she focused on the doomed men before her.

The legion had made good distance while Lyrium waited for confirmation on the message, but it only took her a dozen or so seconds to reach leaping distance. She dove towards the centre of the legion. Her powerful legs braced and launched her, the earth below passing by at a dizzying pace, before she saw a single pair of terrified eyes.

Dead. Crushed effortlessly by the massive, ethereal werebeast.

Lyrium's new form lashed out at the soldiers around her while her feet remained firmly planted on her first kill. Like an alpha defending her right to eat first, she crushed those close to her. Her glowing claws tore armour and rendered the flesh below. Corpses were hurled to the side, deemed irrelevant in what was quickly becoming a rampage.

The men tried to disengage.

Once there was no one alive within her grasp, Lyrium pursued the first target she saw. Her aura deepened, and the beast around her clamped down on a fleeing soldier's torso. Like parchment, the man crumpled.

Then onto the next.

A pair of men helping a third with a broken leg. All three driven into the dirt as the beast struck from behind. Killed instantly on impact.

The beast threw back its head and howled at the sun. Through the rage and bloodlust, both the creature and its wielder felt something change. The atmosphere shifted, and they knew what had happened even before they looked down.

The battlefield had turned silent. No sounds of fleeing knights, no screams of terror. Nothing.

Beast and Vassal nodded as they pivoted on the spot, watching the backs of the suddenly frozen knights. Her gaze rested on one; there was nothing about him that stood out until he turned on the spot, lifted his helm and grinned. The knight's short brown hair began to grow and darken, his eyes turning from soft green to sinister amber, his skin from sun-kissed to pale and bloody.

It wasn't Jex, not fully. It was an amalgamation of the two people, as if Jex was forcing himself to the surface from within. But it wasn't limited to one knight. The others turned simultaneously, removing their helms in unison as Jex forced his influence upon them.

Lyrium was surrounded.

Surrounded by hundreds of contaminated victims, all with

the painted face of a grinning maniac.

"You just keep making mistakes, don't you?" The gargle of countless abominations made it difficult to decipher the words.

The beast around her panted, confused by the lull and ready to continue the rampage.

"Now I know your face," the knights rasped. "Aren't you angry at yourself yet?"

A tortured sound of bloodied throats echoed around her as the compromised legion laughed.

The beast roared, a terrifying sound that demanded to be heeded over the cacophony of doomed men. Lyrium latched onto her error, the revelation only fuelling her desire to crush anything wearing her enemy's face. She reinforced it with the excuse that killing those the enemy controlled weakened him.

The force rushed her from all sides. They lumbered awkwardly, but obeyed the curse nonetheless. Both beast and Vassal turned feral, crushing the first group to reach them with a single swing of their massive paw. The beast lashed out unpredictably, its moves desperate. The weapons collided with the aura and while Lyrium felt the dull throb of impacts, it only ignited her fury further and deepened the ethereal glow around her.

"COME ON!" Lyrium screamed as the beast roared and crushed another three men. "GIVE ME MORE! HIT ME! I WILL CRUSH YOU ALL!"

She was descending into a berserk state of mind and she relished it. Her vision was shrouded in a sepia aura, yet she saw everything. She could feel her mind embracing the fury, submitting to it. She saw each individual enemy as a target to be destroyed, and the power enabled her. The impacts of weapons upon the aura ceased to sway her. She had achieved the perfect rage.

Bodies flew, and bodies crumbled. The sight of tainted blood only sustained the rampage, though it never touched her. She ripped at the torso of a knight, his blood spraying away from the aura, as if compelled to avoid it. A dozen soldiers rushed her and a dozen fell. There was no stopping her, and she was at peace with the mayhem rioting within her. The light of sanity was fading, and she felt compelled to let it.

Until...

"That's it, fellas! Bury the bastards!" A familiar voice... A voice lost in the chaos reigning within and around her. One that had meant something before this; one that might still.

Her ears rang with the sound of something colliding with steel. Behind her, past the wall of corrupted knights – what was it?

She marched. She marched *through* the knights, tossing them aside carelessly like toys she had grown bored with. There was something new she wanted, and she was going to find out what it was. The soldiers threw themselves at her aimlessly. She caught glimpses of their perpetual, bloody smiles and horror-filled eyes, but she didn't care. They were tools of her enemy, and they would fall.

She faltered upon reaching the outer edge of the soldiers. The beast around her attempted to lunge forward at the sight before it, but Lyrium kept their feet grounded.

Hundreds of hunters rushed forward, slowed only by preparing their bows and letting arrows fly.

The sky was filled with the arrows of her brethren, and

surely some must have connected with her. The rage couldn't, or *wouldn't* discern the difference; everything was fuel to it. Lyrium's head pounded suddenly, as if boulders were falling on it. She recognised the feeling. She was trying to claw her way back to sanity.

Damn it! she screamed internally. *Why must I give up one for the other? How can I choose?*

She received no response from the being within the stone, and yet an answer appeared before her. On the front lines, lumbering between his father and distant cousin from the west, was Arok, roaring with primal passion. The hunters cried back in unintelligible confirmation.

Lyrium threw back her head and screamed towards the sky, adding her fury to the din of the hunters. Within the aura, she slammed fist into palm before turning and leaping straight up into the air. As she crashed to the ground, her lover and his entourage met the enemy head on. Lyrium drove her ethereal fist into the earth, and splintering out from the impact point, the ground cracked and shifted.

The soil beneath the soldiers erupted with life. Glaives of earth ascended from the ground, impaling and slaughtering dozens. Vines restrained their victims long enough for the hunters to destroy their bodies. In the centre of it all was Arok, swinging his mighty, indestructible weapon with the force of a falling comet. His face was one of grim fortitude, his body a bulwark for his people. As Lyrium filled the soil with her essence and commanded it to do her bidding, Arok was the champion the others followed into the fray.

The earth began to respond in other ways, seeming to know what was expected of it. As a pair of bloodied knights descended upon some younger hunters, they suddenly found themselves bound to the ground by nature's tethers. Knives of bones quickly found their throats and the hunters moved onto the next.

Lyrium could see the combat thinning out. The knights had given up trying to pierce her aura and were desperately trying to kill the hunters. It left Lyrium in a state of peace in the dying chaos, undisturbed as she devoted her energy to calling upon the land. Her aura was lightening, but it didn't matter. The combat would be over momentarily.

This is the second time... the voice within her stone said quietly.

Lyrium was about to hiss at the voice and remind him of their agreement not to speak when another voice responded.

The number of times is irrelevant. I have requested you release her.

Female, silky smooth and completely unrecognisable. Her words echoed within Lyrium, sending chills and shivers through her body.

I will. But you have chosen poorly.

Have I? the female voice asked kindly. *Then how is she able to hear me?*

The connection broke. "Who are you?" Lyrium cried, desperation to know welling up within her. *"Who are you?"*

She was still staring at the ground, screaming the same three words over and over, until she was lifted to her feet and Arok stood before her. He was covered in dirt and had streaks of smouldering blood on his clothes, but was otherwise fine.

"It's over," he said hoarsely, concern written on his face.

Lyrium looked around at the battlefield. Scorched and bloodied corpses were everywhere. There wasn't a direction she could turn without seeing death. Her aura was gone, though she barely cared.

"It's… over?" Lyrium struggled to breathe, her desire for an answer still lingering. "How many did we lose?"

"A few. Few more injured. Gaia favoured us this day. We should return to the forest," Arok spoke in stilted statements, his stoic face hiding his emotions from everyone but Lyrium. He was terrified, but he rallied.

As would she.

"Right. The forest," she muttered, letting her arm rest over Arok's shoulder as they began to trudge over the sea of corpses towards their sanctuary.

Lyrium kept her eyes forward, allowing Arok to guide her. She stumbled slightly at one point, and her eyes fell on the face of a soldier impaled by a large, sharpened bone. The man's face was lifeless and almost peaceful. There was no way to tell what kind of life he lived before Aquiocia fell to corruption, but Lyrium wondered if he – no, if *anyone* deserved to be returned to Gaia the way he had.

To her horror, the man's lips spread into an agonised grin. Her body seized up as a single eye opened, causing the knight to appear to be winking.

"Give chase, and I will send more to die –"

The cursed knight's face disappeared under Arok's boot, and they kept walking.

CHAPTER 43

A FLEEING KING

Bah, ridiculous, Arissam scoffed internally. *How did that man get into my chambers so easily? I don't care what he said – I know he was after my life.*

The King was a slender man, but he wasn't in shape. Even scurrying along the level, masterfully crafted stone of the castle's corridors left him wheezing.

I should have known there would be other organisations out there looking for my head. Arissam's mind was as frantic as his feet, trying to make sense of the situation. *But if they were after me, then why did he go after the enchanted parchment instead?*

He knew why. He just didn't want to admit to himself that the enemies he'd forbidden entry to were now free to wander into the castle at their leisure. Because that was what they would do.

They'll come through the walls and floors and – SHIT!

The King came to a sudden halt at the sight of a dark silhouette at the end of the corridor. Its outline was alight with the dying rays of a departing sun invading the palace through one of the ornate stained-glass windows. The orange glare didn't reveal any details of the figure, but he knew exactly who it was. It didn't matter that they were on the same side – his presence made the King uneasy.

"Jex."

"Arissam," the silhouette replied evenly.

There was no bid to be called "King".

"Forgive me, Jex, but I must attend to –"

"You're running," Jex observed with a hint of humour. Stepping forward, his features were illuminated by the glow of the departing sunlight. His face didn't display loathing, contempt or even the usual dash of lunacy. It was almost as if…

"You look at ease," Arissam said with a glance past his undesirable company.

"Oh, I am. Everything has gone precisely as intended."

Jex's body flashed with a dark aura that trailed as he blazed forward, now a few feet away from the flinching King. The dark light faded as he released its hold and Jex's voice maintained the same serene tone.

"Everything is as I predicted, right up to you fleeing like a cowardly dog that's been kicked in the guts." Venom laced Jex's tone at the last few words.

Arissam attempted weakly to object before he found Jex's hand wrapped around his throat.

"Don't speak, coward."

Arissam couldn't reply if he wanted to. He was weak; it was highly unlikely that he'd be able to win a brawl with an intoxicated adolescent, let alone the most dangerous man in Aquiocia.

"Pathetic," Jex sneered, throwing the King to the ground as easily as a child might discard a piece of trash. "Farewell, Your Majesty."

"F-f-farewell?" Arissam spluttered. "W-what –"

"What do I mean?" Jex finished, never halting his casual saunter away. "Do you not understand? This is the endgame. Everything I've done, I've done for this moment. The fact that it might disrupt my plans is the only reason you're still alive. Your death might offer the royal bitch some semblance of hope."

"I could kill myself —"

"But you won't. You're a dog. I've seen enough men like you in my time. You bark. Oh, how you love to bark. But you never bite. Someone else must do that in your name. No, you'll do what you always do — you'll run. So do it. Run. Run fast and run far. Because after I deal with the Princess, I won't have any reason to leave you breathing."

Arissam didn't reply. Instead, he remained on the ground in a bewildered stupor as Jex continued to walk away, before disappearing entirely. Arissam had always known who — and what — he was. "Coward" was an apt name for him, but it wasn't the name itself that bothered him so much. It was the fact that Jex was the first to call him one since he had seized power.

He'd heard the whispers of other royals. Whispers about his aversion to the battlefield and to fighting. He'd always sought to silence the talk, and he'd thought himself successful in doing so. But to have someone so ruthless and cruel, someone so clearly unstable, someone like Jex, call him a coward to his face...

Damn it. Damn him!

Arissam pulled himself to his feet and rubbed his throat. It felt uncomfortable, but not painful — Jex had meant it when he said he didn't mean to kill him yet.

There was nothing else for a man like Arissam to do at this point.

He ran.

CHAPTER 44

A SQUIRE'S ESCORT

Over a month had passed, though Jex wouldn't have known it. He knew hours had turned to days, and days to weeks, but there was no way to keep track of exactly how long he'd resided in his cell. The only visitor he'd had was an older lady who would enter the cell once a day to replace his bandages. He always asked the same questions about what was going on outside, and if she had heard anything about the Warmaster or the King. The woman would simply brush away the stray silver hairs from her face, reminding him that she was just a nurse and knew nothing of the kingdom's proceedings. It didn't stop him from asking, and had eventually become a joke between the pair. Jex realised the old woman was the closest thing to a friend he'd had since Clareen.

Jex felt a stinging sensation in his chest. It took him a moment to realise it wasn't a physical pain that was poking at him. The agony from the blade's handiwork came and went at its own leisure, sometimes striking quickly for a few seconds of writhing anguish before dispersing. Other times it would supply an uncomfortable sensation that caused his entire body to seize up for hours at a time. But this new feeling wasn't either of those, and though it took him a while, he soon saw it for what it was. Guilt.

It was gone as quickly as it came, and part of him thought he might have imagined it from restlessness and boredom. Before he had any time to reflect on finally feeling any form of guilt, the cell bars suddenly sprang open and in waddled the kindly old woman, gauze in one hand, a bucket filled with hot water in the other. Jex greeted her with a small smile and she returned a friendly grin. As Jex sat up and the woman set to her work, he asked a question he'd never thought to ask before.

"I can't believe I've never asked, but what is your name?"

"Oh, I hadn't realised. They call me Idi, dear," she replied as she started to peel away the bandages caked in blood. "Ah, today is one of the bad ones, it seems."

"Hard to imagine a good one anymore. What is this, your fifteenth visit?"

"My forty-fifth, dear." Idi frowned, looking over the flesh that had been magically scorched beyond belief. It was reluctant to heal; the skin was slowly repairing, but every time it managed to stitch itself back together, blood would gush from the wounds and the process would repeat. Idi had declared it to be an infection, but Jex suspected she knew better.

He paused a moment until silence had well and truly set within the cell.

"Do you think I will ever get out of here?" he asked.

"I don't think so, dear," Idi said with a genuinely apologetic tone.

"I figured." Jex gazed towards the roof of glowing stone and settled in for another lonely stint.

The solitude didn't worry him so much. It was the fact that he hadn't managed to make much of an impact in his time outside of the walls around him. When he thought about it, it was all he could do to contain the rage within. He'd had his chance. He'd had the blade, his key to unreal power, and an avenue to make his mark. But he'd overlooked the Chairman. He had underestimated him and as a result, he had blown his one chance. Now he was to sit there and do nothing with his days.

Not even the Princess had deemed him worthy of another visit. That was a small victory, but a victory nonetheless. He couldn't afford to get angry in front of her again.

Idi seemed to notice his reverie. Without looking up from dressing his wounds, she said, "Tomorrow you may just get a chance to tell your side after all."

Jex's eyes flittered down to the nurse.

"What makes you say that?"

"All right! That's enough time to change a damned bandage!" a rough voice called from outside the cell.

"Time's up, it seems," Idi announced. As she got to her feet and the guards entered the cell, she whispered in Jex's ear, "Good luck, my dear."

Jex was left to his own thoughts as Idi departed with the accompanying soldiers. He had little idea what she meant, and absolutely no concept of what time of day it was. But he knew someone was obviously coming for him, and that at the very least, tomorrow would be more interesting than his most recent days.

Whatever happens tomorrow, I will be ready.

❖

Of all the people Jex thought may have come to see him, the Warmaster was not amongst them. He had barely awoken from his slumber when he saw the impressive, crimson-haired man standing in the centre of the cell, encased in full-plate azure armour with the Aquiocian Rose etched into its front. The most surprising part of it all was the fact that the Warmaster was smiling – no, *grinning* directly at the sleepy-eyed prisoner.

"Warmaster…?" Jex said through the thickness in his throat.

"Maxim is fine, Jex," he said, gesturing towards the door. "Shall we?"

Jex was lost for words as he followed the gloriously dressed man from the cell and up a staircase leading to sunlight. It was then that he realised he was not in the prisons where regular criminals were kept. As he let the fingers of his uninjured hand run across the narrow walls lining the staircase, runes glowed with lights of every colour. Wherever they were, he was never going to get out unaided.

This just makes the Princess' visit all the more impressive.

As the pair reached the top of the staircase, Jex cowered momentarily from the harsh exposure to natural light. Maxim waited patiently for him to recover, and once he had, he took in his surroundings for the first time. The first thing he saw was the western side of the Aquiocian palace across the way. His gaze swept over the palace and steadily made its way back to where he stood, on its way taking in memorials, flowers and tombstones by the thousands. In each direction he could make out well-maintained paths and clearings designed to make visitors' navigation of the cemetery easier. Along the paths were the occasional pairs of knights who would look towards them, see Maxim and nod with respect before continuing their patrols. They were obviously supposed to look like they were patrolling the cemetery, but it was obvious they had been watching over him.

Jex let the air escape his lungs slowly.

"A tomb. I was locked in a tomb," he said, more to himself than his companion.

"Yes. Not many know about the various prisons around the kingdom like this one," Maxim explained as they started their walk towards the palace. "You were kept here as it allowed for you to remain out of sight and yet close at hand. I apologise for the distinct lack of visitors, but no one, save for a select few soldiers here, myself, Setz, and of course the King, knew you were even here."

"It's fine. I had Idi for company on a daily basis, along with a visit from the Princess herself."

Maxim seemed to be about to ask about Idi, but his duty trumped his curiosity.

"The Princess visited you?"

"It's impossible to tell when exactly, but towards the start of my imprisonment."

"That'll make it difficult to find out who was on duty the day she escaped their watch, then. Unfortunate."

"You might as well scold everyone who has ever watched anything to do with the castle. The Princess has memorised the patrol routes along with the times that patrols begin and end for the entire castle," Jex revealed. "The grounds as well, it seems."

Jex caught a hint of a smirk on Maxim's face before it vanished. The Warmaster wasn't going to give anything away voluntarily, but he was obviously impressed by the Princess' feat. He had personally designed every patrol route and schedule himself, and while it was steadily becoming more difficult to monitor as his workload increased, he'd thought them almost infallible. Clearly, he had not accounted for Princesses who were too clever for their own good.

Jex himself had found that he was falling into a state of numbness. During his stay in the tomb-prison, he'd felt pangs of various emotions, none more so than anger. Yet now he felt the way he had before the events involving the blade. He realised that until now, he hadn't even considered the possibility that perhaps the blade had instilled the lasting bursts of seemingly random emotion. But at this moment, he was confronted by the sensation of feeling nothing upon leaving his cell. Was it the room causing the surges of emotion? One thing that had definitely been affected by the cell was his ability to hear the heartbeat of others. He noticed this when he flinched as he walked past a group of guards. Surprisingly, he couldn't seem to home in on Maxim's.

"That talent seems to have a drawback or two. Not sure I'd like it myself," Maxim observed.

"Ta-talent?" Jex stammered, trying to gain his bearings from the sudden onslaught of heartbeats.

"Blood Sense," Maxim said knowingly. "Unimaginative name aside, it's quite a rare ability. You won't find much about it in your regular library."

"What do you know about it?" Jex asked, dropping the act entirely.

Maxim shrugged beneath his armour. "Not a lot. It's a rare ability. I've heard it is derived from manipulation of

Dark Magic combined with another force. What the other is, I don't know. I've heard that even those aligned with the correct elements stand very little chance at actually having the aptitude for it. It chooses the wielder rather than the other way around, it seems."

"How did you find all this out?"

Maxim clicked his tongue thoughtfully as they made their way along the stone path leading from the cemetery to the palace's courtyard. For the first time in Jex's life, the Warmaster seemed uncertain of what to do or say.

A question. A question is what brings a man of his prestige to a stop. Ridiculous.

"Believe it or not, Jex, I do try to understand each of my men. That in itself is a near insurmountable task – I know this. So, I prioritise helping those who need it most. But do not think of it solely as pity. I put you in charge that day for a reason, and that reason is that I wholeheartedly believed you had the ability to lead those men. For what it is worth, I still do." Maxim's voice was cold despite the sentiment, and it only hardened as he went on. "But you made a mistake, and a heinous one at that. The worrying aspect of all this is that none of us know whether you meant to do it or not. But that's not the most terrifying part at all."

"What is, then?" Jex asked, scratching at his bandaged arm.

"The terrifying part of it all, Jex, is that you don't know whether you meant to do it or not."

The younger man fell silent at the Warmaster's words. He knew the truth; realistically, they both did. The two men both knew well that they saw through each other, but neither wanted to accept the conclusions they had come to.

"You think I'm a monster?" Jex didn't know if he was asking or stating it.

"No," Maxim replied without hesitation as he pushed open the grand doors to the audience hall. Jex hadn't even realised they had made it to the palace grounds, let alone across the entire courtyard. As they entered the hall, Maxim rubbed his left temple as if in thought. Jex might have asked if he was unwell had he not noticed the countless guards within the hall. There were at least a hundred men wielding crossbows, and as their bolts took aim at the newcomers, Jex felt a surge of excitement. The idea of fighting for his life greatly appealed to him, despite being unarmed and somewhat malnourished from the imprisonment.

Wait... I didn't eat once in that cell. How is that possible? Jex wondered, before accepting that it must have had something to do with the enchantments surrounding the cell itself.

"I do not think of you as a monster, Jex," Maxim continued as the soldiers lowered their weapons and another impressive man rose from the throne at the end of the hall. As Jex recognised King Axeal, the Warmaster added but a single word before leaving his side.

"Yet."

CHAPTER 45

A SQUIRE'S TRIAL

"Ah, Jex!" Axeal greeted the prisoner as he waved away the countless guards. Within moments there were only a dozen left stationed within the hall, as was the norm. "It has been a while indeed! I apologise for not seeing you sooner. I was considering a rather pressing matter."

"You owe me no apologies, Your Majesty. I am hardly worthy of your time now," Jex said humbly, hoping he wasn't overplaying the act.

Jex noticed that while the King hadn't sensed any insincerity, Queen Adele revealed herself by standing from her own throne and giving him a sceptical eye before silently taking her leave. Jex found himself slightly relieved by the Queen's departure; it was no secret that Alicea had inherited Adele's intelligence and cunning. To have either one of them present during the meeting with the King would spell almost certain disaster – they were simply too perceptive. King Axeal proved that he wasn't completely oblivious by noticing the exchange of expression on Jex's face at the sight of the Queen.

"Adele will not be taking part in this – let's call it a *conversation*," he confirmed with a stroke of his full beard. "But please do not think this will be a simple matter to delve into. Walk with me, young man."

Jex had a full minute to take in the image of his King as they turned and walked towards the staircases behind the thrones that led to the upper floors. He was wearing a massive, cerulean cape adorned with white furs over pure silver armour that clinked ever so slightly as he walked. His deep-brown hair was combed back under a small golden crown that he wore day-to-day – he was supposed to wear one at all times in the public eye. His ceremonial crown was much larger and grander by comparison. Following the King upstairs in silence, Jex couldn't help but feel the tension surrounding the great hall from his place on the balcony. The knights who remained behind were giving the pair sideways glances before and after bowing to the King.

Finally, Axeal came to a single door guarded by four soldiers, who immediately stepped aside to allow the pair access.

"Here we are. Please, make yourself comfortable," Axeal offered, gesturing inside the room.

Jex took a hesitant step inside. The doorway opened into a medium-sized chamber, its walls lined with countless portraits of the royal family. Many of the faces he didn't recognise, but he quickly found the image of King Axeal and Queen Adele holding an infant Alicea. They radiated happiness; Jex looked away in muted disgust. He shot a quick glance towards a portrait of a man with thinning brown hair. He recognised the man as one of the younger Council members, but couldn't recall his name. He looked out of place in his official-looking robes compared to the other people on the wall, and Jex knew the reason why. Almost every royal and noble in Aquiocia fought in the military and was often away from the grand kingdom they were sworn to protect. As a result, they were rarely seen by the public, but it was the Aquiocian way.

Finally, his eyes lowered to a grand and glorious table and high-backed chairs in front of a roaring fireplace. Rising from one of the chairs was Setz, who didn't meet Jex's eye as he nodded to his King. After a hushed exchange about a man called Locke having found the Princess outside the castle, Setz was gone.

Axeal prompted his subject to take the seat on the right as he removed his heavy cape and crown, hanging both on the seat opposite Jex before sitting down. Before them was a strange four-foot-wide tabletop that looked like a bird's eye view of a mountain range. Jex noticed that there were even clouds moving across the surface of the image, as if a day was continuing its course despite being locked into a piece of furniture.

"Tell me, Jex. You're an intelligent man; have you heard of The Elemental Chronicles?"

"The... game?" Jex asked slowly, to which Axeal nodded. "The board game that creates a replica of the player by reading their consciousness, or some ridiculous notion. The higher officers play it."

"Indeed. The game drags the players' minds into it, where they must utilise their real-world abilities to undertake a task on a fictional playing field-turned-battlefield. This game allows for a person to truly be themselves. I suggest you think about why you're here, Jex," Axeal advised, handing him a seemingly normal block of timber. "I encourage you to keep your previous actions at the very forefront of your mind as we sit here today. Consider this chamber your courtroom, consider me your judge, but above all, consider this *ridiculous* game your trial. Let us begin."

CHAPTER 46

A SQUIRE'S CHANCE

Jex was soaring through the air. He felt liberated, as if recently freed of all responsibility and sin. He had been gifted a fresh start, a new beginning, and he was flying towards it.

Then his stomach fell and his body followed. He wasn't rising anymore, and he wasn't moving forward. He was plummeting through the blackness and the passing winds whispered rumours of a doomed man falling to his fate. He didn't see the ground before he hit it feet-first. His legs bent but didn't buckle, the force absorbed instead by the world forming around him.

Ripples reverberated through the air before stabilising. He was now a part of the game.

"So… This is The Elemental Chronicles?" Jex murmured to himself as he gazed around at the sheer cliff sides surrounding him.

He was in a valley, from what he could see. A glance behind him revealed other paths that opened into separate sections of the land. It didn't matter which way he turned – he was trapped between steep cliffs crafted from earth and stone that would be suicide to climb.

Thankfully, although the walls ran parallel to one another, they offered a comfortable gap that could fit several small houses side-by-side in most sections. As Jex took his first step towards a destination he had no knowledge of, small pieces of debris fell from the stone wall to his right. Instincts took hold as Jex crouched down and examined the wall's surface. There was nowhere that indicated instability, which left only the very top as a plausible culprit.

The King, perhaps... Jex pondered. *Oh, who cares? Isn't the point of this game to kill your opponent? He didn't say anything about doing otherwise.*

Jex kept walking. The sun was high in the sky, which was unnerving as he continued his journey to nowhere. Weaving through the canyon for what he swore was hours, Jex began to question why the sun hadn't descended at all. It had been midday for too long. He wasn't worried, but he could identify a pointless task when presented with one.

Just as he was about to re-evaluate his plan, something caught his eye in the everlasting sunlight. A shine – no, a shimmer of light on steel. Jex ducked his head as he approached the new fixture wedged in the ground before him. He knew well that it could be a trap.

As he reached the strange item, he identified it as an Aquiocian longsword, its blade half buried in the dirt. The angle of the sun and the blade made it impossible to look directly at the weapon, so Jex pulled it free the moment he reached it to prevent himself from being blinded. Then he heard it all. The roar of men, the resonance of war horns and the chaos of battle above him.

His head jerked upwards to see the sun finally moving through the sky at an accelerated rate, the darkness of night in pursuit. It had gone from midday to dusk in seconds; Jex would have questioned it if he wasn't suddenly distracted by the sound of grinding stone a short way ahead of him. He watched on as large sections of the walls on either side crumbled to the ground, reforming into expansive stone roads leading up and out of the valley.

All I did was pull the sword free – this doesn't make any sense. Obviously, logic will only get me so far here.

With cautious eyes, Jex examined the roads that were once walls, listening to the din of combat above him. He figured that maybe he was safer in the valley than emerging from its embrace. He could just turn around and run, but he could already feel something building up inside him. His blood felt like it was burning in his veins and he felt the desire to leave the valley's confines. Before he could fully comprehend that he'd made a choice, he had already reached the impasse. Looking down each of the paths revealed little, as if something was obscuring his vision from seeing further than the path wanted him to.

What he could see of the two paths was identical in every way except one. Littered along one path were countless glimmering, azure petals that caught what little remained of the dying sun's light. The other was smattered with drops of blood, as though hundreds of wounded men had traversed the path without treatment or gauze.

Jex knew which one he wanted to follow. He also knew that in the real world, he was on trial for following his instincts.

What do I do?

His thoughts were drowned out by the sound of a throbbing heartbeat echoing in his ear. The pulse moved through his being until his entire body was alive with the beat of a heart growing faster in excitement. Jex assumed it was the same sensation young men felt when an attractive woman entered the room. He felt a little giddy, yet more in control than ever. He knew what he wanted, and unlike a puberty-ridden teen, he could take it without consequence.

It's just a game, after all. Besides, the goal is to find and strike down your opponent. The King probably found this fork in the road before me. Knowing him, he'd have followed the blood to make sure whoever it belonged to was safe. So I will follow it myself, find my opponent, and win this game.

Whether Jex knew his mind was tainted by something else, offering convenient excuses to follow the trail of blood, was anyone's guess. But he felt something as he strode down the path of bloodstained stones. Perhaps not happiness or joy, but a manic and exhilarating elation of his body and mind, marching through his veins at the prospect of the wounded people's pain.

I feel all this merely at the sight of blood? I haven't even seen the people it belongs to yet.

❖

The perpetual sound of battle grew louder as Jex traversed the path stained with blood. The sound, his enthrallment and the amount of the precious red resource strewn across the stone all escalated with each step he took. It wasn't long before the squelching sound of a thick liquid came from beneath his boots as each time his foot descended, it found a deeper puddle to dive into.

Suddenly, the world around him seemed to stop. He could

no longer hear the chaos of battle, only the persistent, irritating ring of silence in his ears. Turning slowly, Jex's eyebrow rose a fraction at the sight before him.

Somehow, he'd reached the top of the valley he was in just minutes before. There was no longer a path, only the large slab of blood-coated stone on which he currently stood. The massive gouge in the earth had expanded greatly, as if the force that had torn it asunder in the first place had struck out at it again, leaving an enormous chasm in its wake. As dusk gave way to midnight in a matter of seconds, a pale, full moon lent Jex its light as he took in the countless rope-and-timber bridges extending from one side of the canyon to the other.

With the platforms often branching off in strange patterns, all connected, and all supporting one another, these bridges weren't simply to get from one point to another. On the strange, wall-less labyrinth were hundreds upon hundreds of soldiers – all fighting for a cause beyond Jex's comprehension.

Though he witnessed people dying by their opponent's blades, or even falling from the precarious structure, it was the fact he couldn't hear a single sound that had Jex's attention. Not the battle, the heartbeats or even his footsteps made a noise as he slowly approached the battlefield, blade in hand. He felt lost. The feeling of enthrallment from moments before had evaporated with his hearing. A familiar hollowness welled up within him, one that was now undesirable after feeling so much.

Is this fear, then? Jex wondered, quickening his pace. *They say it has the power to slow or even cripple a man. I can't allow that to happen. Not now. Not after feeling what I have felt. I don't like this. I don't WANT it!*

Are you under the impression that you can have one emotion and not another? a familiar voice broke through.

You. The blade. How are you here?

It only makes sense, Jex. The Elemental Chronicles drags you unto itself – all of you. I am part of you. Through mind, through memory, the voice explained cryptically. *Through body.*

Jex doubled over and let loose a silent scream as he grabbed at his bandaged arm. He couldn't tell if he'd managed to stifle the wail of pain, or if the silence had nullified his voice. All he knew was that his bandaged arm had begun to bleed so profusely that the bandages were already stained crimson. He knew that soon the bandages would be completely redundant.

Would collapsing to blood loss end this game? he wondered through the pain.

Probably. But that isn't the way you want this to end. You know what is at stake, and I know what you desire. So why don't you get to your feet and pursue it? You will have my aid, of course.

The same aid that killed thousands in an instant? Jex scoffed, though he knew he'd like nothing more than a second attempt at wielding the weapon's power. *The blade isn't here – how will you help me?*

Once one wields the blade, they are never alone. Though very few survive. I admit I wanted nothing more than devour your life force entirely. It is my primary desire and purpose. But another interfered just in time. It was barely enough, and only by catching me by surprise did they succeed in severing the connection between the blade and yourself. But the other was not so quick as to be able to prevent me from imprinting on you anyway.

I don't understand. Jex rose to his feet, removing the pain from the forefront of his mind. *I don't care. You want to help me win this stupid game? Do it.*

A fine and cavalier attitude.

Isn't it just? Jex mused. *I know there will be a price in accepting you, but I will pay it again. I loathe feeling nothing after everything that has happened. Anything is better than being left feeling hollow again.*

I feel honoured that you "accept" me. As if you ever had a choice.

Jex ignored the remark. He knew what he was doing was reckless. Though the circumstances had changed, the struggle he was undergoing at that moment was precisely what had landed him in the strife he was currently wading through. He didn't care. He was going to win. Because that was what was around him: a game to win. He knew his adversary was more than competent in swordplay, magic and war. To stand even a sliver of a chance, Jex needed everything at his disposal.

The easiest way to defeat a body of people is to take off its head. Jex sneered as he began to stride confidently towards the bridges. *I'm coming to find you, Your Majesty. I'm coming for victory.*

CHAPTER 47

A SQUIRE'S JUDGMENT

Jex stepped onto the unusual battlefield. Granted, he didn't have the ideal weapon, manpower or strategy to do, well, anything. But he had full faith in his own capabilities. After all, how difficult could it be to find and slay one man amongst hundreds of combatants fighting upon countless interlocked bridges suspended over a chasm that seemed to grow in breadth whenever it deemed necessary?

Just kill or be killed, the absent blade's voice rang through Jex's mind.

It was exactly what he had planned and begun executing the moment his feet hit the first accessible bridge. Two men with swords were immediately on him. They weren't the burliest of opponents in their light armour, silver and blue ribbon wrapped around their arms. Jex immediately noticed that each had a single such ribbon, guessing they had attached them to their clothing personally. This made it easy to deduce which arm was the dominant one.

Jex casually stepped back from the pair's respective swings, impaled one of the men with his sword and sent the wounded man hurtling into his ally. The men collided and fell from the narrow platform, screaming in terror the whole way down.

Jex sniffed. He hadn't counted on them falling before he

could make them bleed more. Disappointment didn't linger long as he looked towards the other bridges branching out in every direction. With a quick glance behind him, he wasn't surprised to find a wall of solid stone stretching out along the length of the chasm's edge. The barricade stood higher than Jex could even make out. He knew that leaving the battlefield was no longer an option and it was a development he was fine with.

Turning back, he was surprised to see two more men running towards him with their swords sheathed. Jex had to exercise every ounce of self-restraint he had to not cut them down immediately, and he had to admit to himself that the only reason he didn't was the sight of the pitch and crimson ribbons on their arms.

"My Lord!" the men cried, each dropping to a knee. "Thank the gods you're here!"

"Gods?" Jex's eyebrow rose at the strange greeting.

"Given the recent occurrences – moving land, enemy troops suddenly appearing…" One of the kneeling men shook his head as if at a loss. "I'm ready to believe in anything."

"I am no lord."

"What are you saying, My Lord?" The men looked up from their bows. Jex noticed they looked almost identical to the two he'd struck down only a minute earlier. "Please, tell us you aren't deserting us, not now!"

"Deserting you? I have no idea what is happening here," Jex said with an even indifference. It wasn't just a case of them looking identical to the pair before that made him feel like they meant nothing. It could have been almost anyone kneeling in front of him. "I am here for my own reasons. I will see them fulfilled."

"My Lord, please understand that despite whatever else might be influencing your decisions right now, we are people as well. We are people who need your leadership – we need your help. Please, aid us in our plight!"

Though he felt nothing save for the twitching of his sword arm, Jex recognised the plea as a social cue designed to make a person listen – to empathise. Try as he might, he couldn't bring himself to care for these men. But perhaps he could force himself to do what he knew would be considered the right thing.

Perhaps not.

Before he could respond further, he felt a forceful yank on his left arm, followed by the sensation of a thick, warm liquid saturating his bandages from the outside. He knew what he'd done even before he saw his sword buried in the whimpering man's chest. His final words meant nothing, and Jex didn't hear them anyway. His interest was focused on the fact that he could feel the difference between the blood of the stranger outside his bandages and his own from within. His own blood burned with contempt and loathing while the dying man's emanated dashed hope and a perpetual despair. Jex could feel everything, and he relished it.

Rather than draw his blade, the second man took off back the way he'd come. Jex could hear his screams warning his comrades of "their Lord's betrayal".

Jex calmly pulled his blade free and dropped the dead man like one would discard unwanted food. A brief, dark shine from his blade caught the moonlight and distracted him for a single moment before his legs were carrying him across the bridge. He quickly reached a series of interchanging bridges, some running parallel to his own, others above, below and even stretched across in front of him.

Irrelevant, the voice told him. The single word was cryptic, but Jex knew what it meant. *Indeed,* he agreed as he leapt from his place on the platform and fell to another much larger one twenty yards below him.

You have great faith that I won't let you fall to your death, the voice mused as Jex watched the dozens of men struggling to win the position on the wider platform below.

Faith? There's no need to insult me, Jex scoffed as he fell through the still air. *I either live, or I die. Your call.*

Jex felt the entity's amusement burst through his being as his bandaged arm shredded through the gauze with dark energy and darker blood. His sword had transformed into the cursed blade; his flesh mimicked its sinister hue, the crimson ribbon wrapped around his wrist the only thing breaking up the darkness, burning and seething with its influence.

If the soldiers saw the ominous light descending towards them, it did nothing to save them from being launched in all directions by its impact. Jex landed amongst the combatants, unharmed and cushioned by the energy enveloping him. The bridge rattled but held. The blade had distributed the energy to give its wielder a safe landing that wouldn't collapse the structure beneath him.

The wails of surprise caused Jex to smirk. Another sensation made its way under his skin. It originated from multiple places, but they all met at the same point – his heart. The precious muscle began to pump erratically; at first, he thought it might explode, when he noticed that he felt no pain stemming from it. There wasn't even the slightest discomfort. That was when he realised it wasn't that his heart was beating rapidly itself – it was echoing the sound of the others nearby. What started as the steady beat of his own heart was now a convoluted din comprised of dozens of soldiers' hearts, picking up in both pace and ferocity.

The instant the phenomenon hit Jex's senses, he knew it was pointless to try to decipher each of the rhythms and their owners. But as he watched the warriors who'd been lifted into the air plummet off the sides of the wide bridge, the discord of heartbeats lessened.

So, if I'm closer I can hear them better. Makes sense, Jex realised as his thoughts cleared. *Is this your doing?*

Mine? the voice asked in genuine surprise. *I can assure you I have absolutely nothing to do with blood. I seek a far greater prize.*

A greater prize? Jex wondered briefly, glancing at his blackening arm.

Do you care about what I seek at this point, or are you just wasting time? the voice countered.

I couldn't care less, Jex conceded as he looked around at the half dozen men who hadn't been forced off the bridge. There were two with crimson ribbons, four with azure, all six faces looking borderline identical. Under normal circumstances, Jex would have suspected them to be siblings.

"That's the enemy commander!" a man with an azure ribbon yelled as he got to his feet. "We kill him and this battle is as good as won!"

"That's no commander of ours, he's a bloody traitor!" cried one of the men who was trying to kill him just seconds before.

"Lies! But I guess there's no harm in helping you kill your

leader!" another called out with a forced laugh that did nothing to hide his fear.

Looking up from the sinister blade in his left hand, Jex glared at the first man his amber eyes landed upon. His long hair fell across his face, but it did little to shield the man from the sheer loathing in Jex's expression. Jex didn't have to keep track of the others and their movements; he could sense their hearts, filled with trepidation as they attempted to flank their adversary. He'd gone deadly still, with only the dark energy of his weapon rising from blade and flesh like an unholy smoke.

There was no way for the soldiers to know it, but their enemy had given himself entirely to the influences that had plagued him his entire life. For so long Jex had felt nothing at all, and to finally experience emotion, however cruel or depraved, wasn't something he'd allow himself to be deprived of. Not again.

"You insects are nothing," Jex hissed as the man he was glaring at glanced to the others. "I see no reason for that which has no bearing on the world to exist. You all look the same."

"Are you mad? We look nothing alike!" the man cried in desperation as Jex lunged forward at an inhuman pace.

The soldier didn't lift his blade. He didn't have time. Jex was on him and all he saw was the terror and despair of the man he was about to strike down. Bringing up his blade, Jex lashed out with a manic laugh, a mirth cut short by the ringing of metal on metal and his body coming to an abrupt halt. Something had stopped him before he could end the man's life, and it took him a moment to realise he was staring into the eyes of the Aquiocian King.

"Greetings, Jex." Axeal grimaced as his opponent took in

the new situation. Their blades were locked, with the King between Jex and the terrified man. "I see you've already made a few choices. I trust you're happy with them – are they the ones you'll stand behind until the end?"

Jex grunted as he pushed back from the deadlock. He was surprised not only that Axeal had stopped his rush with ease, but that the dark blade hadn't overwhelmed him. He also couldn't sense the King's heartbeat, though he could feel the hearts of the soldiers easing.

The King's very presence brings these insects peace?

Yes. I wonder what would happen to their resolve should their King fall here?

"Your Majesty," Jex greeted him between clenched teeth.

"Jex, please." The King smiled as he stroked his beard with his spare hand, looking up from his undamaged, gloriously ornate longsword. "Call me Axeal."

❖

"Get to safety." Axeal's soft command carried to the ears of the men around him.

"You're our enemy!" one of the men yelled as he pointed at the King's crimson adornment.

"The true enemy within any great battle is the one borne from even greater misunderstanding. War can be a crutch upon which one leans when they hate what they cannot fathom, or it can be a bridge to bring people closer. Now, get to safety."

Whether the men gathered there felt moved by the King's words, or were just scared of the newcomer who had somehow launched dozens of warriors off the suspended platform, was irrelevant. They ran, and Jex didn't even bother to watch them leave. He could feel their heartbeats disappearing into the maze of bridges around him. He also noticed that the night had gone completely silent; even the presence of the voice within his blade was hushed by the King's arrival.

I didn't even sense his approach. How long has he been watching me?

"Might I be blunt in my questions, Jex?" Axeal asked politely as he sheathed his blade in an equally beautiful scabbard. The weapon and its home would have seemed ostentatious had it not been for the King's choice in armour, catching the moonlight brilliantly upon its exquisite design of cerulean and silver. It was full-plate, but articulated to its wearer, and did nothing to slow the King as he paced back and forth across the platform. He was looking everywhere that Jex wasn't, as if thoroughly enjoying his examination of their surroundings.

"You're the King," Jex replied with a bitterness that got away from him.

"I am, aren't I?" Axeal chuckled as he gazed at the stars strewn across the black velvet sky. "Now, what kind of fool allowed a lout such as I to ascend the throne?"

"I… What?" Jex stuttered. *Is this even the King?*

"We've never had the opportunity to speak in person. Well, not freely." The King smiled widely, finally looking at his former soldier. "Do you think the blade came to you because it sought you out, or because you longed for its strength?"

The sudden question caught Jex unawares, though it didn't show on his face, which still clutched its scowl of defiance.

"Both," he said finally.

"Probably." Axeal tilted his head casually and resumed his pacing. "I understand that you've met Alicea on a number of occasions."

"I... have met Her Highness, yes," Jex replied hesitantly. He'd been haunted by the child throughout his training.

"Her Highness?" Axeal openly laughed, a full and hearty sound that would lighten any normal situation. "*Her Highness* has been quite difficult to keep an eye on at times!"

Jex didn't answer. He didn't know if he was supposed to join in the jokes or if insulting the Princess in front of the King was a bad idea. He also didn't know if he cared about the King's reaction if he did.

"I can't keep up with her, you know," Axeal admitted, his voice full of happiness and pride. "Adele knows exactly what Alicea is up to at any given moment, but she's long since left me in the dust!"

Adele always knows what Alicea is up to? Jex wondered before the realisation hit him.

"And Adele *always* fills me in." Axeal's tone dropped, though his smile remained.

The following moments of silence might have been agony to anyone else, but Jex felt his excitement growing. Somewhere down the line, Alicea would have told her mother at least *some* of her thoughts on him, and in turn, the Queen would have informed Axeal. The conversation was finally interesting to Jex. His hand tightened around the hilt of his blade slightly. The ribbon responded, constricting his wrist harder with the burning sensation.

The movement wasn't lost on Axeal, though he didn't address it verbally.

"Blood Magic, is it?" he asked, cheerfully changing the subject. "Adele has been researching it. Perhaps it would have been better had she seen out your trial here."

"Why are you here instead, then?"

"Because Adele would have killed you where you stood well before the game began," Axeal revealed casually. "Couldn't have that."

The Queen wants me dead?

"Indeed, she does," Axeal nodded, answering Jex's question before he could even voice it.

"My original question stands," Jex replied forcefully. While he'd been taken aback by the Queen's perception of both him and her daughter, he had also realised it meant nothing in the grand scheme of things. The truth was that the situation he was in couldn't be altered. Not yet, anyway.

"I am here because I listened to Maxim. He claimed you deserved a trial, and although you've made some undesirable choices, along with Adele being less than pleased with me, I'm glad I saw out your trial personally."

"Why did Maxim vote for a trial?"

"He's a traditional man who wanted his King to address the issue personally." Axeal shrugged before his eyes finally hardened. "Please don't misunderstand, Jex. There was no vote. Had there been one, you'd already be executed."

Jex didn't reply. Instead he met the King's firm gaze with his own. He knew he stood in front of the judge who would decide his fate, and the time of judgement had arrived. Here, on a bridge suspended over a chasm, in a fictional world crafted by a board game's magic, he would be informed of what would happen next. If he had to, he would fight.

Fight for what? Even if I kill him here, I will be apprehended in the real world. Jex finally realised the magnitude of strategy the King had implemented to have a smooth "trial". He was even more trapped than he had been in the prison.

"So far I've witnessed you embrace the power of the cursed blade willingly and murder those who trusted you. I've seen you elect the path of bloodshed time and time again, and I only speak of the events in this game. Jex, I implore you to say something – *anything* – in your own defence!"

Jex took a measured breath before the first genuine smile he'd ever experienced found its way to his face.

"Well, Your Majesty, I will recite the words that a King once said to me." The man consumed by darkness shrugged, and the King's confidence faltered for a fraction of a second at Jex's next words. "This game allows a person to truly be themselves."

CHAPTER 48

A SQUIRE'S PUNISHMENT

"So be it!" Axeal roared as Jex's blade collided with his own. The faces of the two combatants came within an inch of each other as they fell into another deadlock.

Jex's eyes were alive with excitement, Axeal's with grim determination. The King had no choice but to lash out. His subject had made his choice. Time and time again he'd insisted on the destructive path with no sign of remorse, and now the King had seen it personally.

I'd hoped that by bringing forth a battlefield, where real people wouldn't be hurt, that maybe he'd... Axeal's mind wandered before he forced it into focus. *No, Adele was right. They all were.*

"What's the problem, Your Majesty?" Jex sneered, his tone mocking. "Can't even cut me down in a fictional world?"

"Jex, how does one man go so horribly wrong?" the King muttered before stepping back suddenly. His opponent fell forward in surprise as Axeal spun on the spot, gripped the hilt of his sword with both hands and brought the shining blade straight through to Jex's chest.

The blow should have killed him. It had the force to cleave through flesh and bone, and had it not been for the dark aura surrounding Jex's arm expanding and intercepting the attack, Axeal would have instantly downed him. Instead his glorious blade glanced off the new barrier surrounding a now hysterical Jex.

"I might be condemned in the real world, Your Majesty. But I'm not going to lose here. You trapped me."

"I gave you a chance!"

"Ha! A chance, you say?" Jex's voice grew more manic by the second. "I never had a chance in this world, much less the one we inhabit! I never stood a chance at living happily amongst people who all nod and agree at the sound of a spineless King's orders!"

"A spineless – watch your mouth, you insolent –"

"Oh, shut your own!" Jex snapped. Axeal looked like he'd been slapped. "You sit on your throne and nearly cry at the sight of the knighted squires, all the while declaring that you're doing the best you can to protect the kingdom. Horseshit. You're a joke. Do you even know that Lucian's at large?"

"Lucian? The knight? That hasn't been proven –"

Jex lost control. "I HAVE SEEN HIM WITH MY OWN EYES, YOU ROYAL FOOL!" Suddenly he was breathing heavily, as if he'd just run a mile. "You pathetic, you... Why, why can't I breathe?"

"Because it's over, Jex," Axeal said with sincere regret.

Through his blurring vision, Jex noticed the King's open palm shining faintly.

"You... The... The air!" Jex fell to his knees as the cursed blade's ribbon expanded to cover more of its wielder's flesh. As Jex's will to fight faded, the ribbon scorched more and more of his skin. Before long, his entire body from the neck down was encased in the ribbon burning away at his being. Despite the excruciating agony, Jex refused to cry out or beg.

"Your desire to see the good in people, your bleeding heart... Your weakness will... It will be the end of you."

"That is something I have already made peace with. Rest now."

Axeal's soft voice echoed throughout the worlds as Jex found himself suddenly free of one set of restraints and bound with others. He was back in the chamber where the game was being held and his arms were now clasped in thick chains.

"I... How?"

"You suffocated and were consumed by your own blade." Axeal sat across from Jex as he flailed against half a dozen knights.

"I suffocated... How?" Jex snarled in his fruitless attempt to break free.

"I was happy to fight with blades alone, but you incorporated corrupted magic, and so I followed suit," Axeal said with a stoic expression.

Jex was suddenly silent. He'd underestimated the King yet again.

"Take him to his cell," Axeal ordered with an even expression. "Jex, understand that I did not want this. You will be executed at dawn. I will see to it personally."

CHAPTER 49

A SQUIRE'S REVELATION

"Get in there, you monster!" one of the knights snarled as the rest of the entourage hurled Jex back into his cell in the cemetery. The force was completely unnecessary; he'd long since given up the fight.

The cell door slammed behind Jex as he glanced around at the pale glow of the walls that had become familiar. The soldiers who had escorted him threw insults in an attempt to provoke him, but Jex ignored them, suddenly solemn. There was no point buying into their petty attempts at goading him; they were inferior and irrelevant. Eventually they grew bored and took their place up the stairs and outside the tomb. It had been approaching dusk when he'd been led through the castle and across the cemetery. The night had just begun.

It's strange that there were so few people in the castle, Jex thought.

It was as if the entirety of the castle's residents had left the palace for the duration of the trial. Save for the King and the knights who had apprehended him, Jex had only caught a brief glimpse of one other person as he was dragged back to his cell – the Queen herself. She had been sitting crosslegged upon the throne, with a stillness that only a statue could boast. With the same ice-blue eyes as her daughter, Adele silently watched on as the man she'd demanded be executed was taken away.

Not a word was exchanged, but Jex's struggle had ceased upon meeting her gaze. He could feel the hearts of the knights fill with reverence and just a slight hint of awe at the sight of their Queen, and it didn't take Jex long to understand that she was truly a force to be reckoned with, despite having never engaged in conversation with her. Suddenly, he understood the Princess' parents like never before – they truly complemented each other. It didn't matter that Adele wasn't of royal blood; the Aquiocian people had the same absolute faith in their Queen as they had in their King. Through the rushing blood of the people around him, it all became clear to Jex.

The King's kindness and compassion sustained his people with the steadfast loyalty that allowed them to wade into battle with a hope unwavering. Axeal could only accomplish this with Adele by his side, a dangerous, intellectual force who was ruthless in preserving the peace of their kingdom. Jex had heard rumours about the King and Queen in battle – they sounded like the tales of great heroes told by bards who depended on a drunk audience to make a living.

Jex had put no stock in the rumours, but feeling the rush of emotions running through the veins of the people, he was almost ready to believe. So why couldn't he feel the emotions directly? Why did he not feel a sense of peace that defied an impending death when the King was near? Why did he not get the sense of utter adulation others received in the presence of the Queen? What did the others have that he didn't? Why could he only access the emotions through them?

It doesn't matter now. In less than twelve hours, I will be dead.

His cynical thoughts sobered him.

Jex suddenly felt like he was being watched and smirked despite his situation.

"Come to see me off, then?" he snarled.

Turning slowly on the spot and looking down at the prison door, he wasn't surprised to see the small, shaking form of the Princess.

"Hello, Jex," Alicea squeaked.

"What do you want?"

"I... I am uncertain." The child Princess faltered for a moment. "I suppose I came to apologise."

Jex's ominous eyes narrowed at his visitor. There had been so much more going on that day that an apology felt like the last thing he'd be receiving, much less something he felt entitled to. He didn't reply, instead striding over to his small bed in the corner and taking a seat on the end of it, staring at the cell door. It appeared as if he was more interested in examining the door than the Princess herself.

"I am truly sorry for the fate my father has decided for you. It was not my intention."

"What are you talking about?" Jex muttered, genuinely confused.

"My mother –"

"She wants me dead. She followed you all those times you appeared around me," Jex revealed, talking over the Princess. It took a moment of observing the uncomfortable look on Alicea's face for realisation to finally hit him. "You knew…"

Alicea bowed her head in silence.

"YOU KNEW SHE WAS FOLLOWING YOU!" Jex wailed. He rose to his feet and threw himself across the room at the bars of the door.

His body slammed into the metal as the frightened girl yelped and jumped back out of reach. Jex attempted to put his arm through the gaps and received a shock that sent him reeling back, howling in pain. It didn't deter him; he launched himself at the bars again and again as the Princess wept and whispered the same phrase over and over.

"I'm so sorry, I'm so sorry, I'm so sorry."

"YOU'RE SORRY?" Jex screamed, his face pressed against the bars, magical energy singeing his hair. "I WILL MAKE YOU SORRY – I WILL MURDER YOU AND YOUR ENTIRE FAMILY! NO, I WILL KILL EVERYONE IN YOUR ENTIRE KINGDOM! YOU'RE FINISHED, ALICEA!"

"This is what I saw…" Alicea said between bouts of tears. Her miniscule amount of courage was trying to shine through.

"YOU *SAW* THIS?" Jex pushed back from the cells and feverishly smashed his fists into the bedframe. The cheaply made furniture buckled and splintered with each of his manic blows. Suddenly his head snapped back to his visitor, and with a whisper far more terrifying than any outburst, he said, "You helped *make* this."

Alicea didn't have a response for that. She saw that the man before her was broken, and perhaps she was somewhat at fault. But she knew Jex was dangerous; she saw it before anyone else. At four years of age, she had sealed away a monster, and while she had hoped for exile, perhaps execution was best. She shuddered at the thought. She might have only been a child, but she was more than perceptive enough to understand bloodshed and its toll. She'd seen it in the eyes of her people.

"Farewell, Jex," Alicea muttered solemnly.

As she ascended the stairs leading outside, she could hear the manic threats of the prisoner below. The last she heard stayed with her far longer than she would have hoped.

"YOU BETTER PRAY THAT MY HEAD COMES OFF TOMORROW, BECAUSE IF BY SOME STROKE OF LUCK IT DOESN'T, I'M COMING FOR YOU, ALICEA!"

The desperate cries suddenly vanished as she pushed open the door leading out of the tomb. The tomb was clearly enchanted to be soundproof so that visitors wouldn't think the dead were wailing out to them. It was morbid, in a sense, keeping a prisoner in a cell masquerading as a tomb, an enchantment masking the sound inside.

"Y-Your Highness!" a knight stuttered as he saw Alicea emerge from the tomb.

"Please escort me back to the palace," she replied coolly as she wiped away the stray tears on her face.

The knight nodded, rushing to her side. "I will take you to the Queen immediately!"

"And tell her what? That you failed to stop her daughter from sneaking into a tomb serving as a prison for a dangerous criminal?"

"I... I don't..." The guard faltered as he searched for the right answer.

"I won't tell if you won't," Alicea offered.

"T-thank you, Your Highness. You are –"

"I am impatient. Less speaking, more escorting."

The bewildered knight nodded quickly and gestured towards the palace.

"Right this way, Your Highness!"

CHAPTER 50

ONE FOR ALL

The corridors of Aquiocia held no secrets for Setz or his companion as the pair made their way through the palace at a brisk pace. As expected, the place was largely deserted. The main force would be on the battlefield, captured or retreating. Everything had gone according to the Princess' plan.

Including her disappearance, it would seem, Setz berated himself.

Though he had a great deal of faith in the Princess, he knew a lot of people would pay for her naivety should her plan fail. Garnet could sense the Guildmaster's hesitation.

"You need not worry," she offered in a soft whisper. "We both know she tends to be blinded by her own kindness. That's why she has so many willing to follow her already. She only wishes to prove her worth."

"I know this," Setz muttered gruffly. "It's not her kindness or her ambitions I hold disdain for; it is the situation in which they're being tested that has me on edge."

Garnet held her tongue for a moment as Setz turned abruptly to one of the bare, pale-blue walls and placed his hand to its surface. A small smile flickered across her lips as the wall disappeared and the pair stepped through into the hidden passage. The wall reappeared just in time to conceal them before thirty soldiers ran past on their way to wherever they had been ordered to go.

"I wouldn't usually comment on your methods, however impressive they might be," Garnet began as they traversed the passage. "But you do realise it's stunts just like that one that give her the confidence her subordinates will get her through whatever idealistic plan she concocts, right?"

"No, that's not the reason at all." Setz shook his head as his hands found the wall at the opposite end. It disappeared at his touch and the pair came face to face with six bewildered knights.

"Gladirus: Coleep," Garnet muttered, and the soldiers fell to the ground in an armoured pile of snoring men. The pair continued, Setz leading the way and Garnet questioning him. "Then why don't you tell me what gives her the confidence to blaze forth with half the facts?"

"It's not her subordinates' talents or power that give her confidence, Garnet. Because she doesn't have subordinates. She would never consider us, Rufus, Lyrium or even the lowest-ranking knight as such," Setz explained as he waved his hand, restoring the wall to its original place. "Anyone who fights alongside the Princess does not have a rank. There is no hierarchy in her mind when the struggle begins; she stands with each person involved."

"I believe there is a point you want to express, Setz," Garnet pushed.

"Alicea doesn't fight her battles with subordinates or an army of underlings. She fights the battle with those she loves. The only reason so many people have rallied behind her, and will continue to do so, is because she would do the exact same for them. You see armies that would die for their Princess. The rest of us see a Princess willing to die for her people."

The pair had completely avoided the audience hall through Setz's network of secret walls. In one instance they found themselves dashing across the courtyard under the royal balcony. The smell of smoke and sulphur hung in the air, but it was fading. The Guildmaster gazed up at the balcony for a moment and gave it a nod, the meaning lost to his companion. It didn't matter. It wasn't for anyone but the three men who had most recently died serving him.

A soft click got Setz's attention; Garnet was pointing across the courtyard to some moving shadows. They might not have been perceived yet, but they weren't alone. Setz pointed towards a wall that branched out from the main palace and the pair dashed towards it, running headlong through an illusion the second Setz's hand met it.

They were back inside the palace, storming down the interior of the north-western corridor.

"Do you miss it?" Garnet asked.

"The palace?" Setz paused. "No."

"That's not the answer I expected."

"After most of the royal family perished, there wasn't a lot to return to. If I'm honest, the enchantment that forbade my men entry was something of a bittersweet gift. Being here…"

Setz trailed off. He had no idea why he was sharing so much with the woman keeping stride down the corridor of portraits. The masterpieces once held the royal family and those who'd done great service for Aquiocia. Setz blinked, the only sign of distaste he exhibited at the sight of two dozen portraits all showing Arissam.

"How does it feel now?"

"It feels... right," Setz said slowly. "Alicea needs to be on the throne. Whatever other feelings I have for this place are irrelevant."

"I noticed we avoided the audience hall?"

"We did."

"Would we not find a false King on the throne?" Garnet asked, showing her ignorance of Arissam's nature. "I assume he is your target?"

Setz allowed a tiny smirk.

"We will find this particular false King hiding in a hole. We are going to smoke him out."

CHAPTER 51

RESTRAINED SALVATION

Time passed, but nothing in the cell changed with the day's end. Jex lay sprawled across the floor in a trance. He didn't know when he'd stopped his frenzied outrage, but he was now lost in the glow of the ceiling, without even the voice of the dark blade to offer him comfort.

Once the Princess had left, he'd turned his screams of anger – of betrayal – to his arm. It hadn't been long before the demands he made of the entity responsible had turned into him begging for a response. Now he lay on the cold stone, defeated and exhausted. He couldn't believe the level of emotion he'd felt in what felt like the past few hours. He couldn't be sure how much time had passed, but he assumed what he'd just felt was not a normal amount for a person to experience every day.

His mind drifted to the Princess once more, and he could feel the anger welling up in him again.

I can feel hatred on command for that bitch. Jex rolled onto his side. *If I had known… If I had the chance… I'd kill that little wretch time and time again. I'd kill them all. I'd kill her last. I'd make her feel loss…*

Jex was so lost in his thoughts that he didn't even register someone at his cell door until they cleared their throat. His body protested as he slowly sat up. Looking at the entrance, he saw a man of average height, with the tunic of someone wealthy enough for a place in the upper district. His trousers were well worn but of excellent quality, and his face was concealed by cloth save for his eyes. It was obvious that whoever he was, he had money, but couldn't afford for his face to be revealed.

"Good evening, Jex," the man said in a slimy tone.

"You here to pass judgement as well?" Jex snarled. "Line up with the rest of the dogs and wait your turn."

"I'm here to offer you something."

"Spit it out already. What do you want?" Jex yelled, pounding his bruised fist into the stone floor.

"What do I want? Why, I want to give you a chance to seek retribution, Jex," the voice answered in the same smooth tone merchants embraced when trying to sell something.

"Retribution?" Jex spat the words before literally spitting on the floor as he rose to his feet. The very word left a bad taste in his mouth.

"Yes, I'm sure a man in your particular predicament would like nothing more than to… Let's say, *confront* the people who've imprisoned and condemned you to death. What would you do with such an opportunity?"

"Who are you?"

"Does it matter?"

"No. Tell me how you can offer me this."

"I can hide you." The man took a deep breath. "I can hide you until it is time for an upheaval of the throne. I can conceal you and your existence until it's time for the rightful ruler of this land to step forward. Then, and only then, could I release you upon the people who so unfairly persecuted you."

"You believe I'm innocent?" Jex scoffed. Even he didn't believe that.

The man shrugged as Jex eyed him curiously. "I believe you're useful."

"This 'rightful ruler'. Who is it?"

"Lucian," the man revealed.

Jex paused. "You're lying," he accused unconvincingly.

"So what if I am?" The man waved his hand dismissively. "What have you got awaiting you by staying in this cell?"

"Death," Jex answered immediately.

"You don't fear it, though, do you?"

"No."

"I figured," the man said triumphantly as he glanced back towards the entrance for a moment and nodded. Someone was signalling him. Turning back to Jex, he said, "You have about ten seconds to make a decision. I cannot tell you how long you'll wait, but I can promise you a chance at retribution."

"You will tell me –"

"Five, four, three…" the man interrupted.

Jex grinned with a manic glint in his eyes. "I'm in."

"Men!"

The cell's bars disappeared before their eyes. Four burly men in cloaks entered the room, grabbed Jex and forced him out of the cell and up the staircase. As his face was met with the cool air outside the tomb, the man's voice sounded directly behind him.

"I can't promise that your new living arrangements will be much more pleasant than your last, but my other promise will be fulfilled. You will get your chance in time."

Jex grunted as he was led through the cemetery and out the

gate leading to the Blue Crystal Mountains.

The man's voice had disappeared. His midnight visitor had left. Jex didn't know any of the nobles personally, so there was very little chance that he'd know who his new captors were until they saw fit to inform him.

The trek they were on seemed to last for hours as they trudged up the side of the mountains. The going wasn't particularly tough – just enough to get a man's muscles to appreciate a break. None of them complained, and nor did Jex. He knew this was the closest thing to freedom he was going to obtain, and that even should he get away, the King would have every soldier looking for him. Best to wait and see what plans unfolded.

"In 'ere," one of the brutes grunted as he pointed at a massive boulder.

"What am I supposed to do with a giant rock?" Jex asked snidely as the man walked over and reached out, his hand to the stone's surface.

Jex's eyebrows rose as the man's arm disappeared into the solid rock before pulling free.

"Illusions. Of course," Jex muttered as he stepped forward and forced himself to walk into the natural fixture.

The boulder didn't budge, nor did it deny him entry. Jex stumbled upon a staircase beneath it. As he awkwardly descended the stairs, his vision through the illusory stone cleared and he saw glowing walls, similar to those of the prison he was in but an hour ago. This chamber was bigger, the bed far larger and more luxurious, but there was no denying that it was another prison.

"I thought I'd be hiding with a sense of freedom?" Jex asked, before realising he was alone.

Turning on the spot and gazing up the stairs he'd descended, he felt the rage of betrayal surfacing again. All he could see at the top of the staircase was solid, glowing stone.

He had been deceived again.

CHAPTER 52

MEMORIES UNDONE

"I reached out to you because of your talents, not your mouth," quipped a young man dressed in noble attire. He'd just thrown the fabric that had served as a cowl across the chamber and into the fireplace for the dying blaze to feast on.

His company sniggered. "Of course, Lord Arissam."

Arissam stood around five feet ten and boasted looks that didn't quite pass as attractive. He was only sixteen years of age, but his awkward teenage years didn't seem ready to leave him yet, with a face full of blemishes and a prematurely receding hairline. His choice of career didn't help him in the popularity polls, either. Unlike the rest of Axeal's royal family, who went into the military, Arissam had chosen politics. Specifically, he'd chosen to join the Council.

Though no one would dare say it out loud, they all knew why. Arissam was a coward. He had been since he was a child, and although Axeal had shown him the appropriate respect, Arissam loathed his much older cousin.

"Can you do as I requested?" Arissam asked, scratching at the first wisps of his pubescent beard.

"But of course. I have received the agreed payment, I am in your debt, and so your will shall be carried out. Tonight, if that's suitable?"

"Tonight would be ideal." Arissam turned to look at his company.

If Arissam was unattractive, then the rat of a man before him was hideous. Boils that had been left unchecked covered most of the hunched-over figure, who looked to be seventy years old or more. His skin was oily, and while parts of his head were covered in thick grey hair, others revealed his dry, flaky scalp. The man was obviously unwell, and yet he moved without hindrance. Something was keeping him going, though Arissam felt he didn't truly want to know.

"Very good. All three, if you will."

"All three, Lord Arissam?"

"Yes. I'd like Alicea done as well."

"My Lord, that is unnecessary. As it is, undergoing the procedure with the King and Queen will completely exhaust me. To then attempt it on even a child would lead to disastrous results."

"Disastrous how, exactly?" Arissam asked casually as he produced a small pair of scissors and began trimming his already miniscule amount of facial hair in the mirror.

"It'd draw attention to something being amiss. If I might explain, the King himself will be a relatively simple task, but the Queen –"

"Yes, you've expressed your concern about the Queen," Arissam cut across coolly, before adopting a scathing tone. "Trust the King of Aquiocia to wed a woman as intelligent as she is beautiful. Whore."

What followed was a small glimpse into Arissam's true nature as he swore and cursed the King and Queen under his breath, before finally turning to the repulsive man, smoothing out the front of his tunic.

"Do what you can, then," he said pleasantly.

"Absolutely." The man grinned, revealing golden teeth flecked with decay. "With your permission, I will take my leave to prepare."

"Go," Arissam ordered with a nod, turning back to the fire as the door closed.

Time for step two. From there, we wait.

❖

The Aquiocian palace hosted a still silence throughout its halls. Even the knights on duty seemed uninterested in talking amongst themselves. It was just past midnight; half of their shift had elapsed – the half they had spent catching up with each other. Now they were tiring, simply looking forward to dawn.

Not one of them noticed the hunched-over man skulking through the audience hall – or rather, none of them *recalled* seeing him. Every time a blunder was made, the man's attempt at stealth was corrected by a few words muttered under his breath, and whoever had seen him suddenly went back to their patrol without protest.

It appeared that the intruder could have simply walked through the castle without worry, but he was the cautious sort. You didn't cheat death as long as he had by charging into dangerous situations without thought. While it was true that he was perhaps overdoing it by trying to sneak up to the royal chambers, he was also trying to preserve the energy he had stockpiled. Each time he had to use his talent on an inconsequential being, a small portion of his reserves was taxed.

He knew his hoarded energy was in surplus when he ascended one of the grand staircases behind the thrones. His legs were already starting to protest, but his mind was alive with excitement and euphoric energy. As he cleared the balcony and shuffled towards the massive double doors and spiral staircases at the end, he permitted himself a few moments of reflection on his magical talents.

He always allowed himself to get momentarily lost in his memories on a big job. It was a bad habit to lose focus, but he hadn't failed yet. He thought about how it had felt when his magic had first become apparent to him: a rush of power and an even greater rush of control. He'd never tried any other way of utilising his strength; after all, what more did you need when you could alter the very memories of anyone who meant you ill will?

His adoptive mother had been his first subject. She'd always cared so deeply for the ugly, screaming child she had found in the mud. She could never have children, and not because she was unappealing. Many suitors had been at the buxom, fire-haired beauty, only to lose interest upon learning of her inability to conceive. Such rejection allowed for her to care for the orphaned child with a love undying.

Love undying is right, the man thought with a sniff as he casually waved his hand at two knights who had appeared in his path. With a quick series of words from the hunchback, the knights were bowing and rushing off to a fictional errand they had just recalled.

The love the woman had held in her heart was the one

thing he couldn't tamper with. He had experimented on his mother's memories while she had slept, and while his magic had the capabilities to convince her that he was the King of a foreign land or a ruthless murderer, her love remained. The fact that he couldn't quash the emotion from shining through had led him to killing her in frustration one night. He had filled her mind with countless memories of her beloved son dying at the hands of bandits, memories so real that she had run into a neighbouring forest to seek revenge. Her body had been found later, impaled by weapons and mauled by beasts in equal measure.

The man smiled at the bittersweet memory. It was a shame, really; he had thought his magic ineffective against love itself. But the truth had been revealed when he had taken to travelling around the land and taking jobs only he could accomplish. He had found plenty of work in altering the memories of people, none so much as in unfaithful men and women who would pay handsomely to have the memory of their partner walking in on them erased for good. He had even accumulated some "regulars" who would call on his service. As they tried less and less to avoid being caught, the man's wallet grew ever fatter. When he had had enough, he simply altered his client's memory to forget him, and moved on.

Back in the palace, he groaned at the sight of the spiral staircase in front of him. He'd been in plenty of palaces and lords' homes, but he never saw the point in stairs. He'd always felt that if one had so much money, why not work on a solution to that particular atrocity?

As he climbed, more and more momentarily confused knights saw and quickly disregarded him. With each wave of his hand, he expected to feel some form of drain on his mind, but none came. It was literally effortless for him to change the minds of the people walking past him.

Either I've grown more powerful, or these knights are the most feeble-minded I've ever met. The man chortled internally. *Probably both.*

It took longer than he'd have liked, but he eventually reached the pinnacle of his ascent. He realised he had risen above the ceiling of the audience hall and was on a beautiful plateau, engraved with the image of a wreath of Aquiocian Roses encircling the current royal family. The entire masterpiece had been carved into the pale blue stone and adorned with countless, priceless gems that had had been cut and smoothed out to allow for the safe traversing of its surface.

The man screwed up his boil-ridden face at the sight of the artwork as he walked across it. If he had the tools, he'd like nothing more than to dislodge the gems and deface the entire masterpiece. He had nothing against the royal family personally; in fact, they were just another job, despite his fascination with the Queen. It was only the sound of shifting metal that tore the man away from his examination.

He looked up, waving his hand, and a velvety darkness twinkled with stars in front of his form. The knights opened their mouths and were a moment away from yelling to raise the alarm when they stopped. After a few seconds, one of them whispered to the other, "Ah, this must be the sorcerer replacing us tonight." He nodded, looking back at the archway about thirty yards behind him, where the King and Queen slept soundly.

"Must be," the second agreed. "It's about time we got some

more magicians in the kingdom."

"Weird they told us not to tell anyone about him, though…" The first's eyes narrowed.

Another wave of velvety brilliance was seen and forgotten.

"No, wait, I remember now. The King himself entrusted us with this," the knight corrected.

"Aye. A test of our covert abilities. Not even to speak to him about it in case it ends in failure," the second agreed, nodding at the newcomer.

The pair of knights quietly walked past the strange man without a hint of suspicion. The mage couldn't help but roll his eyes as the pawns he had just manipulated left him with the King and Queen. For a second, he couldn't believe his luck. He knew most people he encountered were mundane and ungifted, but he always exercised a little more caution when things were going too well.

The man stepped towards the large archway leading to the royal chambers, leaving the beautiful plateau behind him. A quick mental outreach to the arch revealed no traps, be they magical or mundane. Could it be that the King and Queen were truly so trusting of their staff? He'd heard that the King always promoted trust and honour within his people, but this seemed downright foolish.

The man had taken it upon himself to do a little research into the hierarchy of the royal family, and it certainly seemed that the Queen boasted the brains in their marriage. Despite this, the final rulings were always from the King himself, and while the Queen had a far more realistic and level outlook on the world, the King wanted to believe in people.

The man realised he was standing at the foot of the royal

bed ten seconds after he'd reached it. He'd lost himself in his own thoughts.

Focus, you fool!

He took a quick glance around the gorgeous chamber, his eyes running over the massive arched window looming over the bed, the beams of a full moon shining through the stained glass. The rays were enough to light up the entirety of the oversized bed. The pattern of countless rose vines upon the stained glass were spread across the covers and, in turn, the two people sleeping before him.

As he examined his new test subjects, he couldn't help but think just how un-royal they looked. Sure, Axeal cut an impressive and exceptionally broad figure as he slept in thin trousers alone, light hair and an abundance of muscle strewn across his chest. He was snoring ever so slightly, with a small smile on his face, and the intruder caught a glimpse of why his client loathed the man so. This was a content King. There were probably very few people in the known world as pleased with themselves as King Axeal.

It isn't hard to see why the royal fool is so pleased with himself, the man thought bitterly as he cast his eyes over the woman lying next to the King.

Adele was a beautiful woman, in a fierce sort of way. The man had examined the Queen from a distance, noticing that while Axeal obtained the respect of everyone he met in some capacity, Adele commanded it. She had a playful and mischievous side to her that came out when she'd poke fun at her husband, but cross her or anyone she cared about, including the Aquiocian populace, and the cold fury in her eyes may just be the very last thing you saw.

The intruder had done his research. He knew that both the King and Queen were adept mages and more than competent in physical combat. He also knew that should they awaken, the biggest difference in reaction between the two would be that Axeal would question his motives for being there. Adele would simply end him.

So, he'd taken the precaution of ensuring there had been a sleeping herb crushed and sprinkled into their traditional wine glasses before bed. Every night they would toast to themselves, the kingdom and their child. It had made drugging them almost easy. Finding someone willing to do it had been more difficult. He'd asked dozens of kitchen staff to do it, only to be refused, wipe their memories and move on to the next. Eventually he'd settled on an incompetent apprentice, manipulating his memories to make him think the crushed powder belonged in the beverages.

The herb wasn't strictly to keep them asleep. It relaxed the mind and thus made it easier to penetrate. As the man prepared himself for the task, he somehow knew he'd need the drug's assistance to break the Queen's mental barriers. He'd heard all too often how tenacious she was. On that note, the man waved his hand in front of the King's eyes.

A mild shimmer of stars on pitch, and he was in. He could no longer perceive the royal chambers, or the people in the bed before him. He was watching a performance. He stood in front of a stage with each of the King's memories flittering by in front of him. It was a production well worth watching, and it was interesting to see how the King thought of his life and the people in it. The man was momentarily surprised by the fact that Axeal didn't think himself more important than anyone else. In fact, even when he found the memories he was looking for – the ones involving Jex – not once did Axeal feel loathing or even a hint of distaste. The King had wanted nothing more than to help – to understand.

The man got to work. With relative ease, he began to pick apart the images before him. The show was no longer allowed to proceed unaided. He was the director of this production now, and it would play out how he desired. It was a simple task; Axeal wasn't a simple man, but the intruder had surpassed the King's mental defences long ago. To him, it was almost a joke. The King was barely better protected than the knights defending him. Within a few moments and the expenditure of minimal energy, the King would awaken the following morning believing that Jex's execution had been taken care of by him alone, as he'd decreed.

Now the Queen just had to believe that as well. That her husband had awoken early in the coming morning, executed Jex and returned to her in bed. It was a difficult series of events to line up and ensure they coincided, but the man had undertaken more difficult endeavours.

I could just make them recall a long period of rest and have them think they awoke at the same time in late morning. I'd have to stay the night to ensure the knights for the morning shift have their memories altered as well… But it'll work well enough. Curse the perfectionist in me. The man allowed himself a moment of humour as he disconnected with his first subject and acclimated himself in the royal chamber once more.

Wiping his lumpy brow, the cretin let out a silent whoosh of air as the warmth of the night became a more relevant factor in his ordeal. The King was still sleeping soundly next to his likewise unconscious wife, but it had taken more of the mage's reserves than he'd first thought. This had always been the case, though – diving into someone's memories caused the caster and victim to become one on some level. They fed off each other's energy without realising it, and it was never apparent until he disconnected with the recipient of his meddling. It was a factor he had never been able to mitigate the effects of, no matter how much he practised or studied over the years.

I should have asked for a higher fee, he thought bitterly. *I underestimated the King's fortitude. Now, the Queen...*

CHAPTER 53

A QUEEN'S DEFENCE

The moon had shifted throughout the man's ritual, and it cast its light solely upon the Queen herself. Despite the man having learnt to undergo his practice in silence decades ago, he was still somewhat surprised that the woman hadn't awoken. This was Queen Adele, known for her perception and fierce magical prowess! Yet here she lay, asleep and oblivious.

The man felt his confidence reforming as his stamina started to return. He'd always been able to recover from magical endeavours at a remarkable pace. It was why he could work night after night, week after week, before finally resting. It was part of why he was once highly sought after; it was also why he held so much wealth. Or he *had* – he'd long since given up on the idea of wealth when he realised he'd outlive the gold's usefulness, and instead started to only take jobs that offered a challenge.

Just like the one in front of him.

He could feel it, the euphoric sensation of a difficult challenge. It was the same thing he'd felt every time he'd dived into the memories of his adoptive mother. The magic felt new again; he felt the rush of power course through him. He was ready. The man thrust his hand towards the sleeping woman's face, stopping an inch from physically touching her as the glitter of countless stars flew from his palms and rested upon her eyelids.

They were connected, and the man felt like he'd run headlong into a wall.

It took him a moment to adjust to what he was seeing. He knew that he was on the outskirts of the Queen's mind, yet all he could see was a monumental wall that expanded for what he assumed were leagues in both directions. The wall was solid and crafted from a material of opaque turquoise. At the sight of the colour there was no doubt in his mind that he'd found his first obstacle, and it was indeed formidable. As long as he was inside someone's mind, he could feel everything, and he knew the wall was crafted through years of mental restraint and discipline.

I may not be physically powerful in the real world, the man conceded. *But as soon as we take a step off the playing field that is reality, you'll come to find that I'm quite proficient in my own personal style of combat.*

The second he'd finished his silent banter, the man took a wild swing at the formidable wall. His gnarled fist connected but did not give way. Instead, a large section of the wall shattered in front of him. The debris disappeared from existence, discarded and unusable. The man continued to throw punch after punch at the wall as he shuffled forward into its centre. What was once a thick barricade was swiftly becoming a makeshift tunnel for him to burrow through.

He'd met plenty of people who'd erected similar walls, and he was surprised that the one he was currently infiltrating hadn't completely shattered upon the first few impacts. Most mages who'd devised some form of defence had thought it enough to simply put it in place and leave it to fend off any coming threats. Not the Queen, however. She'd nurtured her defences, and it showed as the man felt himself starting to tire.

I suppose a short break is in order.

He crouched down, the sickly thin legs beneath his robe groaning in protest. His breathing was a little ragged as he looked back the way he came. He couldn't see the entrance he'd crafted behind him anymore, though he was sure that he was carving a linear path. For a moment he worried that perhaps he'd bitten off more than he could chew, but quickly reassured himself.

I still have plenty of tricks should the need to reveal them arise, he thought with a grin filled with rotten teeth.

He allowed himself a few minutes of silence and felt his breath and reserves return, as he knew they would. It didn't matter how many times he was forced to rest – so long as he could, he'd crush the challenges before him sooner or later. It was but a simple matter of time.

Just as he was about to strike out at the cracked wall again, a voice stopped him in his tracks. The Queen's voice.

Greetings, vile man.

Your Majesty! he replied with barely concealed surprise. *A pleasure to make your acquaintance!*

Is it?

The simple question made the man falter for a moment. There was a distinct coldness in both her words and the surrounding stone. An involuntary shiver went up the intruder's spine and he reached out to touch the surface of the stone. What he felt was a cold so bitter that it shot through his hand and up his arm before he pulled away with a yelp of shock.

I see that the influence you have is quite… chilling. The man smiled. It was true that he was unnerved. No one had ever addressed him while he poked around their mind. There had been those who had fought back, of course. But it had been primal, a flailing attempt to resist a far more powerful foe. This was different.

But he was in his element, and he knew he could win. He just had to find the key to locating her memories. There was always a key, and it was always the thing the person trusted in most.

It'll probably surface as a manifestation of her husband, or a friend of some description.

Looking for something? Adele's voice queried before adding, *It doesn't matter – not really. You are not the first to try to infiltrate my mind, and although I know your motives differ to those who seek to outright destroy me, your fate will be identical to theirs.*

You speak some rather pretty threats. However – The man's retort was cut off by the sound of shifting rock behind him. A quick glance revealed that the way he'd entered had closed over and the tunnel was sealing at a rapid rate towards him.

Was he surprised? A little. Scared? Perhaps. Invigorated? Absolutely.

The man knew what would happen should he die here within the Queen's mind. The connection would snap and the part of his mind within hers would be forever trapped in limbo. What remained in the real world would be sent mad in an instant. The insanity would hit so quickly and so forcefully that he'd likely become a drooling mess incapable of controlling his bowels, let alone weaving magic.

In short, undesirable.

The cold stone surrounding him started to grind towards him slowly and he did nothing to stop it. He wanted it to consume him. He wanted the woman who'd trapped him to do what she felt she had to. She was about to learn that he wasn't an amateur.

The moment he felt the turquoise stone press against every inch of his body, he rallied the same energy he'd used to shatter pieces of the wall and discharged it in every direction. There was no sound, just the sudden flood of twinkling against darkness that devoured the stone threatening to become his tomb. The light didn't stop there; it continued its journey outwards, and as it consumed each massive portion of the once solid material, the light pressed forward with greater zeal. The perfectly devised trap vanished as quickly as it had approached.

It wasn't without a toll, and the man found himself breathless once more. This time he elected to sit as he gasped for air and took in the woman standing before him. She appeared to be around her mid-twenties, but he knew she was easily in her early thirties. Her shoulder-length ebony waves and limpid blue eyes defied her true age as her fierce gaze settled on him. He could see his opponent had felt the impact of her barricade being decimated, but he could also see that her pride didn't allow her to show such weakness. He always could read people better inside than outside their minds.

"Direct telepathy just seems redundant when face-to-face, don't you think?" The man grinned as Adele's eyes narrowed.

"No more so than actually talking. Your mind will perish here, and once it does, I will imprison your physical being in a magic-negating cell for the rest of your days."

"But where *is* 'here'?" The man tilted his head slightly from his place sprawled across the floor of the Queen's mind.

"What a ridiculous question. This is…" Adele's fierce poise faltered for a second as she looked around at the emptiness surrounding the pair. "This is…"

"Don't strain too hard, now," the cretin chortled. "Focus on what you came here for, that's what is important!"

He slowly rose to his feet and enjoyed the flow of his energy returning once more, though at a far slower rate. Between Adele's mind attempting to fight back and his efforts to tweak her memories to his benefit, he wasn't receiving the regular return of energy that he was familiar with.

Looking up at the confused Queen, he nodded to himself. It made sense that the Queen would trust herself above anyone else. It wasn't so much that she didn't trust anyone at all, but more that she wouldn't have wanted anyone else to get hurt should a different image of a person appear before an intruder in her mind. Had she instilled her full faith in a family member, their image would have appeared after the destruction of her defences instead of her own. She had no idea that it would be him to worm his way into her mind, or that he had little interest in doing anything that wasn't what he was paid to do.

"What I came here for…?"

Adele's mind was slipping. He'd wipe her memory of the confrontation gradually so he could work more thoroughly on his goal.

She couldn't focus on what she'd come to do, or even *where* she'd come to. She'd been forced to dive into her own mind plenty of times before, but the man had been sure to pluck out those memories of recognition and place them to the side. She could have them back later. If she spent the entire time trying to put together a puzzle that he'd confiscated the pieces to, all the better.

He was done. Or so he thought; he had to check.

"What are your thoughts on Jex?" he asked suddenly.

"I try not to think of the atrocity. Tomorrow my husband will see to his execution personally. I'm thankful that today was the last I, along with anyone else, will see him." The Queen's eyes hardened. "Is that who you're working with? Who are you?"

"Oh ho ho!" The old man wheezed out a breathless guffaw. "There is no point in telling you my name. Nobody remembers it anyway, and that's by my own design."

Adele's face screwed up. She'd decided to lash out at him, but it was too late. He'd vanished. Her annoyance and fury subsided as quickly as the strange place she was standing in began to fade. Suddenly, she couldn't remember who she was mad at, or if she had even been upset with anyone. She felt tired – exhausted even. It was time for rest; it was time to sleep.

She couldn't help herself. Her body led her slowly to the ground, where she found comfort lying upon its dissolving surface. As sleep took her, Adele's dreams and tampered memories became her own once more.

❖

He was back in the royal bedchambers. Exhausted, but he'd made it out of the Queen's mind without being consumed. The man took a shaky couple of steps away from the bed and saw his most recent target's face turn from a look of turmoil to one of serene peace. Her mind was intact. Slightly shuffled, but in working order.

The hunched man's smoky eyes turned upwards to the stained glass and saw that the moon's light was waning. It was approaching dawn, which was worrisome for a fraction of a second, before he felt his energy beginning to replenish at the slowest rate it had ever done. He was getting barely even a trickle, and he knew why – the Queen had been far more formidable than he'd been prepared for.

If this woman had even a modicum of strength more… This would have had a different outcome. Had she even another few days to fortify her defences, she'd have crushed me. Me!

The man shuffled out of the chamber, thankful for the sleeping drug they'd been fed, because he couldn't lift his feet to prevent them scuffling along the stone. He stole a quick glance to the east wing of the chamber out of curiosity. Despite it clearly being a library of sorts from the bookcases lining the walls, he could feel something magical within its confines. It was a magic that he'd never come across, and he knew that even if he had a chance to study it further, he'd never understand it. The magic seemed to almost not understand itself, as if it was incomplete.

Suddenly, the sensation vanished, as if it had concealed itself.

He didn't care. His job was done, and he could hear the knights coming to relieve their comrades from their shift. The new pair of knights had barely stepped onto the ostentatious plateau when their memories were altered, and they were bidding farewell to the sorcerer they "knew" would be waiting for them, before forgetting about his existence entirely as the hunched man made his exit.

Mission accomplished. Time to make myself scarce and check in when a few years have passed.

CHAPTER 54

HISTORY'S BLAZE

The cathedral stood in all its ruined splendour just as it had every day since Chase and Temperance's arrival, and for two centuries prior. It wasn't difficult to see what the cathedral once looked like with its thick, cracked walls. Enormous statues depicting dragons adorned an ostentatious altar at the far end of the massive, open room.

The rows of damaged pews still stood defiantly despite the destruction that had once been unleashed upon the building. The wrath of the elemental stone had left a wound on the cathedral similar to the one upon the rest of the once grand city – crippling and everlasting.

The Nameless had gathered within the cathedral on either side of the centre aisle. Chase escorted Temperance along the aisle with stiff posture and a stiffer expression. He was unnerved by the sight of forever-scorched men and women preparing for a forbidden ritual. At least, in his mind it was forbidden.

Probably should have nurtured that belief earlier... he thought with a glance at Temperance. Although he still felt guilty, he couldn't be sure he would undo what he'd done if given the chance. When he looked at Temperance it all became so... confusing.

They reached the group standing in complete silence at the end of the aisle. Chase took a step back away from the gathering and watched on. Namier bustled past to join them and muttered a few words that neither Chase nor the others heard, but Temperance climbed the stairs towards the top of the display, where a long, rectangular stone object lay. It took a moment for Chase to realise that the large stone feature was actually a sarcophagus.

He was about to blurt out questions and objections when Temperance lay on top of the stone casket rather than inside it. Chase felt his apprehension recede slightly and continued to watch on anxiously. He couldn't put his finger on it, but he could feel that not all was as it seemed.

What about this actually looks normal? he asked himself in irritation.

With Temperance lying atop the sarcophagus and eight of the Nameless surrounding her, Namier addressed everyone who had gathered to witness the ritual.

"Thank you all for attending this momentous occasion!" he began in good cheer. "As each of you is aware, a short while ago the Vassal of Fire graced us with her presence and allowed us to take part in preparing her for the coming struggles. This honour was much more than any of us could have ever hoped to receive in our endless stasis."

The rest of the Nameless remained silent, nodding in unison at their leader's speech. The Nameless always thought as one – it was something Chase had become accustomed to, despite it still making him feel uneasy.

"This woman is our hope, our light and above all – our guidance. Though young in years, she is one of the six and therefore has the power to make a difference. We exist only to serve her! So if it is her wish that we attempt to remove the stone from within her, then doing so is our duty!"

Another nod throughout the cathedral. Chase was too fixated on the long dagger in Namier's hand to care about the Nameless' odd tendencies.

"Let the ritual commence!" Namier screamed suddenly, and with one vicious movement he plunged the dagger deep into his own stomach. "For the Vassal! For Our Flame!"

"For Our Flame!" the Nameless chorused.

What? Why...? Chase thought with surprise as he watched Namier's blood gush from his body.

The other Nameless began chanting as one and Temperance's body started to glow in a familiar, fiery aura. Chase watched his friend rise into the air until her now limp body hovered a full three feet above the sarcophagus.

The Nameless' chanting intensified, as did her aura, turning into a white-hot haze that filled the air with unpleasant heat. The sensation was familiar to Chase; he could feel his scorched hand start to itch within its glove. He was a third of the chamber's length away from Temperance, yet he still wanted to get away from the heatwave emanating from his friend.

Strangely enough, Temperance appeared completely at ease. Her face was placid, and it wasn't until Chase glanced at Namier again that he realised what was happening. Somehow, Namier had taken the pain of the ritual onto himself. It was a cruel task to place upon anyone, but Chase knew that, come morning, it would be as though he had endured nothing. The blade in his stomach and the sensation of every cell in his body burning up was only temporary.

He's felt this before.

Chase's trance was broken when a piercing white ray of light launched itself from Temperance's limp body towards the high ceiling of the grand cathedral.

The blaze exploded and fanned out across the surface of the roof. The light began to twist and meld before finally coming together in a massive, slightly transparent image. An image that made the Nameless fall to their knees in reverence; an image that made Chase draw his blade.

The image of a crimson dragon.

CHAPTER 55

A SWORDSWOMAN'S INTERROGATION

"Scourge!" Chase spat in awe.

The legendary beast's claws appeared to be buried in the ceiling of the cathedral. His neck twisted so that his fierce face could look down at the shocked masses below. Chase assumed that, from Scourge's point of view, it was they who clung to the ceiling. He also assumed that his energy might have been better spent thinking of a way to survive the encounter rather than marvelling at the physics surrounding it.

"My, you just seem to find trouble wherever you go, huh?" a female voice echoed through the cathedral. Chase turned hesitantly towards the entrance. It wasn't one of the Nameless speaking. "It's not enough that you get exiled, you have to start a dialogue with an extinct civilisation and a dragon? You pair really are something else."

Chase took in the sight of the lightly armoured woman, a thin blade at her hip and an abundance of confidence in her stride.

"Katarina. You caught up," Chase noted, panic threatening to consume him as he joked. "You will have to excuse me for not dropping everything."

"Given the circumstances, I will forgive you this once." Katarina smiled with pained humour as she looked up at the vicious form of Scourge.

Encompassing most of the cathedral's ceiling, the dragon made his statues seem like oversized children's toys. His baleful crimson gaze was enough to make Chase feel like he was burning up. His scarlet scales, though transparent, shimmered with a light that they seemed to conjure upon themselves. His long tail whipped back and forth irritably, with enough power to easily crush everyone who stood before him.

The only thing holding Chase's courage together was the reasoning that it couldn't be the real Scourge – or at least, Scourge himself could not possibly be in the same room as them at that exact moment. It was common knowledge that dragons resided on a completely different plane of existence to humans. After the last disaster, surely the Nameless were not so reckless as to attempt summoning the real specimen again.

"Go back to where you came from, dragon!" shouted Chase, dumbfounded and terrified.

A roar silenced him. "Close your ignorant mouth, human. It is your actions that are to blame for my being here. Does your insignificant race never learn? Or do I have to set alight your entire world?"

"You can rest assured that we had no intention of disturbing you, oh mighty dragon!" Namier had found his voice, his wound having already returned to the scorched yet intact flesh of the curse.

"Then what is it you are attempting?" Scourge sniffed, a thick grey cloud blowing from his giant nostrils towards Chase.

The smoke did not irritate Chase's nose. He let go of the air trapped in his lungs. His theory had been right; Scourge was not truly with them.

They weren't going to have to fight a god-like reptile.

Why does he not look at anyone else? There's a Vassal – the civilisation that he had a hand in cursing... Chase barely had time to register the fact that this confirmed the dragon was within Temperance. He glanced at Katarina. *There's also Kat. I don't know her very well… But surely she's more interesting to Scourge than I am.*

"We merely wished to remove the stone from within the Vassal," Namier answered meekly.

"Unacceptable. This woman is now bonded with my stone, and furthermore – with me," Scourge snarled. "She is mine."

"You're the one within her stone after all!" Chase exclaimed before scolding himself.

"Yes, though I do not find it prudent that I answer your questions anymore, human."

"You will answer all the questions we like now! Temperance commands your power. That includes you answering our questions!" Chase replied in triumph.

The entire cathedral filled with scentless smoke as Scourge exhaled, growling in a fashion Chase assumed was the dragon's rendition of laughter.

"I answer to no one. My power is my own, as is this woman."

"But that's not quite the entire truth, now is it?" Katarina piped up. She'd long since learnt to analyse before acting. It was a lesson she intended to pass on to Chase. "You have consumed a great deal of humans who have tried to take on your power. I've seen the mountain of corpses at Neibel-

Haven; I've heard the legends surrounding this city and its people."

Scourge snapped his massive jaws in irritation, as if readying to eat the tiny woman who dared to confront him. It was something he would have been capable of doing with relative ease had his corporeal form been present.

But that wasn't the case, and Katarina clearly knew it.

"It is obvious your process in selecting a Vassal is a little different to the way I was chosen by my own guardian. The entity within my stone sought me out, but that is a story for another time. My point is that you prefer potential Vassals to seek you out instead. In return for those craving your power, you crush them both physically and spiritually." Katarina smiled before adding, "But Temperance can handle the onslaught, can't she? I assume she is the first?"

"You... You're a Vassal after all..." Chase stuttered. He had assumed as much, but to actually hear her admit it was still a shock. *We spent years trying to create one in the underground and now another just wanders through the front door...*

"Don't look so surprised, Chase." Katarina winked. "It's hardly a secret."

"The Vassal of Wind, is it?" Scourge growled. "I could sense the coward concealing itself within the stone you bear. Why do you offer that information so willingly to those around you?"

"Temperance is my ally in this, whether she knows it yet or not. These people follow and support her unconditionally. Therefore, I am their ally as they are mine." Katarina shrugged. "My stone has fallen completely silent; I cannot sense a single trace of the being within it. It is the first time it has felt like that since I was chosen. I assume it is avoiding you?"

"What would make you think I have anything to do with your stone and its owner? I have no interest in what other Vassals or their stones' guardians do. I simply acknowledged its cowardice," Scourge replied dismissively.

"Yet again, you do not speak the entire truth. I believe my stone's guardian is avoiding you. I believe that perhaps the guardians within the stones have more of a connection than any of you are letting on," Katarina pressed with the same smile.

Does she feel no fear? Chase wondered.

"If I was there, human, you would have been dead before you could have asked even one of these irrelevant questions." Scourge let a deep roar fly from his mouth and the fake smoke filled the chamber once more. The sound was impressive, but did nothing to harm the ears of the dragon's audience.

Even the sound the dragon creates has little effect on the surroundings...? Chase wondered, wishing Temperance was awake to decipher what that might mean.

"I do not question your ability to kill me, especially given that the being within my own stone is unwilling to speak to you, much less fight you. But even if I was on my knees, sword and stone forfeited, even if I was bleeding out, I would still ask these questions. It is my duty as a Vassal." Katarina spoke with a level of sheer courage Chase had not thought possible.

"Humans are weak," the dragon announced. "But sometimes they display great bravery. Whether that is borne from genuine courage or blatant stupidity remains to be seen. However, you have earned your answers."

Everyone, including Chase and Katarina, had fallen

completely silent.

"There is indeed a deeper connection between the stone's guardians that you are not yet aware of. You will not be able to remove me from the Vassal, as I do not wish to be removed. I will return to being dormant within her, and only when the time is right will I relinquish my hold on her. I cannot speak for the other Deities, but I would not ignore the possibility that they may one day desire their own stones to become one with their respective Vassals."

"What of her being the first to control your power?" Katarina asked.

Scourge didn't reply. The light that had made up his image was distorting and deteriorating at a swift pace, and it soon disappeared. Temperance's body gently lowered to the surface of the stone casket.

Chase ran up the stairs of the altar and shook his friend with concern.

"Temp! Wake up!"

Temperance's body responded by lurching into a sitting position. In a voice that was not her own, she growled, "No, there was another, and should you not hurry in your quest, you will find yourself confronted by her. Beware the Silent Maiden of Imperishable Flames!"

Temperance fell back, breathing deeply, leaving everyone to ponder her words.

CHAPTER 56

THE SMILING SWORDSWOMAN

"I could have sworn I asked you to wait at Hearthgrim!" Katarina exclaimed as she spun around to look at the two people trailing her. Walking backwards, she grinned at Temperance's pale face and Chase's concerned expression.

The Nameless scurried off in all directions, as if an inaudible order to vacate the vicinity had been given. Soon enough, the trio was wandering through the ruins of the destroyed city alone and with no destination. Neither Chase nor Temperance replied until Katarina slowed and nudged the swordsman roughly.

"We are sorry," Temperance offered.

"You're sorry?" Katarina asked in bewilderment. "What could you possibly have to be sorry for?"

"We were going to stay there and wait, but I wanted to visit Scourge again," Temperance explained.

"That makes sense after your last trip here ending prematurely," Katarina nodded. "I assume you found what you were looking for?"

"Of sorts, yes." Temperance nodded timidly in return. She seemed put off by the more confident woman.

"You know about her abduction?" Chase's gaze fell to the dirt and ash he walked upon.

"I do. I know everything I need to know about what happened at Neibel-Haven, and a bit even before that." Katarina winked at Temperance. "It was a mess to be proud of. Truly, you two don't do things by half measures. An underground tower, what looked to be scorched corpses, and then I hear that you nearly wiped out the city itself to boot. That's not to mention luring out the Vassal of Darkness, either."

"So it *was* you who confronted the other Vassal!" Chase spluttered.

Katarina grinned proudly. "Yes, but how did you know that?"

"We had our theories when the Nameless told us they could sense things around the land," Temperance explained. "They told us there had been multiple energy spikes where Neibel-Haven is."

"Our first meeting was too strange to be coincidence," Chase added before frowning. "Wait, where is Amelia?"

Katarina responded simply by glancing at Chase and back ahead in silence.

"I see. My condolences."

"I assume you pair have rallied your senses in your time here in Scourge?" Katarina asked, changing the topic.

"We have had time to discuss our predicament, though we have no real ideas on what to do next," Temperance conceded.

"We have been honing our skills here alongside the Nameless and learning more and more about its history. What you saw today might be considered a breakthrough," Chase finished uncertainly with a glance around at the everlasting destruction.

"Oh, you mean the dragon that just so happened to greet

me as I walked through the front doors?" Katarina laughed loudly. "Yes, that counts as a breakthrough, I'm sure!"

"You seem to be taking all of this in rather easily," Temperance said quietly.

"How am I supposed to take it?"

"Well, I would have thought a person would react quite differently if they found out I was a Vassal and what I had done."

"Oh, don't worry about all that. I knew you were the Vassal of Fire before I'd even laid eyes on you. Secondly, the people of Neibel-Haven are currently choking on their own harsh words towards you pair. I would have been here much sooner had I not had something to take care of first. I will say, though, you seem…" Katarina took a moment to look over the exhausted pair. "Well, you seem more *something*."

"How could you possibly have known I was the Vassal when I don't even have my stone anymore?"

"That's not to say I can't sense the stone within you. As for how I knew you were the Vassal – you practically stink of magical energy. Any mage worth the title could tell that you are something entirely different to the regular species. People who aren't particularly gifted in any of the elements can't sense it, but other mages, especially another Vassal, can sense it as easily as breathing in air."

"Wouldn't that make her a target, then?" Chase blurted out, his concern getting the best of him yet again.

"Can you feel her energy, Chase?" Katarina asked with an amused expression.

Chase let his mind reach out towards Temperance, but he recoiled quickly at the feeling that greeted him. Her energy felt cruel and violent despite her timid appearance. Above all, it felt as though it was in a rage, ready to consume any who contested it.

"I can feel it," Chase stammered. He swore the temperature rose around him for a second.

"Would you attack her after feeling that?" Katarina grinned as Chase shook his head quickly. He knew she was oversimplifying the situation, but it was good enough for now.

"I do not like this conversation anymore," Temperance said quietly.

"Then let us finish it and start another," Katarina responded, unabashed. "I need to tell you everything that happened at Neibel-Haven, just as you two need to tell me everything that happened in my absence. We will then decide on what we shall do next."

"Why are you helping us?" Chase asked suddenly.

"I wish to help."

"But why?" he pressed, with a slight hint of accusation.

"Chase, stop asking why I'm here, or why I'm helping you pair," Katarina ordered politely with a glance at the silent Vassal of Fire. "You two somehow managed to piss off a dragon in the short time I left you alone. Trust me, you're my kind of people."

"So, you're staying with us?" Chase asked, his suspicion not wavering.

Katarina laughed again. "You will have a great deal of difficulty getting rid of me now."

Chase fell silent. He didn't know how to feel about this. Part of him had known Katarina wouldn't leave after catching up with them.

"You will want to leave this place," Temperance assumed. For some reason she was avoiding calling the city by its name, a cue that Katarina picked up on.

"Indeed, I certainly will. I daresay you'll feel the same once we sit down, rest and have a chat."

"I want to learn more about this place."

"And you'll have a chance to," Katarina promised as she fondled the pommel of her sword. "After we deal with what we've been entrusted with."

Questions filled both their minds, but Temperance and Chase knew to wait.

Katarina had found the closest thing to an intact table and chairs and was leading them to it. She made a show of dusting off the cracked stone that once served as solid seating blocks. The large, round stone that served as a table was split through the middle, half toppling to the ground. Despite half of the arrangement being destroyed, Temperance and Chase found plenty of space to sit. Chase helped lower the exhausted Vassal onto a smooth slab of granite and sat beside her with ever-present concern.

Katarina swiped at the dust on a ruined seat across from the pair before shrugging and opting to stand, pacing back and forth and stretching as she went. Chase's eyes moved from Vassal to Vassal, taking in Katarina's form for the first time since meeting her on the side of the road.

She didn't look much different since their last encounter, despite losing her sister. He didn't know what differences he expected to be apparent, as he didn't know the woman at all. What was it about her that was so intriguing? Her courage? The way she openly laughed in the face of danger?

How did she not even blink upon laying eyes on a dragon? Did she really fight another Vassal? What was that battle like? How is she so different to Temperance if they are both one of the chosen?

"Hrm." The sound came from Temperance; she was looking directly at Chase with an eyebrow half-cocked. Clearly, she had noticed his staring.

"I –"

"You have questions!" Katarina interrupted with a clap of her thin gauntlets. "Lay 'em on me!"

Suddenly, every question Chase had left his mind. Thankfully, Temperance had it covered.

"Why did you protect me?"

"Straight to the big questions, eh?" Katarina's hazel eyes twinkled. "I like you, Temperance."

A silence fell on the trio again.

"Thank you?" Temperance said hesitantly. "But my question…"

"Was just answered. I like you. I like Chase as well. I protect what I like." Katarina grinned like she had just told the world's best joke. "Not good enough?"

Temperance answered with continued silence.

"Fine. Remember when I said Vassals reek of magical energy?" Katarina said, pushing away from the table. "Those with a little aptitude might sense a fledgling Vassal. They probably don't know exactly what the large magical signature is, but they would feel it. Those with training would know there's a mage with immense power in their vicinity, perhaps even what element they are aligned with. Superb mages would not only know of the fledgling Vassal and alignment, but would be able to locate her and even have a good idea of her energy levels, and perhaps some of her capabilities."

Katarina grinned again. "Then there's people like me."

"People like you?" Temperance had perked up, as she always did at an educational lecture.

"Yup. See, within the geyser of magical energy that a Vassal exudes are remnants of their emotions and character. Things like confusion, torment, misery…" Katarina let her eyes rest on Temperance for her last words. "Or hope."

"Hope." Temperance muttered the word bitterly.

"What drives you, Temperance?" Katarina asked suddenly. The woman grinned as Temperance eyed her warily. "Look."

Katarina spread her arms as she stepped back and slowly pivoted, a grand gesture towards the ruins surrounding them.

"You were, what – dragged into a dungeon beneath a city and forced to become one with a supernatural force? And what do you do?" Katarina clapped her hands together, her fingertips now directed at Temperance. "You got up and stumbled right back here to Scourge. Why?"

Temperance didn't reply. She felt Chase stiffen at Katarina's overview of what had transpired.

"Because you don't let *anything* stand in your way. You continued travelling with Chase – yes, I know his part in it. Why?"

Chase recoiled, but Katarina's gaze held no judgement.

What is her angle? Does she not think me a monster?

"Hope," Katarina answered herself. "Now, doesn't that sound cheap?"

Chase's guilt was starting to get the better of him. Thankfully, a figure behind Katarina caught his eye.

"Namier?"

The Vassals joined in looking at the scorched man, who looked sheepish. The Nameless never interrupted other conversations without good reason.

"My apologies to all." Namier bowed quickly to show he meant his words. "The Nameless and I understand that you might be leaving soon."

He's referring to himself separately from the rest of the Nameless? Chase noted, wondering if Temperance had noticed herself.

"It was our – no, *my* wish to have one last sparring session with Chase," Namier revealed. He spoke slowly, as if hoping not to offend.

Chase sat in surprised silence for a moment before nodding. "Of course. I'd never deny you a match, but…" He faltered, unsure of himself. "This is the first time you've ever asked me."

"Forgive me, but I believe I've come to you numerous times for our sessions."

"Yes." Chase nodded again, reaching up and over his shoulder to his longsword. "But this isn't scheduled. Never mind, let's do it!"

A grin spread across the cursed man's face, a look of genuine delight, as Chase's excitement began to overflow into his step.

"Good." Katarina watched the pair retreat to an open patch of blackened soil across the way. "Now we can *really* talk!"

CHAPTER 57

THE WORLD'S CRY

Temperance followed Katarina tentatively through the smouldering ruins of Scourge. They had left Chase to his final match against Namier, his enthusiastic cheers since vanishing from earshot as the women wandered the long roads in silence.

Dilapidated houses and places of worship lined the paths, each a sobering reminder of the power Temperance held inside her. A power that, according to the records she had studied, was similar to the strength Katarina wielded. She analysed the carefree swordswoman, her confident stride and cheerful disposition. On the surface, she seemed to be someone who would take on anything without hesitation, and yet logic dictated there had to be more.

For the first time, Temperance found herself more interested in deciphering a person than the ruins surrounding her. She caught herself staring and barely averted her gaze in time for Katarina to suddenly stop.

"There really is nowhere in this city we won't be watched, eh?"

Instead of replying, Temperance took in her surroundings. They had reached the southern wall. Even with the lingering damage, it was obvious this wall had been less fortified than the northern or western ones. The burnt-out barracks and sporadic watch towers had once overlooked the ocean, wary of seafaring enemies.

"A real gap in their defences here…" Katarina said wistfully, striding towards the main gate.

Temperance found herself following again. From a distance, the massive timber gate and steel portcullis appeared to be in a salvageable state. Up close, however, they found flaky charcoal and twisted metal. There were chunks of the gate missing, allowing someone to climb through if they were careful enough.

"Phew, that heat is something else…" Katarina muttered. She was sweating, her forehead shining with moisture. Despite the discomfort, she grinned at Temperance. "But you don't feel it like I do. Bit jealous of that."

Temperance looked back at the gate. It was true; even the angry glow of the warped portcullis gave off no heat that she could feel. She instinctively reached out for the metal, but Katarina slapped her hand away.

"What —"

"Wouldn't recommend that," Katarina warned cryptically. "Give it time. It's not what we're here for, anyway."

Katarina guided Temperance to the side of the gate as a gentle breeze flowed through the gaping holes in the wood. Once the pair were clear of the road, the wind picked up from outside the wall. Temperance heard the wailing of a gale before burnt wood and singed metal burst from the gate into the city.

"Shall we?" Katarina gestured to the massive cavity that had appeared in the southern gate.

"Was that necessary?" Temperance asked, lifting her dress

slightly to avoid getting black dust on its hem.

"Would you have preferred me picking you up and flying you over?"

Temperance didn't answer, instead murmuring, "We shouldn't leave the city…" Her statement trailed off as she took in the sight before her.

A long path led down a slight cliff to the ocean. What remained of the dockyards lined the shore, undamaged but neglected. Even from a distance, Temperance could see the lack of destruction. The people of Scourge had never been particularly interested in the sea, but they had enjoyed its bounty. Fishing had been a cornerstone of their survival.

The water was choppy, as if angered by something. The wind was wild, forcing Temperance to hold her glasses in place to examine what she soon realised was a roaring storm in the distance. But this was no ordinary storm. The sky was clear and deep blue, yet heavy rain fell upon the ocean. There were no clouds, yet webs of lightning ravaged the sky. The waves glittered and shimmered, as if blanketed by jewels.

A chill filled the air, cold but refreshing.

"What is this?" Temperance wondered aloud.

"You want the long answer or the short?"

"Both."

Katarina didn't reply for a moment, analysing the phenomenon before them.

"This is the world crying for help," she finally answered. "This is the world falling apart. The weather is the first thing to go. The one within my stone said so."

Temperance felt the wind around her dying down as the other Vassal spoke. The storm continued in the distance, but the bluster didn't touch the pair.

"These chaotic storms have been happening more and more frequently. In fact, this is a mild one – it'll pass shortly," Katarina continued.

"Their cause?" Temperance asked. The scholarly part of her was intrigued.

"I don't know."

"A hypothesis, then."

Katarina paused before reaching out towards the storm. The waves roiled and cursed the shore, but several shimmers flew forward from its surface. They gathered in her hand, fragments of shining essence. She barely had time to show her companion before the shards of light faded from existence.

"You know that everyone is aligned with an element," Katarina stated more than asked.

"Of course."

"And surely you acknowledge the theory that everyone is made up of the elements living in harmony, with one being dominant over the others?"

"I do not know if it's truly the case, but yes, I know of the theory," Temperance said, eyes narrowing.

"If that theory was to be proven, would it not follow that the elements make up *everything*?"

"Perhaps," Temperance conceded. She saw where Katarina was going with the thought and couldn't deny its credibility. "The elements make up the world. Should the elements fall out of harmony, the world falls apart. In theory."

"In theory," Katarina repeated.

The pair stood in silence for a moment, allowing the sound of crashing waves to wash over them, the chilled air resting on their skin.

"Are you hunting Lucian?" Temperance asked, and for the first time since meeting her, she caught Katarina off-guard.

"Amongst other things, yes," Katarina replied quietly.

"You're recruiting," Temperance said.

The remark hung in the air. From another mouth it might have sounded like an accusation, but from Temperance it was an observation.

"I am."

"Will you make me come if I say no?"

"No." Katarina met Temperance's inquisitive gaze. "But it will make my life more difficult, because I will have to watch over you from afar."

"I am safe enough here, I think."

"You're a fledgling Vassal with enough raw power to recreate this." Katarina gestured to the ruined city behind them. "You command the power of a god, and you haven't picked a side."

Temperance turned back to the storm. It had weakened; the waves were smaller and the flashes of lightning had subsided. The glimmering on the surface had all but vanished. She knew what Katarina was suggesting, but it didn't frighten her. Having seen this phenomenon, part of her had already made a decision. More answers were required, and for those answers to be found…

"Where are we off to, then?" Temperance asked, smoothing down her dress as if ready to set out immediately.

"I'm so glad you asked!" Katarina exclaimed, placing a hand on her new ally's shoulder. "Have you ever been to Nimbus?"

CHAPTER 58

A SQUIRE'S RETREAT

The days passed, and they weren't easily endured. Although Jex had completely lost any sense of time, he'd spent the first few weeks screaming out to anyone who might be listening. He'd yell at the top of his lungs until exhaustion got the best of him and he succumbed to sleep.

He would awaken to the same glowing walls, the same bed and the same menial existence. Whenever he slept, he awoke to find lavish spreads of food laid across the wooden table in the corner. He'd tried many times to feign sleep in hopes of capturing the person delivering the food, but they knew when he was and wasn't conscious.

Eventually, Jex accepted his lot and realised there was little he could do, and though it made him sick to his stomach, he had to put his faith in the man in the cowl who'd broken him free from the ceremony. He would often turn to the voice in hopes of conversation, and not a day went by that he wasn't disappointed by its silence. He had no idea what he would even discuss with it, but he was rapidly reverting back to how he was as a child – hollow and emotionless.

He could identify that this relapse wasn't a full reversion. The anger and loathing for the royal family rested in his chest like a stubborn splinter that refused to be removed. The only way he'd ever be free of it was to obtain his revenge. With that revelation, he got to work. He gorged on the food supplied, namely the heavier foods like potatoes and meat. Then he got to exercising. Day in and day out, he'd undergo countless exercises designed to strengthen his body. He'd never be as broad as the men who'd taken him from the cell, but it gave him something to keep himself occupied.

He was relatively pleased one day when he found some large chunks of stone with handles carved into their sides so they could be lifted with a single hand. His captors were watching and trying to accommodate him as best as they could.

Even more than developing his physical strength, he thought. He thought about everything that had happened up until that point, over and over again. Every time his mind drifted to the Princess' apology, he would shudder with a rage he'd thought gone. Each time the fury took hold, it took what felt like an eternity for him to get it under control until eventually, he started to use it as a tool. It took months of incomprehensible time, but Jex trained himself to suppress the feelings until he started to feel hollow again. Only when he had almost completely reverted to feeling nothing would he allow himself to think about the King, the Queen and their daughter.

It was more than enough to drive the emptiness away and force him to his feet, a fit of rage resulting in the destruction of the furniture around him. In the early months, he'd tear at himself as well. He'd drive his fists into whatever part of his body he could reach and throw himself into the walls. He didn't let his mind push down the pain; he relished in it – it sustained him. Then he'd collapse in exhaustion and wake up to see his wounds treated and the furniture replaced.

His left arm had its bandages replaced daily, and its bleeding never stopped, despite the magic-negating glow of the room. His downtime consisted of him investigating the wounds left by the blade's ribbon. He missed the weapon, along with the searing agony it sent coursing through his body. It was strange to think that even though the wound was a result of a powerful magic leaving its mark on his body, the room couldn't prevent its bleeding. Jex didn't know much about magic in general, but after pondering it for so long he felt it stood to reason that maybe the burns caused by the blade's restraints weren't connected to the bleeding at all.

The more he thought about it, the more his theory made sense and the more questions arose. Why did he experience no negative effect from bleeding so much? Why had Lucian mentioned blood at their meeting? Why could he hear the beat of most people's hearts, yet he couldn't recall hearing the rhythm in the chests of any visitors to his cell? Axeal had mentioned Blood Magic – was it possible that he was a mage?

His questions didn't go completely unanswered. After a few tireless days of examining his wounds, he awoke to find the typical meal along with a tome on magic – Blood Magic. Inside the cover was a short note that read, "So you finally recognise one of your talents. I hope that this tome will be of some use. Though you'll find the practical side rather difficult in your current dwelling, I'm sure it will provide some answers."

It was a thin tome, but Jex relished the opportunity to read something. The first few chapters were about the basics of magic, things they'd been taught as squires about mages and their limits. It also gave some insight on what to do when confronted by one as a soldier. It was slow going, Jex having only grasped a basic understanding of letters and numbers through his studies as a squire. But once he reached the second half of the book, he started to understand why it was gifted to him.

The art of Blood Magic is one offered only to very few. It is a field of magic that not only requires the innate affinity of two elements, but manifests from those affinities into something much darker. Due to its rarity, many scholars claim it a myth. Those who have witnessed it firsthand, however, are often of the opinion that it should be forbidden because of the toll it takes on the person wielding it. Though as powerful as any other field, many shun the very idea of Blood Magic altogether.

Jex's interest was genuinely piqued. He couldn't remember ever being interested in any literature; even that which he was given as part of his training to become a knight was read once and discarded.

Very few great Blood Mages were ever recorded during the course of history. It is believed that this is because of their eradication. Times have changed since then, and it remains unclear whether there are any remaining in the world, or if perhaps they are all in hiding.

"Is this the reason the Queen was researching Blood Magic?" Jex wondered out loud, his voice hoarse from using it solely for bursts of outrage since coming to his new lodgings.

Though tremendously powerful with the right training and environment, Blood Mages run the risk of going mad from the effects of the magic. As a result, their lives are often ones of isolation.

He had no idea exactly how many times he read that same tome over the time he spent hidden away, and despite more books being delivered to him on various topics, the original was his favourite. It was almost a comfort having it close by. It was the only thing he'd come across that came close to understanding him.

CHAPTER 59

A SQUIRE'S PRISON

Jex hurled his plate across the room and placed the book he was holding onto the table. He couldn't tell exactly how much time passed between each book delivery, but he guessed a couple of days on average. The only measurement of time he had was how long it took him to read the material in each leather-bound volume.

There was a reason for his excitement as he pushed away from his newest table. This furniture in his little hovel had lasted the longest of any he'd had before. The table, chairs and even his bed had lasted half a dozen book deliveries. However long that was.

His anxiety grew at the prospect of what was to come next.

Today, no, tonight, no... Jex thought. *Bah, IRRELEVANT! IT'S TIME!*

The prisoner made his way to the bed, stretching and arching his back to the point of almost snapping. In his constant training, he'd realised he was quite flexible. He had no idea where he'd inherited such a strange ability, but he had a theory. A theory that coincided with the experiment he was about to undertake now that he was sitting comfortably on his bed.

He produced a small eating knife from his pocket. It was

simply decorated with a small sapphire embedded in its silver handle, and he knew it was from a noble's table. He hadn't concealed it to hide it from his captors, as they surely knew he still had it. He'd placed it on his person because once he'd seen its royal appearance, he knew it had to be the one to experiment with.

Jex stretched out his right arm, wrist pointing down. Without hesitation, he slashed at his upper arm, clipping the skin and opening a thin wound. The flow of blood was light, but it was a starting point. After a moment he lashed out again, deepening the wound. He smiled, satisfied by the flow of rich crimson now cascading down his arm.

Now for the tricky bit.

Jex's grin didn't disappear, but it faltered as he attempted what the tome had dictated. His mind attempted to stretch out at the blood running down his arm. He had no idea what to expect, or if he'd even find success – or know it if he did. He'd never dabbled in magic; not willingly, anyway. It wasn't a matter of hating or disliking it – he simply hadn't had the opportunity or been exposed to it. So, it was an immense surprise when his mind hit a wall so forcefully that he felt his body recoil.

A wall? It's preventing entry to... something. He could feel the barricade's forbidding nature, but he also couldn't pull away effectively. Whether that was because it had entrapped him or because his own will wouldn't allow it was unclear.

One thing he did know was that he didn't want the daydream to end until he'd broken down the mental barricade. It was absolute, and getting past it was like trying to recall something you'd never experienced, but there were a few things Jex could discern about the obstacle. The first was that it wasn't a part of him; the wall was a separate entity from himself. He could tell it was an outside force by the way it repelled not only his mind, but his body.

The second conclusion he reached was that it wasn't discriminating against him; it was discriminating against his attempt at reaching for the magic he'd been studying. It was then that he realised what the wall was.

My opponent is my prison itself.

❖

"Argh!" Jex flung himself across his bed in frustration. His annoyance lasted only as long as it took for his body to connect with the stone wall. The sudden halt in movement made him chuckle.

Ah, what an exhilarating challenge!

Jex spent the next few moments rolling around on the bed's covers like a pig in fresh filth. He had too much pent-up energy, and it was coming out in more and more peculiar ways. His body jolted upright suddenly as he reached out to the familiar wall just outside his mind.

It was a perplexing situation, having been enlightened to his magical capabilities only to have them immediately bound. So far, he'd deduced that the walls surrounding him were enchanted with the same charms as the cells in the Aquiocian dungeons. He'd also worked out that everyone around him seemed to have been aware of his magical abilities apart from himself. He'd always assumed the magic belonged to the one within the sword; now he wondered if it had simply unleashed his own. Of course, that theory was only given merit by the voice's sudden absence from his mind.

Where have you gone? Jex lamented. *You're the only voice I long to hear...*

Brooding aside, Jex was on his feet, and with a quick leap he was horizontal across the ground, briskly performing push-up after push-up. After his mental count reached thirty, he reached for the dormant magic within himself. Rather than trying to draw from the pool of his reserves and lash out at the mental block surrounding his mind, he allowed himself to stew within it.

He barely noticed it at first, the steady pace of his exercise increasing with each repetition allowed the euphoric sensation to course through his body. He knew his latest theory would surely be disproven, and sure enough, he soon felt the foreboding presence of the magic-defying aura reach out to him. It was the first time it had come to him, but it was no less determined to crush any attempt at magical endeavours within its confines. As he felt the enchantment rest upon his skin and begin to soak through, he grinned.

You've punished me each time I've reached out to you, but you're on my grounds now. I've housed more pain in my body than you could ever deliver!

Jex's resolve faltered briefly when the first wave of resistance hit his system. The crushing feeling made itself at home in his body, offering a slightly uncomfortable and forced presence before striking out at its host. Jex flinched but didn't utter a sound. He hadn't counted on it diving into both his body *and* his mind. It took him a confused moment to pinpoint exactly where it was striking out, until he realised that while the presence was filling his entire body, the most forceful surges of its strength hit him as his heart gave each panicked beat.

Ha! It's in my veins! Whatever it's trying to destroy is tied to my own blood!

Jex's eyes closed, his arms not letting up as his efforts intensified. He could feel his muscles burning, but the minor discomfort vanished the second the aura redoubled its efforts. His arteries felt as though they were being forced closed. He had no idea how the prison's enchantment negated magical endeavours originally, but he knew it had given up its efforts in doing so. Localising his newfound magic had lured the charm onto his own terms, and negating the source of a magical attempt was proving far more arduous than simply negating the result. Now it only sought to crush the source.

But it wasn't going to be successful. Jex forbade the notion as each push-up forced the blood in his veins to expand violently. Now it was time to undertake the one step he had no idea how to initiate.

Help me! his mind ordered.

He could feel the lucid, searing sensation of his energy deep within his being, but he had no idea how to call upon it. The pain was getting worse, and each pump of his heart became more of a stretch for it to reach, as the effort yielded diminishing returns. It steadily became evident that he'd made a miscalculation as he swapped from push-ups to sit-ups to tap into a new source of blood flow.

The realisation did nothing to damper his feverish euphoria. He didn't care if his body caved. As far as he was concerned, there was a good chance he'd never be released. His thoughts raced with the memories of his time in the prison, scattered throughout the abstract concept of the prison's timeline.

The memories lacked variety; there wasn't much to recall if you took away the outbursts of anguish, the destruction of furniture and the simmering lunacy that roiled within him as he studied the precious tomes he was gifted from those outside. The only things he had left were the desires to master whatever was within him and to seek his revenge. If he couldn't do both, then he might as well keel over right now, alone and irrelevant.

The blood can't... flow. His thoughts were scattered, unfocused. *The... blood... needs to flow... freely.*

Jex rolled over and hurled himself towards the table across the cell. The cutlery scattered, much to his dismay – it had been his target. Frustration flashed in the front of his mind and he felt his left arm react, striking out at the already damaged table. He struck the table two, three, four times before its top buckled under the onslaught, leaving four sharp, splintered legs rising from the ground like small timber stalagmites.

Jex didn't hesitate, his instincts taking control as he grasped one of the wooden stakes and drove the dangerous tip into his stomach. The countless timber spines pierced his skin and dove into his flesh. Jex screamed. Not in pain, but rather ecstasy. It was exhilarating to feel the blood being expelled from his body, rushing from the new wound in a geyser of dark liquid.

He felt some relief as he stared down at what he'd done to himself. His blood was tainted with the colour of midnight, as though mixed with swirls of black paint. Surprisingly, it appeared to be seething angrily upon the pale, glowing stone floor. The soft glow was fading the closer it was to the spilt blood, and was all but non-existent in Jex's immediate vicinity.

I must spill more! Jex realised. *I can cover the entire cell with –*

Idiocy! The voice reverberated around Jex's mind with more force than the prison's enchantment. He shuddered, not because of its volume, but rather the fact that he hadn't heard another voice in so long. On top of that, it was one he recognised.

How long has it been? Fight this battle where it's localised. Your war is within.

What are you talking about? Jex roared internally. The voice and his own thoughts felt close, so close that the pain of his arteries slowly collapsing felt an eternity away when they spoke. Despite this, he couldn't ignore what was about to kill him, not now that the one person – if you could call a disembodied voice a person – he wanted to speak to had finally reached out to him. Suddenly, he had a stake in living again.

You'll fall here if you don't destroy that which has you at knifepoint, the voice observed calmly. *A common tactic in winning a battle is to remove the head of your opposition. An efficient way to accomplish that is to invite them onto a battlefield of your own choosing. You've done the latter, now do the former.*

Jex felt the voice vanish, its presence suddenly void. Fighting the urge to lash out at whatever he could reach in frustration, he focused on the insight offered to him by his companion.

Remove the head... Jex looked down at the grotesque mess of blood, flesh and singed wood. His blood had scorched the timber's surface and he realised he should have already bled out. At the very least, his organs should have sustained heavy damage, and yet all he could feel was the tightening grip around his veins.

The pieces began to connect, forming a picture that still didn't quite make sense. His magic was tied to his own blood. Whatever miracle this was began with what was flowing through his veins – the blood was both a shield with which to protect himself and a sword with which to remove the heads of those who would oppose him.

He just needed to wield it.

The blood simmers… Jex smirked as he issued a command internally. *You – will – BOIL!*

The effect was instantaneous. He felt the aura's grasp recoil like a child's hand from an open flame. Jex could feel the scalding uproar that was coursing through his veins, yet it wasn't painful. Rather, the entire experience was soothing, as though his entire being was embraced by a warm sense of comfort. He could tell a battle was being waged within him, and his opponent was trying to retreat, only to be ripped back and reduced to nothing as his own energy swallowed and absorbed that which once kept him prisoner.

He knew he didn't control the magic, but he trusted it. It was his in title, but title alone.

"Is every mage's experience the same as my own?" Jex wondered aloud. He quickly realised that his words weren't laboured, that his body felt a certain peace it hadn't before.

Looking down at the wound again, he noticed that the shaft of the primitive weapon had burned and decayed, and the gash had healed over. In its place was heavily scarred tissue and restitched flesh. The surrounding blood seemed to have vanished – to where, he had no idea.

Furthermore, he felt no internal damage. His instincts

suggested that the shock of the experience was clouding his ability to feel the distress his body must be under, but a far more rational part of him knew that whatever damage his organs had suffered had been restored by the tainted miracle that was his magic.

His head found the stone wall as he leant back roughly and let fly a sigh of relief. He'd done it. He could feel the presence of the magic-defying aura surrounding him, but it made no move to stifle him in any way. The erratic and feverish blood flow settled after a few moments, returning to a steady and regular rhythm as though nothing had transpired.

Because nothing DID happen, Jex smirked as he looked around at the ransacked cell. *They'll come when I sleep and they'll think I simply destroyed the furniture out of frustration.*

A plan was already forming in his mind as the pieces steadily fell into their convenient places.

I can hear my own heartbeat... Jex realised. Another thought dawned on him so suddenly that his head jerked forward, and he leapt to his feet in excitement. *I can sense my own heartbeat again! Which means...*

Looking around at the pale glow of the walls, Jex yelled triumphantly. He let himself get lost in the energy as he threw himself across the room and thrashed the mattress on his bed over and over, before finally lying perfectly still.

I can't wait to have my first proper visitor. Jex grinned as his eyes closed.

CHAPTER 60

A SQUIRE'S RETURN

Jex was in the corner of his chamber, wide-eyed and alert. He could hear something. No, he could hear people. He hadn't heard people in... How long *had* it been? Days? Months? Years? In that moment it didn't matter to the man grinning from ear to ear. If they had come to release him, then a great time was about to be had, and if they hadn't – well, he'd at least have fun with whoever was walking down the staircase of glowing stone and dirt.

His expression of manic ecstasy didn't falter at the sight of Arissam. He'd gotten older. From what Jex could discern, the Council official had aged at least a decade. His hair had thinned further and while the acne had dispersed, the scars remained. Arissam was scratching at the beginnings of a beard that couldn't quite spread its influence across his jaw, resulting in patches of thin brown hair scattered across his skin.

One thing that had improved the otherwise unattractive man's appearance was the royal blue coat wrapped around his form, falling to just above his knees with matching trousers, both trimmed with fine silver. His fingers were almost overwhelmed by the sheer amount of silver rings encrusted with jewels, shining even in the pale glow of the cell. Whatever

Arissam had done in the time that Jex was locked away, it had improved his standing in the kingdom.

"Greetings, Jex. I see you made it." Arissam waved dismissively at the prisoner as if his survival was irrelevant.

Jex didn't reply, instead continuing to grin like a kid who'd just found himself.

"You'd have thought after the better part of fifteen years you'd be more talkative," Arissam said as he walked across the chamber to the table that had been repaired countless time while Jex had slept. Picking up the tome on Blood Magic, Arissam smiled. "I see that you got quite a lot of use out of this. I'm glad that I could make your stay more... comfortable."

Arissam didn't notice Jex move to stand right behind him. He had no way of knowing until Jex's long hair fell upon his shoulder as Jex peered over it. Arissam had no delusions that the man he was speaking to could kill him instantly, but he also knew it was imperative that the prisoner understood he was in charge.

"I *did* enjoy that book," Jex whispered in Arissam's ear. It took every shred of Arissam's self-restraint to stop himself from cringing. "The first couple of hundred times I read it, I found it very insightful. So, it was a member of the Council who took a shine to me..."

"Your time here has treated you well," Arissam noted without moving.

"Do you speak of my appearance?" Jex asked, chortling. Arissam couldn't help a mild shudder when Jex whispered into his other ear, answering his own question. With a wave at the books littered around the prison, he continued, "Of course you do. I finally understand. I am different. You probably assumed that this cell would preserve my body by causing my innate magical energy to go into a stasis. That's how a magic-negating area works, right?"

"Were my sources incorrect, then?" Arissam asked with a mild yet genuine concern.

The response he received was a loud crashing sound behind him. Spinning around, he found himself rooted to the spot when he realised there was a large, wooden stake an inch from his throat. He could make out the debris behind Jex that had been a fully constructed bed less than five seconds earlier. The man had completely ruined the furniture and returned with a weapon in a flash. Noticing the faint, dark aura surrounding Jex's body, there was no way for Arissam to deny that magic was the cause.

"So," Arissam began uncertainly, his eyes returning to the crude weapon at his throat. "How long have you been free of the cell's influence?"

"Free?" Jex's manic grin returned briefly before he screamed in the man's face. "YOU CALL THIS *FREE*?"

Arissam didn't know if it was outright fear causing his mind to malfunction, or his heart slamming so forcefully that his chest felt ready to explode. He'd misread the situation, perhaps gravely. He had expected the experience to break Jex, to make him more submissive. He'd always known the violent side of his prisoner would be in there somewhere, but having so much time in a magic-negating cell did things to a man – it was how they were designed. Short-term, it could hold a prisoner before a hearing without risk of jailbreak. Long-term, it gnawed at the resident, stifling their outward magical aptitude and eventually scraping off pieces of the prisoner themselves. Like sharpening a sword with a whetstone, each stroke took a tiny piece away from the whole. Whatever effect it had had on Jex had been the opposite; the experience had added something. How had he managed to escape its influence?

And why hasn't he escaped...?

Jex's attention had been caught, and Arissam knew what had captured it. Jex could sense his terrified heartbeat and it captivated him. It took Arissam a moment to realise that it was more than that as Jex hastily brushed his hair aside with his spare hand. Using the same hand, he reached out and cradled Arissam's throat, gazing into his horrified eyes. Jex could see something within, Arissam knew that. But what it could have been was beyond his own understanding.

He could see the interest – the enthrallment – in his captor's intense gaze. Jex's sinister eyes were twitching ever so slightly, as if allowing him to take in a scene playing out before him. The stake moved, and Arissam gasped as Jex hurled the weapon behind him. The Councillor had thought it all over for him, but instead, his former prisoner took a step backwards and bowed deeply with a gesture towards the exit.

"I believe you had something to give me once my time here had come to an end," Jex said, his tone suddenly amicable.

Whatever Jex had seen in Arissam's eyes had just saved his life. Arissam couldn't help but wonder what it was, despite being thankful that the madman had seen it at all. He forced his trembling legs into action and walked stiffly towards the staircase, desperate to keep any of his composure intact.

The giant stone still rested across the hole, and Arissam barely stifled a whimper when Jex hugged him from behind, resting his grinning face on Arissam's shoulder. Arissam knew why; Jex wasn't going to let him walk through the illusion without him. He also knew there was a good chance that Jex will kill him when he was free, but it was his only chance.

"I apologise for the sudden intimacy, but I can't let you just leave me here for another – how long did you say it was? Fifteen years?" Jex whispered in Arissam's ear as they awkwardly took the staircase one step at a time. Arissam couldn't help but notice that Jex smelt like… Well, nothing. He hadn't bathed once since being left in the cell, and while his clothes had frayed and worn, he himself was as fresh as a new day.

"Not a problem," Arissam responded shortly.

"Then do you know what you're going to do?" Jex asked quietly. Arissam shook his head. "You're going to deliver your promise and give me a chance at the King and Queen. They are still alive, yes?"

"Th-they are," Arissam stammered, not from fear but from relief. Jex was still bent on revenge, meaning he still had use for Arissam. "They are very well."

"That'll change soon, I trust?" Jex snickered as they reached the boulder and began to pass through its false image.

Upon emerging into the moonlight for the first time in fifteen years, Jex got his answer.

"I-indeed, they are planning a very important operation as we speak. One that you're going to be a part of, and one that you'll see go awry," Arissam breathed as he was released.

Jex reached over to the Councillor's robes and tore off a long strip of fabric from his arm. Reaching up to his own face, he tied back his long, dead-straight hair and laughed at the waning moon. The sound sent chills through Arissam and even the men watching on who served as his guard. It was a horrible realisation when Arissam noticed that he didn't feel remotely reassured of his safety even with ten men there to protect him.

"Oh!" Jex snapped out of his vile mirth with a look of thoughtfulness. "Oh oh oh! It's almost time, gentlemen, can't you feel it?"

No one knew what he was talking about, but that didn't matter. Jex got the response he desired: almost a dozen terrified hearts racing. He could sense them fully; there was no distortion, no interference from the cell's influence. Jex drew large, almost comical gulps of air, as if the terror from the onlookers somehow sustained him. It wasn't a ridiculous theory.

"Lead the way, gentlemen. It has been too – bloody – long!"

CHAPTER 61

THE LAST GIFT

Jex strode out of the house as though he owned it, which, for all intents and purposes, he did. The house looked like any other in the lower class, crafted from gorgeously carved blue stone sourced from the mountains behind the kingdom, and finished with silver filigree and small gemstones lining the "15" on its door. The house had been bought up by Arissam in the early years of his scheming and now housed Jex throughout the day.

Arissam had been quite cunning in his execution, claiming that he'd purchased the house solely for a place to get away from the tribulations of each day and enjoy some quiet drinks and card games with his fellow Council members. Within a couple of weeks, nobody thought anything odd of the small group of Council members entering the otherwise abandoned house. Nobody expected the night Arissam and his entourage arrived escorting the man who had been called the "Reaper".

Jex had almost blown their cover entirely when he broke into hysterics at the sight of the number fifteen, but they'd managed to shove him through the front door as Arissam smiled at the people peeping through their windows across the road. With a quick shrug and a mime of taking a drink, the Councilman managed to quell the people's suspicions with ease.

Half an hour after the meeting concluded, Jex set out into the city lit by moonlight. He'd been told to not wander the streets aimlessly, or to leave the house at all. He'd also been told that Arissam didn't expect him to listen, instead being implored to at least try to keep his existence hidden. The Councilman knew it would be borderline impossible to restrain Jex again, and Jex knew he had complete freedom in that regard. But Arissam had underestimated his hold over Jex in one single facet.

If hiding away is what gives me my chance to confront the royal family, then so be it, Jex thought, chortling out loud as though he'd been the one putting away the mead at the meeting an hour prior.

Jex turned down the first alley he came across in the backstreets. He walked bare-chested and barefooted, his only clothing the fading trousers that he'd worn for a decade and a half. He took no precautions in disguising himself, his dead-straight hair falling across his face. He didn't look a day older than he was when he was first imprisoned. Anyone who laid eyes on him had the potential to recognise him as the monster from the rumours surrounding the private execution fifteen years ago, but he did nothing more to hide his presence than to avoid the main streets.

He didn't know where he was going, as he didn't have a set destination. He simply found a morbid nostalgia in traversing the city streets he'd memorised in his knightly training. Some of the houses' ornaments had changed with new tenants coming and going, and there were a few more stray animals skulking around the streets, but for the most part, nothing had changed. There was no new construction, no new defensive measures or even any more patrolling knights. It was like walking the streets a decade and a half ago. It was like he had never existed; he hadn't made the slightest difference.

That'll change quickly this time, Jex thought viciously as his pace inadvertently quickened. *Only a pretentious city like Aquiocia could suffer the losses they did and not feel the need to bolster their defences. Their impertinence towards what was a very real threat is nothing short of idiotic. The threat is back, you mongrels. And he has a few ideas on how the royal family and their people should atone for their ignorance.*

He didn't know where his good mood had gone, but it returned in short order when he stumbled across one of the main hubs for merchants. He'd somehow traversed the backstreets long enough to arrive at the enormous, grandiose courtyard housing the first new feature that Jex had noticed – a larger-than-life depiction of Princess Alicea.

He hadn't laid eyes on the Princess since his release, yet he had little difficulty identifying the masterfully crafted blue stone standing proud in the likeness of his enemy. It was fortunate that the courtyard was deserted, because Jex abandoned any effort to remain hidden as he openly approached and circled the wondrous sculpture. His face reflected outright awe at the woman depicted in front of him, and then the craftsmanship itself. He knew the artist had spared no detail in capturing the Princess as a young adult.

She was shown in a light, full-length dress with a split straight up the left leg. A shawl was tossed over her shoulder and left to drape down to her lower back, joining the ends of her meticulously arranged hair. More and more detail came to him, and despite clearly looking like a stone replication,

Jex couldn't help but feel that he was looking directly into the eyes of his nemesis. How he loathed the "woman" in front of him, even more so now after seeing that throughout the term of his imprisonment, she had only flourished as a Princess, and as a person.

His livid gaze fell to the base of the statue and he openly sneered at the short pedestal it stood upon. There were countless gifts of gems, money, wreaths of flowers and even letters of adoration for the Princess. The sheer number of gifts stood in dozens of mounds, each over a foot tall. Each of the priceless gems was worth more than any amount of coins he might have earnt as a knight, and the way the people of Aquiocia just discarded their possessions at the feet of a statue dedicated to the woman who had secured his imprisonment filled Jex with a fury he couldn't contain. His stomach filled with a molten hatred that had been simmering for years upon years.

Before he knew it, he had dived amongst the gifts and begun to ravage the offerings. The letters he tore into shreds, scattering the remains into the night air. He found toys and other wooden crafts and crushed them against the stone pedestal. Coins and gems were hurled into the air and directly at the ground before his mania got the best of him and he scaled the sculpture itself. Despite the depiction being larger than life, Jex was able to wrap his legs around the sculpture's hips while he screamed and pounded his fist over and over into the beautiful face of the Princess.

When his unbound fist split, he swapped arms, and he could feel the sharp impact jolting through his chest with each swing. The assault of the inanimate object continued for several minutes before he stopped suddenly as a familiar sensation filled his mind: the feeling of anxious hearts approaching his location.

Soldiers, eh? Jex's eyes darted all around from his vantage point. His manic desire to lash out had evaporated and his curiosity had returned. It wasn't long before he saw the light of lanterns approaching from the northern district. They must have heard his wails. It was time to move.

Running was the last thing he wanted to do. It was only the thought of his chance at revenge being squandered on no-name knights that spurred his effort to escape. It wasn't difficult; he'd come to realise the vast expanse of magical energy he housed within himself, and even more importantly, he'd learnt to hide his magical signature for feats involving low volumes of the precious resource.

Ten seconds passed, and he was a block away. In twenty, he covered a further three. He only channelled a miniscule amount of energy into his bursts of speed. He'd been warned about an organisation that might or might not exist, and he wasn't going to risk letting his energy get away from him and blowing his cover.

That ought to do it! Jex stopped suddenly, grinning as though deeply proud of himself.

He couldn't hear the anxious hearts of the soldiers anymore, but a new sound had replaced them. It beat in a steady rhythm – the heavy tink of metal on metal, of hammer on steel. With a quick pivot and a wave of his hands, Jex greeted the blacksmith tending to his creations in a forge lit with an angry, orange luminescence.

"Ho!" The blacksmith greeted him with a nod and a twitch

of his auburn beard. His stout stature and the burns up and down his upper body told countless stories about his craft. They were stories Jex was suddenly interested in.

"And 'Ho' to you also!" Jex exclaimed, overenthusiastic as he looked around at the expansive wares of the forge. There were countless ingots and sheets of metal behind the blacksmith, waiting to be turned into more of the weapons he was tirelessly crafting. It was early even for the blacksmiths to be starting their workdays, but Jex knew why this man was already awake and working.

Jex knew the blacksmith had noticed his curiosity, knew he was watching Jex's eyes moving throughout the shop at a feverish pace. Though his excitable gaze took in every piece of crafted metal, he couldn't help but feel like he was looking for something. Something that wasn't there.

"Let me know when you've finished searching, then," the blacksmith grunted knowingly before turning back to his work.

What does he know? Jex's neck snapped back to the man. *More importantly, what do I want him to know? Odd for him to say "searching" rather than "looking". As if he thinks I know what I'm searching for – as though he might know what it even is. I don't even know what it is!*

Jex's internal monologue was met with a vocal burst of uncontrollable laughter. The whole paradox was hilarious to him. Jex only stopped relishing his impromptu hysterics when he noticed the man was all but ignoring him.

"What do you know?" Jex verbalised the question in a suddenly threatening tone that suggested he was no longer amused.

"Only what my master allows me to," the man muttered,

barely audible between the crackling heat and the ring of metal colliding with metal.

"Master? The King?" Jex asked, carefully preventing his voice from shaking with rage.

"King?" The man finally looked back at Jex. "The King, he says! Ha!"

Jex's face lit up with a grin at the unexpected response. Could it be that he had inadvertently found someone who didn't respect the King of Aquiocia?

"The King of Aquiocia!" the gruff man declared in amusement. "He's an idol to many, that man!"

"But not to you, then?"

"Bah! He's a powerful man, in a lot of ways, that's a fact." The man nodded thoughtfully as he plunged the searing blade of a longsword into a barrel of water. "But even the most impressive of men are but footnotes in the story that is my master's seemingly endless journey through life and beyond!"

Jex was lost. The words made no sense to his already scattered mind. For a moment, the only sound hanging in the night air was that of the cooling blade sizzling away as its craftsman began work on another. Suddenly, Jex lunged for the blacksmith's wrist, grabbing it in mid-air, the hammer's descent abruptly halted. Jex could see no trace of surprise or alarm on the man's face as he pushed his own closer to take in every feature possible. His examination was cut short by the blacksmith's indifferent expression, and Jex realised that was the very affirmation he needed.

"You're not concerned at all." Jex grinned when he noticed the absence of the man's heartbeat in his ears. It didn't matter how much he strained to hear; there was no heartbeat to be heard. "I could try to kill you right now, but you wouldn't fall like the others who have crossed my path, would you?"

The man's smirk broke through his beard. "Perceptive. What was your first clue?"

"You don't speak like any blacksmith I've ever met." Jex's grip tightened around the man's wrist, but no pain washed over his captive's face. "I can't hear your heartbeat, and you speak of a master on an endless journey through life and beyond."

Jex couldn't control his shaking body. He was too excited – too anxious. He was close, he could feel it. He had all but given up the idealistic dream of meeting with him again, but maybe...

"Take me to him," Jex ordered quietly. The blacksmith's expression didn't change. "NOW!"

"No," the man replied simply.

"WHY NOT?" Jex roared in his face. He'd gone from hopeful to irrationally angry in an instant.

"Because he does not wish it," the man replied, unflinching. At first Jex figured his defiance came from him being more fearful of his master than the lunatic holding him hostage. But he knew before long that a different motive drove him. The blacksmith respected his master, irrevocably so.

"He... He still deems me unsuitable?"

The rejection hit hard, and so surfaced a wound long since covered. Before Jex knew it, he was finally experiencing the myriad unpleasant feelings that stemmed from truly desiring something and being denied. Jex released the man and took a step backwards, shaking his head slowly. He'd passively stifled the feeling countless times throughout his life, including the first and last time he'd met with the knight who had terrorised his village. But if there was one pure and undeniable side effect that had been borne from the past years, it was that he could feel.

Erratically and irrationally, he attempted to endure the rejection without lashing out. He couldn't risk detection; it was bad enough that he'd already raised his voice.

"When you're finished." The blacksmith grunted again, returning to his work.

Jex lowered himself to the ground as his eyes stung with an unfamiliar irritation. He couldn't explain it; the bitterness was so foreign. It didn't make him want to lash out or laugh. It didn't make him want to maim or kill. He didn't want to retaliate by inflicting pain on another; instead he only sought relief from his own misery. The extremes of sadness rioted through his body, sudden thoughts of self-harm and even suicide racking his consciousness for the first time. He'd never hesitated in inflicting pain upon himself to achieve his goals, but this was different – he wanted to mask pain with pain.

"He's not uninterested, you know," the blacksmith offered casually as Jex began to sob.

"Wh-what are you saying?" Jex asked as he slapped the tears away from his face.

"There's a reason we met tonight. My master may not have taken you under his wing personally like he has with myself and others, but he has kept a keen eye on you."

Jex's heart beat ever so slightly faster as the excitement began to douse the misery.

The blacksmith simply watched on with a slightly raised eyebrow, thrusting another blade into the forge. The crunch of metal being buried amongst searing coals brought Jex back to the present.

"The reason," Jex stated rather than asked.

"Aye, he knows about the Council's plans."

"Why would a man like him care about the events of a kingdom? Especially one like Aquiocia, which primarily engages in trade?" Jex asked in one of his rare moments of genuine curiosity. The rest of the world seemed so dull – so futile. Yet the moment the knight was mentioned, he was all ears. "Rumours tell of his desire for stones of immense power – does he plan on seizing Aquiocia and its resources to –"

"His motives are not yours to question," the blacksmith interrupted. "Just know that what you are planning could be greatly beneficial to my master's plans. Reports are unclear, and my master has been uninvolved in this world's affairs due to… certain circumstances."

The blacksmith sniffed, as if genuinely disgusted in something. Jex could sense that it was irritation at himself for giving away too much, although Jex had little idea as to what the information could be used for.

"I'm here to give you a reward. It has been a long time coming. Long enough for me to have become quite the accomplished blacksmith, anyways." The man shrugged as he tossed the searing blade into the barrel with the rest.

There was no way the weapon could have been ready, yet it appeared that the craftsman couldn't care less as he reached under a table and dragged out a heavy, ostentatiously gaudy chest. Jex's first assumption was that the chest was a display of great wealth, but as the stones embedded into its frame lit up at the man's touch, Jex knew them for what they were:

safeguards.

What the blacksmith revealed was nothing like what Jex expected – not that he knew what he was supposed to be anticipating. Something was handed to him, a contraption seemingly made of dark metal yet folded as easily as one might fold parchment. The object was longer rather than wider, with a strap designed to be slung over one's shoulder. Along one side of the object's length was what appeared to be a long, curved blade, its dangerous edge folded inwards to prevent injury to its owner. The peculiar item held Jex's attention like nothing else, even before the sound of thousands of steadily beating hearts invaded his eardrums.

Jex almost looked around in alarm; it felt as though a legion was marching towards him. Instead, he stared longingly at the item, suddenly desperate to embrace the single gift that had meant anything to him. He didn't know what it was, exactly. He knew it had to be a weapon of some description, but none of that mattered. He'd been given a gift from the single person he'd ever felt he truly understood. It had its own heartbeat, or rather, its own populace of hearts thumping in unison, and they beat for him alone.

"What am I to do with this?"

"Find a use." The blacksmith shrugged as he lifted the heavy black-stained apron over his head. Tossing the heavy garment dismissively into the blazing coals, the man stepped out from his forge. With an almighty stretch accompanied by an over-exaggerated yawn, he gazed up at the starry night.

Jex didn't ask any more questions – he knew the conversation was all but over. Instead he slung the strap over his shoulder, commenting, "Huh, it sits perfectly."

"It'll do that. Enchanted weapons are something else entirely. The truly remarkable ones come in all forms, and their power – well, imagination is the only limit I found." The man paused, looking out onto the street. "It is time…"

"You made this," Jex observed, attempting to keep the conversation alive.

"Did I?"

They were the last words he heard from the blacksmith before he was left alone. The man walked away, content with a mission finally completed. As Jex watched on, he saw the man approach a tall, slender silhouette bathed in moonlight. The newcomer was silent, with an expression far more solemn than any teenager should wear. Jex recognised the adolescent's attire as the roughly spun clothes worn by the denizens of Aquiocia's neighbouring villages.

The blacksmith shared a few words with the lanky teenager before turning and nodding at Jex. Then they faded away before his eyes, whether into the shadows or from existence itself, Jex would never know.

CHAPTER 62

ALICEA'S PART

This was it: the chance they had all worked for. Alicea stole a moment to reflect on the situation as she swiftly made her way through the sewers of Aquiocia, her long, dark hair billowing out behind her like a shadow in hot pursuit.

Every faction at her disposal had played their part admirably. The warriors of Tremel had succeeded in drawing the enemy out of the kingdom via the main gate. She knew Setz would be successful in breaking through, ordering his army of thieves and assassins to emerge from the Underbelly via the countless manholes and passages. They would use the element of surprise to defeat all resistance the cursed knights of Aquiocia presented.

Rufus had led his own small team – himself and the twins – into the city to create a diversion after the warriors of Tremel had caught the attention of the military at the main gate. Alicea knew they had been successful after the earthshaking explosion of fireworks that had made the city shudder.

The Princess felt a quick pang of concern for any civilians who might have been caught in its detonation, before banishing the thought entirely. There were measures in place; she had been there when her mother had placed the wards in the walls of the warehouse. Adele had been adamant about seeing to it personally.

Alicea had to have faith that it had all worked out – she had to force herself to keep putting one foot in front of another. She ran down the length of the canals to the area where Setz had told her there was a secret passage into the kingdom. He'd imparted the knowledge early on in her life in case she ever had to flee the castle. She'd never used it; with her ability to memorise where guards would be at any given moment, she hadn't needed it.

There was a reason she had picked this passage in particular. It ran directly parallel to the city above, meaning it was the most likely to share the enchantment's influence. Setz had intended on accompanying her, but she couldn't allow it. The Princess knew a large portion of her force was wondering why they should be there risking their lives for her. All her tactics for peace were well and good, but she also knew she had to prove her own personal strength to inspire the people watching and fighting for her.

She would find Arissam. She would prove she was worth fighting for.

No, I will prove that I am worth fighting alongside!

To do that, she would need to find the man now leading her kingdom. He would either be in the audience hall or the Council chambers. She didn't know Arissam particularly well. However, she knew him well enough to know he'd be at a place of power. He was a glutton for authority and never one to get his hands dirty. He'd be squirrelled away while Jex addressed the force at his front door.

Fortunately, projecting her voice magically was a technique covered in the books Garnet had given Alicea to pass the time.

She had learnt a lot from the pages and even developed some of her own strategies and styles of magic, but in subduing Arissam, it was the voice projection that would hopefully bring everyone to heel.

The Council will fold when they see the rightful Queen at the top of the kingdom. I do wonder what Jex will do.

Apprehensive, the Princess came to a staircase that was in surprisingly good shape due to lack of use. As Setz had explained, even though it was constructed long before she was born, few people had used it. It had been designed so that the royals could escape unnoticed, should the castle ever be attacked. It wasn't a cowardly manoeuvre, but rather designed so they could regroup and launch their own assault from within.

Only the late King and Queen, Setz and Alicea knew of its existence. The Princess entertained a moment of guilt for taking off without Setz when he turned his back, but suppressed the thought so she wouldn't be distracted from the task.

Mr. Thief would lose his mind if he found out about this now. It would have made his task of kidnapping me a lot easier, Alicea thought. Smiling at the realisation, she decided to tell him about it the next time he annoyed her.

She climbed the stairs at a brisk pace, trying her best to muffle her footsteps as Rufus had taught her. It was a practice the thief had insisted on imparting to her, and while she hadn't mastered it like Rufus had, it was becoming second nature.

The staircase was exceptionally steep, yet she barely broke a sweat. Training with Garnet and Rufus every day had paid off. Now she was fitter, stronger and faster than she had ever hoped to be. Her stature was often gravely underestimated in training exercises and she allowed a small smile at the memory of her last spar with Rufus.

Look at me reminiscing about Mr. Thief, Alicea thought. *Focus!*

When she reached the top of the stairs, she nodded at the small swan sitting on a lever protruding from the wall. To anyone else, the aqueous bird would have been a strange and out-of-place sight, but it had known her plan even before she had enacted it.

"Hello, my little friend. Waiting for me?" Alicea addressed the bird and it ruffled its supernatural wings restlessly as if it was tired of waiting.

Alicea stretched her arm out and the bird jumped on and hopped up to her shoulder. The Princess wrapped her hands around the heavy lever and, with a deep breath to calm her nerves, pulled it downwards. The effect was instant as the wall in front of her dissolved before her eyes, revealing the royal audience hall in front of her.

The lever triggers a magical illusion... Alicea thought as she entered the great hall for the first time in months.

It was a peculiar feeling, looking around at the once comforting walls of her kingdom. She had been away from it far longer than any time before. To walk – no, sneak – into its confines now left a bad taste in her mouth.

She took a moment to gaze around the deserted hall, taking in the gorgeous designs on the walls: interconnecting vines adorned with Aquiocian Roses. The Princess even allowed a small moment to lose herself in the fountain's splendour in the middle of the hall. It was a surreal experience after years of walking past and paying little heed to its existence. Now, however, she appreciated the fountain and the precious liquid launching from the various cavities of its simple, elegant design.

Finally, her eyes moved to rest on the thrones at the far end of the enormous hall. Her heart leapt into her throat when she noticed that someone was sitting in her late father's seat.

"Tell me something, Princess," a cruel voice called from the throne. "Did you truly expect one such as me to fall for your little ruse?"

The man slowly rose to his feet, as if allowing Alicea a moment to take in his form. A long, frayed coat fell open to reveal a scar-plagued chest of lean muscle. His long, jet-black hair fell across his face, partially covering his amber eyes and poorly concealing his wide, manic sneer.

Alicea felt the panic rise within her.

She had made a mistake.

CHAPTER 63

FAREWELL

"It's time!"

The deep and cheerful voice of the Aquiocian King echoed around the royal chambers. His wife wore a deadpan expression as she tightened her travelling cloak around her slender shoulders.

"If you could sound a little less enthused about going into battle, then perhaps people wouldn't assume that your mind is going," Adele quipped.

"Do people really assume that?" Axeal stopped mid-cheer to question her raised eyebrows. "Bah! You're just having me on!"

"I wish I was." Adele smiled as her husband ignored the bait.

"Think about it, my love!" the King declared as he directed Adele towards the balcony on the west side of their chambers. Adele sighed but humoured her husband, allowing him to gently lead her out of the castle and into the open air as dawn made its debut. "There won't even BE a battle!"

Adele took a moment to take in the slowly rising sun that was steadily devouring the last of the night's shadows.

"Are you completely mad?" she asked incredulously. "You're about to march a legion of soldiers into a conflict that has broken out between two entities of immense magical power, but you truly believe that a battle might not even take place?"

"Why do you keep questioning my sanity?"

"What's really upsetting you?" Adele countered suddenly.

The question took the King by surprise, but only for a second. By the time his wife flicked her fringe away from her face, he had already accepted that she'd seen straight through him.

"An hour ago…"

"I was there," Adele stated sharply.

Axeal's grin and mirth evaporated as he suddenly became exceptionally interested in the sunrise. It was a few minutes before he found the words, and Adele waited in patient silence.

"I have full faith in us accomplishing anything. Whether it be ruling a kingdom, or marching into a potential battlefield against the gods, I know that with you, I can triumph."

"You're very sweet. But I asked you a question."

"Leaving Alicea is difficult," Axeal admitted.

It was a new problem. Or rather, a more severe version of an older one. Neither the King nor the Queen liked the idea of leaving the Princess alone, much less this time when almost all the royal family was to march with them. It had been a ruling that Axeal had felt necessary after the Queen had expressed her concerns that the two entities might be some of the Vassals. It wasn't a theory shared beyond the royal family themselves, but it had been agreed that they would march together.

"You do not need to worry about her. I know it isn't easy, and her outburst wounded you. But she's strong," Adele said kindly. "After all, she's your daughter."

Axeal smiled despite his doubt. He already felt better as he wrapped an arm around his wife's waist.

"If I may interject…" a soft voice interrupted. The King and Queen both turned to the man in a dark cloak who joined them on the balcony. "The Princess is in safe hands. I can assure you of that."

"We know, Setz," Adele said quietly.

"Why are you here?" Axeal asked in surprise, abandoning his embrace.

"I suppose I'm here in one last-ditch attempt to convince you to allow me to accompany you in –"

"No," Axeal interrupted.

"At least allow me to send –"

"No," Adele contributed.

Setz's face flickered with the slightest hint of annoyance, a luxury he allowed himself on occasion with the royal family. He knew he could get away with it.

"You, and your men, need to remain here," Adele said firmly. "You will protect the Princess from the shadows. It is your sole responsibility."

Setz didn't reply. He knew he'd be able to help on their mission, but he couldn't deny a direct order. He didn't have an army in the same sense as the Aquiocian military, but he had more than a few competent men who could be trusted with ambitious tasks. The King and Queen knew that, which was precisely why the men were on guard duty. Setz often entertained the thought that his hands wouldn't be so frequently tied if they simply allowed him to operate autonomously.

"My men have been confined within the castle perimeter for a few weeks now," Setz started, before seeing the pair's unamused faces and adding, "And there they shall remain."

Adele changed the subject suddenly. "I assume the other task involving the selected candidates is going well?"

"As well as it has been every other day you've enquired about it," the Guildmaster replied quietly. He turned to Axeal and addressed him directly. "Do not change. No matter what is before you – do not change."

"Wouldn't dream of it!" Axeal grinned. "I leave the kingdom in your hands. Adele, do you have anything you want to add?"

"Yes," Adele said as she set her cold, all-seeing eyes on her husband's advisor. "I sincerely hope that your preparations will be sufficient if and when the time comes."

Setz didn't pause, nor did his gaze leave the Queen as he responded.

"And I yours. All the best to the pair of you. Farewell."

CHAPTER 64

THE CHAIRMAN'S SUCCESSOR

The Council chambers were deserted when Setz and Garnet pushed open the great doors. Garnet seemed perplexed but the Guildmaster simply sighed quietly to himself.

"What now? Have they fled?" Garnet whispered.

"They have indeed fled, as expected. But if my assumption is correct, they have not gone far," Setz replied as he crossed the chambers, his long cloak brushing across upturned chairs that had been hastily pushed away from the table.

Garnet followed at a slower pace, taking in her surroundings. While she would prefer to be amongst nature, she had long since conceded that the Aquiocian palace was beautiful. Even now as she saw sides of it she hadn't yet laid eyes on. Her last visit hadn't been a happy occasion and perhaps this one was an even more miserable affair, but one thought kept her mind and heart at peace.

This was the Princess' home, and just like her parents before her, she was prepared to fight for it.

Garnet's bittersweet reverie was cut short when she noticed her companion staring at her. In his hand he held the cloth of the great flag showing the Aquiocian Rose emblem. He had pulled it down from the wall, and underneath, a thick timber door was revealed.

"Another one of your little secrets?"

"Hardly," Setz scoffed. "This attempt at a secret passage is leagues away from holding a torch to my own talents."

"Careful, Setz," Garnet warned. "I've found it's the men who brag the most that are often lacking in other facets of their lives."

"I've found there to be a monumental difference between bragging and making a statement of truth," Setz said, before pushing open the heavy door.

Behind the door they found a dark passage whose walls were lined with unlit torches. Setz took a moment to look at the strong stone walls and at the first torch in the corridor. Garnet joined him, and the pair shook their heads in disbelief at the same time.

"Did they truly believe we would fall for something as juvenile as this?" Garnet asked with a slight hint of humour.

"It is obvious they have been lit and doused recently so as not to attract attention to their escape, should this passage be found. It would have been a last-minute precaution, I would think."

"What makes you think that?"

"This passage leads into the mountains themselves. It is the most direct route through them to the other side. It isn't exactly an Aquiocian secret that this is here, but it isn't a fact we like to parade because of what is on the other side."

"And what might that be?"

Setz took a moment to glance up the dark corridor and then to his companion.

"I have no issue with seeing in the dark, as I hold a strong affinity with it. Lighting the torches would only attract attention to our approach. How will you navigate the darkness?"

He had barely finished voicing the question when Garnet's body mutated in front of his eyes. A long slender snout protruded from her face as her body lowered towards the ground onto all fours. Red fur burst from all over her body as sharp ears and a red bushy tail appeared. Where Garnet stood moments before lay a pile of clothes, a fox climbing out from within.

I shall be able to navigate just fine. Her voice echoed throughout Setz's mind as the fox used its mouth to pick up the clothes.

Setz's scarred face almost looked impressed as he nodded at the fox. With a small gesture towards the tunnel, he turned and broke into a swift yet silent sprint down the corridor. Try as he might, he could barely make out the soft patter of fox paws directly behind him. Despite being unable to hear her sometimes, he knew she never stopped her pursuit.

It may not be in the same field of magic, but Garnet is astonishingly versatile with her skills, Setz thought, feeling genuinely impressed. *She has been nothing but a boon in our efforts here.*

Keep up with the flattery and you may just be the first person to make an old fox blush, Setz, Garnet chortled.

How did you hear that? Setz asked in mild surprise. *Telepathy only works both ways if all parties allow it.*

We are connected mentally. I established the connection when I transformed. I've done it many times with Kurok, Lyrium, Arok. I've even managed it with the Princess and her thief companion, Garnet explained as they ran through the bleak passage.

That doesn't answer my question – how did you establish a connection to my mind without me feeling it?

Oh, you felt it. Your mind just had no hesitation in connecting with me. Now, what does that tell you?

It tells me that this conversation is over, Setz replied.

❖

After they had been running in silence for ten minutes, Garnet's red ears flicked towards the sound of people ahead. The pair had ceased conversation to focus on whatever was going to happen should they find the Council members.

Setz had clearly sensed something as well. He slowed to a walk as Garnet shifted back to her human form and donned her loose dress once more. She then turned her attention to flickering light in the distance.

"Torches," Setz muttered.

"So, then, we have found them – how many by your estimate?"

"There *should* only be three or four Council members and maybe a handful of actual knights."

"You're going to base our next move around how many there *should* be?" Garnet asked sceptically as the pair began their much slower advance.

"Numbers are hardly relevant when it comes to us, Garnet," Setz muttered.

"I'd appreciate it if you would keep me out of your boasting," Garnet said. "Why don't you tell me what is important, then?"

"Arissam," Setz muttered under his breath. "He is the one who initiated the treachery and he is the one Alicea wants brought before her."

"Is he a threat?"

"I do not know." Setz shook his head. "From the information

I have obtained, I do not think so. He is not a threat to us directly, but he truly believes in the ideas Lucian has placed in his mind. His faith is unwavering and that may cause him to become unstable."

"You're concerned that he may make it impossible for us to present him alive to Alicea," Garnet said, before falling dead silent as the corridor ended abruptly and opened into a chamber. The light of the torches' flames finally revealed what was within.

The hidden chamber was massive, and its walls were made of the same blue stone as the castle behind them. But unlike that with which the castle was built, this stone was rough, jagged and clearly uncut. From the hundred-foot-high ceiling hung precarious-looking stalactites, their sharp points facing downwards to the ground. Embedded within the mundane blue stone were light blue crystals that shimmered in the light of the flames. The number of crystals varied between each body of stone, with no discernible pattern.

Spread around the cool stone ground were fragments of the formations above that hadn't been able to hold on any longer. A few knights from the castle were sitting on various shattered pieces of stone in a semi-circle, shielding a handful of noble-looking men. They were so busy talking amongst themselves that they hadn't yet noticed their new company.

Leading the conversation was an irritable and flustered Arissam attempting to gain control of the others.

"Shut your mouths, damn it!" he yelled. The exclamation was clearly designed to be commanding but lacked conviction.

The knights responded hesitantly. Each time they attempted to resist, small wisps of dark smoke rose from within their armour. Neither Garnet nor Setz understood exactly how the curse worked, but they could tell it was weakening. Something about the situation had changed.

Has Jex fallen...? Garnet wondered, knowing full well how unlikely it was as she glanced over the shimmering crystals.

"Listen here, mongrels," Arissam snarled, lowering his voice pointlessly as it echoed around the cavern. "I selected you lot because you were the closest at the time. I have given you all the opportunity to flee with me. You will be saved from the monster attempting to overthrow Aquiocia and –"

"Who is… the monster?" one of the knights asked hesitantly.

It was evident Arissam's lies were beginning to lose their effect alongside the curse. Arissam looked genuinely surprised by the question before a look of fury took its place.

"Did I give you leave to speak?" he shrieked with a rising hysteria. The more he attempted to keep hold of his position in charge, the flimsier his grip seemed.

Garnet nodded at the Guildmaster before moving towards the scene, stopping only when Setz grabbed her arm. With a slight shake of Setz's head, the pair continued to watch on from the darkness.

"Is it true?" another knight asked, nervous at first but more confident as his brethren looked up. "Is it true that our Princess hasn't been held captive?"

"What horseshit is this?" Arissam asked, incredulous. He wasn't surprised so much at the question but at the audacity they had to ask it.

"Is she the one coming for the throne?" another piped up.

"Is she the monster?" the original spoke again as he rose to his feet.

The Council members standing beside Arissam regarded the questions, as well as those asking them, warily. They shrunk behind their leader as if he was the hero who would see them through.

"What's happening...?" Garnet whispered.

"Heroics of the grandest kind," Setz said solemnly, reflecting on those he'd sent to die. "Heroics that are not expected to be acknowledged."

"Kill this man!" Arissam ordered suddenly, eyes darting to each knight standing before him. "I order you all to kill this man – he is inciting betrayal!"

"No," the knights replied in unison, the dark wisps of the curse evaporating.

"What do you mean, *no*?" Arissam shrieked again, taking several steps back. "I am your King! I will –"

"You have done enough." Setz's voice echoed through the chamber finally, drawing all eyes to his dark form emerging from the shadows.

"S-Setz!" Arissam stuttered, his mind whirling. "Y-you're back!"

"I never truly left, Arissam," Setz said, lifting the left sleeve of his cloak. Scars upon scars were torn across his flesh as if a pack of wolves had ravaged his arm. But that wasn't what caught the tyrant's attention.

At the top of Setz's torn bicep, seared into his ripped flesh, was the same brand that was upon the enchanted parchment Arissam had once kept so close to his bed.

"Y-you... You're the a-assassin... I-I don't –"

"It's over, Arissam," Setz said quietly, nodding towards the knights, who inched forward.

Arissam grabbed a cowering Council member with each hand and pulled them forward in front of him.

"Not so fast, Setz!" he cried with hollow triumph. "Shouldn't you be more concerned with the Princess' whereabouts than mine?"

Setz's eyes narrowed slightly. The thought had occurred to him – Alicea wasn't with Arissam. He had hoped he'd find her confronting him.

"What I'm doing is of no concern to you anymore, Arissam," Setz said, his voice barely above a whisper.

"He knew she'd rush off a-alone, you know," Arissam stammered, a bluff that was closer to the truth than he knew. "H-he didn't march with the army for a r-reason."

The knights were hesitating, staring at Setz for a response. Or a command.

"You're grasping at straws. A coward until the –"

"The passage leads to the audience hall!" Arissam cried in desperation, leaving the cavern in silence.

Garnet took the initiative. With a nod towards her companion, she was gone.

"How did you find that?"

"Lucian knows all!" Arissam replied triumphantly. "He has people everywhere and –"

"The late King and Queen must have been aware of Lucian's people within the walls," Setz said over the tyrant's rambling.

"They were, but they couldn't find every single one." Arissam laughed. Then a thought occurred to Setz.

"So, Lucian consciously left the stone within these walls for decades, and yet never bothered to come and get it, knowing full well that a Vassal had been born into the royal family?"

"He – I…" Arissam stammered. "He is far too powerful to care about trivial facts such as that!"

"He didn't know." Setz nodded. "Just like he didn't know that she would struggle this much. Just like he didn't know that the people of this world would put up a fight. I don't expect an underling as pitiful as you to know, but what is keeping him from this world and its Vassals?"

"That is none of your business!" Arissam roared.

"I'm afraid it is. I do not answer for the whole world, but I do speak for Aquiocia and its royalty. The way I see it, there is only one thing that could distract someone like Lucian from the proceedings of this world." Setz glared at the despicable man before him. "It sounds to me that the old myths might have more truth to them than people give them credit for."

"You do not know as much as you think you do!" Arissam snapped.

"And yet so much more than you assume," Setz muttered as smoke began to rise from his form. "Seize them!"

The knights responded, as though relieved to finally have an order. The three Council members were grabbed by rough hands and forced to the ground. Arissam turned to flee, only to come face-to-face with Setz. Before he could comprehend that the Guildmaster had seemingly teleported, he felt something course through his veins and bones. A sudden fatigue.

"The games are over, Arissam," Setz whispered. "Pray the Princess lives to dole out your sentence, lest it fall to me."

CHAPTER 65

SHOWDOWN

Jex leant forward on the throne, staring directly at the Princess with a triumphant smirk. He was supposed to be on the battlefield; they had even received reports to that effect. It stood to reason that he would be wherever it was most likely that people would die. It didn't make any sense for him to be in front of Alicea, despite her previous dreams.

Those dreams... Is the fact that I found Jex here just a coincidence, or is there more to it? Alicea thought. *I've made a grave miscalculation...*

"Is something wrong, Princess?" Jex asked mockingly. "Oh, of course! My lack of manners is putting you off! After all, this is no way to talk to the almighty and magnificent Princess of Aquiocia!"

Jex doubled over at his own jest, his laughter filling the otherwise silent audience hall. Alicea stole a glance towards the staircases on each side of the throne. There was no way around him, and the only favourable part of the situation was the fountain between them, spraying endless streams of clear water.

"I know you are hoping for a peaceful resolution, but surely even one as naïve as you can see that it simply isn't going to happen," Jex said, after recovering from his outburst.

"I suppose a blood-bather such as yourself wouldn't be able to see anything but death as recourse in this situation," Alicea replied coldly, barely concealing her fear.

What is it about him that scares me so?

"Then we understand each other," Jex replied shortly as he rose and strode towards her.

He stopped on the other side of the fountain so that Alicea's view of him was slightly obscured by the jets of liquid.

"Allow me to start over," Jex said, his mocking tone returning with the clearing of his throat. "Welcome back, Your Highness! Welcome to your broken kingdom. Both I and your pathetic subjects have missed you so, we –"

Jex's taunt was cut short as the fountain's water suddenly mutated into countless staves and propelled themselves at him.

He moved with uncanny speed, his form encased in a dark aura as it weaved through the flying staves. His body bent at impossible angles before finally rushing towards Alicea.

In response, Alicea called the water of the fountain to her. It answered her mental cry by becoming a wave. Jex reached Alicea, but the moment before he could grab her, she danced gracefully backwards, her bird taking flight and colliding with her enemy as she retreated.

Jex barely felt the attack. He looked both surprised and amused as the wave of water came crashing from behind him. The dark aura surrounding his body intensified and braced against the water as it descended upon him, following through to its master. As the water gathered around Alicea like a shield, its essence became deadly still until she stood within a liquid dome.

Her bird had recovered and flown into the water shield's surface, reforming on the inside and taking its place on Alicea's outstretched arm.

"My, the Princess can defend herself after all!" Jex scoffed.

"I'm also rather accomplished at attacking," Alicea threatened weakly from within her bubble. "If you'd like to test that, then you will be going head-to-head with a Vassal herself."

"Surely you jest, Your Highness!" Jex retorted, his cruel joy slowly subsiding. "I have killed countless men, women and children alike; I revel in death. Tell me, how many lives have you taken?"

Alicea remained silent. Jex had a point, albeit a sadistic one. She commanded one of the elemental stones, and that offered an advantage in battle that very few could wield.

But this man was a killer – and a powerful one.

"This still surprises me," Jex began thoughtfully as he paced around the water-shield. "I can see someone's death, even before I take their life. It's intriguing that, of all people, I still can't see yours."

"Perhaps that is a sign you should leave me alone," Alicea replied coldly.

"You are quite the jester. No, I will take your life. It will be quite the experience to kill someone without seeing their death beforehand," Jex said, his excitement growing with each word. "Come, Princess. It will be our little experiment before I make your corpse my greatest trophy."

Jex lunged at the wall of water surrounding Alicea. Amidst his charge, he channelled dark energy into his right arm and thrust it into the Princess' shield. The shield held, but Alicea felt a sharp drain on her consciousness.

A single attack and the integrity of my shield flinches? Alicea realised, fear rising within her.

Jex seemed surprised at the fact he had not destroyed the Princess' magical creation in one fell strike. He began to pace around her liquid sanctuary, looking carefully at every inch of it, trying to find a weak point. Alicea couldn't help but focus on the fact that Jex had the same odd contraption slung over his shoulder as he did at the confrontation in Tremel.

At Tremel, the item hadn't seemed important. But now Alicea knew that should he use it, she would be finished. Everything from the dream had become reality; even his pacing around her shield had repetitively played a part in her dream.

Thankfully, she didn't feel intoxicated like she had in the other instances.

Her gaze moved to his left arm. It was wrapped in dark burgundy bandages, not a single inch of flesh to be seen. As a child, Alicea had written it off as an injury sustained from his last mission. Sixteen years on, she knew the wound wasn't natural. She needed to know everything she could about her enemy.

And she needed to prevent the dream from becoming reality. *In my dream I attempted to hold my position until he crushed me. Whatever that thing on his back is… As soon as he made to draw it, I would die, and my dream would end. So, if I can't just fight defensively…*

Alicea reached out to the precious item in the secret pocket of her tabard that Rufus had installed to keep it hidden.

The stone responded instantly. It felt as if it was happy to finally be allowed to help, and their connection sparked and blazed brightly within Alicea. She hated to rely so heavily on the stone's power, but there was just no denying that the sensation of power washing over her like cool spring water was addictive.

Jex turned his attention from the shield to its master as he sensed the power shift. He smiled in amusement when he spoke.

"So, this feat is without the stone's aid? You have grown strong, Your Highness. I do wonder if it will be enough."

His actions haven't changed much from the dream, but his words have – and that's something, though I doubt it is enough. I must attack, but not leave my defences without attention.

Alicea commanded the small swan to transform and it obeyed, switching its form to the staff of still water that the Princess was adept at wielding.

She then reached out to the water of her shield and called small amounts towards her body. The water came to its conjurer and took its place upon her skin, covering her entirely as her pores soaked up the liquid.

Jex watched on curiously. His eyes ran over the Princess' form; it looked as though she had just bathed and put clothes on without drying herself.

Alicea was confused as to why her enemy hadn't attacked again. Then she realised that for him, this was all just part of the game.

He wants to kill me when I'm at my absolute best! That's why he isn't on the field where he could kill as many people as he'd like. It's because killing me means more to him than killing countless others. If I died here… would he leave?

Alicea's consciousness lashed out again towards the now

filled fountain, grasping at the water. She felt the drain of so many connections, but it wasn't unpleasant. She knew she still had a while to go before reaching her limit. She only hoped the techniques she'd mastered over the months would be enough.

The fountain erupted again, long, slender beams of water spewing forth at her enemy. Jex grinned widely at the assault as his body unnaturally weaved through the water. He didn't see the opening in the Princess' shield, and Alicea sprinted through with her staff in hand.

She swung the staff with all the force and discipline instilled in her through her training, striking Jex around the side of the head. He recovered quickly, but he was no longer as sure-footed as he had been. He spun around and immediately jumped back as Alicea brought her unusual weapon up to strike him again.

The pair danced around the fountain, Jex barely an inch out of the reach of each precise and well-honed swing from the Princess. Alicea noted that Jex was bleeding from the left-hand side of his head – though the liquid was not red, but black.

Jex finally got his bearings and stepped into an overhead swing of Alicea's, gripping her staff with his bandaged hand and bringing his spare fist forcefully into her stomach. But she had already analysed his movements as he dodged her attacks. Although his body moved unnaturally, it did have its patterns. As soon as he tensed between strikes, Alicea knew he was about to counter.

She shifted her focus from combat, mentally tightening her grip around the water resting in her pores, and Jex's fist met the resistance of a stone wall. Shock registered on his face as excruciating pain shot up his arm. Alicea grimaced, spinning backwards before lashing out with her staff. The end of the blunt weapon found its mark, smashing Jex right between his surprised eyes.

The Princess wasn't finished. Her mind gripped the water still serving as a stationary wall and brought it forth to crash into Jex with the force of a small tidal wave. The unexpected impact sent his body sprawling across the ground.

Jex struggled to all fours, his manic laughter erupting around the hall.

"Yes, yes, YES!" he exclaimed as he leapt to his feet and pushed his drenched hair out of his face. "This – is – incredible! What a development! The Princess, no less! Nay! The Jewel of the Kingdom, the Rose of Aquiocia – can actually fight!"

Alicea could only stare at the deranged man as he started to pace frantically. It was as if he couldn't control his own movements.

"Oh, Your Highness, I am unworthy of your presence!" Jex laughed, his voice laced with mockery as his hand reached for the contraption strapped to his back. His eyes were wide and excited as his voice turned cold. "Oh no, I'm most certainly not worthy, but you better believe I'll do my damned best to be so."

Alicea braced herself; this was it. This was the end in her dream. When Jex unleashed whatever weapon was behind his back, it always spelt the end for the Princess.

Jex's hand gripped the contraption and he spun it up and around over his head.

The strange item unfolded into what seemed like a long pole with long blades emerging from the centre at one end. The blades were the colour of raven feathers and each appeared to be dripping constantly with a black liquid, similar to the blood leaking from Jex's head wound.

As Jex slung the mighty weapon over his shoulder, Alicea noticed two things. The first was that it looked like a large, dark version of the sickles farmers used in the fields. The second – far more worrying – was that Jex swung it as easily as Rufus swung one of his daggers. Whatever this thing was, it was just as dangerous as its wielder.

"Beautiful, isn't it? I was gifted this scythe by Lucian himself when he contracted me to his service," Jex explained with pride. "It took me years to find any trace of him again, but it was worth it. He said I showed promise, and I haven't let him down."

"Lucian? A myth is what drives you?" Alicea accused weakly. There had been too many strange occurrences to completely discredit the idea anymore.

"The very same, Your Highness. And guess what!" Jex sneered. "He's back, and he isn't pleased."

"Impossible!" Alicea laughed. "You expect me to believe that this knight is centuries old?"

"Older than centuries, Your Highness. If you don't believe me, then how do you explain that you have known me since you were a child, and yet the man in front of you appears to be your age?" Jex smirked.

Alicea fell silent. This was something she had pondered her whole life. In fact, it was the reason she grew up being so unnerved by Jex. He never changed. Battle never wore on him; struggles were shrugged off. Nothing about life left its mark on the man's body. Everyone around her weathered life's embrace, with new shadows in their eyes from each experience. Over fifteen years after he was supposed to be executed, the man before her had scars, yet time had ignored him.

If I survive, I'm sure I will have a lot to think about.

She did have one answer at last: she knew what drove him.

"So, the legend is true," Alicea said, looking down at her staff and gripping it tightly.

With her spare hand she reached into her pocket and produced a shining hair tie encrusted with diamonds. With a quick flick of her wrist and fingers, her hair was in a messy yet restrained ponytail. Her mind lashed out to the water filling the fountain along with the liquid that had drenched the stone floor.

"Sure, take your time, Your Highness, no rush!" Jex laughed, but allowed her to prepare nonetheless.

"Now I know who the enemy of my kingdom is and who has made so many suffer. You –" Alicea shook her head slowly before continuing. "You will merely be a stepping stone to pave our way to Lucian. You will be nothing more than a footnote in the story of how we clipped the wings of anyone who deliberately brought pain to the innocent."

"You are mistaken, Your Highness. He is not the enemy of your kingdom – he is the rightful owner!" Jex declared, sprinting towards her with his scythe's blade down at his side.

Alicea commanded the water to return to her, but she knew there was no way it would get to her in time. She had counted on him to continue speaking. She was forced to spread her feet apart and meet the brutal weapon with her own as Jex flipped around effortlessly into a downwards swing.

The scythe's blade bore down on Alicea from Jex's greater

height as she struggled to keep the weapon away from her flesh. It slowly inched downwards as Jex steadily overpowered her with a single hand. The blade was still dripping the dark liquid and a few stray drops fell upon Alicea's skin. She thought nothing of it until she felt a searing pain where the liquid had landed.

Alicea cried out in shock and jumped back from Jex, who was laughing again.

"An interesting weapon, is it not? It's enchanted – but you, of course, would know that," Jex mused, staring at the weapon thoughtfully. "It has seen thousands of deaths and drunk the blood of each of the victims. It has been busy the past year, as have I. It enchants the blood with a technique known as Blood Manipulation. That is what you feel upon your skin: the blood of thousands manipulated by my will."

Blood Manipulation? I know nothing of that, Alicea thought hopelessly.

Because it is not a common choice amongst mages, came the voice within the stone. It was a surprise to hear it speak when she hadn't heard from it in months, despite trying to make contact. *It mutates the essence of magic within the blood and bends it to the wielder's will. It allows the master to control blood itself and is no small feat. It is, however, an abomination.*

"Shall we take a break, then?" Jex offered, lowering his guard and stretching casually.

How do I fight this? From the stories, Lucian's soldiers could not be quelled while Lucian lived.

Kill him, was the short reply from the stone.

Lucian's men can't be killed so long as Lucian lives! Alicea repeated in exasperation as her mind raced through the stories she'd been told around Tremel's bonfire.

He is not bound. The dead cannot command blood, as it is a resource of the living, the stone explained. *This man has given his body and services to Lucian willingly. Though his soul is clearly twisted, it is not bound to the Forgotten Knight.*

I understand... I think... Alicea replied. *But I can't kill him...*

Why not?

Because I... Alicea's mind clouded with memories from sixteen years ago. *I already gave this man a death sentence. I condemned him... It was me.*

You will lead your people to salvation or perish alongside them. The sobering words echoed around Alicea's mind before the voice added, *this conversation is over. Now be the Queen you're destined to be and end this.*

The words were like a slap in the face. A slap that brought forth the image of every person she had met in the past few months. The people who had thrown their lives on the line for the Princess and her kingdom. Months of memories relived in a moment, showing the very same people she was searching for a reason to abandon.

I truly am a selfish brat, Alicea thought bitterly as she pictured Rufus' face.

Shaking her head, she reached up and tightened the priceless hair tie before turning her gaze of newfound determination on her enemy.

He may be powerful, but he can also be killed.

Jex took her turning her attention back to him as an invitation and lunged at her again. Alicea channelled the water she had called to herself into a wall separating them.

Jex collided with the wall and bounced back. This time he

didn't hesitate in swinging his bloody weapon at the barricade, and Alicea watched in despair as her liquid protection started to darken. The blood from Jex's weapon began to seep through the water, causing it to spread and decay.

Alicea released the magic instinctively, sending water spraying throughout the audience hall, only to see Jex glide through the moisture unharmed. He reached her effortlessly and swung his long weapon downwards.

Alicea sidestepped and brought her staff upwards into Jex's ribcage. The blow glanced off and Jex lashed out with his spare bandaged hand, violently knocking the Princess to the ground. The maniac wasn't mocking her anymore. His eyes were fierce as he went for the kill.

Before he could deliver the killing blow, a shadow glanced past Alicea's eyes so quickly that even she didn't quite recognise the person. Jex's face registered confusion as he looked down to see someone between him and his prey. It suddenly occurred to him that he had been wounded. Two long knives were buried in his stomach, in a precise strike that was designed to bleed someone out – this person knew how to assassinate. Jex stumbled back, the blades still lodged in his gut.

The newcomer stood upright and flipped the hood of his cloak to reveal an unshaven face and light-green eyes. The man pushed his hair back off his face out of habit before touching the scar near his right eye at the sight of the roses upon the castle walls.

"Mr. Thief!" Alicea spluttered in surprise. "I wasn't sure if you'd make it…"

Rufus turned and smiled at the Princess, extending his hand

to help her to her feet. "You're hurt," he said, referring to the growing bruise across her eye.

"I am fine," Alicea said slowly. The adrenaline had kept the pain at bay.

"Damned maggots can never do anything alone," a vicious voice spat from behind the pair.

Both Princess and thief turned to their enemy with surprise. Jex was still standing, though he was clearly in pain from Rufus' vicious assault. He began stretching his body before letting out a wail that sounded like a dying animal as the daggers' hilts fell from his body. Dark blood spewed onto the ground from his wounds. It sizzled angrily, burning holes in the stone beneath the wounded man.

He melted the blades! Alicea realised.

Yes, his blood devoured the blades. Blood is forever wanting, the voice agreed. *His body should have been disintegrated by such a stunt. Impressive.*

You may not know this, but praising the enemy is less helpful than you might think! the Princess snapped.

Jex's wounds had closed and another vicious scar was now healing at a rapid rate on his already torn and slashed torso. His face was filled with fury as he grabbed at his bound arm and pulled roughly at the restraints. The bandages gave way to reveal an arm with skin and muscle as black as night.

With a flash of dark light, an unexpected force soared from Jex's arm and sent Alicea flying. Rufus howled in anger and lunged at him. He had two more knives in his hands and plenty of other tools on his person; he'd find one that would kill his enemy. Jex barely acknowledged the man sprinting at him, swinging his blackened arm around and slamming it into the thief's gut.

Rufus stumbled, winded, and Jex lifted him into the air and slammed him down onto the stone floor. Rufus writhed in shock and pain. He barely processed the sight of Jex looming over him before the shaft of Jex's weapon drove into the side of Rufus' head.

It was effortless, almost laughably so, to dispatch the so-called guardian of the Princess.

Worthless. Jex laughed as he turned his attention to Alicea.

Alicea barely had time to tighten her focus around the water in her skin before her petite frame was lifted by a violent blast of dark magic from Jex's blackened arm. The blast didn't harm her as the water cushioned the blow, but she felt her energy start to leave her body as she soared across the hall and through one of the stained-glass windows. Suddenly free of the hall's confines, the Princess sprawled out in the courtyard, lying face-down in the wet grass as cold rain pelted down from above. The water bound to her skin joined the rain running down her body. She couldn't hold it there.

She climbed to her feet despite the overwhelming urge to collapse, turning just in time to see Jex launch himself out of the shattered window after her, illuminated only by the erratic flashes of lightning.

He held his scythe in his right hand as he raced towards her and grabbed her fiercely with his dark, twisted arm, pulling her up off the ground with superhuman strength. The now unbound arm was impossible not to notice, whether by physically looking at it or sensing its undeniable magical presence. Whatever those bandages had been, they had been keeping the arm's secrets hidden. Now Alicea was eye-level with the furious Jex, too dazed to even think of a way out of the situation.

"You pathetic excuse for a Princess – you have nothing! Your friend lies unconscious inside. I'll torture him until he begs for death and gives up all the little secrets about your allies. I'll make him cry blood and just before he passes into the next life, I'll drag him to Lucian. His cries of agony will be heard for an eternity and then longer still! Do you see?" Jex screamed in Alicea's face before throwing her across the courtyard. "I asked you a question! Do – you – see? You can't save anyone! All you have done is brought pain to those who have thrown their lives on the line for you. THIS IS YOUR DOING, YOUR HIGHNESS!"

"That's not true!" Alicea cried as she struggled to her feet again, her face covered in tears blending into the rain and dirt. "They believe in a better way…"

"And what good has that done you all?" Jex bellowed angrily. "You're just like your parents, believing everything will be fine with your delusional ideals."

"DO NOT TALK ABOUT THEM LIKE THAT!" Alicea screamed. "YOU DON'T KNOW THEM!"

To this Jex laughed, but not maniacally. He had control now and he was genuinely amused.

"Oh, Princess. Allow me to fill you in on your parents' story before I finally kill you. I want you to understand just how wrong you are so that you can fully grasp how little you've accomplished."

He paced for a moment before continuing.

"Your parents weren't horrible rulers," Jex started, his anger appearing to die down to a simmer. "They continued what your grandparents and their parents before them had started. They constructed a kingdom with a foundation of peace, and *that* they managed to do well."

Alicea listened closely despite already knowing what Jex was saying. She picked herself up off the ground and rested on her knees as Jex continued.

"Aquiocia is very wealthy. Well, it was, anyway. It's under Lucian's control now, and the treasury has taken hit after hit as he uses it to motivate people to his side."

"Why would he be buying people off? He has proven that he could just enslave the lot of us. Where is he?" Alicea spat. The rain had soaked her to the bone, but she felt no chill.

"Lucian understands that to get what he wants he will need a bigger force than his last attempt on the stones. Look at me, Princess. I am gifted in Blood Manipulation, a tool that he would not be able to make use of should he bind me to him. It took me a while to realise why I was rejected…" A small pause. "As a result, he has a growing army that is terrified to resist. One day, when the force is large enough, I will offer it to Lucian. He will accept me."

This is all for him to be accepted by a myth…? Alicea thought with disgust. *People are tormented and dying so he can be praised by Lucian.*

"But we are getting off topic. Your parents had all this gold accumulating in their precious treasury, but what did the military see of it? Nothing, that's what!" Jex's rage seemed to be resurfacing. "While the gold kept coming in, the once great army of Aquiocia was left to go stagnant. The skill of the soldiers diminished more and more with each new squad – the exception being me, of course. I do what needs to be done."

"What is your point, Jex?" Alicea asked coldly. "It is a ruler's duty to ensure that the kingdom and its people flourish and prosper. It sounds like my family has done a good job of that."

"Oh yes, they did a marvellous job of making Aquiocia weak and passive," Jex sneered. "Aquiocia could have had firm control over the whole land if the past rulers weren't so spineless. From there, even the sky wasn't a limit. If Aquiocia had played its cards right with the settlements below the mountains, even Nimbus itself wouldn't have been able to resist!"

"Conquest is not what Aquiocia is about!" Alicea protested. "It never was and never will be!"

"And that was ultimately the downfall of us all, Your Highness!" Jex bellowed. "We could have resisted Lucian and any other threat if we were stronger and not so fixated on our wealth! We even had a Vassal in the royal family, and another in the hovel of savages. We could have brought this land to heel!"

"We? You speak as if you were once united with this kingdom!" It was Alicea's turn to scoff. "The fair Kingdom of Aquiocia would never voluntarily be in allegiance with a bloodthirsty monster like you!"

Jex ignored her. "Two things happened that amounted to the end for Aquiocia. The first was your spineless parents on the throne. Your father had some degree of courage until he took that bitch commoner as a wife. The second was that pathetic, peace-loving *Warmaster* Maxim."

"Maxim? Where is he?" Alicea demanded, kicking herself for not finding him.

"You will be going to meet him soon enough, Princess," Jex said snidely.

An overwhelming mix of emotion hit Alicea when she realised what he meant.

Maxim was dead. Grief and anger brewed within her. She barely caught herself before breaking down. She knew. She had known for a while, but refused to admit it. She knew she couldn't succumb to grief, but she found it difficult to want to stand.

"He was on your side!" She lunged clumsily at her enemy, only to be caught and hurled back the way she came. The grief within her twisted and manifested into loathing as she looked at the smirking face of a man relishing her pain. "He was one of the only people who believed you and you… You just…"

"There is no one left for you, Princess. Everyone you have ever loved and called family is dead. You had a chance to take the kingdom's reins and lead its people properly against Lucian, but you weren't interested. You were too captivated by your own self-pity and now everyone is dead, from the fool Warmaster to your spineless parents. This is your doing."

"They weren't spineless! They led the charge to stop the conflict at the Plains!" Alicea screamed, desperate to ignore her sadness.

"And they may have succeeded under other circumstances!" Jex shrugged.

"What are you talking about?" Alicea demanded, her voice breaking.

"Maxim was to lead the troops. Your parents wanted to speak to the Vassals to try to work it out peacefully. As if that would ever work!" Jex spat on the ground as if disgusted by the idea. "But the Warmaster suddenly fell ill before the march, thus making him incapable of leading the troops. I wonder how that happened?"

"What are you talking about?" Alicea repeated, her voice rising.

"I'm talking about the fact that when they got to the Plains, they met with the Vassal of Light and the conflict resumed with your parents aiding her. How is it that an entire army, both of your parents and even the Vassal of Light fell to just one woman?"

"The enemy Vassal was too powerful…" Alicea said, repeating the same story she had been telling herself for over a year. She was having trouble believing it now.

"That's one theory, yes." Jex smiled cruelly. "Another might be that the army was compromised."

Alicea let this new theory roll around in her head. Try as she might, she couldn't dismiss its credibility. It had never occurred to her – the Aquiocian knights were traditionally loyal to a fault.

Then she finally managed to see the piece she had been missing for the past year. She looked at Jex with loathing as all the pieces finally came together.

"You only recently resurfaced. Where have you been?" Alicea asked coldly, before outright screaming when she saw Jex's smile grow. "WHERE WERE YOU WHEN MY PARENTS WENT TO THE PLAINS, JEX?"

"It's simply wonderful that you are standing here and

screaming at me for answers," Jex sneered, his voice full of dark humour. "A little over a year ago, your parents did the exact same thing."

CHAPTER 66

SHIMMER

"Heads high and eyes forward, my friends!" Axeal's voice boomed throughout the savannah. His content demeanour hadn't diminished a fraction in the week-long journey to the north-east.

A thousand of Aquiocia's finest followed him in an organised legion. It had been a shame that the Warmaster had taken so ill, but a thousand soldiers were the norm for an Aquiocian force, and the King had led similar numbers many times before.

Axeal grinned at the beautiful woman riding side-saddle on the horse next to him. He couldn't help it; the day was gorgeous, the nature surrounding them was luscious, yet it all seemed so ugly when compared to his wife.

Adele smiled back slightly before inclining her head towards what lay before the legion of cerulean and silver. Both King and Queen's faces turned grim and a collective murmur rippled through the ranks of soldiers. The ground ahead had had both turf and soil ripped up by an unknown force.

The entire legion shifted slightly, and the front line raised their shields before cautiously moving ahead at half their original march speed. The King and Queen hadn't needed to say a thing; the knights were trained far too well.

As the company moved ever closer, more and more features started to become clearer. Like the scattered, fully grown trees that had been uprooted and launched from their resting places in all directions. Multiple feet of soil had been dug up and strewn everywhere, though from no tool known to man. The destruction of nature spread out for leagues, the only differences being in the cavities now within the earth. They ranged from a few inches deep through to gashes dug ten feet into the world's flesh.

The King's hand rose slightly, and the company stopped at the edge of the disturbed land. It was then that Adele saw the shining energy in certain parts of the soil and identified the site for what it was.

"The arena," the Queen muttered, her voice carrying through the strained silence.

The murmuring amongst the troops resumed but was cut short by Axeal's hand rising once more.

"It's close. You can feel it, can't you, my love?"

"I would not call her an 'it' – I fear that might cause offence." Adele smiled, looking directly at a shimmer in the distance that only she was able to perceive. "Greetings. Might I have a word?"

Everyone fell silent as the Queen dismounted her horse and adjusted her royal garb in one fluid movement before stepping towards the upheaved, unstable soil. Her boots sank on the uneven surface, but she didn't stumble. She was confident, she was graceful, and falling wasn't something Queen Adele was known for.

The entire force, along with the King, waited in anxious stillness. They all knew she saw something they didn't. While a few amongst them were learned in the magical arts, they all knew Adele's magical senses were far more attuned than the rest of them combined. All they could do was wait and see what happened next.

Adele paid no mind to the legion behind her as she walked forward and addressed something they couldn't see. The shimmer didn't change or increase in intensity, nor did it run or try to hide. The Queen could feel its nature as it twinkled in its semi-existence, like the glare of sunlight upon the sand of a shore. She knew it was a person, and she knew nobody was supposed to be able to see them.

She'd crossed a considerable distance before the shimmering essence rose from the soil in countless tiny, shining lights, congregating into a human outline. Adele couldn't make out any details of the shining silhouette, but from its natural curves, her initial theory that it was female seemed correct. The more the Queen tried to look into where she supposed the shining woman's eyes would be, the more the illusion resisted. She could feel her energy expiring the more she attempted to examine the silhouette. Whatever the woman was, she didn't like people prying into her appearance.

Despite the entity's withdrawn nature, Adele could sense two forces directly before her. One was housing the other, and the visitor boasted a level of power that made even the Queen's mind cloud a little. She could feel a third energy signature in the distance beyond the shining woman, but it felt dormant, as if awaiting a command.

Suddenly, Adele felt another sharp tug on her reserves, and she knew that probing at the other energy signature was another forbidden act.

Her disappointment was short-lived when the shimmering spectre spoke with a soft voice of illusory brilliance that made even the imposing Queen's eyes widen slightly at its almost song-like tune.

"Greetings, Queen Adele of the Aquiocian kingdom."

Adele's bottom lip fell slightly. Her composure was clinging to what remained of her regal poise. The woman's voice wasn't natural; it transcended human nature, and the Queen couldn't help but entertain the possibility that the being before her wasn't of this world.

"An... an angel..." Without meaning to, Adele voiced her stray thought.

"No." The shimmer radiated a warmth that calmed the Queen's racing mind. "I'm simply a human who has had more time than most to refine themselves. The brilliance before you is the harnessed potential that lies within all aligned with the Light."

"I don't understand," Adele said, trying desperately not to be completely captivated by the woman's voice. It wasn't an intoxicating or debilitating sensation, but rather a feeling of benevolence. Whoever this was, she meant no ill will, least of all to the enemy she had heard reports of.

"You will exhaust yourself," the spectre said in a tone that Adele felt belonged to a woman who would smile kindly as she looked over someone she cared for.

"I'm fine." Adele shook her head slightly. The warmth surrounding her refused to evaporate. "Who are you, and how do you know my name?"

"The time for talking is not now." The voice's tone had turned to concern, and the Queen could feel the third energy signature flashing brightly in the corner of her mind. "It appears that the next round has begun."

The Queen had no chance to respond as the shimmering silhouette turned away and glided across the destroyed land at the speed of a charging horse. There was no way for Adele to match the spectre's pace before the sound of a colossal collision echoed throughout the plains.

The ground shook, and cries of surprise from the legion joined the din. Several crashes joined the first, but it was the visual spectacle that held Adele's intense focus. Across from where she stood were two shimmering lights dancing around what had become a battlefield once more. Where the second light – a massive ball of brilliance – had come from was anyone's guess as the pair collided with their enemies: a dark silhouette accompanied by a similar companion of violet shadows.

The two spectres were deadlocked, and although Adele couldn't make out the specifics of any of the combatants, she knew what they were. They had to be Vassals. The sheer energy being thrown around was enough to make her temples throb. She had no idea who or what the two orbs of contrasting light were, but they were bounding around the field and launching themselves at each other.

Are the orbs manifestations of their energy? Adele mused as she attempted to take in what she could about the combatants without looking directly at them. Gazing at them for even a second burned her eyes mercilessly. Each time the great spheres of light lunged at one another, their brilliance would intensify, leaving onlookers seeing double as they attempted to refocus.

Too much exposure to this will leave permanent damage, Adele thought grimly. She knew she had to suppress them.

"Soldiers!" Adele called back to the bedazzled legion, enhancing her voice to be heard through the chaotic crashes behind her. "We are here to quell this confrontation that they have no interest in ceasing. We march!"

The Queen's message was met with a courageous chorus of cheers, none louder than King Axeal's as he dismounted his horse, slapped its backside so it knew to flee, and ran to his wife's side. The legion charged forth, the steady shuffling of marching armour joining the din.

"THIS DISTURBANCE ENDS NOW!" Adele's voice boomed across the torn plains.

She received a short reply from an apathetic voice, as if its owner was bored.

"What a joke – they actually came. Do it now."

King, Queen and army had no idea what the cryptic message meant, but their march didn't slow.

CHAPTER 67

A SQUIRE'S BETRAYAL

"Phew, did ya see that?" a young knight exclaimed to the dozen others who had retreated from the main force upon the order to march. They were one of the supply corps, armed with only longswords and massive, sturdy horses pulling the carts of supplies. They weren't fighters, with good reason.

"Aye. I don't envy the soldiers' jobs right now," another agreed, thankful to be putting distance between them and the confrontation.

The thirteen terrified cooks, servants and scouts all murmured in agreement. They weren't amongst the bravest of men, and they knew they only had one job when battle ensued: survive and meet up with the other supply corps – a task that was about to become a great deal more difficult.

"Good afternoon, peasants," a cruel voice broke through the muttering knights.

Looking around, they all realised something was deeply wrong with their numbers.

"Wait a minute…" one man muttered.

"We have an extra…" another trailed off.

It was too late.

Beneath the helm of the knight hanging back, an amber blaze erupted. As the intruder steadily stripped himself of the pieces of armour clinging to his form, the squad of troops began to writhe in a nauseous haze from their places in the saddle. Moans escaped their throats, and with each piece of armour the assailant shed, the knights' agony intensified.

It wasn't long before a few of the afflicted men recognised the person clad in all black and sneering at them. But when they attempted to speak, all that came forth was the gurgle of blood looking for an escape. Thick red liquid spilt from their lips and down their chins as they frantically attempted to remove their helmets in hopes of being able to breathe.

The beating of drums echoed through each of their skulls as their eyes begged the man to cease his cruelty. Instead of relief, they found themselves weeping the same thick, burning substance escaping their throats. Through the terror and anguish, one man managed to choke out the question, "Why?"

"Why not?" Jex shrugged dismissively. "I've been dying for the day that I'd be freed. You know, I almost gave up."

Jex was grinning as he dismounted his horse, his long, fading coat flapping in the gentle breeze as he made his way to the knight who'd managed to speak.

"But I came back, didn't I?" Jex brought his face within an inch of the man being tortured by his own lifeblood, openly laughing when he choked and sprayed his terroriser with blood. "How disrespectful! Don't you know that I own you?"

Jex's laughter was met only with gargled whimpers. Turning back to his horse, he addressed the distraught men sobbing tears of blood.

"You'll fight your own," Jex said quietly. "You, along with the other supply corps, will charge the main force. You will have the element of surprise, and you will die. You will die at the hands of your own kind. Your fellow soldiers, your comrades-at-arms, your military family – they will be the ones to strike you down. I will feel their blood quicken with the regret and fear of what you've become as they bring about your end. And I will rejoice! Do you want to know why? Because that royal bitch is next!"

CHAPTER 68

THE BATTLE OF A THOUSAND BLADES

The laughter of a madman joined the cries of the Aquiocian legion marching to battle. The pace of the soldiers had slowed somewhat on the rough turf, making it easy for the corrupted supply units to catch up.

Jex kept pace with the supply units, clearing the field with a haste that no regular human could possibly keep up with. No man stepped within a dozen paces of him, but he didn't feel exposed. They were doing his bidding, after all; dozens of scattered and shambling men were racing erratically at the main force.

There was no tact or strategy in their charge, and even when they hit the uneven earth, their pace barely slowed. They didn't have any concern for sprained ankles or even broken bones. The dark influence of their blood being manipulated kept their bodies together and running headlong at their comrades. Any resistance shown by the men was immediately rewarded with a searing sensation of liquid magma coursing through their veins.

The Aquiocian military were known for their bravery and their loyalty. But to have a foreign magic thrust upon them with no prior training or warning was too much. How do you fight a force when you have no idea what it is, much less how it works?

Every resistance was met with excruciating agony that blinded the minds of the victims and forced the sorcerer's will ever further forward. It wasn't long before their minds surrendered, and after a few short waves of anguish, anything that made the soldiers human was erased, replaced with puppets fuelled by blood and cruelty.

At first the collective resistance of dozens of men had made Jex flinch, but with each renewed assault, the control became easier. He knew he wasn't to seize control of their minds, but their bodies. At first he'd thought his power was controlling the minds of his victims, but that wasn't the truth.

Mind control seems like such a mess. Jex laughed once more at the thought. *Control someone's body with enough force and their mind will fall in line with the rest of them. Punish the individual severely enough and their will can be moulded as easily as their flesh. The result is a puppet that is literally dying to do your bidding. They become compliant, and their existence is finally granted meaning.*

Jex was so lost in his joyous reverie that he almost didn't notice that his shambling party was almost upon the main force. As they crossed the rough terrain, a few of his numbers stumbled and fell to the dirt, only to be forced to their mutilated feet.

"On your feet, mongrels!" Jex's voice boomed across the torn prairie.

The tortured men wailed as their limbs twisted and contorted. The flesh within their steel prisons bulged and split from the burning blood pumping through their veins. The shredded meat of their legs pushed forward, carrying each blood-seeping carcass that was once a living being forward.

Their shrieks could still be heard from under their helms. The foul magic had not offered the victims a true death, their grasp on life forged by desperation.

By this point, the main force had noticed their supply units making their way back towards them, and Jex could feel the soldiers' hesitation in the way their hearts fluttered. They were still too far away for the legion to notice the men were suffering, but their return was still something to be worried about.

Then they saw Jex, shrugging as if to say, "Surprise!"

The soldiers' chanting steadily died off as more became aware of what was going on behind them. A path was made through the centre of the legion as they shuffled out of the way to allow the King to approach. Axeal's look of surprise was shattered as quickly as it appeared, replaced with a look of grim determination. The King would never allow himself to be shaken on a battlefield, whether by two Vassals of the elements or a man who had risen from the dead.

"Jex!" Axeal's commanding voice reverberated around the land.

"Make it quick, Your Majesty!" Jex hollered back with a grin. "These mongrels have a job to do before they fall apart!"

"I've executed you once – I will do it again!"

"You've failed to execute me once, and will fail to do so again!" Jex corrected, bursting into hysterics so overwhelming that he doubled over mid-march.

Axeal didn't reply, instead charging directly at the cackling lunatic.

Jex's mirth ceased, an air of cruelty adopted seamlessly in its place as he screamed, "Kill them! Kill your comrades! Kill your King! Royalty and gods be damned – KILL THEM ALL!"

The sound of steel colliding with steel was immediately drowned out by the roar of men meeting in battle. It had worked; Jex could feel it in the hearts of all around him. Trepidation, panic and then resolve – the resolution to kill the enemies before them.

The sheer conviction of the Aquiocian knights is absolute, Jex thought as his body flashed with a dark, sinister light and he casually dodged the wrath of the King's sword. *But ever so predictable.*

Jex turned slowly to see King Axeal standing with rough poise upon the uneven ground, rising to his tall, broad stature with ornate longsword in hand. The royal wasted no time on words, lunging at Jex only to find his target an elusive one. With each swing of his deadly blade, he found only air as his enemy dodged effortlessly. Jex was moving unnaturally swiftly, and the King knew that some foul magic aided his every movement.

Finally, Axeal reached out and surprised Jex by grabbing him roughly and pulling him close. Jex had no chance of defying his sheer physical strength and was forced to gaze into the stern eyes of the Aquiocian King.

"This game you're playing is over, Jex!" Axeal snarled, and his spare hand ran the royal blade through the madman's stomach.

Jex reeled back, the sword twisting before he yanked it free. He wailed wildly, head thrown towards the sky. The shrieks of shock dissolved into gurgles of blood and a failing voice. The King had mortally wounded his enemy, and all he could do was stare in morbid fascination at the man he swore he'd executed fifteen years earlier.

The dying man fell to his knees, and the King's hope faltered. Jex began to exude crimson liquid from every orifice of his body. Streaks of red streamed from his eyes and down to his jawline as the sockets themselves flooded with blood. Before Axeal could even comprehend what was happening, the same crimson began to escape Jex's pores. It was as if the blood was moving to the surface of his skin through whatever means necessary. Bone and muscle structures began to sink into the bloody mess until all that was left was a pile of bones, muscles and what appeared to be boiling blood singeing the remains.

And then laughter. The laughter you'd expect from a cruel jester who had successfully pulled the greatest stunt of his career.

Axeal couldn't think – he couldn't focus. He couldn't comprehend how Jex had even appeared after he had executed him personally. Now, he'd struck him down a second time, and yet a crimson pile of human sludge devouring itself remained.

And a madman's mirth.

Axeal realised it was the laughter he needed to locate – or rather, the person it belonged to. He moved in a haze, his ears barely registering the sound of combat around him as the cruel hysterics continued, an ever-constant ringing.

My men are still fighting? Axeal thought in concern. *They should have quashed that threat in seconds.*

The King didn't have any time to look around and take in the battle's proceedings. He'd found what he was looking for.

He'd found Jex – again.

The tall, slender man stood just fifteen yards away, clothed in dark leather trousers and equally dark boots. He wore the same long coat of faded black he was imprisoned in, and bandages were wrapped tightly around his heavily bleeding arm. He was in hysterics.

"H-how…?"

Jex's eyes snapped wide open, his humour gone as he glanced around at the fighting men.

"Do you have any idea what is going on around you, Your Majesty?" Jex asked casually. Despite the sounds of weapons, armour and people colliding, Axeal had little trouble hearing him.

"You've incited a mutiny. You've infected my men with some form of contagion…" Axeal trailed off, his eyes never leaving Jex.

At first, Jex didn't respond, instead looking around at the battle and nodding thoughtfully, as if he'd been given something to ponder deeply.

"Yes… A contagion. That's an excellent deduction," Jex commended, proud of his creation.

"It's in their blood!" Axeal spat, anger and indignation crushing his confusion as he steadily realised what was going on.

"It is. Every body is full of blood, so taking control of it means that you can take control of them. The precious liquid becomes tainted – and do you know what the quickest way to spread any contagion is?"

"Contact…" Axeal muttered. His eyes widened in horror as he took in the battle around him fully for the first time.

The once laughable balance that had firmly been in the King's favour had shifted, and as he gazed around at the commotion, he realised there appeared to be an even amount of men fighting on each side. The corruption of the legion's ranks had become so deeply embedded in the afflicted men that it looked more like a free-for-all gladiator match than an alliance with a few turncoats in their ranks.

The screams of soldiers meeting their ends sounded different. They sounded...

Pure. It was an accurate description, the King was forced to admit, and it made him physically recoil. *They are dying, and the pain they are feeling isn't a result of Jex's magic. It's a result of them embracing the relief that death brings a tortured soul. Exactly what is this monster capable of?*

Axeal felt beaten, as though utter defeat was nibbling at his heels and he was barely keeping ahead of it. He wanted nothing more than to kill Jex, to strike him down and avenge those who'd suffered at his hand. But he had already slain the monster twice, and both times he had failed. What would stop Jex from appearing again and again each time he was killed? Axeal didn't understand how Jex's power worked, but he understood that his legion was melting around him, and that it was far too late to save the soldiers with any real semblance of their lives intact.

The Aquiocian King only snapped out of his bitter trance when a cerulean blaze soared from his right, aiming directly at Jex. The blur caught Jex by surprise, and the image of the Queen balling her fist and driving it directly at her enemy's face was truly a sight to behold.

Then she redirected.

Slamming her fist into the ground a few strides from where Jex was standing, Adele's mind reached into the soil and effortlessly carved its way through the earth's essence, rallying all moisture to her mental cry.

Jex looked mildly curious as he leapt away from a geyser of water that burst violently from the soil. The fierce jet of liquid soared into the air before cascading back down in a pleasant drizzle. And then another pillar of water exploded from its earthen prison. Then another. And another, until dozens of the torrential pillars tore through the already destroyed plains.

Jex couldn't believe his eyes. At first he thought Adele had intended on striking him with the assault, but apart from the initial spike, she hadn't come close to hitting him. It didn't feel like a concentrated attack designed to hurt him directly; it felt more like a single step in a far grander plan. It felt like a set-up.

He wanted to react, though he wasn't sure how. He wanted to strike out at the Queen, but he noticed the King wasn't standing in the same place he had been just moments ago.

Damn it, where is he? Jex scolded himself. *I should know by now that these two feed off each other, that he'd find a will to fight once she was on the scene.*

Jex took a risk in turning his attention away from Adele in search of her husband, and it almost cost him dearly as the Queen lunged forward. In her hands were short swords formed from liquid, which she thrust at his open chest. He barely avoided the blades by side-stepping behind one of the geysers of pure water. Dancing around the pillar, he came face to face with Axeal. Jex allowed for a moment of uncertainty before ducking instinctively to avoid the blade aimed at his head.

Jex ran. He scrambled over the torn, muddy earth, between

the jets of the seemingly never-ending liquid.

How much water is under the ground? Where is she calling all of this from?

The soil had become thick and sludge-like as Jex ran through the labyrinth of water and mud. Then he felt it – a chill. A chill that ignored skin and muscle alike and settled directly into his bones. He wasn't just shivering; his entire body was shuddering involuntarily from the sudden temperature change. Comprehension failed him as he looked up to see the twinkling of crystals falling from the geysers to the earth. It took a few of the beautiful shimmers landing on his frigid skin for him to realise that they were particles of ice, and that what he was seeing was a shower of frost – a veritable phenomenon in Aquiocia. He didn't understand how or why she was able to perform a feat that defied the weather, but he knew beyond a shadow of doubt that he had sorely underestimated the Queen.

His body was numb, only the burning of the frosty air registering in his mind as he forced his protesting legs into action. He didn't know where he was going, and it didn't matter as Adele appeared from behind one of the sleet-spewing gashes in the earth. The Queen looked magnificent – a majestic and striking specimen of a mage in absolute control. The cold did nothing but enhance her intimidating presence as her still, cerulean eyes bored through the freezing man.

"You first." Adele's gaze didn't waver. "Then the one shrouded in darkness, and finally, should there be a need, the one akin to an angel."

Jex's mind was sluggish from the cold, and it took him a moment to understand what the Queen was insinuating. It was the order in which she would crush each of them. It was a promise that she had every intention of keeping.

The magical airwaves were electric. If there was one thing he could feel more than the bitter cold, it was the combination of energies melding and existing in a strained harmony. It was as if the various forces knew that combat was imminent, and they were anxious for it to begin. Jex wasn't as gifted as some at sensing the nature of magic – he was far more adept at sensing the state of the hearts around him. But again, he could read nothing of King Axeal's heart, and found a similar result trying to feel for Adele's. They had clearly steeled themselves.

Despite all that, Jex couldn't deny the sensation of Adele's cold demeanour and magical signature melding with Axeal's courage and devotion. Jex's senses were in overload as he pieced together everything happening around him. It wasn't Adele's efforts alone causing the impromptu winter; she was seamlessly connected with her husband. It was too late to react.

Jex felt the cold intensify as a calm breeze blew past him. The breeze carried the essence of a wintry impending death, picking up in ferocity as it navigated through the maze of massive, frozen spires that towered towards the sky.

The gale pushed his numb body forward, and he couldn't help but stumble and fall roughly to the ground. His bandaged arm tried and failed to break his fall, instead buckling under his own mass as his face hit the ground.

Help me, damn it! Jex screamed internally in attempt to get the voice's attention. *What are you doing that could possibly be more important than this?*

The voice he heard next wasn't the one he'd expected – it

wasn't one he'd heard at all. It was female and laced with a confident apathy.

"It has become obvious that I'm to do everything here."

The voice was gone, and with its disappearance, silence fell between the combatants. Jex didn't know who it was, and nor did the Queen. The King was still out of sight, but that was the least of Jex's concerns as the light surrounding the maze of torrential fountains dimmed slightly. Jex's head snapped towards the sky to find the sun up high and shining with its standard brilliance. It wasn't the sun's influence being diminished, but the area around him being overshadowed. The realisation did nothing to answer any of his questions.

An ominous voice flooded his mind. You're focusing on unimportant details again.

Jex froze. Until that moment he hadn't felt an ounce of fear. He didn't fear death, torture or even isolation. He was determined to succeed in his task, and he became angry with himself whenever he thought of failure. But he wasn't scared of it. Then the voice had spoken. The voice that had deserted him upon his imprisonment, leaving him in his own company for fifteen years.

The implications of the voice returning were pushed aside when Jex caught sight of a brilliant, violet blaze coursing through the maze of spires before soaring towards the Queen. Without a hint of emotion, Adele waved her hand at the energy and the force redirected into one of the towers of water and frost. The impact echoed across the plains, an intimidating roar of two forces at odds meeting for the first time.

Jex exploded with laughter, the same enjoyment a child might feel during his favourite play. He watched on as the

Queen glanced towards the impact of the deterred missile. A silhouette appeared a few feet behind her. The Queen's cold and cautious eyes turned back to her enemy a second too late.

The silhouette behind the Queen was bathed in shadows, smoke rising from her form. At first glance, the woman appeared incorporeal, but after watching her movements as she lashed out at the Queen, Jex knew that the shadowy woman was simply shrouding herself in her own energy. The newcomer leapt into the air, bringing her leg up and around the side of the Queen's head. There was nothing anyone could do, and even Jex stood rooted to the spot in complete surprise at the brutally precise strike.

Adele fell, and she fell hard. The side of her face was burnt black, as if held over an open fire, and the damage was spreading. Jex's body shuddered with a joy that came in waves. The first was mild, and he was uncertain what he was feeling, but by the third wave of mirth, he knew he was in a state of ecstasy. He might have been robbed of the pleasure of taking the Queen down himself, but he could still seize the satisfaction of dealing the killing blow.

"YOU ACCURSED LUNATIC!" Axeal was close.

To your left.

Jex followed the mental order instinctively, expecting to see the enraged King rushing him. Instead he found the dark being standing an arm's length away from him. How had he not sensed her?

"Why did you help?" Jex sneered. He was curious about this new turn of events. He hadn't expected his plan to go so poorly, much less to have any assistance once it did.

"You're a tool – an instrument in the palm of a man who'll

change this world." The woman didn't look away from the Queen writhing in shock and pain.

"Lucian... Does he find me useful after all?" Jex asked eagerly.

"Clean up your mess."

The woman vanished into a cloud of smoke, leaving Jex to focus on the King marching towards him. Any hint of the compassion and kindness the King once exuded had vanished – nay, it had been beaten down. The spark that had insisted on seeing the good in people to offer them a chance at redemption had been slaughtered, leaving only a distraught man's wrath.

The frigid air picked up again, this time with the ferocity of a twister that made Jex stumble and fall to one knee as he struggled to keep his bearings. The wind wasn't as cold as before, as though one of the two forces was being overshadowed. The King's accomplice had been incapacitated.

It was getting harder to breathe. Jex recognised it as the same strategy the King had employed during the confrontation in the board game so many years ago – he planned to suffocate him.

"DO IT!" Jex screamed into the gale drowning out his words. "KILL ME! SEE IF IT BRINGS BACK YOUR BITCH OF A WIFE!"

"ADELE!" Axeal's voice boomed as the force of the wind intensified and knocked Jex clean off his feet. The quickly forming cyclone was powered by sheer emotion.

What is this? Jex wondered in glee. He knew the Queen was as good as dead, and the King was unstable with grief.

Seems to be a source of power that eludes you.

Shut it, voice! Jex snarled internally. *You have no right to offer an opinion after leaving me alone in my prison.*

Would you like a moment to feel sorry for yourself? the voice countered mildly. *Perhaps you'd like an apology? Or maybe you will find it within yourself to stop this self-destructive path derived from nothing more than self-pity.*

Jex swore. He cursed the voice, he cursed the incapacitated royals and knights around him, and he cursed the wind forcing him to lie flat on the saturated soil as it roared inches above his head. But most of all, he cursed himself.

It wasn't long before the words of the voice stopped making sense as they echoed through his mind. Just as they began to fade away, they'd redouble their efforts to be heard over the din around him.

Jex resorted to swearing louder at the voice in an attempt to be heard. His curses turned to threats, his threats to pleas, his pleas back to curses – the cycle repeating endlessly as the man embraced his lunacy.

"NO, NO, NO!" Jex shrieked as his body launched into the air like a doll being thrown across a room. His being projected a sinister aura that coated his entire body. It was the colour of pitch at first, before steadily fading and thinning.

The wind around him diverted before making contact as Jex landed on his feet and shakily rose to his full height. The ominous aura pushed back the King's energy, offering Jex a small radius of literal breathing room. The aura had become comfortable in its new existence and had all but faded from view, leaving Jex gasping and profusely sweating blood. The blood fell from his eyes like crimson tears borne of the greatest joy.

The voice quietened as Jex tore at his bandaged arm. He

had to see it. The sheer rapture of the flesh scorched black from the sword's curse filled him with a euphoria he couldn't comprehend – and he had no interest in trying to. He had shattered the cycle, if only long enough to briefly address what he'd come for. His body was unstable, but given what he'd already endured, the torturous steps towards his prizes were nothing.

My apologies for keeping you waiting, insanity, Jex chortled through cracked lips wet with blood. *I've got something to take care of before I dive into your alluring embrace.*

CHAPTER 69

A SQUIRE'S MARK

Axeal fell to his wife's side. The wind bound to his call didn't touch the pair, and despite the disruption in his magical wavelength he felt just moments before, he felt safe. The sound of Jex's cursing carried on the wind to its master's ears. The King took a grim satisfaction from his enemy's distress.

"Ax-Axeal… My love…"

"Shush – we are going to get through this!" Axeal declared in a tone that made the Queen almost believe his words. He had always been confident in everything working out for the best, despite it often being a result of her pulling strings in the background.

Adele's once fierce beauty had been consumed by the ugly burns left by the dark being's vicious assault. The flesh of her face and neck was steadily being eaten away, like a slow-burning flame upon a thick sheet of parchment. Her smirk didn't fade; it was the same one she regularly wore for the King. The smirk that displayed her admiration and yet demanded his best be tested, that he become better than he was.

He spent many years trying to remove that very expression from her face. He only stopped trying when he realised the reason she wore it was that she believed in him. Regardless of the titles he obtained, or the reverence he accrued from the people around the land, Adele had always been there to push him – to challenge him. He came to love her for that.

There was nothing to say. He'd said everything he'd ever wanted to the dying woman in his arms throughout their time together. The most mundane of tasks had been enriched, and the momentous occasions made even more brilliant throughout the life he'd spent with the woman he'd met in a small village to the south of his kingdom. She had never asked for anything and had only worn the royal attire when requested to after their wedding. She'd never been interested in his wealth or his kingdom; instead, she'd seen his courageous and foolishly idealistic heart and fallen for it. In return, Axeal had spent so long trying to impress the Queen that it felt like he'd loved her since first laying eyes on her.

And she knew it. She was always one step ahead.

"My dear…" Adele murmured, the dark burns spreading across her lips. "I…"

"I know!" Axeal blurted out, tears welling in his eyes. In a softer voice, he repeated, "I know. She will be alright – I promise you that."

No further words were exchanged as the familiar smirk faded from the Queen's scorched lips. There was one final and glorious sign of life: the dying woman's eyes overflowed with colour and the surrounding vortex dropped to a freezing temperature. The wind carried ice and grief as the King lowered his love to the ground, where she lay motionless. The King's silence spoke louder than the howling blizzard circling himself and the dark silhouette standing behind him.

Two sides of a great battle clashed in the distance, one trying to rush towards him while the other blocked their way. He couldn't make out the exact nature of either of the forces at work, and he didn't care for them. As he turned and confronted the deranged man soaked in his own blood, he already knew the outcome of this struggle.

It didn't stop him. The King rushed the lunatic who had wrought the devastation of yet another company of soldiers, along with the Queen herself. Hundreds of the royal family had been amongst the ranks, along with hundreds more soldiers who had dedicated their lives to protecting Aquiocia – all of them reduced to human waste to be carried away on the wind. Axeal's grief was too much, and even the thought of his daughter was barely enough to keep him from breaking then and there.

He reached Jex, and swung his glorious longsword wildly.

He missed. He swung again. He missed again.

Every wild assault met only air as his adversary effortlessly moved out of reach in the last split second. Axeal barely saw the evasive manoeuvres, they were so unnaturally swift, but his will to watch his enemy's movements was broken. He just wanted the man to die. He wanted Jex to fall so that he might drive his blade deep within his own heart and join his love on the ground.

After another awkward swing of his blade, Axeal suddenly found himself choking. His focus was so erratic that he could barely comprehend that Jex had him by the throat. The blood seeping from Jex's pores scorched the King's skin, but he didn't scream – not once. The poisonous blood wouldn't draw a sound out of him. Jex's sudden display of superhuman strength was another phenomenon Axeal had little hope of understanding as he was lifted to the tips of his toes by his enemy's grasp.

"I'd say you've failed, but don't feel too bad – everyone has their shortcomings," Jex hissed between gasps. "It's just unfortunate your greatest downfall was your inability to kill me."

"Wh-what now, Jex?" the King wheezed as his throat threatened to close from the pressure and the stench of burning flesh.

"Now?" Jex's eyes widened with excitement at the King's question. "Why, now the city of Aquiocia will grieve. They will weep, and they will wail. Then, after enough time has passed, the Council will take the throne and Aquiocia will kneel."

The pair of men glared at each other for a moment lasting an eternity, one with a life force crafted of morbid cruelty, the other fading quickly.

"I meant… for you… What's next, lapdog?"

Whether it was the fact he was choking to death or the unpleasant sensation of the searing blood gradually entering his system, the King didn't seem surprised by the betrayal of the crown.

"Oh, there's only one other thing I'm interested in, Your Majesty." Jex winked. "Or should I say, one other person?"

Axeal's misty eyes filled with realisation before his throat was crushed and mangled with a single flash of dark light that burst from Jex's arm. Axeal's life was extinguished, and at that moment, a kingdom lost its King, a Princess lost her parents, and a lunatic walked away from yet another battlefield alone.

CHAPTER 70

LIGHT, DARK AND FROST

The Vassal of Darkness felt the disappearance of the two origin points for the King and Queen's energy signatures. Amongst the exchange of vicious blows between herself and the being of light across the field, she could feel something big coming towards her – something powerful.

She invited it.

Turning on the spot, she saw a tidal wave of wind and frost roaring towards her, spreading out for hundreds of yards in each direction. It wasn't difficult to discern what had happened. This was their last stand, their final attempt at quashing the disturbance. For whatever reason, the fools had marched to the plains to settle things, and this had been their fall-back plan in the case of their death.

The Vassal's eyebrows rose ever so slightly in interest at the level of power the pair of royals had commanded at the time of their death. The billowing wall of frost devoured the warm air of the day and turned it into cold, bitter fuel. It drowned the surface of the land, leaving a thick layer of sleet in its wake.

It was impressive for two people who weren't attuned to one of the stones to command such raw power, but the Vassal knew more than she'd let on. She knew the harmony of the world's elements had been compromised. It wasn't unexpected that there might be more people commanding great power being born every day.

Her opponent had noticed the bluster tearing towards them, and for a fraction of a second, the light dimmed enough for the Vassal of Darkness to make out the form of her enemy. There was nothing about her she recognised, but she couldn't help but wonder why she never instigated the battles between them. In that single realisation, the woman shrouded in smoke felt something familiar stir within her. Perhaps she once knew that feeling, before she came under Lucian's command.

The respite was broken when the being of light called out to her again. She'd been doing it for days whenever the fighting hit a lull, sometimes even during the exchange of attacks.

"You have to stop this!" the woman bellowed, her voice amplified.

"So I'm told, and yet you haven't supplied a single believable reason why I should."

"You aren't like this – I know you aren't!"

"What do you know?"

There was no time for further words; the blizzard was upon them. The dark being readied herself to escape when she noticed that the other woman had erected a shield of brilliant light to face the impending blast. The figure amidst the light had her hand stretched out in front of her, the energy of the barricade branching out from her fingertips. The being of light intended on trying to weather the assault. It was her chance to tip the scales and she took it.

The Vassal of Darkness blazed across the ruined soil and cut through the chilling air, riding on her own smoky reserves. She was only a few yards from her opponent when she readied her strike and was intercepted by a force that sent her reeling towards the bluster of wind and frost. Her head snapped up to see a massive glowing ball bouncing around the woman behind the barricade. It annoyed her that the ball of light seemed so overjoyed with its efforts, but it was the least of her worries as the blizzard hit.

It was everything she could do to rally her defences in time to avoid being snap-frozen. The cold was unbelievable, and the Vassal had travelled to plenty of places whose winters had large and regular death tolls. Her own strength wasn't enough, so without a word, the stone concealed on her form responded, fuelling and co-existing with her own efforts to repel the blizzard's embrace. She hadn't been ready for it and it cost her greatly. It was a wonder how the man she'd assisted had survived within its confines for as long as he had.

She attempted to focus on her enemy, though she knew it was a fruitless endeavour. There was no chance of seeing her amongst the disaster, and she found it painful to reach out for her energy signature. Every time her mind attempted to reach out, she felt the final will of the dead royals quashing her efforts and forcing her back. They had all but locked her down, both physically and mentally.

I have to move…

She felt a sudden warmth coming from above. It was faint at first, but swiftly gaining strength, almost as if it was building up to something. Something above her. It was a pointless act, looking up at the white-blue storm of ice. The cold had lessened somewhat as her stone's energy rallied to protect her with a shroud of thick smoke. Whatever was gathering above her suddenly changed in nature, and the dark Vassal threw herself out of the way of a searing column of light falling from the sky and scorching the ground she stood upon just moments before.

While the sudden beam of light was designed to envelop her, the Vassal felt it wasn't a malicious assault. She felt the same gathering of energy and found herself running blind through the blizzard. She didn't know why she was running; the shining brilliance cut through the frozen hurricane time and time again, and she could tell it wasn't designed to hurt her. But it was from her enemy, and she couldn't trust it.

The woman commanding the light clearly wasn't sure of her opponent's location, but the fact that she was at ease casting beam after beam told the dark Vassal her opponent wasn't hindered by the blizzard as much as she was.

Then the beams of light stopped.

Her breath was slightly ragged from drawing in the blistering air, but she'd long since trained herself in breathing techniques and calmed herself immediately.

Why is my stone's power not enough to nullify the effects of this blizzard? Were those two so strong?

A flash of dark light caught the corner of her eye, and had she not felt the disturbance in her mind, she might have dismissed it. But she knew what had happened and she sprinted towards the commotion. Another flash and she was upon them.

If the shimmering spectre could show surprise, it would have done so then. The dark Vassal had encroached upon the pair trying to pin down the massive dark counterpart to her enemy's orb of light. She got under the spectre's guard and struck quickly. She was almost surprised when she connected with a solid being. Despite having collided time and time again in the past week or so, the woman bathed in transcendent light truly did appear as an angel.

With three quick blows to where the angel's kidneys and abdomen would be, the dark Vassal finished the flurry with a sweep of her leg behind her opponent's, and she fell. The orb of light roared with the ferocity of a great beast and lunged at its master's assailant, only to be pinned by its counterpart. The sound of vicious snarls filled the thinning air, and somewhere in the back of the Vassal's mind, she realised the blizzard was steadily dispersing.

She didn't have long. The being of light would be recovering in short order, and there was only so long her ally could keep its own opponent occupied. She moved fast, reaching out with her own mental waves to the origin of the woman's power. She found it. Concealed inside a pocket hidden within her outfit. She couldn't make out the woman's attire through the blaze of intensifying heavenly light, but it didn't need to be seen. With a motion too quick to be noticed clearly by the untrained eye, the Vassal of Dark snatched the precious commodity and ripped it out through the fabric.

The dark Vassal's foot found the recovering woman's stomach and a cry of surprise sounded within the light. Turning away, she stole a glance at the glorious diamond that was losing its lustre by the second. It was in the wrong hands, and her master had been right. She had just stolen the stone housing the element of Light, and the woman behind her was its Vassal. She wasted no time in summoning a dark portal borne from her own stone, and was surprised when no last desperate grab for the stone took place. The great orb of darkness broke free of the deadlock and bounded through the portal.

"Please, stop…"

In spite of herself, the victorious Vassal turned and locked her bored, crimson eyes on her defeated opponent. She was only a few feet from escape, and she knew that the former Vassal of Light would be unable to follow her, but she also knew she was risking being attacked from two sides, her own ally having escaped. But the pair bathed in light seemed uninterested in attacking.

"Your mistake was holding back," the Vassal of Dark said lightly.

"Regardless of what happens here, I do not consider that a mistake."

The pair stood in silence as the Vassal of Light's aura steadily dimmed. There was still no hope of seeing through it to the conjurer, but she was weakening. The shadowy woman knew that crushing her enemy would be a lot simpler now should she choose to, and yet she had no desire to. She had her prize.

"Sometimes people just choose the wrong side of a battle to join." The dark Vassal turned and entered the portal.

"I couldn't agree more," the defeated Vassal of Light muttered sadly, as the other woman disappeared.

CHAPTER 71

UNFORGIVABLE

Alicea broke. She felt as though her mind was wiped clean before layer after layer of rage was applied directly to it. She couldn't recall reconnecting with the stone, but the blaze in her mind was burning brighter than ever before, and she kept taking more.

Young one, be cautious of how much you take –

Shut up, stone! Alicea lashed out at the stone's consciousness, forcing it to retreat from her mind.

She didn't know how she managed to push down a being as powerful as the one within the stone, or where the sudden brutish outburst came from, but she knew she had to ride the feelings to keep her resolve intact.

Jex was staring at her with the same smug grin, though his eyes were curious and uneasy. He was obviously trying to stifle whatever was causing him discomfort, but the Princess' sharp eye missed nothing in the flashes of lighting illuminating the sky at regular intervals. As the storm grew in intensity, she saw the small flecks of discontent in her enemy's eyes.

Good, fear me! Alicea thought viciously.

The rain altered its course, each drop erratically changing its direction as it descended towards the earth.

Alicea's mind felt as if it was being ripped in thousands

of different directions as it lunged out at every particle of water it could find. Her energy was draining, but instead of stopping, she drew more and more from the stone's seemingly endless pool.

Jex had noticed the change in the rain's pattern. He had also noticed the pale azure aura bathing the Princess. Jex looked up at the sky and saw that no liquid was falling on his body anymore – it was all gravitating around Alicea. A look of alarm crossed his face when he finally realised he had made the biggest mistake possible when going after the Princess. He had practically bestowed the greatest weapon he could upon his enemy.

He had given her the rain.

Did she plan this? No, surely not.

Jex wasted no time in raising his weapon and lunging at the Princess. He discovered it was a poor time to initiate another assault when Alicea's body erupted with ethereal light. The blast launched Jex back the way he came before taking its place covering every inch of the courtyard. The otherworldly light illuminated the area around them as effectively as the midday sun, despite it being the middle of the night. The bushes in the gardens revealed Aquiocian Roses, crimson from the bloodshed surrounding them, contrasting with the radiance that emitted from the Princess.

Alicea stared at the ground from her place within her personal aura. Her drenched hair had fallen over her face, but the moisture was leaving it at a rapid rate. The Princess held such perfect control over her element that it dared not step out of line. As a result, her hair was dry within moments as the excess moisture formed with the rest of its kin at her feet.

Jex climbed to his feet and watched on, waiting to see what would happen next. He was as excited as he was anxious; he knew the Princess wasn't the same as she was before. He knew that, at that exact moment, she was a very real threat.

An odd sound echoed around the gardens, amplified and distorted. At first, it was unclear where the sound was coming from.

Then Jex realised it was coming from the Princess. She was crying.

The sound of her sadness ricocheted off the great stone walls surrounding the garden, amplified by the magic coursing through and around her body. Jex braced himself, unsure of how to proceed. She had seemed so angry before – was she breaking down? Alicea's head snapped upwards before Jex could analyse the situation any further. He could see her tear-stricken face within the aura as she pointed an accusing finger towards him.

"I – I'm going to kill you!" Alicea screamed.

"Yes…" Jex smiled and nodded slowly; he had broken her. "That's what I want to hear! Come, Princess! Struggle for me!"

Alicea shook her head violently, trying and failing to clear her mind. Instead, she reached out to the water around her and issued a mental command. The strain was apparent, but she drank deeply from the stone's energy as the water came together, forming a replica of her swan standing at twice her own height. Jex ran at the Princess, his cursed arm lobbing blast after blast of dark energy. Alicea responded by raising her arms; large volumes of water flowed from the sky towards her. At the last second, the massive bubbles of liquid altered their course towards the oncoming energy. The two forces collided in mid-air and exploded, cancelling each of their masters' magic.

Jex reached Alicea and swung his mighty scythe directly at her as she grasped at the moisture beginning to flood the garden. Her body was propelled into the sky, the water on the ground forcing her upwards. The savage blade of Jex's weapon met only the trail of water behind the elusive Princess. Alicea's body soared through the air as the water pushing her skyward slowly turned darker, blood running through it from the deadly weapon.

Alicea was in a state of pure serenity as her petite body gracefully glided through the air. She severed the connection to the infected water and it erupted with a sound like that of a boulder landing in a small pond.

Jex's blackened arm was a blur as he hurled blasts of dark energy at his adversary, only to be intercepted by countless swans forming from the rain.

As Alicea started to descend, she spread her legs as if she were to hit the ground flat-footed. Instead, her feet found the back of her giant swan, which had taken off to catch its master. The swan's wings went into overdrive to carry itself and the extra weight skyward.

The Princess looked back down at the garden she was soaring above. She located Jex and issued an order to every drop of liquid her mind could reach. In response, thousands of replicas of her flying companion formed and dive-bombed the enemy below.

Young one! You need to slow down, you are taking on too much!
I said shut up! I'll kill this traitorous mongrel!
If you take on – The stone was cut off; Alicea silenced it and

blocked it from her mind as she looked towards the ground.

Jex was still fighting, his scythe a deadly blur as he cut down the flock of vengeful birds descending upon him. Amongst the frenzy was something coming back towards Alicea. The light from the aura allowed her to see a large number of her swans returning to her. But something was different; they were now darker in colour.

How did he corrupt them? Alicea wondered, as she released the magic binding the birds.

The sky exploded with lightning and the rain kicked up again as both water and blood fell from above. Alicea's body stiffened when Jex's voice rang upwards to meet her.

"IT IS TIME, YOUR HIGHNESS! THIS IS IT! THIS IS WHERE IT ENDS!"

CHAPTER 72

FAITH IN FRIENDSHIP

Lyrium crouched at the forest's edge. Her drenched face snapped upwards to see a light-filled sky through the breaks in tree branches. The hunters shifted anxiously, awaiting a command. There wasn't one to give; they had been routed. Striking again would cause more death on both sides, and so they waited in the heavy rain. In the darkened skies, something broke. Something changed.

Lyrium felt it.

A desperate cry for vengeance. It wasn't a plea, or the result of a woman begging for what she considered to be just. It was the awakened bloodlust of a pacifist. It was the war cry of a torn woman who had endured far too much to stand idly by and watch the heinous acts of villains continue any further.

A rough but sure hand planted itself on her shoulder. With a panicked glance, Lyrium found comfort in her lover's smile. She couldn't work out if it was her mundane or magical senses that informed her what was happening as she fixed her gaze solely upon the castle of Aquiocia in the distance.

On the eastern side of the castle, rising from behind the walls, was an otherworldly, azure radiance that threatened to pierce the sky. Despite the brilliance of the unreal luminescence spreading its influence across the castle, it wasn't what had caught the bulk of Lyrium's attention. The angry clouds that had been gathering all afternoon had amalgamated and combined their efforts, filling the air with torrential rain and sky-splitting streaks of lightning. The rain was no longer falling on the forest and plains in front of the kingdom. She could already feel her body beginning to dry, and was relieved when she wiped her face and found it wasn't immediately drenched again.

Her eyes occasionally caught sight of the rain's trajectory, and she knew that it wasn't simply a matter of the rain falling in an odd pattern. The water was being dragged down from its place in the sky – it was being summoned. The atmosphere of the night and the battlefield had radically shifted to accommodate the intense magical presence of a Vassal truly realising her cause.

"Arok," Lyrium said with a shuddering breath.

"Aye?" he responded, leaning casually against his war hammer and staring straight ahead.

"Do you have any idea what is happening here?" she asked, with little hope of her lover comprehending.

"Aye, of course," Arok said, an oversimplified answer that made Lyrium grin despite the battlefield before her. "Someone just went and pissed off the Princess. I wouldn't worry too much. I'd wager they'll only do it once."

CHAPTER 73

THE ROSE AND THE REAPER

Alicea released every magical connection she was holding onto, save for the one holding the giant swan she flew upon. The sound of water exploding echoed between the booms of thunder from the strengthening storm overhead.

From her elevated point of view, she had lost sight of her enemy. Her head kept snapping from each side of her magical mount as unease brewed in her heart and mind.

What did he mean by it ending here?

Above you! the stone's voice cried out.

Alicea barely had time to direct her mount out of the way of the shadow descending upon her. The massive swan dove downwards to her left, the shadow missing her by mere inches. A glint of lightning flashing off the surface of dark metal was the only thing she was able to catch sight of.

It returns, young one!

Alicea chose to weave to the right this time, but the sluggish response cost her. The swan threw its head back in an inaudible scream of pain as its right wing was brutally slashed and removed from the rest of its body.

Alicea recovered quickly, calling on the rain to restore the swan's lost wing as she rapidly lost altitude. The bird's wound was quickly healed and Alicea homed in on the assailant's energy. It was a beacon in the night, easily discovered in the dark sky.

She kept summoning the water from the sky to her liquid mount and it continued to grow. She also called the rain to her right hand, forming her familiar staff and arming herself as best she could. The airborne Princess chose not to summon the water to her pores as she had done earlier. She knew that should the vicious weapon connect with the water, it would contaminate her body instantly.

How is he even able to reach me at this altitude?

By the time the shadow chose to strike again, the bird beneath her was massive. Its wingspan was over a hundred paces long and growing still. As Alicea stood upon its huge back, the shadow chose not to slash at her mount as it had before. This time, it landed on the opposite end of the swan to her.

Despite watching the silhouette descend and land upon her creation, the Princess had difficulty believing that this was actually the enemy she had been fighting all this time. It was Jex, but not as he was before. Between flashes of lightning, Alicea could make out that every vein in his body was violently pulsing through his skin.

Jex was bleeding heavily from the wound on the side of his head, and the skin on the right side of his face was singed from the infected blood. But that wasn't what disturbed her the most about her enemy's new appearance.

Jex's backbone had grown out of his body and fanned out in a web-like spread, forming wings of the darkest crimson. Blood fell steadily from the wings onto the bird's back as it tried to repel it, water washing the blood away as the rain repaired the cavities it left in the swan's back.

If the rain keeps up I can stay airborne, Alicea thought confidently.

You must end this right now, young one. You don't feel it now, but fighting like this is starting to damage your body. At this point you will recover with rest, but much more –

I'm aware. Just keep this bird in the air and flying level. I will take care of him myself, Alicea ordered with conviction. She wouldn't allow her confidence to waver at the sight of Jex's transformation.

Understood. Now kill him, young one!

I will, Alicea replied with finality. She was ready.

Jex raised his weapon, though the action seemed somewhat laboured. He grunted from the effort and yelled across the ever-growing arena.

"This is so exhilarating! Wouldn't you agree, Your Highness?" His voice was a mix of excitement and desperation. "Very few get to fight in this kind of situation – no one can say you didn't struggle before you died!"

Jex's spare hand shot forward, pointing directly at the Princess as something assaulted her body. It came from within, a burning sensation in her veins. The temperature rose within her and she heard a small chuckle in her mind. The searing sensation eased, replaced by a cool rush flowing through her veins.

Jex's manic expression betrayed a moment of confusion as his own body caught a chill. It wasn't as potent as the last time he felt it, but it was the same bitterness he had felt from the blizzard just over a year ago. It was the kind of cold that had little interest in skin or flesh, but instead riddled one's bones.

He knew there was little hope of bending the Princess to his will. For whatever reason, the curse wouldn't take hold.

He had questions. He expected a reaction from the Princess, yet she said nothing.

She telepathically ordered the bird to turn. It responded, arching sharply to the right and causing Jex to lose his balance for a moment. It was all the Princess needed as she sprinted across her mount's back and swung her staff at her enemy.

Jex took the strike without flinching and returned with his own wild swing that Alicea parried with ease, following through to thrust the end of her staff into his chest. He took a step backwards from the force, and for the first time since the beginning of the battle, he gripped his weapon with both hands.

But it was too late.

Alicea had spun her staff around her body with the grace of the being she fought upon and struck the man again. As the blow connected, she manipulated the water that was her weapon into a sharp point that pierced Jex's flesh. He brought his weapon around and Alicea abandoned her own as she rolled across the surface of the swan, leaving the spear lodged in Jex's body.

As she expected, her weapon was already darkening, and she was already forming another from the rain. She saw how little Rufus' blades had done to him; one spear was not going to be enough.

I will have to inflict a blow that'll end his life instantly, or overload his body with so much pain that it shuts down. It is the only way to stop him from healing.

Jex swung downwards, but it was a wild swing and easily

evaded by the Princess. He suffered another piercing assault, this time in his side, and fell to one knee in pain as his blood boiled, attempting to repair the damage from the wounds.

Alicea ran at her wounded adversary and threw her small frame into him. The impact caused him to stumble backwards. As he attempted to regain his balance, the bird made a sudden turn, throwing him off its back, his expression one of outright surprise.

Jex's wings of contaminated blood had barely started correcting his fall when a violent blast of water collided with him from above, forcing his body downwards like a comet falling upon the land. The ground rushed upwards up to meet him. The details of the kingdom's walls and towers quickly became more distinguished until his wings finally started working in his favour.

Alicea was upon him, smashing her mount into his falling body. The massive swan's bosom smothered Jex's flailing body as it corrected its form. In his struggle within its breast, the contamination from his blood began to spread rapidly throughout the swan's body. Alicea gave the order to land, and the darkening bird alighted roughly in the main courtyard of the kingdom. The ends of its wings collided with the castle walls and exploded into massive showers of black liquid.

Alicea could barely keep control of the swan as she rolled off its body and landed face-down on the soft grass. She felt the wind leave her lungs from the impact and crawled to all fours to see Jex within the prison of her plagued familiar.

People had begun to return to the castle, but now they were running in all directions. Alicea barely noticed them as her once beautiful companion started to disintegrate.

Jex felt the shift of power in the water. Just before his lungs exploded, he found he could breathe again and fell to the cold stone pavement. He drew in large gulps of air and laughed between gasps. He was wheezing at the Princess' failure to suffocate him, but the mirth was short-lived as he looked up towards his opponent.

His mind only had a few seconds to acknowledge the hundreds of liquid spears soaring towards him before his entire body erupted in pain. He writhed in agony as he was pushed to the ground by the countless piercing impacts. The tainted magic within him was completely overwhelmed, his body crushed beneath the storm of spears. He finally experienced what those who had lost their lives to him had felt. For but a moment, he felt the fear of dying that anyone would experience, before allowing himself to bask in his newfound, grim respect for the Princess.

She had done what was needed. As a child and now as a Queen.

As his sight began to flicker to blackness, Jex remembered the words of the Warmaster he had so callously assassinated before setting out for Tremel.

Long live… the Rose of Aquiocia, Jex thought, as a death long overdue laid its claim.

CHAPTER 74

A HERETIC'S REALISATION

Garnet heard the crash of something massive colliding with the outside walls, though she had no idea what it could have been. Her paws slid to a halt in the audience hall; a quick transformation and swift flick of her wrist over her head had her striding across the hall in human form, completely clothed.

She stopped when a heap on the ground caught her attention. She noticed the man was still breathing and gently nudged him with her foot. "Get up, Rufus."

Receiving no response, she placed her hand softly on his face and closed her eyes, allowing her energy to trickle into his skin. A sudden shock pulsed through her and she was forced to retract her hand. Something within him rejected her Earth Magic.

Seems you DO have a secret or two yourself, Rufus.

Garnet had little time to ponder the implications before her attention returned to the now spluttering man trying to get to his feet.

"What was – my skull feels like it has Arok's hammer constantly hitting it!" Rufus exclaimed, following up with a string of curses.

"Are you going to stand around swearing, or would you like to find the Princess with me?" Garnet quipped.

"The Princess?" Rufus muttered to himself as he struggled to bring her to his mind. "Alicea…?"

"That is her name, yes," Garnet replied warily, glancing over the thief. "Rufus, are you feeling alright?"

"I don't know. My head is spinning…" the thief admitted.

"Can you walk?"

"Aye, I think so," Rufus muttered, shaking his head violently. "It's coming good now. Which way?"

Garnet answered by breaking into a swift pace towards the great doors at the end of the hall, leading to the courtyard outside. Together they reached for the doors and pulled them back.

Why can't I remember what happened? Rufus thought in alarm. *I… attacked him and… Did he hit me with something?*

With the great doors open, the pair ran into the courtyard and scanned the drenched gardens and pathways.

Garnet noticed the stones in the pathways were burnt away and stained black in a lot of places. The mysterious burns would have to wait to be investigated until she found the Princess.

I missed! Rufus suddenly remembered, his mind struggling to grasp at the recollection. The side of his face pulsed with dull pain. *He put me on the ground so damned easily…*

With another shake of his head, Rufus decided to put his thoughts aside for now and immediately saw a large group of knights gathering in the corner of the courtyard. To make matters even worse, more knights by the dozens were filing through the front gates.

"We can't win this!" Rufus spluttered as he reached for his daggers, only to remember they had been destroyed. "We definitely can't win this!"

"Well, we can't leave. See that group?" Garnet pointed towards the original mass of knights, beginning to stride towards them. "They have the Princess."

"How do you know that?" Rufus asked in surprise. "I can't hear her."

"Take it from a schooled mage. I'm familiar with her energy patterns from her training. She is there."

"And the cursed knights surrounding her?" Rufus insisted.

"They are no longer cursed, are they?"

By this point, the pair had reached the group and the knights had turned their attention to the newcomers. They looked at Garnet in surprise before turning to Rufus. Then the whispers started.

"Isn't that the thief?"

"What thief?"

"It is him! I would know that face anywhere!"

"What are you talking about?"

"He's the one who kidnapped the Princess!"

"Well, not again!"

"Oh, would you lot belt up already?" Rufus roared over the whispers. To his surprise, the knights simmered down.

"I will not deny this man's crime, nor will he," Garnet began, and the crowd started to shift anxiously. "But are you all so short-sighted and blinded by the Council's lies that you cannot see this man's actions saved your Princess – no, *our* Princess – from the same torment that you have all endured? This man set in motion the events that led to your Princess returning, breaking the curse, and saving her people. Are you so quick to condemn him?"

Garnet's not-quite-truthful speech had worked. The knights nodded in uneasy unison as they shuffled to make a path between them for the pair. It was obvious the knights were confused and searching for some hope that everything would be as it was before.

At the centre of the group was an unconscious woman, drenched to the bone, with noticeable bruises developing on her face. Her long, dark hair was sprawled over the pavement, fanning outwards in all directions. Her skin was paler than usual from over-expending her magical energy and under her eyes were black and blue bags of utter exhaustion. The Princess looked as if she had aged a decade from her ordeal.

"Has she been examined?" Garnet asked calmly.

Rufus was not so reserved, sprinting through the guards.

"Hey! Not so fast –"

"Leave him!"

The entire courtyard fell quiet. Hundreds of men and women clad in armour stood in the rain, waiting in silence as if they anticipated some grand display.

"Damn it! No, no, NO!" Rufus snarled under his breath.

"Rufus, she –"

"BELT UP, DAMN IT!" Rufus screamed as his hand ran over his friend's face.

The light drizzle was starting to fall heavier again, but not one of the people present cared. No amount of rain or cold could deter the gaze of those there to witness the failure of a man to his friend.

It all came back to him. Alicea's appearance returned to his memory with a force that he didn't think possible. Her eyes were closed, but he knew that when they were open, anyone gazing upon their cerulean splendour would be captivated. He brushed the hair from her face, feeling the weight of silence. The silence of everyone watching in anticipation. The silence of the Princess. What he wouldn't give for her to awaken and scold him for leaving her in the rain, or for not having a change of clothes for her, or even just for staring at her – anything.

What he received was silence.

"I'm so damned sorry, Alicea," Rufus blurted out, his voice catching. "I wasn't fast enough, or strong enough, and you paid for it."

"She will awaken," Garnet offered softly.

"Get Lyrium!" Rufus ordered. "Tell her to do the thing with the two stones again!"

"That will not work this time," Garnet said quietly as the sky lit up with lightning and the rain came in force. "We should move inside –"

"Why wouldn't it work?" Rufus yelled. He didn't want reason; he wanted results. He wanted her awake.

"Last time Alicea expended magic like this, it was a simple display of taking on a task too far beyond her capabilities. This is different; this struggle was for her people, against a man who has tormented her since childhood. As soon as strong emotion is the fuel of magic, there are not only wonderful perks, but also potentially horrendous side effects."

"Meaning what?" Rufus asked, turning back to Alicea.

"Meaning that the trauma may in fact prove to be too much for her body and mind to endure," Garnet explained. "You can't feel it right now, but her entire being is in absolute chaos. Her magic is entwined with the rest of her functions. Her body and mind are currently trying to quell the wave of her magical energy from consuming her entirely. But she must do it alone, without the aid of the stones. She needs rest, Rufus. Rest, and time."

"This can't be happening." Rufus felt the burning of his eyes as tears threatened to rush forward.

"She did it for all of us, Rufus," Garnet said kindly before adding in a more forceful tone, "Now, may I please move the Princess inside so we don't add illness to her list of ailments?"

"Just do it," Rufus snapped, wiping his eyes.

Garnet quickly delegated two knights to pick up the Princess and carry her towards the palace. She gave the rest the order to be on standby and return to barracks, and to spread the word that the battle was over.

The knights did not hesitate in following the orders of the strange older lady from Tremel. Some of them arranged to watch each of the entrances for any suspicious activity, despite not being on duty.

With an almighty roar of "For the Princess!", the knights scattered, and Rufus was alone.

As he climbed to his feet, he noticed something of morbid interest.

It was Jex's corpse.

Rufus walked over slowly, wary of Jex even in death. Standing over him, Rufus took in the grotesque figure. He could barely recognise the man with every vein on his body ruptured and dried black blood covering more of his body than it didn't.

Jex's entire body seemed to have been repeatedly punctured by sharp projectiles. His limbs were all bent at jarring angles and his face was twisted into a mangled smile. Alicea had destroyed him, and yet he looked as if he was happy to meet his end.

"You cannot blame the Princess for being terrified of him."

Rufus heard Setz before he saw him appear out of thin air beside him. A second body sprawled forth onto the ground beside Jex's.

The man wriggling to get free appeared to be bound by chains crafted from shadows. Every time he got close to gaining freedom from the restraints, the chains tightened mercilessly and twisted his already crushed wrists.

"There appears to be plenty of other people with terrifying traits for her, should she wake up," Rufus quipped.

"Yes, her current state is unfortunate. However, there are –"

"I swear on what little in this world that can still be called holy, if you say there are 'other things to be done' I will pick up Jex's weapon and run you through with it!"

The pair stood in silence for a long moment as they stared at Setz's prisoner, who seemed to have momentarily resigned himself to his fate.

"You are clearly too upset to be of any use in fixing anything at this point," Setz conceded to the now silent Rufus. "I will not ask you to do anything for the next few days. But after that I will be calling on you, and you will come."

"Whatever. I don't care," Rufus muttered.

"Wallow in your grief all you like, but do not lie to me," Setz said.

Rufus opened his mouth to reply, but instead changed the topic.

"Who is this man?"

"This man's name is Arissam," Setz revealed. "He is the

one who incited treachery within the Council and effectively bought the people's trust before betraying it to Lucian himself."

"Is he the cause of the curse?"

"No. Our theory is that the curse was made possible by Jex himself, though Lucian may have been part of his motivation."

"So, Lucian is nearby?"

"No, I believe Jex was the carrier of the curse. Since the Princess has removed him, the curse is no more."

At Setz's mention of Alicea, Rufus looked away again and sighed sadly. Setz clicked his fingers and two more figures appeared.

"Sir!" The figures bowed.

"Take this man to the prisons and post both Aquiocian guards and our own men to watch him. If he somehow escapes, your heads will be taken as compensation."

"As I would expect, Sir!" One of the men nodded towards Jex's lifeless body. "And him, Sir?"

"The same treatment, but prepare the disintegration procedure. We cannot risk this man having any more cards to play." The men nodded, disappearing with their new cargo.

Setz turned to Rufus again.

"I expect you to take the next few days to be checked over by the healers and reflect on your failures here today."

"I think it's your reassurance and support that gets me through!" Rufus snarled.

"I wasn't finished, Rufus," Setz said coldly. "It wasn't a lack of strength in character that ultimately held you back today. You defied my orders and rushed after the Princess."

"I do not regret that," Rufus muttered.

"I should hope not. You ran after the Princess because you gave a damn about her wellbeing. I'm relieved to see you have found something worth getting off your arse for."

"It's nothing. I did what anyone would do."

"What did I say about lying?" Setz asked. "Play it down all you like, but the fact is that both of you have come a long way. Gather your thoughts and feelings, heretic. I will call upon you in due time."

Rufus had no time to reply before Setz disappeared into wisps of dark smoke and the thief was left alone again. He heard the title, yet he left it. He couldn't take anything more at that moment. Allowing himself a grimace, he looked up to the sky and felt the refreshing chill of the cold rain washing over his face.

I can't believe the Princess took down someone like Jex, he thought before his reverie took a despairing turn. *I couldn't even scratch him. What use for a guardian like me does she have now?*

CHAPTER 75

INHERITANCE

Alicea woke with a shudder. Her body instinctively sat up and she barely suppressed a scream. She was sweating profusely under something holding her down.

What... A blanket?

Throwing the covers aside, she realised where she was. She recognised the gorgeous walls lined with artwork. In between each piece was pale blue stone, freshly scrubbed for a reason she didn't know.

There were no portraits of the royal family like those lining the palace corridors. Instead, there were depictions of landscapes from all over the world. Painted by a master artist, there were dozens of masterpieces showing different parts of the world. Alicea spotted her personal favourite – a glorious rendition of the sparkling ocean, captured from atop the Blue Crystal Mountains. It had been a favourite of her mother's as well.

"She climbed the mountains alone to paint that one," said a voice with an air of wistfulness. "It is heart-warming to see her daughter climbing her own."

The Princess didn't respond, not even to look at Garnet sitting in the back of the room. Words felt... inadequate. What could she say that wouldn't lead back to a conversation about what had happened?

"You will tell me if and when you would like to speak about it," Garnet said kindly, reading her mind. "People are entitled to their feelings, Alicea. Do what you must to avoid being crippled by them."

Half an hour passed before Alicea finally turned her grey eyes towards the older woman reading in the corner. The dying light of whatever day it was barely illuminated the room at all. Soon, they would find themselves sitting in darkness.

"I... I wish to work..." Alicea mumbled as Garnet lowered her book with an analytical gaze. After a moment, the older woman nodded slightly, and a shadow appeared in the doorway. Setz entered the chambers.

"I have something to show you, Your Highness," the Guildmaster said in a businesslike tone that Alicea appreciated.

"If it gets me out of this room, then —"

"It doesn't," Setz said bluntly, adding with a gesture towards the King and Queen's personal library, "At least, not quite."

"I have to get out..." Alicea mumbled to herself.

Setz stopped as if pondering something, before muttering an incantation. The room filled with a soft light emitting from his hand. A small, glowing orb slowly rose from his grasp and hung in the air. It was an obvious bid to make the Princess feel a little more at ease.

It worked, somewhat.

"Do not fear the darkness itself, Your Highness, as it is not inherently evil. I assure you, the light can be just as harrowing," Setz said with a wave towards the archway.

Alicea's movements were stiff, but her body thanked her for the motion with satisfying aches and pains as she stretched out. It was nice, feeling something. Garnet snapped her book shut and gave Setz a measured look. Something silent passed between them, and Garnet left.

Alicea noticed, but couldn't bring herself to care at that point. She barely cared about whatever it was Setz was going to show her. It was only sheer will, and a sudden irrational fear of being alone in the dark, that made her cross the chamber towards the library.

Do what you must to avoid being crippled by them...

Setz walked towards the doorway leading to the library as Alicea's mind presented countless memories for her to relive. The memories were immaculately recreated in appearance, but something was missing.

The emotion behind them.

How many times had she disappeared from her parents' sight as a child, only to be found in here with every book she could reach on the floor? Tomes would be scattered everywhere, and she would be in the centre of them, reading one after another.

On multiple occasions, her mother had found her buried amongst the literature. The Queen never got angry and would clear a spot to sit and read with her daughter. They were happy memories, amongst her favourite. But at that moment they seemed... bland. As if they belonged to someone else and she was looking in on a mother and child with no attachment to either.

Alicea came back to reality and saw Setz looking up at the books before fetching the ladder from the far end of the room. Her emotionless gaze swept over the perfectly arranged spines as she wandered the single extensive corridor. As she read each title, her mind filled with passages from the pages within. She attempted to grasp onto certain lines, the ones that had made her feel something when she had first read them – nothing.

Setz returned with the ladder. He climbed to the top and his fingers brushed gently against a single book. Alicea wandered back to the Guildmaster and caught a glimpse of the tome that held his interest.

Animals of Gaia? Alicea thought, blinking in disbelief. The title had changed. *Guildmaster…*

With a yank, Setz pulled the book free and quickly climbed back down the ladder to re-join the Princess. Tossing the book behind him onto a different shelf, the bookcase he had first scaled began to rattle and shake. Before their eyes, the entire bookshelf slowly descended into the floor beneath them.

Standing behind where the bookcase was a moment ago was a glowing pedestal of pale blue and green light. Upon the short structure was an item that made the Princess momentarily snap out of her trance.

Hovering an inch above the pedestal was a large tome that stood almost as tall as the retainer below it. Its cover was an oversized image of the Aquiocian Rose, adorned with countless small diamonds and sapphires. It was a display that must have taken the uninterrupted attention of several master jewellers.

As the great tome slowly rotated in the air, Alicea's eyes widened at the sheer number of pages between the covers. There was no less than two hand spans' worth of fine parchment filled with whatever text the magnificent book might contain.

After a moment, the rear of the tome was revealed along with the image of the six rings that the Princess once wore on her hand at all times. The image was much simpler than the first, but it also proved that without a doubt, the tome was for her.

Alicea's eyes finally fell on the oversized silver clasp that held the book closed. The buckle branched out over the book's surface into strong straps that she supposed would allow someone to attach it to something.

Oh, so you can carry it strapped to your back... Alicea realised. *Well, I can't carry that around; it will weigh far too much.*

"Connect with your stone," Setz commanded. Alicea hesitated.

Before connecting with the stone directly, she reached out towards the being within it. She could feel the stone's resident, but it felt distant. Alicea felt as if she was trying to catch the attention of someone in the distance and they weren't interested in responding. While she was curious about the tome, she couldn't bring herself to be worried about the ignorance of the being at that moment. She connected with the stone and latched onto the small amount of intrigue she was feeling.

She felt the stone go cold in the hidden pocket within her shirt, the connection sparking and blazing in her mind. As the connection grew stronger, she noticed she could feel another presence nearby that wasn't Setz's or her own. She realised that in her mind's eye, the book in front of her was giving off a strange aura. She reached out with her mind towards the new source of energy and felt it welcome her.

The book snapped open so suddenly she feared it would fall

from its place in the air. The connection between her and the stone severed, and a page fell from the tome to the ground. Setz had picked it up before Alicea even had a chance to absorb what had happened. The Guildmaster handed her the page and Alicea recognised her mother's handwriting in its beautiful calligraphic style.

"My mother wrote this." It was a statement more than a question.

"She did, although only you can read it – your mother was a gifted mage. Perhaps more so than even myself," Setz said. "She said that she had enchanted both that message and this book so that only the Vassal of Water would be able to read them. The tome itself cannot even be opened unless you are of Adele's bloodline. I was told to pass this on should your parents pass in the Battle of a Thousand Blades."

"What?" Alicea spluttered. "How could she possibly know that I was the Vassal?"

"I, too, received something after they had passed. They gave me a letter before they left for the battle that I was only to read should the Council of Aquiocia prove corrupt and the grief threaten to smother you. It said to show you this. They also requested, once you had recovered from your grief, to let you know that they knew you were the chosen Vassal of Water at birth."

"How?"

"After your birth there was a great ceremony to celebrate. When your parents retired to their chambers with you, your mother commented to your father that your eyes swapped between the shades of blue that the large sapphire in their treasury shone with," Setz stated, relaying a message he had clearly read multiple times. "Your father went personally to retrieve the stone from the treasury and brought it back to your mother and you."

"Then what?" Alicea pressed.

"The stone reacted, sealing your fate as a Vassal." Setz smiled. "The voice from the stone spoke, telling your parents what your destiny will entail in time. However, at the time you were far too young, so the stone was hidden away in a separate treasury. The one I had Rufus raid when the time was right, before having him ensure that it got to you."

Setz chuckled to himself before continuing.

"Your mother was crafty. Even I didn't realise for a long time that I was acting as she predicted. She was truly a great Queen indeed."

Alicea allowed a small smile at Setz's admiration for her mother and looked down at the letter that only she could read. Setz made to leave the room so that Alicea might read it privately when she stopped him.

"You have been nothing but loyal to my parents in both life and death. If you would like to hear the contents of this letter, I would be happy to share."

"I…" Setz seemed taken aback. "I would be honoured, Your Highness."

Alicea unravelled the letter after tearing her gaze from the massive, rotating tome. After taking a deep breath, she began to read aloud.

> *To my dear Alicea,*
> *By now we are no longer amongst the living.*
> *It breaks both your father's and my own heart to think of*

leaving you alone in this world. But we must protect this kingdom in any way we can.

I leave it in Setz's hands to see that you get this letter and tome after our passing. I know that just like every other time we have relied upon him, he will not let us down.

This may seem unfair, but your fate has been pre-determined since your birth. I know deep in my heart that you are both capable and willing to see your duty through.

Please do not look at our passing as a cruel twist of fate, but instead as the next step in what I'm sure is going to be an incredible life for you.

We have been in contact with Setz constantly and we know what it is he is doing. Know that it is with our blessing.

This tome is filled with everything I know about Water Magic, along with various pieces of lore that I've gathered over the past years – the knowledge from the talented mages I've met, along with a lot of what I've taught myself.

The tome itself also holds many enchantments. These are ones I've bestowed upon it myself. Amongst them are charms to make it almost indestructible, along with one that makes it near impossible for anyone besides its owner to lift it.

Learn from me, my daughter. Surpass me as a mage in the same way that I know you will as a Queen.

I know of the young thief. Do not judge his appearance rashly. He will be just as important as you in the coming struggles. We know that there will be conflict between the two of you, but please promise me you will not throw this book at him.

Trust in the thief, trust in Setz, and above all, trust in yourself.
Always remember, Alicea,
That we love you.

Alicea tried to choke back the tears but failed as they fell down her exhausted face. Even Setz seemed somewhat moved by the letter's contents as he stood there with his hand on the sobbing Princess' shoulder. She tried to rally herself to a rational level of composure, but instead turned and buried her face into the Guildmaster's cloak. Setz tentatively wrapped one arm around her.

"It's not fair!" came a muffled exclamation from Setz's torso.

"No, it most certainly isn't," Setz acknowledged. "But you must get it together, Princess. You have a tremendous number of things that require your attention, and you are overlooking one very important thing."

"What?" Alicea asked, pulling away and looking at the mysterious tome once again.

"Your parents have left their legacy to you, and only you. Your mother has left her secrets in this tome that only you may view. Your parents had, and still have, unwavering faith in you," Setz said.

"But what if I fail to live up to their expectations?" Alicea asked. "Their sacrifice will be for nothing."

"Their sacrifice will never be for nothing," Setz said kindly. "Because you will never let them down. Look at all you have done already."

"What I've done was only possible because of everyone's help!" Alicea protested, pushing away from him.

"Then you are already living the life that your parents envisioned for you, one where you change things for the better. One where you are surrounded by friends. You are honouring their memory in the best way possible." Setz smiled. Alicea didn't reply.

"Tell me something, Alicea."

"What is it?"

"Are you happy?"

Alicea paused for a moment to reflect on her life. It felt like a mess. In a few short months, she had gone from being an immobilised Princess confined to her castle by her own grief, to Aquiocia's saviour. She didn't feel heroic, and the idea of looking her people in the eye felt like a horrifying idea. People died and she... She had killed.

If I hadn't... She stopped the dive into self-deprecation when she thought of those close to her. None of them would have let her finish that thought; she wasn't going to allow herself.

After her silent reprieve, she looked up at Setz again.

"I am... getting there."

"That is all your parents ever wanted. There is nothing wrong with grieving or missing someone, but do not allow it to consume your entire life," Setz advised.

"You're right," Alicea said, wiping her face and examining the enormous book. "First, I must figure out how to carry this. I do not wish for it to be out of my sight."

"Then pick it up and we will be on our way."

"Yes, my mother wrote that only I may pick it up," she replied, approaching the strange artefact slowly as if ready to be attacked.

Hesitantly, Alicea reached out with both hands and

attempted to wrap her arms around the giant book. Preparing herself to take on an immense burden, she threw her body backwards with all the strength she could muster.

The result was not what she expected. Setz watched the Princess effortlessly hurl both herself and her inheritance across the floor.

The tome fell on top of Alicea as she looked up from the stone floor in surprise and embarrassment.

"It doesn't weigh anything!" she exclaimed.

"To you it doesn't," Setz smirked.

"You knew this would happen!" Alicea accused.

"Would you have warned me, had the roles been reversed?"

Alicea shoved the giant tome that now encompassed most of her body away and sat up.

"No, I suppose not," she smiled.

Setz watched the Princess in amusement as she crossed her legs on the ground and pulled her new reading material closer. His own memories came forth of him silently walking into the chambers to speak to the late Queen. Dozens of times, he had decided what he had to say could wait when he spotted both Queen and Princess sitting on the cold stone floor, laughing together as they read. Adele had always sought him out straight after her reading sessions with her daughter; she had known he'd been there. It was never mentioned, but the Guildmaster knew she appreciated the lack of disturbance in those moments.

He knew he was staring, but it didn't matter. He saw the young girl that the Princess once was sitting on the floor, escaping reality. He rarely allowed himself reprieve from the real world; there was too much that required his unwavering attention. But in those moments, he allowed himself to be taken in by another time. A time long gone, a time that had led him to now. The memory of a childlike Alicea faded gently when her adult counterpart looked up from the book.

"We... We have only just begun, haven't we?" she asked.

Setz simply smiled.

EPILOGUE

A TYRANT'S TRIAL

Both Setz and Garnet were speaking, advising, from their positions either side of the throne. Alicea had taken a tentative sitting position on her mother's side after critically analysing her late father's. It was true that Aquiocia's head had always been a male, a King. Now, she sat in her mother's throne, deciding it was simply another thing that would change. It practically already had.

Her advisors hadn't skipped a beat in what swiftly became outright lectures. Their voices hushed but continued as a select few people filed into the audience hall from different paths. Alicea didn't lock eyes with any of the visitors, instead looking around at the hall that had been a duelling arena a week prior. There were still a few places upon the stone floor that looked discoloured from the burns of contaminated blood. It was obvious the servants had attempted to remove the taint, but it had been insufficient. Sections of the stone itself would have to be replaced.

Her eyes flickered across the hall at the window she had been sent through. The fragmented glass had been cleared away and some pieces of scaffolding left beside the pane. The repairs were suspended for what was about to happen.

Alicea sighed lightly, suddenly wishing she was back in her

late parents' chambers, reading.

"Acknowledge them." Garnet's whisper broke her reverie.

"Hmm?"

"Your people – acknowledge them."

Alicea finally met the gaze of the people standing by the fountain and watching her. They look apprehensive, even anxious. But at a glance, the Princess could see the prevailing emotion upon their faces.

Hope.

Alicea bowed her head in a respectful nod, partly to reassure that she was there for them, and partly because she hadn't spoken a full sentence in days. It hadn't been needed. She had slept through the days and read through the nights. She had been making disheartening progress through the immense tome, as if something aside from its enormous size was preventing her from devouring its contents.

"Silence!" Setz demanded loudly, quelling whispers from the crowd Alicea hadn't even noticed. "Bring him forth!"

A few grunts of surprise emitted from the crowd when three shadows appeared before the throne. The shadows formed into men who threw a fourth figure onto the ground in front of the throne before disappearing again. The man on the ground struggled against the inky restraints wrapped around his wrists. His pleading eyes met the Princess' hollow gaze. There was nothing in her expression to exploit; she had been through enough.

"You stand witness to the judgement of Arissam, former head of the Council of Aquiocia and false King of this kingdom. He stands before you all, including the rightful Queen, on the charges of conspiracy, treason, murder, fraud, fearmongering and tyranny. Make your voices heard if this is the man of which I speak!"

The small crowd roared to life, screaming insults and threats at the man on trial. Setz raised his hand and the crowd fell silent.

"What say you?" Setz asked, watching the grovelling prisoner with a passive expression.

"I – I… I did it for this kingdom, I did it for Aquiocia…" Arissam whimpered weakly.

"Rise," Alicea croaked, her voice strained.

Arissam struggled to his feet without the use of his hands. He met the Princess' cold gaze with a pathetic one of his own. He was shaking and sweating so feverishly that he might have caught pneumonia.

"We now await the judgement of the greatest authority currently in this kingdom. Princess Alicea, rightful Queen of Aquiocia, what do you decree in regard to this man's fate?"

A moment passed. Long enough for everyone around her to shift slightly, but short enough not to reignite conversation.

"Death," Alicea stated as she rose to her feet. "Tomorrow. Your final meal will be tonight, just short of midnight. You will dine with me. Dismissed."

The Princess vacated the hall, leaving the wailing of a doomed man and the cheers of his victims in her wake.

❖

The Princess was already at the candlelit table in her parents' chambers when Arissam arrived with half a dozen guards. The massive bed had been removed and replaced with a long table that boasted a spread so glorious it might have been organised to welcome royalty home from a long journey. She stood in greeting and gestured towards the only other seat at the opposite end of the table.

Arissam relaxed slightly when the guards backed out of the room. He even took a moment to absorb the image of the Princess. In the candlelight he took in the full-length, shimmering cerulean dress that fit her form perfectly. Slivers of silver lined the edges of the garment, from the small vee at her neck to the split up her left leg. The gown was sleeveless, showing wrists adorned with countless silver bracelets, six rings lining the fingers of her right hand. Her hair was tied up in impressive curls and obviously freshly pampered by its sheen in the dim light.

She looked beautiful, but the point of the effort in her appearance eluded Arissam as he took his seat.

"Your Highness, I –"

"Call me Alicea, Arissam. We are family, after all," the Princess interrupted.

Arissam struggled to find words.

"Alicea, I apologise for everything. You have to understand – Jex was out of control."

"I don't doubt he was," Alicea said with a deadpan expression. She gestured at the food. "Eat. It is a dinner."

Arissam hesitated. Food was the last thing on his mind. He also didn't think too highly of receiving orders from the woman he had attempted to have killed. Still, if there was a chance at living through the following day…

He selected a large, roasted potato garnished with half a dozen herbs and spices, and took small bites from it. The bruises and swelling up his wrists still burned mercilessly, but he was happy to be free of the restraints. Alicea nodded slightly, and the only sound for several moments was the sound of cutlery upon plates. As Arissam finished the last of the potato, he attempted to appeal to the Princess again.

"He was not the only one to blame," Arissam started, his host's eyebrows rising slightly. "Lucian, he…" He trailed off as Alicea's eyes fell back to the food she was pushing around her plate. She had lost interest. She had been briefed on the nonsense Arissam had been spewing to Setz during interrogation. He had come clean almost instantly about what he had put the kingdom through, but the horror stories had been accompanied by excuses. She didn't want excuses.

Another long, silent moment passed as Arissam attempted to calm his nerves with a large glass of wine. It worked, somewhat. A new tactic formed in his mind.

"I am surprised you would see me alone like this. Especially in the current circumstances."

"Why is that?" Alicea asked with a hint of curiosity. "What makes you think we are alone?"

Arissam hesitated as his host smiled slightly.

"You may relax. Have another drink, if it helps. We are alone. There is no one on this floor of the palace, by direct order."

"Why would you risk me escaping, or harming you?"

Alicea's smiled widened, and from across the table, he saw the ethereal glow of her eyes. He caught a glimpse of what had thwarted him and destroyed Jex. He wasn't going anywhere; they both knew it. He helped himself to another long drink.

"So, you see no fault in what you did at all?" Alicea asked

as he finished the last mouthful and began refilling his glass again.

"My hand was forced, Alicea. I had to do *something* about the stagnation of Aquiocia," Arissam explained in a tone attempting to be diplomatic.

"And that something was usurping the throne and releasing a monster on the people of Aquiocia?"

"Lucian is –"

"Irrelevant," Alicea said, selecting a napkin, dabbing slightly at her mouth and placing it back down. "Lucian, at this particular moment, is irrelevant."

"I don't understand," Arissam said, uncertainly taking a sip from his glass.

"I am discussing your actions, not Lucian's. You have offered no true justification for what you have done."

"I – that is…" Arissam's head whirled. Had he drunk too much? No, he was a seasoned wine drinker.

"Midnight approaches, its arrival imminent," Alicea observed, watching her guest closely.

"What? I don't…" Arissam's head spun again, his vision blurring. Through the haze, realisation dawned on him. "Poison – you poisoned me!"

"Aquiocian executions are rarely made public. I would never tarnish Aquiocian tradition on someone so loathsome as yourself."

Arissam got to his feet – or rather, he tried to. He rose and stumbled onto the table, flailing and sending food and cutlery everywhere as he shakily stood upright. His muscles were already seizing up.

"You… You'll lose, Princess!" he slurred. Alicea rose at

the other end of the table. Through the swirling visage, he took in her image one last time and realised the reason for her appearance. "Lucian will kill you! We could have... Jex, he... I –"

"I've practically eliminated two out of the three monsters you've mentioned. What's one more?" Alicea pushed away from the table as Arissam collapsed back onto it. His body was giving out and losing control of its nerves. He would be dead in a few moments.

"I hope you fare well in the next life, Arissam. For in this one, the Rose of Aquiocia lives on." Alicea's eyes flashed as she turned and made for the archway leading out of the chambers.

She felt cold, though not unpleasantly so. The chill felt comforting, as though it knew and supported what just happened in the chambers of the late King and Queen.

Father... Mother... You have been avenged. The kingdom is safe... Alicea's expression hardened as she left the chambers to inform Setz of what had happened.

For now.

AUTHOR'S NOTES

I hope you all enjoyed The Elemental Chronicles: Reaper.

It's not particularly well known, but Reaper wasn't originally going to be the second book in the series. In fact, Reaper was not going to be a title at all. However, I found that people were curious about Jex's origins and there was so much to him that was left unsaid, so I decided to dive in and tell his tale.

It came with its own challenges, but with the support of my friends and family (and my editor), I am proud to have brought you the story of Jex the Reaper. If you have a moment, feel free to jump online and review it. I'd love to see what you thought.

Next in the series is Illumination. The third title will see the themes and struggles of the world on a far larger scale. I look forward to bringing it to you all.

Thank you to everyone. Whether you were there from day one, picked this up online or at a convention, your support is invaluable and beyond appreciated.

See you for the next instalment, and always remember to leave your mark.

Ross Kingston.

Milton Keynes UK
Ingram Content Group UK Ltd.
UKHW011841050324
438776UK00001BC/11